OXFORD

VIRGINIA WOOLF

# *A Room of One's Own*
## and
# *Three Guineas*

*Edited with an Introduction and Notes by*
MORAG SHIACH

**OXFORD**
UNIVERSITY PRESS

# OXFORD

UNIVERSITY PRESS

Great Clarendon Street, Oxford OX2 6DP

Oxford University Press is a department of the University of Oxford.
It furthers the University's objective of excellence in research, scholarship,
and education by publishing worldwide in

Oxford New York

Auckland Bangkok Buenos Aires Cape Town Chennai
Dar es Salaam Delhi Hong Kong Istanbul Karachi Kolkata
Kuala Lumpur Madrid Melbourne Mexico City Mumbai Nairobi
São Paulo Shanghai Taipei Tokyo Toronto

Oxford is a registered trade mark of Oxford University Press
in the UK and in certain other countries

Published in the United States
by Oxford University Press Inc., New York

Introduction and Explanatory Notes © Morag Shiach 1992
Biographical Preface and Select Bibliography © Frank Kermode 1992
Chronology © David Bradshaw 2000

The moral rights of the author have been asserted

Database right Oxford University Press (maker)

First published as a World's Classics paperback 1992
Reissued as an Oxford World's Classics paperback 1998
Reissued 2008

British Library Cataloguing in Publication Data

Data available

Library of Congress Cataloging in Publication Data

Data available

ISBN 978-0-19-953660-3

4

Printed in Great Britain by
Clays Ltd, St Ives plc

# CONTENTS

# BIOGRAPHICAL PREFACE

VIRGINIA WOOLF was born Adeline Virginia Stephen on 25 January 1882 at 22 Hyde Park Gate, Kensington. Her father, Leslie Stephen, himself a widower, had married in 1878 Julia Jackson, widow of Herbert Duckworth. Between them they already had four children; a fifth, Vanessa, was born in 1879, a sixth, Thoby, in 1880. There followed Virginia and, in 1883, Adrian.

Both of the parents had strong family associations with literature. Leslie Stephen was the son of Sir James Stephen, a noted historian, and brother of Sir James Fitzjames Stephen, a distinguished lawyer and writer on law. His first wife was a daughter of Thackeray, his second had been an admired associate of the Pre-Raphaelites, and also, like her first husband, had aristocratic connections. Stephen himself is best remembered as the founding editor of the *Dictionary of National Biography*, and as an alpinist, but he was also a remarkable journalist, biographer, and historian of ideas; his *History of English Thought in the Eighteenth Century* (1876) is still of great value. No doubt our strongest idea of him derives from the character of Mr Ramsay in *To the Lighthouse*; for a less impressionistic portrait, which conveys a strong sense of his centrality in the intellectual life of the time, one can consult Noël Annan's *Leslie Stephen* (revised edition, 1984).

Virginia had the free run of her father's library, a better substitute for the public school and university education she was denied than most women of the time could aspire to; her brothers, of course, were sent to Clifton and Westminster. Her mother died in 1895, and in that year she had her first breakdown, possibly related in some way

# Preface

to the sexual molestation of which her half-brother George Duckworth is accused. By 1897 she was able to read again, and did so voraciously: 'Gracious, child, how you gobble,' remarked her father, who, with a liberality and good sense at odds with the age in which they lived, allowed her to choose her reading freely. In other respects her relationship with her father was difficult; his deafness and melancholy, his excessive emotionalism, not helped by successive bereavements, all increased her nervousness.

Stephen fell ill in 1902 and died in 1904. Virginia suffered another breakdown, during which she heard the birds singing in Greek, a language in which she had acquired some competence. On her recovery she moved, with her brothers and sister, to a house in Gordon Square, Bloomsbury; there, and subsequently at several other nearby addresses, what eventually became famous as the Bloomsbury Group took shape.

Virginia had long considered herself a writer. It was in 1905 that she began to write for publication in the *Times Literary Supplement*. In her circle (more loosely drawn than is sometimes supposed) were many whose names are now half-forgotten, but some were or became famous: J. M. Keynes and E. M. Forster and Roger Fry; also Clive Bell, who married Vanessa, Lytton Strachey, who once proposed marriage to her, and Leonard Woolf. Despite much ill health in these years, she travelled a good deal, and had an interesting social life in London. She did a little adult-education teaching, worked for female suffrage, and shared the excitement of Roger Fry's Post-Impressionist Exhibition in 1910. In 1912, after another bout of nervous illness, she married Leonard Woolf.

She was thirty, and had not yet published a book, though *The Voyage Out* was in preparation. It was accepted for publication by her half-brother Gerald Duckworth in 1913 (it appeared in 1915). She was often ill with depression and anorexia, and in 1913 attempted suicide. But after a bout of violent madness her health seemed to settle down, and in 1917 a printing press was installed at Hogarth House, Richmond, where she and her husband were living. The Hogarth Press, later an illustrious institution, but at first meant in part as therapy for Virginia, was now inaugurated. She began *Night and Day*, and finished it in 1918. It was published by Duckworth in 1919, the year in which the Woolfs bought Monk's House, Rodmell, for £700. There, in 1920, she began *Jacob's Room*, finished, and published by the Woolfs' own Hogarth Press, in 1922. In the following year she began *Mrs Dalloway* (finished in 1924, published 1925), when she was already working on *To the Lighthouse* (finished and published, after intervals of illness, in 1927). *Orlando*, a fantastic 'biography' of a man–woman, and a tribute to Virginia's close friendship with Vita Sackville-West, was written quite rapidly over the winter of 1927–8, and published, with considerable success, in October. *The Waves* was written and rewritten in 1930 and 1931 (published in October of that year). She had already started on *Flush*, the story of Elizabeth Barrett Browning's pet dog—another success with the public— and in 1932 began work on what became *The Years*.

This brief account of her work during the first twenty years of her marriage is of course incomplete; she had also written and published many shorter works, as well as both series of *The Common Reader*, and *A Room of One's Own*. There have been accounts of the marriage very hostile to Leonard Woolf, but he can hardly be accused of cramping her talent or hindering the development of her career.

# Preface

*The Years* proved an agonizingly difficult book to finish, and was completely rewritten at least twice. Her friend Roger Fry having died in 1934, she planned to write a biography, but illnesses in 1936 delayed the project; towards the end of that year she began instead the polemical *Three Guineas*, published in 1938. *The Years* had meanwhile appeared in 1937, by which time she was again at work on the Fry biography, and already sketching in her head the book that was to be *Between the Acts*. *Roger Fry* was published in the terrifying summer of 1940. By the autumn of that year many of the familiar Bloomsbury houses had been destroyed or badly damaged by bombs. Back at Monk's House, she worked on *Between the Acts*, and finished it in February 1941. Thereafter her mental condition deteriorated alarmingly, and on 28 March, unable to face another bout of insanity, she drowned herself in the River Ouse.

Her career as a writer of fiction covers the years 1912–41, thirty years distracted by intermittent serious illness as well as by the demands, which she regarded as very important, of family and friends, and by the need or desire to write literary criticism and social comment. Her industry was extraordinary—nine highly-wrought novels, two or three of them among the great masterpieces of the form in this century, along with all the other writings, including the copious journals and letters that have been edited and published in recent years. Firmly set though her life was in the 'Bloomsbury' context—the agnostic ethic transformed from that of her forebears, the influence of G. E. Moore and the Cambridge Apostles, the individual brilliance of J. M. Keynes, Strachey, Forster, and the others—we have come more and more to value the distinctiveness of her talent, so that she seems more and more to

## Preface

stand free of any context that might be thought to limit her. None of that company—except, perhaps, T. S. Eliot, who was on the fringe of it—did more to establish the possibilities of literary innovation, or to demonstrate that such innovation must be brought about by minds familiar with the innovations of the past. This is true originality. It was Eliot who said of *Jacob's Room* that in that book she had freed herself from any compromise between the traditional novel and her original gift; it was the freedom he himself sought in *The Waste Land*, published in the same year, a freedom that was dependent upon one's knowing with intimacy that with which compromise must be avoided, so that the knowledge became part of the originality. In fact she had 'gobbled' her father's books to a higher purpose than he could have understood.

# INTRODUCTION

In these two essays Virginia Woolf develops an innovative and politically challenging analysis of the causes and effects of women's exclusion from British cultural, political, and economic life. Starting from a consideration of the troubled relations between women and fiction in *A Room of One's Own* (1929), Woolf moves on to a much broader analysis of the political and cultural implications of women's oppression in *Three Guineas* (1938).

*A Room of One's Own* is perhaps Woolf's best-known essay. Despite its very polemical style, its concentration on questions of literary form and literary history has made it accessible to readers of Woolf's fiction. The recent increase in feminist studies of Woolf's life and writing has also led to very significant interest in *A Room of One's Own*, which has been seen by many critics as the first sustained essay in feminist literary theory. *Three Guineas*, on the other hand, is a relatively unknown text. Although Woolf conceived it as a sequel to *A Room of One's Own*, its density, its range of references, and the extremity of the political positions it advocates have pushed it to the margins of Woolf's texts, with even feminist critics expressing unease about its apparent 'empty sloganeering and cliché' and its 'stridency'.[1]

In fact, *Three Guineas* is the result of ten years of research by Woolf, which builds on the arguments she

[1] Elaine Showalter, 'Virginia Woolf and the Flight into Androgyny', in *A Literature of their Own: British Women Novelists from Brontë to Lessing* (London: Virago, 1978), 263–95, p. 295; and Carolyn Heilbrun, *Towards Androgyny: Aspects of Male and Female in Literature* (London: Gollancz, 1973, p. 164).

developed in *A Room of One's Own*. Throughout the 1930s Woolf read memoirs, biographies, books of social theory, official reports, and newspapers, with the aim of furthering her understanding of the social and cultural role of women. The political events of the decade made her political focus both more urgent and more radical. The coming to power of Hitler in 1933, the Spanish Civil War of 1936–9, the polarization of British society in an atmosphere of economic recession and massive unemployment, forced Woolf to consider the political implications of the patriarchal structure she had identified throughout both public and private institutions. Thus, in *Three Guineas*, her object is the identification of the social forces that have led to the growth of Fascism. Seeing these as inextricably linked to the institutions of patriarchal power, Woolf then goes on to advocate a form of radical political action in which women would form themselves into a society of 'Outsiders' in order to challenge the rise of Fascism and the drift towards war.

In *A Room of One's Own* Woolf begins by considering the implications of the historical relations between 'women' and 'fiction'. From three deceptively simple topics—'women and what they are like', 'women and the fiction that they write', and 'women and the fiction that is written about them' (p. 3)—Woolf develops a complex theory of the relations between gender and writing. She begins by examining the exclusion of women from educational institutions, and the relations between this exclusion and the unequal distribution of wealth. Thus, she tells the story of a day spent in 'Oxbridge', where her attempts to develop her ideas about women and fiction are constantly interrupted by her encounters with inequality and exclusion. Her desire to consult a manuscript is thwarted by her

## Introduction

inability to enter the library of an all-male college. Her aspiration to discuss the problem with women scholars is curtailed by her recognition of the poverty of their institutional resources. Such inequalities and exclusions become symbolic of a whole history of negation and exclusion of the intellectual and economic demands of women: 'thinking of the safety and prosperity of the one sex and of the poverty and insecurity of the other and of the effect of tradition and of the lack of tradition upon the mind of the writer' (p. 31). Her argument is advanced through a series of narratives, anecdotes, and apparently random observations, which build up into a picture of 'what a difference a tail makes' (p. 16). Against this image of lack, she insists on the importance for women of gaining both a space, 'a room', and a degree of financial independence.

The next phase of her journey takes her to the British Museum, and to a realization of the vast number of texts that have been written about women by men 'who have no apparent qualification save that they are not women' (p. 34). She finds in these texts a bewildering array of categorical, but contradictory, statements about the nature of woman. What surprises her particularly, however, is the anger that she finds in these texts. This leads her to conclude that men have a strong emotional and political stake in the social inferiority of women, since 'Women have served all these centuries as looking-glasses possessing the magic and delicious power of reflecting the figure of man at twice its natural size' (p. 45). This recognition of strong psychic investments in existing power relations prefigures much recent work by psychoanalytic feminist critics, who have tried to understand the unconscious processes which lock individual subjects into particular social or symbolic structures.

## Introduction

Leaving the figure of 'woman' she has found in texts by men, Woolf moves on to consider fictional and poetic writing by women. Once more, her emphasis is economic and historical. As if to answer the frequent charge that 'there has never been a woman writer as great as Shakespeare', Woolf invents the figure of Judith Shakespeare, William's sister. Judith's desire to become a writer is compromised by her lack of education, and by the fact that she cannot contemplate a career as an actor. Finally, however, she is destroyed by the social codes that immediately identify a woman in public as sexually available. Having been befriended by an actor–manager, she becomes pregnant, and kills herself.

Her fate thus echoes that of the fictional Mary Hamilton who haunts *A Room of One's Own*. Woolf began *A Room of One's Own* by eschewing any fixed identity: she will tell many stories from many different points of view in order to construct a textual and theoretical collage. Indeed she says, 'call me Mary Beton, Mary Seton, Mary Carmichael or by any name you please' (p. 5). These three Marys are characters in a well-known ballad, which is sung by a fourth Mary, Mary Hamilton. Mary Hamilton, having had a child as the result of an illicit relationship with the King, is about to be put to death. Since Woolf identifies the other three Marys at various points in the essay, there is an increasing sense of Woolf's own identification with the fate of Mary Hamilton, and thus also with Judith Shakespeare. Woolf writes: 'who shall measure the heat and violence of the poet's heart when caught and tangled in a woman's body?' (p. 62), and thus signals the troubled relation between women writers and the bodily which continues to preoccupy feminist critics.

In Chapter IV Woolf moves towards a stylistic consid-

## Introduction

eration of the problems facing women writers. Once again, she finds the traces of exclusion and oppression in texts by women. Even when women had access to the financial and social resources necessary for writing, Woolf finds their texts marked by a 'flaw in the centre' (p. 96), which is the legacy of their anger and indignation. Woolf's critical judgements at this point, her privileging of Jane Austen and Emily Brontë over other women writers, have a degree of arbitrariness, but her overall argument is clear. She insists that women writers have suffered from the lack of a literary tradition, of a prose style in which they can produce female subjectivity without strain. Her remark about 'a sentence that was unsuited for a woman's use' (p. 100), which has struck many critics as either idealist or mystificatory, has to be understood in relation to her unease with the status of the first-person pronoun in contemporary prose-writing: 'a shadow seemed to lie across the page. It was a straight dark bar, a shadow shaped something like the letter "I"' (p. 130). Such a powerful subjective presence cannot express the complexity, fragmentation, and plurality which she sees as typical of women's experience.

When Woolf goes on to discuss an imaginary fictional text, *Life's Adventure* by Mary Carmichael, however, she finds innovation and hope not principally in its style, but in its representation of relations between women. For centuries, women had been represented as rivals, or as mediators in relationships between men, but now 'Chloe liked Olivia' (p. 106). Woolf finds in this fictional representation of women's friendship a powerful symbol of transgression, which allows for the development of a form of writing that will not be marked by defensiveness and anger.

Such enthusiasm, however, turns to unease, as Woolf questions the wisdom of praising her own sex. This leads

# Introduction

her to a consideration of the conceptual limitations implicit in thinking of the two sexes as distinct. Observing a man and a woman entering a taxi-cab, and citing Coleridge as her authority, Woolf explores the imaginative and political resources of the concept of androgyny. Woolf argues for the importance of a unified creative mind, which would express both masculinity and femininity, arguing that 'it is fatal for anyone who writes to think of their sex' (p. 136). This move has angered many feminist critics, who have seen it as evasion on Woolf's part, as a failure to face up to the implications of the oppression she has documented and explored so fully in the first five chapters. Indeed, Elaine Showalter has written of Woolf's use of the concept of androgyny as 'the myth that helped her evade confrontation with her own painful femaleness' and thus as a betrayal of any feminist project.[2] Certainly it is true that the enormity of her discoveries seems at times to unsettle Woolf's writing: her insistence that anger should be avoided functions uneasily in a text which has represented so clearly the historical causes of that anger. Still, it does not seem that Woolf's conclusion can be dismissed as simply the result of a failure of conceptual or political nerve. Instead, she can be read as seeking to move beyond the representations of 'man' and 'woman' which have produced so much anger, exclusion, and violence throughout *A Room of One's Own*.

Woolf never questions the historical, political, or bodily significance of sexual identity. What she does challenge is the rigidity with which the categories of 'man' and 'woman' are produced in contemporary fiction. Yet un-doing dominant categories of thought can never be easy, and, when Woolf tries to find an image of the androgyous mind at

---

[2] Showalter, 'Virginia Woolf and the Flight into Androgyny', p. 264.

work, she finds herself caught in a fairly uncomfortable embrace: 'The writer, I thought, once his experience is over, must lie back and let his mind celebrate its nuptials darkness' (p. 136). The difficulty of finding an androgynous image to express her creative and political aspirations is an index of the dimensions of the issues with which Woolf engages in *A Room of One's Own*. Insisting that 'it is natural for the sexes to co-operate' (p. 127), what Woolf actually finds is a history of conflict and inequality, which marks and restricts the whole field of creative writing.

Woolf's interest in the significance and understanding of sexual identity is also clear in her mock-biographical text, *Orlando* (1928). This novel has a central character whose gallop through literary and political history is complicated by his changing into a woman. The stress this puts on the linguistic and structural resources of the novel is considerable, and the resulting text is a hybrid of the fictional, the biographical, and the satirical. Its generic confusion thus mirrors its gender confusion, in ways that foreshadow the rhetorical and narrative complexities of *A Room of One's Own*.

The formal implications of radical conceptual change became even clearer for Woolf, however, as she moved towards her sequel to *A Room of One's Own*, which was to have been called 'Answers to Correspondents', or 'On Being Despised', but ended up as *Three Guineas*. The idea for this text can be found initially in a speech which Woolf gave to the London/National Society for Women's Service in 1931. This society consisted mainly of professional women who were struggling to increase the presence of women in higher education and in the professions. Woolf's involvement with this group was part of her network of relationships with political groups, ranging from her early

# Introduction

involvement with suffrage groups, to work with the Labour Party and the Women's Co-operative Guild. Woolf's speech, later published in a modified form as 'Professions for Women', addressed the difficulties faced by women in entering the literary profession.[3] The main barrier, Woolf argued, was the figure of 'the Angel in the House', the historically and culturally embedded representation of an ideal of femininity. Woolf can see no escape from this figure, except through violence: 'I turned upon that Angel and caught her by the throat.'[4] This violence is justified by a plea of self-defence, since the Angel's ideals of charm, selflessness, and purity have been the death of so many women writers.

The violence implicit in *A Room of One's Own* has here become explicit, and it is blamed on the destructiveness of patriarchal culture. Woolf's sense of the need for new forms of literary production to encompass the perceptions and experiences of women is also intense: she imagines her powers of rationality turning in frustration on her imagination and saying 'I cannot make use of what you tell me— about women's bodies for instance.'[5] This exploration of a new literary form in which to capture the subjective and the bodily was also being carried on in Woolf's writing of *The Waves* (1931).

By early 1932 Woolf was trying both to extend her thinking on gender and education, and to develop an

---

[3] For the text of the speech, see Mitchell A. Leaska (ed.), *The Pargiters by Virginia Woolf: The Novel-Essay Portion of 'The Years'* (London: Hogarth Press, 1978), pp. xxviii–xliv. 'Professions for Women' is in Leonard Woolf (ed.), *Collected Essays of Virginia Woolf* (4 vols.; London: Hogarth Press, 1966–7), ii. 284–9.

[4] *The Pargiters*, p. xxxi.

[5] Ibid., p. xxxiv.

entirely new literary form. She started writing *The Pargi-ters*, which was to be a 'novel-essay', alternating fictional explorations of the history of the Pargiter family since the late nineteenth century with discussions of educational opportunities for women, the destructiveness of the profes-sions as presently constituted, and the troubled relation-ships of women to their own bodies. This experiment, however, was never to be concluded. Instead, Woolf produced two separate texts: *The Years* (1937), a novel which explored the subjective, economic, and political development of a middle-class family from 1880 to the 1930s; and *Three Guineas*, an extended analysis of the social and economic position of women, and a political treatise against Fascism.

Woolf presents her argument in *Three Guineas* as a reply to three letters which she has received, asking for her political and financial support for different causes. The first letter is from a middle-aged, prosperous barrister, who asks her opinion about the most effective way to combat the drift towards war. He also asks her to sign a petition, to join his society which is working to preserve peace by protecting culture and intellectual liberty, and to give a donation to this same society. The second letter she receives is from the treasurer of a women's college, asking for a contribution to its Rebuilding Fund; the third asks her to donate money to a society which aims to promote the entry of women into the professions. Woolf considers each of these requests in turn, ultimately deciding to send each correspondent the sum of one guinea. Her reasons for doing so are, however, complex, and involve her in an analysis of the history of women's education, the political and individual values which dominate public institutions, the relations between militarism and masculinity, and the fear and anger which structure relations between men and women.

At first, Woolf represents herself as ill qualified to pronounce on the drift towards authoritarianism and war, and ill-equipped to organize politically against them. She identifies her social position as an 'educated man's daughter', a definition that draws attention to the difficulties of defining class in relation to women who do not participate in relations of production. As such, she has had little formal education, and thus declares herself unable to determine the economic or political reasons for war. Women, she argues, cannot fight for peace, cannot use the pressure of great wealth, cannot preach sermons or negotiate treaties.

Thus, Woolf argues, if women are being asked to function effectively as a political force, they must approach the business of power and influence in a new way. They do have one 'new weapon', which is their recently acquired legal right to enter the professions, and thus to achieve a modest degree of economic independence. This is a vital first step, since Woolf asserts that economic dependence has always locked women into a reproduction of patriarchal values. Beyond this modest independence, however, women also need to develop a critical distance from dominant political and cultural values—something Woolf achieves by a critique of the rituals and distinctions that structure daily life in educational, legal, and religious institutions.

Such a critique, however, like the political strategies suggested by her correspondent, fails to address the enormity of the violence which she sees in photographs of children who have been killed by Fascist bombardment during the Spanish Civil War: 'the emotion caused by the photographs would still remain unappeased' (p. 166). In order to understand this emotion, Woolf argues for the need to develop an alternative understanding of the role of education, the definition of cultural freedom, and the values of the legal, medical, and literary professions on the basis of a history of the social and cultural role of 'the daughters of educated men' since the mid-nineteenth century. Her task is thus 'to discover where the difference lies' for women who are united by their historical experience of exclusion, and thus form 'a whole made up of body, brain and spirit, influenced by memory and tradition' (p. 175).

Such a sense of the political potential inherent in women's shared experience of oppression is, however, unsettled by Woolf's examination of the case her second correspondent puts up for a donation to the Rebuilding Fund of a women's college. Woolf hesitates, unsure whether she can see the entry to higher education as a progressive political force for women. Firstly, she argues, a woman entering Cambridge University will not find intellectual stimulation and freedom, but rather conflict and competition: she thinks, 'not how she can learn, but how she can fight in order that she may win the same advantages as her brothers' (p. 195). Woolf supports her argument by reference to the history of women's struggles to gain access to both Oxford and Cambridge Universities, a history of widespread hostility and constant financial insecurity. By picking Oxford and Cambridge, which she refers to as 'the two universities', Woolf is, perhaps, making her argument too easy. Other universities, both in Scotland and in England, found the admission of women a less traumatic affair. However, since Woolf's interest is in the education of members of the ruling class, of civil servants, politicians, and prominent intellectuals, such blindness to the diversity of higher education in Britain does not necessarily invalidate her overall argument.

Woolf finds that in both Oxford and Cambridge the values of competition, acquisition, and militarism dominate both research and teaching. She imagines a different approach to higher education, where buildings would be new, and immune from the demands of 'tradition', where libraries would be open to all, subjects would be interdisciplinary, lectures would be abolished in favour of discussion, and awards and honours would disappear. Yet, as soon as she has put such ideas on the agenda, she steps back: how would such an education allow women to enter the professions as presently constituted? Reluctantly, she accepts the dominance of her own first principle, that the key to political influence is economic independence, and agrees to send one guinea to the treasurer of the women's college.

The greatest barrier to the radical reorganization of education, then, is the economic and social structure of the professions. In order to pursue this connection, Woolf turns to her third correspondent, who has asked her for a donation to a society which aims to promote the entry of women into the professions. Woolf's first response to this letter is to wonder why women, who have had access to the professions for nearly twenty years, should be so short of money. Examining the constitution of different levels of the Civil Service, Woolf sees women as the victims of a system of informal patronage, which discriminates against them in terms of both selection and promotion. She identifies such discrimination with the conviction that 'Homes are the real places of the women who are now compelling men to be idle' (p. 227). Such categorical and authoritarian attitudes she identifies, in turn, with Fascism.

The moves Woolf makes at this point are perhaps too swift: there are surely important distinctions to be made between mechanisms of institutional patronage and preferment, and the wholesale exclusion of women from the public world. Yet, the argument has a compulsion, which is derived mostly from the quantity and range of texts Woolf brings to her case. To find such varied sources of unease about the entry of women into the professions certainly adds to the plausibility of Woolf's later claim that we are dealing with something more than rational self-interest.

Confronted with the fact of discrimination against women in the professions, Woolf is inclined to send off her guinea. Yet, she still expresses 'doubts and hesitations', as she considers what entry to the professions will mean for women. What she finds in professional life since the nineteenth century is a history of competitiveness, exclusion, and conflict. The establishment of professional identities seems to her to be intimately connected to the jealous protection of property rights, to vanity and greed. The organization of professional life involves the exclusion of friendship, travel, leisure, and art in the interests of career advancement. Woolf argues, 'we, daughters of educated men, are between the devil and the deep sea' (p. 261), faced with the choice between obscurity and dependence on the one hand, and jealousy and greed on the other.

Rejecting the first solution that proposes itself—'Had we not better plunge off the bridge into the river; give up the game' (p. 261)—Woolf instead tries to imagine a different relation to professional life, which would reflect the social and political values women have acquired as a result of their exclusion from power. She suggests that women can enter the professions without endorsing authoritarianism if they follow four principles. The first is the principle of poverty: to which Woolf gives the unsettling definition of 'enough money to live on'. Perhaps this would be better expressed as the principle of modest financial independence. The second principle is that of chastity: a refusal to sell your brain for the sake of money. The third is derision: a refusal to promote or advertise; and the fourth is a freedom from unreal loyalties, by which Woolf means loyalties to tradition, or to particular educational institutions. Woolf is aware of how radical the action of these principles would be upon the organization of professional life, and also accepts that, for economic reasons, they would be hard to sustain. Yet, she believes that women have more chance of realizing at least some of them, since, ironically, both law and property are in this case on the side of women, easing their path to poverty and derision.

Having imgined the terms in which women could have access to economic independence without subscribing to authoritarian values, Woolf turns once more to her first correspondent, and his request that she work to protect culture and intellectual liberty. Again, her first response is an ironic disbelief: why should men, who have controlled the institutions of education and of cultural production, need to turn to women for help? Once more, however, she pursues the implications of the apparent diminution of intellectual freedom, and lays out the contribution which women could make to the preservation of cultural liberty. Like their role in the professions, women's role is to be that of resistance to hypocrisy, competition, and hierarchy. Woolf asks women not to 'commit adultery of the brain' (p. 290), to find new forms of publication and distribution which avoid the mechanisms of mass marketing.

At this point, Woolf decides that she will, after all, send

## Introduction

a guinea to her correspondent's society, whose aim is to prevent war. To celebrate this momentous achievement of political alliance, Woolf then suggests a symbolic act: the eradication of the word 'feminist'. Again, as in her turn towards androgyny in *A Room of One's Own*, this move has provoked significant controversy. Woolf's reasons, however, are quite explicit. She rejects the project of 'feminism' for its narrowness, its concentration on the winning of particular rights for women. Instead, she proposes a more radical transformation, a fight by both men and women against 'the tyranny of the patriarchal state' (p. 303), against the rising forces of authoritarianism.

There are, however, limits to the degree of co-operation which Woolf can imagine between herself and her correspondent: she agrees to send a guinea, but refuses to join his society. Instead, she proposes the formation by women of a Society of Outsiders, whose very difference from existing political organizations would be the reason for its strength. Such a society would pursue all of the economic, political, and cultural values Woolf has argued for in the essay: a refusal to fight with arms; an attitude of indifference towards 'patriotism'; modest financial independence; state financial aid for housewives; the refusal of honours or distinctions; and a widespread rejection of acquisitiveness and competition. This society would also work for peace, 'by the means that a different sex, a different tradition, a different education, and the different values which result from those differences have placed within our reach' (p. 320).

Typically, however, Woolf does not allow such a conclusion to rest unchallenged. Throughout *Three Guineas* Woolf has expressed the complexity of her argument, and her hesitancy, by the use of ellipses. Those 'three dots'

## Introduction

come to stand for doubts, for the difficulties of finding a language adequate to her ideas, but also, finally, for the silence inspired by fear. Even as she struggles to imagine that 'unity that rubs out divisions as if they were chalk marks only' (p. 365), she has had to confront the intensity of fear and of anger that surrounds relations between the sexes. Beyond rational self-interest, or simple conservatism, she argues, lies profound hostility. Using the very inexact concept of 'infantile fixation', Woolf tries to identify the unconscious forces that lead men to resist any transformation of the private or public role of women. The task is enormous, and the stakes are high, since Woolf argues that the concept of domination is 'connected with manhood itself' (p. 359). This, finally, is the focus of Woolf's analysis. Citing the example of Creon's cruelty and tyranny in the *Antigone*, Woolf insists that 'masculinity', as a socially produced category, is fundamentally implicated in authoritarianism, in violence and clamour. To challenge the rise of Fascism is thus, for Woolf, to challenge the logic and the history of the patriarchal state: something which she can only do as an 'Outsider'.

The radicalism of this conclusion has certainly alienated many of Woolf's readers. Q. D. Leavis's description of the book as 'nasty', 'dangerous', and 'preposterous' has been endorsed by several critics; most have preferred to ignore the book completely.[6] From the very moment of its publication readers responded to the text as an aberration, and expressed disappointment that Woolf had apparently moved away from the ambiguity and fluidity which they so valued in her prose. Woolf was impatient of such

[6] Q. D. Leavis, 'Caterpillars of the Commonwealth Unite!', *Scrutiny*, 7 (1938), 203–14.

[ xxvii ]

*Introduction*

criticisms, writing to Vita Sackville-West, 'how sick I get of all this talk about "lovely prose" and charm when all I wanted was to state a very intricate case as plainly . . . as I could.'[7] Yet many of the questions Woolf poses remain important, and unanswered. The threat of war, and increasingly authoritarian government, continue to dominate political thinking, though not always with the urgency Woolf brought to them in 1938. The extent to which higher education should foster intellectual and cultural liberty, in the face of pressing economic demands from industry and government, is still unresolved. Finally, the role of women in the professions is equally uncertain: the struggle to transform and the need to assimilate continue to produce political and personal tensions. As women move closer to the 'inside' of educational, professional, and economic institutions, the social and political challenge of Woolf's 'Society of Outsiders' remains: perhaps now harder to realize, but compelling to imagine.

[7] *The Letters of Virginia Woolf*, ed. Nigel Nicolson and Joanne Trautmann (6 vols.; London: Hogarth Press, 1975–84), vi. 243.

# NOTE ON THE TEXT

THE text of *A Room of One's Own* is based on the first edition (London: Hogarth Press, 1929); the text of *Three Guineas* is based on the first edition (London: Hogarth Press, 1938). Typographical errors and inaccuracies of reference have been corrected.

This edition makes minor adjustments to hyphenation, word division, ('tomorrow', 'tonight', 'someone', etc.), 'ize' for 'ise', the dropping of the full point after 'Mr' and 'Mrs', and the use of single rather than double quotes, in order to be consistent and to follow current standard usage.

# SELECT BIBLIOGRAPHY

BIBLIOGRAPHY

KIRKPATRICK, B. J., *A Bibliography of Virginia Woolf* (2nd edn.; Oxford: University Press, 1980).

BIOGRAPHY

BELL, QUENTIN, *Virginia Woolf: A Biography* (2 vols.; London: Hogarth Press, 1972).

POOLE, ROGER, *The Unknown Virginia Woolf* (Cambridge: University Press, 1978).

ROSE, PHYLLIS, *Woman of Letters: A Life of Virginia Woolf* (New York: Oxford University Press, 1978).

WOOLF, LEONARD, *An Autobiography* (2 vols.; Oxford: University Press, 1980).

EDITIONS

*The Diary of Virginia Woolf* ed. Anne Olivier Bell, assisted by Andrew McNeillie (5 vols.; London: Hogarth Press, 1977–84).

*The Letters of Virginia Woolf*, ed. Nigel Nicolson and Joanne Trautmann (6 vols.; London: Hogarth Press, 1975–84).

GENERAL CRITICISM

BENNETT, JOAN, *Virginia Woolf: Her Art as a Novelist* (Cambridge University Press, 1945, 1964).

BOWLBY, RACHEL, *Virginia Woolf: Feminist Destinations* (Oxford: Blackwell, 1988).

BREWSTER, DOROTHY, *Virginia Woolf* (London: Allen and Unwin, 1963).

DI BATTISTA, MARIA, *Virginia Woolf's Major Novels* (New Haven, Conn., and London: Yale University Press, 1980).

FLEISHMAN, AVROM, *Virginia Woolf: A Critical Reading* (Baltimore, Johns Hopkins University Press, 1977).

# Select Bibliography

FREEDMAN, RALPH, *Virginia Woolf: Revaluation and Continuity* (Berkeley: University of California Press, 1980).

GUIGET, JEAN, *Virginia Woolf and her Works*, trans. Jean Stewart (London: Hogarth Press, 1965).

LEASKA, MITCHELL A., *The Novels of Virginia Woolf* (New York: John Jay Press, 1977).

LEE, HERMIONE, *The Novels of Virginia Woolf* (London: Methuen, 1977).

MAJUMDAR ROBIN, and MCLAURIN, ALLEN (eds.), *Virginia Woolf: The Critical Heritage* (London: Routledge and Kegan Paul, 1975).

MARCUS, JANE (ed.), *New Feminist Essays on Virginia Woolf* (London: Macmillan, 1981).

MARDER, HERBERT, *Feminism and Art: A Study of Virginia Woolf* (New Haven, Conn., and London: Yale University Press, 1968).

MCLAURIN, ALLEN, *Virginia Woolf: The Echoes Enslaved* (Cambridge: University Press, 1973).

MINOW-PINKNEY, MAKIKO, *Virginia Woolf and the Problem of the Subject* (Brighton: Harvester, 1987).

MOODY, A. D., *Virginia Woolf* (Edinburgh: Oliver and Boyd, 1963).

THAKUR, N. C., *The Symbolism of Virginia Woolf* (London: Oxford University Press, 1965).

WARNER, ERIC (ed.) *Virginia Woolf: A Centenary Perspective* (London: Macmillan, 1984).

ZWERDLING, ALEX, *Virginia Woolf and the Real World* (Berkeley: University of California Press, 1986).

## ON *A ROOM OF ONE'S OWN* AND *THREE GUINEAS*

BLACK, NAOMI, 'Virginia Woolf and the Women's Movement', in Jane Marcus (ed.), *Virginia Woolf: A Feminist Slant* (London: University of Nebraska Press, 1983), 180–97.

BOWLBY, RACHEL, *Virginia Woolf: Feminist Destinations* (Oxford: Blackwell, 1988).

CARROLL, BERENICE A., ' "To Crush Him in our Own Country":

## Select Bibliography

The Political Thought of Virginia Woolf', *Feminist Studies*, 4: 1 (1978), 99–131.

FOX, ALICE, 'Literary Allusions as Feminist Criticism in "A Room of One's Own"', *Philological Quarterly* (Spring 1984), 145–61.

KAMUF, PEGGY, 'Penelope at Work: Interruptions in "A Room of One's Own"', *Novel*, 16 (1982), 5–18.

MARCUS, JANE, *Virginia Woolf and the Languages of Patriarchy* (Bloomington, Indiana: Indiana University Press 1987).

MOI, TORIL, 'Who's Afraid of Virginia Woolf?: Feminist Readings of Woolf', in *Sexual/Textual Politics: Feminist Literary Theory* (London: Methuen, 1985), 1–18.

SHOWALTER, ELAINE, 'Virginia Woolf and the Flight into Androgyny', in *A Literature of their Own: British Women Novelists from Brontë to Lessing* (London: Virago, 1978), 263–97.

SILVER, BRENDA R., '"Three Guineas" Before and After: Further Answers to Correspondents', in Jane Marcus (ed.), *Virginia Woolf: A Feminist Slant* (London: University of Nebraska Press, 1983), 254–76.

# A CHRONOLOGY OF VIRGINIA WOOLF

| *Life* | *Historical and Cultural Background* |
|---|---|
| 1882 (25 Jan.) Adeline Virginia Stephen (VW) born at 22 Hyde Park Gate, London. | Deaths of Darwin, Trollope, D. G. Rossetti; Joyce born; Stravinsky born; Married Women's Property Act; Society for Psychical Research founded. |
| 1895 (5 May) Death of mother, Julia Stephen; VW's first breakdown occurs soon afterwards. | Death of T. H. Huxley; X-rays discovered; invention of the cinematograph; wireless telegraphy invented; arrest, trials, and conviction of Oscar Wilde. Wilde, *The Importance of Being Earnest* and *An Ideal Husband* Wells, *The Time Machine* |
| 1896 (Nov.) Travels in France with sister Vanessa. | Death of William Morris; *Daily Mail* started. Hardy, *Jude the Obscure* Housman, *A Shropshire Lad* |
| 1897 (10 April) Marriage of half-sister Stella; (19 July) death of Stella; (Nov.) VW learning Greek and History at King's College, London. | Queen Victoria's Diamond Jubilee; Tate Gallery opens. Stoker, *Dracula* James, *What Maisie Knew* |
| 1898 | Deaths of Gladstone and Lewis Carroll; radium and plutonium discovered. Wells, *The War of the Worlds* |
| 1899 (30 Oct.) VW's brother Thoby goes up to Trinity College, Cambridge, where he forms friendships with Lytton Strachey, Leonard Woolf, Clive Bell, and others of the future Bloomsbury Group (VW's younger brother Adrian follows him to Trinity in 1902). | Boer War begins. Births of Bowen and Coward. Symons, *The Symbolist Movement in Literature* James, *The Awkward Age* Freud, *The Interpretation of Dreams* |
| 1900 | Deaths of Nietzsche, Wilde, and Ruskin; *Daily Express* started; Planck announces quantum theory; Boxer Rising. Conrad, *Lord Jim* |

# Chronology

| | | |
|---|---|---|
| 1901 | | Death of Queen Victoria; accession of Edward VII; first wireless communication between Europe and USA; 'World's Classics' series begun. Kipling, *Kim* |
| 1902 | VW starts private lessons in Greek with Janet Case. | End of Boer War; British Academy founded; *Encyclopaedia Britannica* (10th edn.); *TLS* started. Bennett, *Anna of the Five Towns* James, *The Wings of the Dove* |
| 1903 | | Deaths of Gissing and Spencer; *Daily Mirror* started; Wright brothers make their first aeroplane flight; Emmeline Pankhurst founds Women's Social and Political Union. Butler, *The Way of All Flesh* James, *The Ambassadors* Moore, *Principia Ethica* |
| 1904 | (22 Feb.) Death of father, Sir Leslie Stephen. In spring, VW travels to Italy with Vanessa and friend Violet Dickinson. (10 May) VW has second nervous breakdown and is ill for three months. Moves to 46, Gordon Square. (14 Dec.) VW's first publication appears. | Deaths of Christina Rossetti and Chekhov; Russo-Japanese War; *Entente Cordiale* between Britain and France. Chesterton, *The Napoleon of Notting Hill* Conrad, *Nostromo* James, *The Golden Bowl* |
| 1905 | (March, April) Travels in Portugal and Spain. Writes reviews and teaches once a week at Morley College, London. | Einstein, *Special Theory of Relativity*; Sartre born. Shaw, *Major Barbara* and *Man and Superman* Wells, *Kipps* Forster, *Where Angels Fear to Tread* |
| 1906 | (Sept. and Oct.) Travels in Greece. (20 Nov.) death of Thoby Stephen. | Death of Ibsen; Beckett born; Liberal Government elected; Campbell-Bannerman Prime Minister; launch of HMS *Dreadnought*. |
| 1907 | (7 Feb.) Marriage of Vanessa to Clive Bell. VW moves with Adrian to 29 Fitzroy Square. At work on her first novel, 'Melymbrosia' (working title for *The Voyage Out*). | Auden born; Anglo-Russian Entente. Synge, *The Playboy of the Western World* Conrad, *The Secret Agent* Forster, *The Longest Journey* |

| | | |
|---|---|---|
| 1908 | (Sept.) Visits Italy with the Bells. | Asquith Prime Minister; Old Age Pensions Act; Elgar's First Symphony.<br>Bennett, *The Old Wives' Tale*<br>Forster, *A Room with a View*<br>Chesterton, *The Man Who Was Thursday* |
| 1909 | (17 Feb.) Lytton Strachey proposes marriage. (30 March) First meets Lady Ottoline Morrell. (April) Visits Florence. (Aug.) Visits Bayreuth and Dresden. | Death of Meredith; 'People's Budget'; English Channel flown by Blériot.<br>Wells, *Tono-Bungay*<br>Masterman, *The Condition of England*<br>Marinetti, *Futurist Manifesto* |
| 1910 | (Jan.) Works for women's suffrage. (June–Aug.) Spends time in a nursing home at Twickenham. | Deaths of Edward VII, Tolstoy, and Florence Nightingale; accession of George V; *Encyclopaedia Britannica* (11th edn.); Roger Fry's Post-Impressionist Exhibition.<br>Bennett, *Clayhanger*<br>Forster, *Howards End*<br>Yeats, *The Green Helmet*<br>Wells, *The History of Mr Polly* |
| 1911 | (April) Travels to Turkey, where Vanessa is ill. (Nov.) Moves to 38 Brunswick Square, sharing house with Adrian, John Maynard Keynes, Duncan Grant, and Leonard Woolf. | National Insurance Act; Suffragette riots.<br>Conrad, *Under Western Eyes*<br>Wells, *The New Machiavelli*<br>Lawrence, *The White Peacock* |
| 1912 | Rents Asheham House. (Feb.) Spends some days in Twickenham nursing home. (10 Aug.) Marriage to Leonard Woolf. Honeymoon in Provence, Spain, and Italy. (Oct.) Moves to 13 Clifford's Inn, London. | Second Post-Impressionist Exhibition; Suffragettes active; strikes by dockers, coal-miners, and transport workers; Irish Home Rule Bill rejected by Lords; sinking of SS *Titanic*; death of Scott in the Antarctic; *Daily Herald* started. English translations of Chekhov and Dostoevsky begin to appear. |
| 1913 | (March) MS of *The Voyage Out* delivered to publisher. Unwell most of summer. (9 Sept.) Suicide attempt. Remains under care of nurses and husband for rest of year. | *New Statesman* started; Suffragettes active.<br>Lawrence, *Sons and Lovers* |

| | | |
|---|---|---|
| 1914 | (16 Feb.) Last nurse leaves. Moves to Richmond, Surrey. | Irish Home Rule Bill passed by Parliament; First World War begins (4 Aug.); Dylan Thomas born. Lewis, *Blast* Joyce, *Dubliners* Yeats, *Responsibilities* Hardy, *Satires of Circumstance* Bell, *Art* |
| 1915 | Purchase of Hogarth House, Richmond. (26 March) *The Voyage Out* published. (April, May) Bout of violent madness; under care of nurses until November. | Death of Rupert Brooke; Einstein, *General Theory of Relativity*; Second Battle of Ypres; Dardanelles Campaign; sinking of SS *Lusitania*; air attacks on London. Ford, *The Good Soldier* Lawrence, *The Rainbow* Brooke, *1914 and Other Poems* Richardson, *Pointed Roofs* |
| 1916 | (17 Oct.) Lectures to Richmond branch of the Women's Co-operative Guild. Regular work for *TLS*. | Death of James; Lloyd George Prime Minister; First Battle of the Somme; Battle of Verdun; Gallipoli Campaign; Easter Rising in Dublin. Joyce, *Portrait of the Artist as a Young Man* |
| 1917 | (July) Hogarth Press commences publication with *The Mark on the Wall*. VW begins work on *Night and Day*. | Death of Edward Thomas. Third Battle of Ypres (Passchendaele); T. E. Lawrence's campaigns in Arabia; USA enters the War; Revolution in Russia (Feb., Oct.); Balfour Declaration. Eliot, *Prufrock and Other Observations* |
| 1918 | Writes reviews and *Night and Day;* also sets type for the Hogarth Press. (15 Nov.) First meets T. S. Eliot. | Death of Owen; Second Battle of the Somme; final German offensive collapses; Armistice with Germany (11 Nov.); Franchise Act grants vote to women over 30; influenza pandemic kills millions. Lewis, *Tarr* Hopkins, *Poems* Strachey, *Eminent Victorians* |
| 1919 | (1 July) Purchase of Monk's House, Rodmell, Sussex. (20 Oct.) *Night and Day* published. | Treaty of Versailles; Alcock and Brown fly the Atlantic; National Socialists founded in Germany. Sinclair, *Mary Olivier* Shaw, *Heartbreak House* |
| 1920 | Works on journalism and *Jacob's Room*. | League of Nations established. Pound, *Hugh Selwyn Mauberley* Lawrence, *Women in Love* Eliot, *The Sacred Wood* Fry, *Vision and Design* |

| | | |
|---|---|---|
| 1921 | Ill for summer months. (4 Nov.) Finishes *Jacob's Room*. | Irish Free State founded. Huxley, *Crome Yellow* |
| 1922 | (Jan. to May) Ill. (14 Dec.) First meets Vita Sackville-West. (24 Oct.) *Jacob's Room* published. | Bonar Law Prime Minister; Mussolini forms Fascist Government in Italy; death of Proust; *Encyclopaedia Britannica* (12th edn.); *Criterion* founded; BBC founded; Irish Free State proclaimed. Eliot, *The Waste Land* Galsworthy, *The Forsyte Saga* Joyce, *Ulysses* Mansfield, *The Garden Party* Wittgenstein, *Tractatus Logico-Philosophicus* |
| 1923 | (March, April) Visits Spain. Works on 'The Hours', the first version of *Mrs Dalloway*. | Baldwin Prime Minister; BBC radio begins broadcasting (Nov.); death of K. Mansfield. |
| 1924 | Purchase of lease on 52 Tavistock Square, Bloomsbury. Gives lecture that becomes 'Mr Bennett and Mrs Brown'. (8 Oct.) Finishes *Mrs Dalloway*. | First (minority) Labour Government; Ramsay MacDonald Prime Minister; deaths of Lenin, Kafka, and Conrad. Ford, *Some Do Not* Forster, *A Passage to India* O'Casey, *Juno and the Paycock* Coward, *The Vortex* |
| 1925 | (23 April) *The Common Reader* published. (14 May) *Mrs Dalloway* published. Ill during summer. | Gerhardie, *The Polyglots* Ford, *No More Parades* Huxley, *Those Barren Leaves* Whitehead, *Science and the Modern World* |
| 1926 | (Jan) Unwell with German measles. Writes *To the Lighthouse*. | General Strike (3–12 May); *Encyclopaedia Britannica* (13th edn.); first television demonstration. Ford, *A Man Could Stand Up* Tawney, *Religion and the Rise of Capitalism* |
| 1927 | (March, April) Travels in France and Italy. (5 May) *To the Lighthouse* published. (5 Oct.) Begins *Orlando*. | Lindburgh flies solo across the Atlantic; first 'talkie' films. |
| 1928 | (11 Oct.) *Orlando* published. Delivers lectures at Cambridge on which she bases *A Room of One's Own*. | Death of Hardy; votes for women over 21. Yeats, *The Tower* Lawrence, *Lady Chatterley's Lover* Waugh, *Decline and Fall* Sherriff, *Journey's End* Ford, *Last Post* Huxley, *Point Counter Point* Bell, *Civilization* |

# Chronology

1929 (Jan.) Travels to Berlin. (24 Oct.) *A Room of One's Own* published.

2nd Labour Government, MacDonald Prime Minister; collapse of New York Stock Exchange; start of world economic depression.
Graves, *Goodbye to All That*
Aldington, *Death of a Hero*
Green, *Living*

1930 (20 Feb.) First meets Ethel Smyth; (29 May) Finishes first version of *The Waves*.

Mass unemployment; television starts in USA; deaths of Lawrence and Conan Doyle.
Auden, *Poems*
Eliot, *Ash Wednesday*
Waugh, *Vile Bodies*
Coward, *Private Lives*
Lewis, *Apes of God*

1931 (April) Car tour through France. (8 Oct.) *The Waves* published. Writes *Flush*.

Formation of National Government; abandonment of Gold Standard; death of Bennett; Japan invades China.

1932 (21 Jan.) Death of Lytton Strachey. (13 Oct.) *The Common Reader*, 2nd series, published. Begins *The Years*, at this point called 'The Pargiters'.

Roosevelt becomes President of USA; hunger marches start in Britain; *Scrutiny* starts.
Huxley, *Brave New World*

1933 (May) Car tour of France and Italy. (5 Oct.) *Flush* published.

Deaths of Galsworthy and George Moore; Hitler becomes Chancellor of Germany.
Orwell, *Down and Out in Paris and London*
Wells, *The Shape of Things to Come*.

1934 Works on *The Years*. (9 Sept.) Death of Roger Fry.

Waugh, *A Handful of Dust*
Graves, *I, Claudius*
Beckett, *More Pricks than Kicks*
Toynbee, *A Study of History*

1935 Rewrites *The Years*. (May) Car tour of Holland, Germany, and Italy.

George V's Silver Jubilee; Baldwin Prime Minister of National Government; Germany re-arms; Italian invasion of Abyssinia (Ethiopia).
Isherwood, *Mr Norris Changes Trains*
T. S. Eliot, *Murder in the Cathedral*

1936 (May–Oct.) Ill. Finishes *The Years*. Begins *Three Guineas*.

Death of George V; accession of Edward VIII; abdication crisis; accession of George VI; Civil War breaks out in Spain; first of the Moscow show trials; Germany re-occupies the Rhineland; BBC television begins (2 Nov); deaths of Chesterton, Kipling, and Housman.
Orwell, *Keep the Aspidistra Flying*

| | | |
|---|---|---|
| 1937 | (15 March) *The Years* published. Begins *Roger Fry: A Biography.* (18 July) Death in Spanish Civil War of Julian Bell, son of Vanessa. | Chamberlain Prime Minister; destruction of Guernica; death of Barrie. Orwell, *Road to Wigan Pier* |
| 1938 | (2 June) *Three Guineas* published. Works on *Roger Fry*, and begins to envisage *Between the Acts.* | German *Anschluss* with Austria; Munich agreement; dismemberment of Czechoslovakia; first jet engine. Beckett, *Murphy* Bowen, *The Death of the Heart* Greene, *Brighton Rock* Orwell, *The Road to Wigan Pier* |
| 1939 | VW moves to 37 Mecklenburgh Square, but lives mostly at Monk's House. Works on *Between the Acts.* Meets Freud in London. | End of Civil War in Spain; Russo-German pact; Germany invades Poland (Sept.); Britain and France declare war on Germany (3 Sept.); deaths of Freud, Yeats, and Ford. Joyce, *Finnegans Wake* Isherwood, *Goodbye to Berlin* |
| 1940 | (25 July) *Roger Fry* published. (10 Sept.) Mecklenburgh Square house bombed. (18 Oct.) witnesses the ruins of 52 Tavistock Square, destroyed by bombs. (23 Nov.) Finishes *Between the Acts.* | Germany invades north-west Europe; fall of France; evacuation of British troops from Dunkirk; Battle of Britain; beginning of 'the Blitz'; National Government under Churchill. |
| 1941 | (26 Feb.) Revises *Between the Acts.* Becomes ill. (28 March) Drowns herself in River Ouse, near Monk's House. (July) *Between the Acts* published. | Germany invades USSR; Japanese destroy US Fleet at Pearl Harbor; USA enters war; death of Joyce. |

# A ROOM OF ONE'S OWN

# A ROOM OF ONE'S OWN[1]

CHAPTER I

BUT, you may say, we asked you to speak about women and fiction—what has that got to do with a room of one's own? I will try to explain. When you asked me to speak about women and fiction I sat down on the banks of a river and began to wonder what the words meant. They might mean simply a few remarks about Fanny Burney; a few more about Jane Austen; a tribute to the Brontës and a sketch of Haworth Parsonage* under snow; some witticisms if possible about Miss Mitford;* a respectful allusion to George Eliot; a reference to Mrs Gaskell and one would have done. But at second sight the words seemed not so simple. The title women and fiction might mean, and you may have meant it to mean, women and what they are like, or it might mean women and the fiction that they write; or it might mean women and the fiction that is written about them; or it might mean that somehow all three are inextricably mixed together and you want me to consider them in that light. But when I began to

[1] This essay is based upon two papers read to the Arts Society at Newnham and the Odtaa at Girton in October 1928. The papers were too long to be read in full, and have since been altered and expanded.

consider the subject in this last way, which seemed
the most interesting, I soon saw that it had one fatal
drawback. I should never be able to come to a
conclusion. I should never be able to fulfil what is, I
understand, the first duty of a lecturer—to hand you
after an hour's discourse a nugget of pure truth to
wrap up between the pages of your notebooks and
keep on the mantelpiece for ever. All I could do was
to offer you an opinion upon one minor point—a
woman must have money and a room of her own if
she is to write fiction; and that, as you will see, leaves
the great problem of the true nature of woman and
the true nature of fiction unsolved. I have shirked the
duty of coming to a conclusion upon these two
questions—women and fiction remain, so far as I am
concerned, unsolved problems. But in order to make
some amends I am going to do what I can to show
you how I arrived at this opinion about the room and
the money. I am going to develop in your presence as
fully and freely as I can the train of thought which
led me to think this. Perhaps if I lay bare the ideas,
the prejudices, that lie behind this statement you will
find that they have some bearing upon women and
some upon fiction. At any rate, when a subject is
highly controversial—and any question about sex is
that—one cannot hope to tell the truth. One can only
show how one came to hold whatever opinion one
does hold. One can only give one's audience the
chance of drawing their own conclusions as they

observe the limitations, the prejudices, the idio-
syncrasies of the speaker. Fiction here is likely to
contain more truth than fact. Therefore I propose,
making use of all the liberties and licences of a novelist,
to tell you the story of the two days that preceded my
coming here—how, bowed down by the weight of the
subject which you have laid upon my shoulders, I
pondered it, and made it work in and out of my daily
life. I need not say that what I am about to describe has
no existence; Oxbridge is an invention; so is Fernham;
'I' is only a convenient term for somebody who has no
real being. Lies will flow from my lips, but there may
perhaps be some truth mixed up with them; it is for
you to seek out this truth and to decide whether any
part of it is worth keeping. If not, you will of course
throw the whole of it into the waste-paper basket and
forget all about it.

Here then was I (call me Mary Beton, Mary Seton,
Mary Carmichael or by any name you please*—it is
not a matter of importance) sitting on the banks of a
river a week or two ago in fine October weather, lost
in thought. That collar I have spoken of, women and
fiction, the need of coming to some conclusion on a
subject that raises all sorts of prejudices and passions,
bowed my head to the ground. To the right and left
bushes of some sort, golden and crimson, glowed
with the colour, even it seemed burnt with the heat,
of fire. On the further bank the willows wept in
perpetual lamentation, their hair about their shoul-

[ 5 ]

ders. The river reflected whatever it chose of sky and bridge and burning tree, and when the undergraduate had oared his boat through the reflections they closed again, completely, as if he had never been. There one might have sat the clock round lost in thought. Thought—to call it by a prouder name than it deserved—had let its line down into the stream. It swayed, minute after minute, hither and thither among the reflections and the weeds, letting the water lift it and sink it until—you know the little tug—the sudden conglomeration of an idea at the end of one's line: and then the cautious hauling of it in, and the careful laying of it out? Alas, laid on the grass how small, how insignificant this thought of mine looked; the sort of fish that a good fisherman puts back into the water so that it may grow fatter and be one day worth cooking and eating. I will not trouble you with that thought now, though if you look carefully you may find it for yourselves in the course of what I am going to say.

But however small it was, it had, nevertheless, the mysterious property of its kind—put back into the mind, it became at once very exciting, and important; and as it darted and sank, and flashed hither and thither, set up such a wash and tumult of ideas that it was impossible to sit still. It was thus that I found myself walking with extreme rapidity across a grass plot. Instantly a man's figure rose to intercept me. Nor did I at first understand that the gesticulations of a curious-looking object, in a cut-away coat and evening shirt, were aimed at me. His face expressed horror and indignation. Instinct rather than reason came to my help; he was a Beadle; I was a woman. This was the turf; there was the path. Only the Fellows and Scholars are allowed here; the gravel is the place for me. Such thoughts were the work of a moment. As I regained the path the arms of the Beadle sank, his face assumed its usual repose, and though turf is better walking than gravel, no very great harm was done. The only charge I could bring against the Fellows and Scholars of whatever the college might happen to be was that in protection of their turf, which has been rolled for 300 years in succession, they had sent my little fish into hiding.

What idea it had been that had sent me so audaciously trespassing I could not now remember. The spirit of peace descended like a cloud from heaven, for if the spirit of peace dwells anywhere, it is in the courts and quadrangles of Oxbridge on a fine October morning. Strolling through those colleges past those ancient halls the roughness of the present seemed smoothed away; the body seemed contained in a miraculous glass cabinet through which no sound could penetrate, and the mind, freed from any contact with facts (unless one trespassed on the turf again), was at liberty to settle down upon whatever meditation was in harmony with the moment. As chance would have it, some stray memory of some old essay about revisiting Oxbridge* in the long vacation brought Charles Lamb to mind—Saint Charles, said Thackeray, putting a letter of Lamb's to his forehead. Indeed, among all the dead (I give you my thoughts as they came to me), Lamb is one of the most congenial; one to whom one would have liked to say, Tell me then how you wrote your essays? For his essays are superior even to Max Beerbohm's, I thought, with all their perfection, because of that wild flash of imagination, that lightning crack of genius in the middle of them which leaves them flawed and imperfect, but starred with poetry. Lamb then came to Oxbridge perhaps a hundred years ago. Certainly he wrote an essay—the name escapes me—about the manuscript of one of Milton's poems which he saw here. It was *Lycidas* perhaps, and Lamb wrote how it shocked him to think it possible that any word in *Lycidas* could have been different from what it is. To think of Milton changing the words in that poem seemed to him a sort of sacrilege. This led me to remember what I could of *Lycidas* and to amuse myself with guessing which word it could have been that Milton had altered, and why. It then occurred to me that the very manuscript itself which Lamb had looked at was only a few hundred yards away, so that one could follow Lamb's footsteps across the quadrangle to that famous library* where the treasure is kept. Moreover, I recollected, as I put this plan into execution, it is in this famous library that the manuscript of Thackeray's *Esmond* is also preserved. The critics often say that *Esmond* is Thackeray's most perfect novel. But the affectation of the style, with its imitation of the eighteenth century, hampers one, so far as I can remember; unless indeed the eighteenth-century style was natural to Thackeray—a fact that one might prove by looking at the manuscript and seeing whether the alterations were for the benefit of the style or of the sense. But then one would have to decide what is style and what is meaning, a question which—but here I was actually at the door which leads into the library itself. I must have opened it, for instantly there issued, like a guardian angel barring the way with a flutter of black gown instead of white wings, a deprecating, silvery, kindly gentleman, who regretted in a low voice as he waved me back that ladies are only admitted to the library if accompanied by a Fellow of the College or furnished with a letter of introduction.

That a famous library has been cursed by a woman is a matter of complete indifference to a famous library. Venerable and calm, with all its treasures safe locked within its breast, it sleeps complacently and will, so far as I am concerned, so sleep for ever. Never will I wake those echoes, never will I ask for that hospitality again, I vowed as I descended the steps in anger. Still an hour remained before luncheon, and what was one to do? Stroll on the meadows? sit by the river? Certainly it was a lovely autumn morning;

the leaves were fluttering red to the ground; there was no great hardship in doing either. But the sound of music reached my ear. Some service or celebration was going forward. The organ complained magnificently as I passed the chapel door. Even the sorrow of Christianity sounded in that serene air more like the recollection of sorrow than sorrow itself; even the groanings of the ancient organ seemed lapped in peace. I had no wish to enter had I the right, and this time the verger might have stopped me, demanding perhaps my baptismal certificate, or a letter of introduction from the Dean. But the outside of these magnificent buildings is often as beautiful as the inside. Moreover, it was amusing enough to watch the congregation assembling, coming in and going out again, busying themselves at the door of the chapel like bees at the mouth of a hive. Many were in cap and gown; some had tufts of fur* on their shoulders; others were wheeled in bath-chairs; others, though not past middle age, seemed creased and crushed into shapes so singular that one was reminded of those giant crabs and crayfish who heave with difficulty across the sand of an aquarium. As I leant against the wall the University indeed seemed a sanctuary in which are preserved rare types which would soon be obsolete if left to fight for existence on the pavement of the Strand. Old stories of old deans and old dons came back to mind, but before I had summoned up courage to whistle—it used to be said that at the sound of a whistle old Professor —— instantly broke into a gallop—the venerable congregation had gone inside. The outside of the chapel remained. As you know, its high domes and pinnacles can be seen, like a sailing-ship always voyaging never arriving, lit up at night and visible for miles, far away across the hills. Once, presumably, this quadrangle with its smooth lawns, its massive buildings and the chapel itself was marsh too, where the grasses waved and the swine rootled. Teams of horses and oxen, I thought, must have hauled the stone in wagons from far countries, and then with infinite labour the grey blocks in whose shade I was now standing were poised in order one on top of another, and then the painters brought their glass for the windows, and the masons were busy for centuries up on that roof with putty and cement, spade and trowel. Every Saturday somebody must have poured gold and silver out of a leathern purse into their ancient fists, for they had their beer and skittles presumably of an evening. An unending stream of gold and silver, I thought, must have flowed into this court perpetually to keep the stones coming and the masons working; to level, to ditch, to dig and to drain. But it was then the age of faith, and money was poured liberally to set these stones on a deep foundation, and when the stones were raised, still more money was poured in from the coffers of kings and queens and great nobles to ensure that hymns should be sung here and scholars taught. Lands were granted; tithes were paid. And when the age of faith was over and the age of reason had come, still the same flow of gold and silver went on; fellowships were founded; lectureships endowed; only the gold and silver flowed now, not from the coffers of the king, but from the chests of merchants and manufacturers, from the purses of men who had made, say, a fortune from industry, and returned, in their wills, a bounteous share of it to endow more chairs, more lectureships, more fellowships in the university where they had learnt their craft. Hence the libraries and laboratories; the observatories; the splendid equipment of costly and delicate instruments which now stands on glass shelves, where centuries ago the grasses waved and the swine rootled. Certainly, as I strolled round the court, the foundation of gold and silver seemed deep enough; the pavement laid solidly over the wild grasses. Men with trays on their heads went busily from staircase to staircase. Gaudy blossoms flowered in window-boxes. The strains of the gramophone blared out from the rooms within. It was impossible not to reflect—the reflection whatever it may have been was cut short. The clock struck. It was time to find one's way to luncheon.

It is a curious fact that novelists have a way of making us believe that luncheon parties are invariably memorable for something very witty that was said, or for something very wise that was done. But they seldom spare a word for what was eaten. It is part of the novelist's convention not to mention soup and salmon and ducklings, as if soup and salmon and ducklings were of no importance whatsoever, as if nobody ever smoked a cigar or drank a glass of wine. Here, however, I shall take the liberty to defy that convention and to tell you that the lunch on this occasion began with soles, sunk in a deep dish, over which the college cook had spread a counterpane of the whitest cream, save that it was branded here and there with brown spots like the spots on the flanks of a doe. After that came the partridges, but if this suggests a couple of bald, brown birds on a plate you are mistaken. The partridges, many and various, came with all their retinue of sauces and salads, the sharp and the sweet, each in its order; their potatoes, thin as coins but not so hard; their sprouts, foliated as rosebuds but more succulent. And no sooner had the roast and its retinue been done with than the silent serving-man, the Beadle himself perhaps in a milder manifestation, set before us, wreathed in napkins, a confection which rose all sugar from the waves. To call it pudding and so relate it to rice and tapioca would be an insult. Meanwhile the wineglasses had flushed yellow and flushed crimson; had been emptied; had been filled. And thus by degrees was lit, half-way down the spine, which is the seat of the soul, not that hard little electric light which we call brilliance, as it pops in and out upon our lips, but the more profound, subtle and subterranean glow which is the rich yellow flame of rational intercourse. No need to hurry. No need to sparkle. No need to be anybody but oneself. We are all going to heaven and Vandyck is of the company—in other words, how good life seemed, how sweet its rewards, how trivial this grudge or that grievance, how admirable friendship and the society of one's kind, as, lighting a good cigarette, one sunk among the cushions in the window-seat.

If by good luck there had been an ash-tray handy, if one had not knocked the ash out of the window in default, if things had been a little different from what they were, one would not have seen, presumably, a cat without a tail. The sight of that abrupt and truncated animal padding softly across the quadrangle changed by some fluke of the subconscious intelligence the emotional light for me. It was as if someone had let fall a shade. Perhaps the excellent hock was relinquishing its hold. Certainly, as I watched the Manx cat pause in the middle of the lawn as if it too questioned the universe, something seemed lacking, something seemed different. But what was lacking, what was different, I asked myself, listening to the talk? And to answer that question I had to think myself out of the room, back into the past, before the war indeed, and to set before my eyes the model of another luncheon party held in rooms not very far distant from these; but different. Everything was different. Meanwhile the talk went on among the guests, who were many and young, some of this sex, some of that; it went on swimmingly, it went on agreeably, freely, amusingly. And as it went on I set it against the background of that other talk, and as I matched the two together I had no doubt that one was the descendant, the legitimate heir of the other. Nothing was changed; nothing was different save only—here I listened with all my ears not entirely to what was being said, but to the murmur or current behind it. Yes, that was it—the change was there. Before the war at a luncheon party like this people would have said precisely the same things but they would have sounded different, because in those days they were accompanied by a sort of humming noise, not articulate, but musical, exciting, which changed the value of the words themselves. Could one set that humming noise to words? Perhaps with the help of the poets one could. A book lay beside me and, opening it, I turned casually enough to Tennyson. And here I found Tennyson was singing:

> There has fallen a splendid tear
>   From the passion-flower at the gate.
> She is coming, my dove, my dear;
>   She is coming, my life, my fate;
> The red rose cries, 'She is near, she is near';
>   And the white rose weeps, 'She is late';
> The larkspur listens, 'I hear, I hear';
>   And the lily whispers, 'I wait.'*

Was that what men hummed at luncheon parties before the war? And the women?

My heart is like a singing bird
    Whose nest is in a water'd shoot;
My heart is like an apple tree
    Whose boughs are bent with thick-set fruit;
My heart is like a rainbow shell
    That paddles in a halcyon sea;
My heart is gladder than all these
    Because my love is come to me.*

Was that what women hummed at luncheon parties before the war?

There was something so ludicrous in thinking of people humming such things even under their breath at luncheon parties before the war that I burst out laughing, and had to explain my laughter by pointing at the Manx cat, who did look a little absurd, poor beast, without a tail, in the middle of the lawn. Was he really born so, or had he lost his tail in an accident? The tailless cat, though some are said to exist in the Isle of Man, is rarer than one thinks. It is a queer animal, quaint rather than beautiful. It is strange what a difference a tail makes—you know the sort of things one says as a lunch party breaks up and people are finding their coats and hats.

This one, thanks to the hospitality of the host, had lasted far into the afternoon. The beautiful October day was fading and the leaves were falling from the trees in the avenue as I walked through it. Gate after gate seemed to close with gentle finality behind me. Innumerable beadles were fitting innumerable keys into well-oiled locks; the treasure-house was being made secure for another night. After the avenue one comes out upon a road—I forget its name—which leads you, if you take the right turning, along to Fernham. But there was plenty of time. Dinner was not till half-past seven. One could almost do without dinner after such a luncheon. It is strange how a scrap of poetry works in the mind and makes the legs move in time to it along the road. Those words—

> There has fallen a splendid tear
> From the passion-flower at the gate.
> She is coming, my dove, my dear—

sang in my blood as I stepped quickly along towards Headingley. And then, switching off into the other measure, I sang, where the waters are churned up by the weir:

> My heart is like a singing bird
> Whose nest is in a water'd shoot;
> My heart is like an apple tree . . .

What poets, I cried aloud, as one does in the dusk, what poets they were!

In a sort of jealousy, I suppose, for our own age, silly and absurd though these comparisons are, I went on to wonder if honestly one could name two living poets now as great as Tennyson and Christina Rossetti were then. Obviously it is impossible, I thought, looking into those foaming waters, to compare them.

The very reason why that poetry excites one to such abandonment, such rapture, is that it celebrates some feeling that one used to have (at luncheon parties before the war perhaps), so that one responds easily, familiarly, without troubling to check the feeling, or to compare it with any that one has now. But the living poets express a feeling that is actually being made and torn out of us at the moment. One does not recognize it in the first place; often for some reason one fears it; one watches it with keenness and compares it jealously and suspiciously with the old feeling that one knew. Hence the difficulty of modern poetry; and it is because of this difficulty that one cannot remember more than two consecutive lines of any good modern poet. For this reason—that my memory failed me—the argument flagged for want of material. But why, I continued, moving on towards Headingley, have we stopped humming under our breath at luncheon parties? Why has Alfred ceased to sing

> She is coming, my dove, my dear.

Why has Christina ceased to respond

> My heart is gladder than all these
> Because my love is come to me?

Shall we lay the blame on the war? When the guns fired in August 1914, did the faces of men and women show so plain in each other's eyes that romance was killed? Certainly it was a shock (to women in particular with their illusions about education, and so on) to see the faces of our rulers in the light of shell-fire. So ugly they looked—German, English, French—so stupid. But lay the blame where one will, on whom one will, the illusion which inspired Tennyson and Christina Rossetti to sing so passionately about the coming of their loves is far rarer now than then. One has only to read, to look, to listen, to remember. But why say 'blame'? Why, if it was an illusion, not praise the catastrophe, whatever it was, that destroyed illusion and put truth in its place? For truth ... those dots mark the spot where, in search of truth, I missed the turning up to Fernham. Yes indeed, which was truth and which was illusion? I asked myself. What was the truth about these houses, for example, dim and festive now with their red windows in the dusk, but raw and red and squalid, with their sweets and their bootlaces, at nine o'clock in the morning? And the willows and the river and the gardens that run down to the river, vague now with the mist stealing over them, but gold and red in the sunlight—which was the truth, which was the illusion about them? I spare you the twists and turns of my cogitations, for no conclusion was found on the road to Headingley, and I ask you to suppose that I soon found out my mistake about the turning and retraced my steps to Fernham.

As I have said already that it was an October day,

I dare not forfeit your respect and imperil the fair name of fiction by changing the season and describing lilacs hanging over garden walls, crocuses, tulips and other flowers of spring. Fiction must stick to facts, and the truer the facts the better the fiction—so we are told. Therefore it was still autumn and the leaves were still yellow and falling, if anything, a little faster than before, because it was now evening (seven twenty-three to be precise) and a breeze (from the south-west to be exact) had risen. But for all that there was something odd at work:

> My heart is like a singing bird
>   Whose nest is in a water'd shoot;
> My heart is like an apple tree
>   Whose boughs are bent with thick-set fruit—

perhaps the words of Christina Rossetti were partly responsible for the folly of the fancy—it was nothing of course but a fancy—that the lilac was shaking its flowers over the garden walls, and the brimstone butterflies were scudding hither and thither, and the dust of the pollen was in the air. A wind blew, from what quarter I know not, but it lifted the half-grown leaves so that there was a flash of silver grey in the air. It was the time between the lights when colours undergo their intensification and purples and golds burn in window-panes like the beat of an excitable heart; when for some reason the beauty of the world revealed and yet soon to perish (here I pushed into the garden, for, unwisely, the door was left open and no beadles seemed about), the beauty of the world which is so soon to perish, has two edges, one of laughter, one of anguish, cutting the heart asunder. The gardens of Fernham lay before me in the spring twilight, wild and open, and in the long grass, sprinkled and carelessly flung, were daffodils and bluebells, not orderly perhaps at the best of times, and now wind-blown and waving as they tugged at their roots. The windows of the building, curved like ships' windows among generous waves of red brick, changed from lemon to silver under the flight of the quick spring clouds. Somebody was in a hammock, somebody, but in this light they were phantoms only, half guessed, half seen, raced across the grass—would no one stop her?—and then on the terrace, as if popping out to breathe the air, to glance at the garden, came a bent figure, formidable yet humble, with her great forehead and her shabby dress—could it be the famous scholar, could it be J—— H——* herself? All was dim, yet intense too, as if the scarf which the dusk had flung over the garden were torn asunder by star or sword—the flash of some terrible reality leaping, as its way is, out of the heart of the spring. For youth——

Here was my soup. Dinner was being served in the great dining-hall. Far from being spring it was in fact an evening in October. Everybody was assembled in the big dining-room. Dinner was ready. Here was the soup. It was a plain gravy soup. There was nothing to stir the fancy in that. One could have seen through the transparent liquid any pattern that there might have been on the plate itself. But there was no pattern. The plate was plain. Next came beef with its attendant greens and potatoes—a homely trinity, suggesting the rumps of cattle in a muddy market, and sprouts curled and yellowed at the edge, and bargaining and cheapening, and women with string bags on Monday morning. There was no reason to complain of human nature's daily food, seeing that the supply was sufficient and coal-miners doubtless were sitting down to less. Prunes and custard followed. And if anyone complains that prunes, even when mitigated by custard, are an uncharitable vegetable (fruit they are not), stringy as a miser's heart and exuding a fluid such as might run in misers' veins who have denied themselves wine and warmth for eighty years and yet not given to the poor, he should reflect that there are people whose charity embraces even the prune. Biscuits and cheese came next, and here the water-jug was liberally passed round, for it is the nature of biscuits to be dry, and these were biscuits to the core. That was all. The meal was over. Everybody scraped their chairs back; the swing-doors swung violently to and fro; soon the hall was emptied of every sign of food and made ready no doubt for breakfast next morning. Down corridors and up staircases the youth of England went banging and singing. And was it for a guest, a stranger (for I had no more right here in Fernham than in Trinity or Somerville or Girton or Newnham or Christchurch), to say, 'The dinner was not good,' or to say (we were now, Mary Seton and I, in her sitting-room), 'Could we not have dined up here alone?' for if I had said anything of the kind I should have been prying and searching into the secret economies of a house which to the stranger wears so fine a front of gaiety and courage. No, one could say nothing of the sort. Indeed, conversation for a moment flagged. The human frame being what it is, heart, body and brain all mixed together, and not contained in separate compartments as they will be no doubt in another million years, a good dinner is of great importance to good talk. One cannot think well, love well, sleep well, if one has not dined well. The lamp in the spine does not light on beef and prunes. We are all *probably* going to heaven, and Vandyck is, we *hope*, to meet us round the next corner—that is the dubious and qualifying state of mind that beef and prunes at the end of the day's work breed between them. Happily my friend, who taught science, had a cupboard where there was a squat bottle and little glasses—(but there should have been sole and partridge to begin with)—so that we were able to draw up to the fire and repair some of the damages of the day's living. In a minute or so we were slipping freely in and out among all those objects of curiosity and interest which form in the mind in the absence of a particular person, and are naturally to be discussed on coming together again—how somebody has married, another has not; one thinks this, another that; one has improved out of all knowledge, the other most amazingly gone to the bad—with all those speculations upon human nature and the character of the amazing world we live in which spring naturally from such beginnings. While these things were being said, however, I became shamefacedly aware of a current setting in of its own accord and carrying everything forward to an end of its own. One might be talking of Spain or Portugal, of book or racehorse, but the real interest of whatever was said was none of those things, but a scene of masons on a high roof some five centuries ago. Kings and nobles brought treasure in huge sacks and poured it under the earth. This scene was for ever coming alive in my mind and placing itself by another of lean cows and a muddy market and withered greens and the stringy hearts of old men—these two pictures, disjointed and disconnected and nonsensical as they were, were for ever coming together and combating each other and had me entirely at their mercy. The best course, unless the whole talk was to be distorted, was to expose what was in my mind to the air, when with good luck it would fade and crumble like the head of the dead king when they opened the coffin at Windsor. Briefly, then, I told Miss Seton about the masons who had been all those years on the roof of the chapel, and

about the kings and queens and nobles bearing sacks
of gold and silver on their shoulders, which they
shovelled into the earth; and then how the great
financial magnates of our own time came and laid
cheques and bonds, I suppose, where the others had
laid ingots and rough lumps of gold. All that lies
beneath the colleges down there, I said; but this
college, where we are now sitting, what lies beneath
its gallant red brick and the wild unkempt grasses of
the garden? What force is behind that plain china off
which we dined, and (here it popped out of my
mouth before I could stop it) the beef, the custard
and the prunes?

Well, said Mary Seton, about the year 1860—Oh,
but you know the story, she said, bored, I suppose,
by the recital. And she told me—rooms were hired.
Committees met. Envelopes were addressed. Circulars were drawn up. Meetings were held; letters were
read out; so-and-so has promised so much; on the
contrary, Mr —— won't give a penny. The *Saturday
Review* has been very rude. How can we raise a fund
to pay for offices? Shall we hold a bazaar? Can't we
find a pretty girl to sit in the front row? Let us look
up what John Stuart Mill* said on the subject. Can
anyone persuade the editor of the —— to print a
letter? Can we get Lady —— to sign it? Lady ——
is out of town. That was the way it was done,
presumably, sixty years ago, and it was a prodigious
effort, and a great deal of time was spent on it. And

it was only after a long struggle and with the utmost difficulty that they got thirty thousand pounds together.[2] So obviously we cannot have wine and partridges and servants carrying tin dishes on their heads, she said. We cannot have sofas and separate rooms. 'The amenities,' she said, quoting from some book or other, 'will have to wait.'[3]

At the thought of all those women working year after year and finding it hard to get two thousand pounds together, and as much as they could do to get thirty thousand pounds, we burst out in scorn at the reprehensible poverty of our sex. What had our mothers been doing then that they had no wealth to leave us? Powdering their noses? Looking in at shop windows? Flaunting in the sun at Monte Carlo? There were some photographs on the mantelpiece. Mary's mother—if that was her picture—may have been a wastrel in her spare time (she had thirteen children by a minister of the church), but if so her gay and dissipated life had left too few traces of its pleasures

---

[2] 'We are told that we ought to ask for £30,000 at least. . . . It is not a large sum, considering that there is to be but one college of this sort for Great Britain, Ireland and the Colonies, and considering how easy it is to raise immense sums for boys' schools. But considering how few people really wish women to be educated, it is a good deal.'—LADY STEPHEN, *Emily Davies and Girton College* (1927), 150-1.

[2] 'Every penny which could be scraped together was set aside for building, and the amenities had to be postponed.'—R. STRACHEY, *The Cause* (1928), 250.

on her face. She was a homely body; an old lady in a plaid shawl which was fastened by a large cameo; and she sat in a basket-chair, encouraging a spaniel to look at the camera, with the amused, yet strained expression of one who is sure that the dog will move directly the bulb is pressed. Now if she had gone into business; had become a manufacturer of artificial silk or a magnate on the Stock Exchange; if she had left two or three hundred thousand pounds to Fernham, we could have been sitting at our ease tonight and the subject of our talk might have been archaeology, botany, anthropology, physics, the nature of the atom, mathematics, astronomy, relativity, geography. If only Mrs Seton and her mother and her mother before her had learnt the great art of making money and had left their money, like their fathers and their grandfathers before them, to found fellowships and lectureships and prizes and scholarships appropriated to the use of their own sex, we might have dined very tolerably up here alone off a bird and a bottle of wine; we might have looked forward without undue confidence to a pleasant and honourable lifetime spent in the shelter of one of the liberally endowed professions. We might have been exploring or writing; mooning about the venerable places of the earth; sitting contemplative on the steps of the Parthenon, or going at ten to an office and coming home comfortably at half-past four to write a little poetry. Only, if Mrs Seton and her like had gone into business at the age of fifteen, there would have been—that was the snag in the argument—no Mary. What, I asked, did Mary think of that? There between the curtains was the October night, calm and lovely, with a star or two caught in the yellowing trees. Was she ready to resign her share of it and her memories (for they had been a happy family, though a large one) of games and quarrels up in Scotland, which she is never tired of praising for the fineness of its air and the quality of its cakes, in order that Fernham might have been endowed with fifty thousand pounds or so by a stroke of the pen? For, to endow a college would necessitate the suppression of families altogether. Making a fortune and bearing thirteen children—no human being could stand it. Consider the facts, we said. First there are nine months before the baby is born. Then the baby is born. Then there are three or four months spent in feeding the baby. After the baby is fed there are certainly five years spent in playing with the baby. You cannot, it seems, let children run about the streets. People who have seen them running wild in Russia say that the sight is not a pleasant one. People say, too, that human nature takes its shape in the years between one and five. If Mrs Seton, I said, had been making money, what sort of memories would you have had of games and quarrels? What would you have known of Scotland, and its fine air and cakes and all the rest of it? But it is useless to ask these questions, because you would never have come into existence at all. Moreover, it is equally useless to ask what might have happened if Mrs Seton and her mother and her mother before her had amassed great wealth and laid it under the foundations of college and library, because, in the first place, to earn money was impossible for them, and in the second, had it been possible, the law denied them the right to possess what money they earned. It is only for the last forty-eight years* that Mrs Seton has had a penny of her own. For all the centuries before that it would have been her husband's property—a thought which, perhaps, may have had its share in keeping Mrs Seton and her mothers off the Stock Exchange. Every penny I earn, they may have said, will be taken from me and disposed of according to my husband's wisdom— perhaps to found a scholarship or to endow a fellow- ship in Balliol or Kings, so that to earn money, even if I could earn money, is not a matter that interests me very greatly. I had better leave it to my husband.

At any rate, whether or not the blame rested on the old lady who was looking at the spaniel, there could be no doubt that for some reason or other our mothers had mismanaged their affairs very gravely. Not a penny could be spared for 'amenities'; for partridges and wine, beadles and turf, books and cigars, libraries and leisure. To raise bare walls out of bare earth was the utmost they could do.

So we talked standing at the window and looking, as so many thousands look every night, down on the domes and towers of the famous city beneath us. It was very beautiful, very mysterious in the autumn moonlight. The old stone looked very white and venerable. One thought of all the books that were assembled down there; of the pictures of old prelates and worthies hanging in the panelled rooms; of the painted windows that would be throwing strange globes and crescents on the pavement; of the tablets and memorials and inscriptions; of the fountains and the grass; of the quiet rooms looking across the quiet quadrangles. And (pardon me the thought) I thought, too, of the admirable smoke and drink and the deep armchairs and the pleasant carpets: of the urbanity, the geniality, the dignity which are the offspring of luxury and privacy and space. Certainly our mothers had not provided us with anything comparable to all this—our mothers who found it difficult to scrape together thirty thousand pounds, our mothers who bore thirteen children to ministers of religion at St Andrews.

So I went back to my inn, and as I walked through the dark streets I pondered this and that, as one does at the end of the day's work. I pondered why it was that Mrs Seton had no money to leave us; and what effect poverty has on the mind; and what effect wealth has on the mind; and I thought of the queer old gentlemen I had seen that morning with tufts of fur upon their shoulders; and I remembered how if one whistled one of them ran; and I thought of the organ booming in the chapel and of the shut doors of the library; and I thought how unpleasant it is to be locked out; and I thought how it is worse perhaps to be locked in; and, thinking of the safety and prosperity of the one sex and the poverty and insecurity of the other and of the effect of tradition and of the lack of tradition upon the mind of a writer, I thought at last that it was time to roll up the crumpled skin of the day, with its arguments and its impressions and its anger and its laughter, and cast it into the hedge. A thousand stars were flashing across the blue wastes of the sky. One seemed alone with an inscrutable society. All human beings were laid asleep—prone, horizontal, dumb. Nobody seemed stirring in the streets of Oxbridge. Even the door of the hotel sprang open at the touch of an invisible hand—not a boots was sitting up to light me to bed, it was so late.

## CHAPTER II

THE scene, if I may ask you to follow me, was now changed. The leaves were still falling, but in London now, not Oxbridge; and I must ask you to imagine a room, like many thousands, with a window looking across people's hats and vans and motorcars to other windows, and on the table inside the room a blank sheet of paper on which was written in large letters WOMEN AND FICTION, but no more. The inevitable sequel to lunching and dining at Oxbridge seemed, unfortunately, to be a visit to the British Museum. One must strain off what was personal and accidental in all these impressions and so reach the pure fluid, the essential oil of truth. For that visit to Oxbridge and the luncheon and the dinner had started a swarm of questions. Why did men drink wine and women water? Why was one sex so prosperous and the other so poor? What effect has poverty on fiction? What conditions are necessary for the creation of works of art?—a thousand questions at once suggested themselves. But one needed answers, not questions; and an answer was only to be had by consulting the learned and the unprejudiced, who have removed themselves above the strife of tongue and the confusion of body and issued the result of their reasoning and research in books which are to be found in the British Museum. If truth is not to be found on the shelves of the British Museum, where, I asked myself, picking up a notebook and a pencil, is truth?

Thus provided, thus confident and enquiring, I set out in the pursuit of truth. The day, though not actually wet, was dismal, and the streets in the neighbourhood of the Museum were full of open coal-holes, down which sacks were showering; four-wheeled cabs were drawing up and depositing on the pavement corded boxes containing, presumably, the entire wardrobe of some Swiss or Italian family seeking fortune or refuge or some other desirable commodity which is to be found in the boarding-houses of Bloomsbury in the winter. The usual hoarse-voiced men paraded the streets with plants on barrows. Some shouted; others sang. London was like a workshop. London was like a machine. We were all being shot backwards and forwards on this plain foundation to make some pattern. The British Museum was another department of the factory. The swing-doors swung open; and there one stood under the vast dome, as if one were a thought in the huge bald forehead which is so splendidly encircled by a band of famous names. One went to the counter; one took a slip of paper; one opened a volume of the catalogue, and . . . . . the five dots here indicate five separate minutes of stupefaction, wonder and bewilderment. Have you any notion of how many books are written about women in the course of one year? Have you any notion how many are written by men?

Are you aware that you are, perhaps, the most discussed animal in the universe? Here had I come with a notebook and a pencil proposing to spend a morning reading, supposing that at the end of the morning I should have transferred the truth to my notebook. But I should need to be a herd of elephants, I thought, and a wilderness of spiders,* desperately referring to the animals that are reputed longest lived and most multitudinously eyed, to cope with all this. I should need claws of steel and beak of brass even to penetrate the husk. How shall I ever find the grains of truth embedded in all this mass of paper? I asked myself, and in despair began running my eye up and down the long list of titles. Even the names of the books gave me food for thought. Sex and its nature might well attract doctors and biologists; but what was surprising and difficult of explanation was the fact that sex—woman, that is to say—also attracts agreeable essayists, light-fingered novelists, young men who have taken the MA degree; men who have taken no degree; men who have no apparent quali- fication save that they are not women. Some of these books were, on the face of it, frivolous and facetious; but many, on the other hand, were serious and prophetic, moral and hortatory. Merely to read the titles suggested innumerable schoolmasters, innumer- able clergymen mounting their platforms and pulpits and holding forth with a loquacity which far exceeded the hour usually allotted to such discourse on this one subject. It was a most strange phenomenon; and apparently—here I consulted the letter M—one confined to the male sex. Women do not write books about men—a fact that I could not help welcoming with relief, for if I had first to read all that men have written about women, then all that women have written about men, the aloe that flowers once in a hundred years would flower twice before I could set pen to paper. So, making a perfectly arbitrary choice of a dozen volumes or so, I sent my slips of paper to lie in the wire tray, and waited in my stall, among the other seekers for the essential oil of truth.

What could be the reason, then, of this curious disparity, I wondered, drawing cart-wheels on the slips of paper provided by the British taxpayer for other purposes. Why are women, judging from this catalogue, so much more interesting to men than men are to women? A very curious fact it seemed, and my mind wandered to picture the lives of men who spend their time in writing books about women; whether they were old or young, married or unmarried, red-nosed or hump-backed—anyhow, it was flattering, vaguely, to feel oneself the object of such attention, provided that it was not entirely bestowed by the crippled and the infirm—so I pondered until all such frivolous thoughts were ended by an avalanche of books sliding down on to the desk in front of me. Now the trouble began. The student who has been trained in research at Oxbridge has no doubt some method of shepherding his question past all distractions till it runs into his answer as a sheep runs into its pen. The student by my side, for instance, who was copying assiduously from a scientific manual, was, I felt sure, extracting pure nuggets of the essential ore every ten minutes or so. His little grunts of satisfaction indicated so much. But if, unfortunately, one has had no training in a university, the question far from being shepherded to its pen flies like a frightened flock hither and thither, helter-skelter, pursued by a whole pack of hounds. Professors, schoolmasters, sociologists, clergymen, novelists, essayists, journalists, men who had no qualification save that they were not women, chased my simple and single question—Why are some women poor?—until it became fifty questions; until the fifty questions leapt frantically into mid-stream and were carried away. Every page in my notebook was scribbled over with notes. To show the state of mind I was in, I will read you a few of them, explaining that the page was headed quite simply, WOMEN AND POVERTY, in block letters; but what followed was something like this:

Condition in Middle Ages of,
Habits in the Fiji Islands of,
Worshipped as goddesses by,
Weaker in moral sense than,
Idealism of,
Greater conscientiousness of,

South Sea Islanders, age of puberty among,
Attractiveness of,
Offered as sacrifice to,
Small size of brain of,
Profounder sub-consciousness of,
Less hair on the body of,
Mental, moral and physical inferiority of,
Love of children of,
Greater length of life of,
Weaker muscles of,
Strength of affections of,
Vanity of,
Higher education of,
Shakespeare's opinion of,
Lord Birkenhead's opinion of,
Dean Inge's opinion of,
La Bruyère's opinion of,
Dr Johnson's opinion of,
Mr Oscar Browning's opinion of, . . .

Here I drew breath and added, indeed, in the margin, Why does Samuel Butler say, 'Wise men never say what they think of women?' Wise men never say anything else apparently. But, I continued, leaning back in my chair and looking at the vast dome in which I was a single but by now somewhat harassed thought, what is so unfortunate is that wise men never think the same thing about women. Here is Pope:

Most women have no character at all.*

[ 37 ]

And here is La Bruyère:

Les femmes sont extrêmes, elles sont meilleures ou pires que les hommes—*

a direct contradiction by keen observers who were contemporary. Are they capable of education or incapable? Napoleon thought them incapable. Dr Johnson thought the opposite.[1] Have they souls or have they not souls? Some savages say they have none. Others, on the contrary, maintain that women are half divine and worship them on that account.[2] Some sages hold that they are shallower in the brain; others that they are deeper in the consciousness. Goethe honoured them; Mussolini despises them. Wherever one looked men thought about women and thought differently. It was impossible to make head or tail of it all, I decided, glancing with envy at the reader next door who was making the neatest abstracts, headed often with an A or a B or a C, while my own notebook rioted with the wildest scribble of contradictory jottings. It was distressing, it was

[1] '"Men know that women are an overmatch for them, and therefore they choose the weakest or the most ignorant. If they did not think so, they never could be afraid of women knowing as much as themselves." . . . In justice to the sex, I think it but candid to acknowledge that, in a subsequent conversation, he told me that he was serious in what he said.'—BOSWELL, *The Journal of a Tour to the Hebrides*, 19 September 1773.

[2] 'The ancient Germans believed that there was something holy in women, and accordingly consulted them as oracles.'—FRAZER, *Golden Bough* (12 vols.; 1913), i. 391.

[ 38 ]

bewildering, it was humiliating. Truth had run through my fingers. Every drop had escaped.

I could not possibly go home, I reflected, and add as a serious contribution to the study of women and fiction that women have less hair on their bodies than men, or that the age of puberty among the South Sea Islanders is nine—or is it ninety?—even the hand-writing had become in its distraction indecipherable. It was disgraceful to have nothing more weighty or respectable to show after a whole morning's work. And if I could not grasp the truth about W (as for brevity's sake I had come to call her) in the past, why bother about W in the future? It seemed pure waste of time to consult all those gentlemen who specialize in woman and her effect on whatever it may be— politics, children, wages, morality—numerous and learned as they are. One might as well leave their books unopened.

But while I pondered I had unconsciously, in my listlessness, in my desperation, been drawing a picture where I should, like my neighbour, have been writing a conclusion. I had been drawing a face, a figure. It was the face and the figure of Professor von X engaged in writing his monumental work entitled *The Mental, Moral, and Physical Inferiority of the Female Sex*. He was not in my picture a man attractive to women. He was heavily built; he had a great jowl; to balance that he had very small eyes; he was very red in the face. His expression suggested that he was labouring under some emotion that made him jab his pen on the paper as if he were killing some noxious insect as he wrote, but even when he had killed it that did not satisfy him, he must go on killing it; and even so, some cause for anger and irritation remained. Could it be his wife, I asked, looking at my picture? Was she in love with a cavalry officer? Was the cavalry officer slim and elegant and dressed in astrachan? Had he been laughed at, to adopt the Freudian theory,* in his cradle by a pretty girl? For even in his cradle the professor, I thought, could not have been an attractive child. Whatever the reason, the professor was made to look very angry and very ugly in my sketch, as he wrote his great book upon the mental, moral and physical inferiority of women. Drawing pictures was an idle way of finishing an unprofitable morning's work. Yet it is in our idleness, in our dreams, that the submerged truth sometimes comes to the top. A very elementary exercise in psychology, not to be dignified by the name of psycho-analysis, showed me, on looking at my notebook, that the sketch of the angry professor had been made in anger. Anger had snatched my pencil while I dreamt. But what was anger doing there? Interest, confusion, amusement, boredom—all these emotions I could trace and name as they succeeded each other throughout the morning. Had anger, the black snake, been lurking among them? Yes, said the sketch, anger had. It referred me unmistakably to the one book, to the one phrase, which had roused the demon; it was the professor's statement about the mental, moral and physical inferiority of women. My heart had leapt. My cheeks had burnt. I had flushed with anger. There was nothing specially remarkable, however foolish, in that. One does not like to be told that one is naturally the inferior of a little man—I looked at the student next me—who breathes hard, wears a ready-made tie, and has not shaved this fortnight. One has certain foolish vanities. It is only human nature, I reflected, and began drawing cart-wheels and circles over the angry professor's face till he looked like a burning bush or a flaming comet—anyhow, an apparition without human semblance or significance. The professor was nothing now but a faggot burning on the top of Hampstead Heath. Soon my own anger was explained and done with; but curiosity remained. How explain the anger of the professors? Why were they angry? For when it came to analysing the impression left by these books there was always an element of heat. This heat took many forms; it showed itself in satire, in sentiment, in curiosity, in reprobation. But there was another element which was often present and could not immediately be identified. Anger, I called it. But it was anger that had gone underground and mixed itself with all kinds of other emotions. To judge from its odd effects, it was anger disguised and complex, not anger simple and open.

Whatever the reason, all these books, I thought, surveying the pile on the desk, are worthless for my purposes. They were worthless scientifically, that is to say, though humanly they were full of instruction, interest, boredom, and very queer facts about the habits of the Fiji Islanders. They had been written in the red light of emotion and not in the white light of truth. Therefore they must be returned to the central desk and restored each to his own cell in the enormous honeycomb. All that I had retrieved from that morning's work had been the one fact of anger. The professors—I lumped them together thus—were angry. But why, I asked myself, having returned the books, why, I repeated, standing under the colonnade among the pigeons and the prehistoric canoes, why are they angry? And, asking myself this question, I strolled off to find a place for luncheon. What is the real nature of what I call for the moment their anger? I asked. Here was a puzzle that would last all the time that it takes to be served with food in a small restaurant somewhere near the British Museum. Some previous luncher had left the lunch edition of the evening paper on a chair, and, waiting to be served, I began idly reading the headlines. A ribbon of very large letters ran across the page. Somebody had made a big score in South Africa. Lesser ribbons announced that Sir Austen Chamberlain* was at Geneva. A meat axe with human hair on it had been found in a cellar. Mr Justice —— commented in the Divorce Courts

[ 42 ]

upon the Shamelessness of Women. Sprinkled about the paper were other pieces of news. A film actress had been lowered from a peak in California and hung suspended in mid-air. The weather was going to be foggy. The most transient visitor to this planet, I thought, who picked up this paper could not fail to be aware, even from this scattered testimony, that England is under the rule of a patriarchy. Nobody in their senses could fail to detect the dominance of the professor. His was the power and the money and the influence.* He was the proprietor of the paper and its editor and sub-editor. He was the Foreign Secretary and the Judge. He was the cricketer; he owned the racehorses and the yachts. He was the director of the company that pays two hundred per cent to its shareholders. He left millions to charities and colleges that were ruled by himself. He suspended the film actress in mid-air. He will decide if the hair on the meat axe is human; he it is who will acquit or convict the murderer, and hang him, or let him go free. With the exception of the fog he seemed to control everything. Yet he was angry. I knew that he was angry by this token. When I read what he wrote about women I thought, not of what he was saying, but of himself. When an arguer argues dispassionately he thinks only of the argument; and the reader cannot help thinking of the argument too. If he had written dispassionately about women, had used indisputable proofs to establish his argument and had shown no trace of wishing that the result should be one thing rather than another, one would not have been angry either. One would have accepted the fact, as one accepts the fact that a pea is green or a canary yellow. So be it, I should have said. But I had been angry because he was angry. Yet it seemed absurd, I thought, turning over the evening paper, that a man with all this power should be angry. Or is anger, I wondered, somehow, the familiar, the attendant sprite on power? Rich people, for example, are often angry because they suspect that the poor want to seize their wealth. The professors, or patriarchs, as it might be more accurate to call them, might be angry for that reason partly, but partly for one that lies a little less obviously on the surface. Possibly they were not 'angry' at all; often, indeed, they were admiring, devoted, exemplary in the relations of private life. Possibly when the professor insisted a little too emphatically upon the inferiority of women, he was concerned not with their inferiority, but with his own superiority. That was what he was protecting rather hot-headedly and with too much emphasis, because it was a jewel to him of the rarest price. Life for both sexes—and I looked at them, shouldering their way along the pavement—is arduous, difficult, a perpetual struggle. It calls for gigantic courage and strength. More than anything, perhaps, creatures of illusion as we are, it calls for confidence in oneself. Without self-confidence we are as babes in the cradle. And how can we generate this imponderable quality, which is yet so invaluable, most quickly? By thinking that other people are inferior to oneself. By feeling that one has some innate superiority—it may be wealth, or rank, a straight nose, or the portrait of a grandfather by Romney*—for there is no end to the pathetic devices of the human imagination—over other people. Hence the enormous importance to a patriarch who has to conquer, who has to rule, of feeling that great numbers of people, half the human race indeed, are by nature inferior to himself. It must indeed be one of the chief sources of his power. But let me turn the light of this observation on to real life, I thought. Does it help to explain some of those psychological puzzles that one notes in the margin of daily life? Does it explain my astonishment the other day when Z, most humane, most modest of men, taking up some book by Rebecca West and reading a passage in it, exclaimed, 'The arrant feminist!* She says that men are snobs!' The exclamation, to me so surprising—for why was Miss West an arrant feminist for making a possibly true if uncomplimentary statement about the other sex?—was not merely the cry of wounded vanity; it was a protest against some infringement of his power to believe in himself. Women have served all these centuries as looking-glasses possessing the magic and delicious power of reflecting the figure of man at twice its natural size. Without that power probably the earth would still be swamp and jungle. The glories of all our wars would be unknown. We should still be scratching the outlines of deer on the remains of mutton bones and bartering flints for sheep skins or whatever simple ornament took our unsophisticated taste. Supermen and Fingers of Destiny would never have existed. The Czar and the Kaiser would never have worn crowns or lost them. Whatever may be their use in civilized societies, mirrors are essential to all violent and heroic action. That is why Napoleon and Mussolini both insist so emphatically upon the inferiority of women, for if they were not inferior, they would cease to enlarge. That serves to explain in part the necessity that women so often are to men. And it serves to explain how restless they are under her criticism; how impossible it is for her to say to them this book is bad, this picture is feeble, or whatever it may be, without giving far more pain and rousing far more anger than a man would do who gave the same criticism. For if she begins to tell the truth, the figure in the looking-glass shrinks; his fitness for life is diminished. How is he to go on giving judgement, civilizing natives, making laws, writing books, dressing up and speechifying at banquets, unless he can see himself at breakfast and at dinner at least twice the size he really is? So I reflected, crumbling my bread and stirring my coffee and now and again looking at the people in the street. The looking-glass vision is of supreme importance because it charges the vitality; it stimulates the nervous system. Take it away and man may die, like the drug fiend deprived of his cocaine. Under the spell of that illusion, I thought, looking out of the window, half the people on the pavement are striding to work. They put on their hats and coats in the morning under its agreeable rays. They start the day confident, braced, believing themselves desired at Miss Smith's tea party; they say to themselves as they go into the room, I am the superior of half the people here, and it is thus that they speak with that self-confidence, that self-assurance, which have had such profound consequences in public life and lead to such curious notes in the margin of the private mind.

But these contributions to the dangerous and fascinating subject of the psychology of the other sex—it is one, I hope, that you will investigate when you have five hundred a year of your own—were interrupted by the necessity of paying the bill. It came to five shillings and ninepence. I gave the waiter a ten-shilling note and he went to bring me change. There was another ten-shilling note in my purse; I noticed it, because it is a fact that still takes my breath away—the power of my purse to breed ten-shilling notes automatically. I open it and there they are. Society gives me chicken and coffee, bed and lodging, in return for a certain number of pieces of paper which were left me by an aunt, for no other reason than that I share her name.

My aunt, Mary Beton, I must tell you, died by a fall from her horse when she was riding out to take the air in Bombay. The news of my legacy reached me one night about the same time that the act was passed that gave votes to women. A solicitor's letter fell into the post-box and when I opened it I found that she had left me five hundred pounds a year for ever. Of the two—the vote and the money—the money, I own, seemed infinitely the more important. Before that I had made my living by cadging odd jobs from newspapers, by reporting a donkey show here or a wedding there; I had earned a few pounds by addressing envelopes, reading to old ladies, making artificial flowers, teaching the alphabet to small children in a kindergarten. Such were the chief occupations that were open to women before 1918. I need not, I am afraid, describe in any detail the hardness of the work, for you know perhaps women who have done it; nor the difficulty of living on the money when it was earned, for you may have tried. But what still remains with me as a worse infliction than either was the poison of fear and bitterness which those days bred in me. To begin with, always to be doing work that one did not wish to do, and to do it like a slave, flattering and fawning, not always necessarily perhaps, but it seemed necessary and the stakes were too great to run risks; and then the thought of that one gift which it was death to hide*—a small one but dear to the possessor—perishing and with it my self, my soul—all this became like a rust eating away the bloom of the spring, destroying the tree at its heart. However, as I say, my aunt died; and whenever I change a ten-shilling note a little of that rust and corrosion is rubbed off; fear and bitterness go. Indeed, I thought, slipping the silver into my purse, it is remarkable, remembering the bitterness of those days, what a change of temper a fixed income will bring about. No force in the world can take from me my five hundred pounds. Food, house and clothing are mine for ever. Therefore not merely do effort and labour cease, but also hatred and bitterness. I need not hate any man; he cannot hurt me. I need not flatter any man; he has nothing to give me. So imperceptibly I found myself adopting a new attitude towards the other half of the human race. It was absurd to blame any class or any sex, as a whole. Great bodies of people are never responsible for what they do. They are driven by instincts which are not within their control. They too, the patriarchs, the professors, had endless difficulties, terrible drawbacks to contend with. Their education had been in some ways as faulty as my own. It had bred in them defects as great. True, they had money and power, but only at the cost of harbouring in their breasts an eagle, a vulture, for ever tearing the liver out* and plucking at the lungs—the instinct for possession, the rage for acquisition which drives them to desire other people's fields and goods perpetually; to make frontiers and flags; battleships and poison gas; to offer up their own lives and their children's lives. Walk through the Admiralty Arch (I had reached that monument), or any other avenue given up to trophies and cannon, and reflect upon the kind of glory celebrated there. Or watch in the spring sunshine the stockbroker and the great barrister going indoors to make money and more money and more money when it is a fact that five hundred pounds a year will keep one alive in the sunshine. These are unpleasant instincts to harbour, I reflected. They are bred of the conditions of life; of the lack of civilization, I thought, looking at the statue of the Duke of Cambridge, and in particular at the feathers in his cocked hat, with a fixity that they have scarcely ever received before. And, as I realized these drawbacks, by degrees fear and bitterness modified themselves into pity and toleration; and then in a year or two, pity and toleration went, and the greatest release of all came, which is freedom to think of things in themselves. That building, for example, do I like it or not? Is that picture beautiful or not? Is that in my opinion a good book or a bad? Indeed my aunt's legacy unveiled the sky to me, and substituted for the large and imposing figure of a gentleman, which Milton recommended for my perpetual adoration,* a view of the open sky.

So thinking, so speculating I found my way back to my house by the river. Lamps were being lit and an indescribable change had come over London since the morning hour. It was as if the great machine after labouring all day had made with our help a few yards of something very exciting and beautiful—a fiery fabric flashing with red eyes, a tawny monster roaring with hot breath. Even the wind seemed flung like a flag as it lashed the houses and rattled the hoardings.

In my little street, however, domesticity prevailed. The house painter was descending his ladder; the nursemaid was wheeling the perambulator carefully in and out back to nursery tea; the coal-heaver was folding his empty sacks on top of each other; the woman who keeps the greengrocer's shop was adding up the day's takings with her hands in red mittens. But so engrossed was I with the problem you have laid upon my shoulders that I could not see even these usual sights without referring them to one centre. I thought how much harder it is now than it must have been even a century ago to say which of these employments is the higher, the more necessary. Is it better to be a coal-heaver or a nursemaid; is the charwoman who has brought up eight children of less value to the world than the barrister who has made a hundred thousand pounds? It is useless to ask such questions; for nobody can answer them. Not only do the comparative values of charwomen and lawyers rise and fall from decade to decade, but we have no rods with which to measure them even as they are at the moment. I had been foolish to ask my professor to furnish me with 'indisputable proofs' of this or that in his argument about women. Even if one could state the value of any one gift at the moment, those values will change; in a century's time very possibly they will have changed completely. Moreover, in a hundred years, I thought, reaching my own door-step, women will have ceased to be the protected sex. Logically they will take part in all the activities and exertions that were once denied them. The nursemaid will heave coal. The shopwoman will drive an engine. All assumptions founded on the facts observed when women were the protected sex will have disap-peared—as, for example (here a squad of soldiers marched down the street), that women and clergymen and gardeners live longer than other people. Remove that protection, expose them to the same exertions and activities, make them soldiers and sailors and engine-drivers and dock labourers, and will not women die off so much younger, so much quicker, than men that one will say, 'I saw a woman today', as one used to say, 'I saw an aeroplane'. Anything may happen when womanhood has ceased to be a pro-tected occupation, I thought, opening the door. But what bearing has all this upon the subject of my paper, Women and Fiction? I asked, going indoors.

## CHAPTER III

IT was disappointing not to have brought back in the evening some important statement, some authentic fact. Women are poorer than men because—this or that. Perhaps now it would be better to give up seeking for the truth, and receiving on one's head an avalanche of opinion hot as lava, discoloured as dishwater. It would be better to draw the curtains; to shut out distractions; to light the lamp; to narrow the enquiry and to ask the historian, who records not opinions but facts, to describe under what conditions women lived, not throughout the ages, but in England, say, in the time of Elizabeth.

For it is a perennial puzzle why no woman wrote a word of that extraordinary literature when every other man, it seemed, was capable of song or sonnet. What were the conditions in which women lived, I asked myself; for fiction, imaginative work that is, is not dropped like a pebble upon the ground, as science may be; fiction is like a spider's web, attached ever so lightly perhaps, but still attached to life at all four corners. Often the attachment is scarcely perceptible; Shakespeare's plays, for instance, seem to hang there complete by themselves. But when the web is pulled askew, hooked up at the edge, torn in the middle, one remembers that these webs are not spun in mid-air by incorporeal creatures, but are the work of suffering human beings, and are attached to grossly material things, like health and money and the houses we live in.

I went, therefore, to the shelf where the histories stand and took down one of the latest, Professor Trevelyan's *History of England*.* Once more I looked up Women, found 'position of' and turned to the pages indicated. 'Wife-beating', I read, 'was a recognized right of man, and was practised without shame by high as well as low. . . . Similarly,' the historian goes on, 'the daughter who refused to marry the gentleman of her parents' choice was liable to be locked up, beaten and flung about the room, without any shock being inflicted on public opinion. Marriage was not an affair of personal affection, but of family avarice, particularly in the "chivalrous" upper classes. . . . Betrothal often took place while one or both of the parties was in the cradle, and marriage when they were scarcely out of the nurses' charge.' That was about 1470, soon after Chaucer's time. The next reference to the position of women is some two hundred years later, in the time of the Stuarts. 'It was still the exception for women of the upper and middle class to choose their own husbands, and when the husband had been assigned, he was lord and master, so far at least as law and custom could make him. Yet even so,' Professor Trevelyan concludes, 'neither Shakespeare's women nor those of authentic seventeenth-century memoirs, like the Verneys and the

Hutchinsons,* seem wanting in personality and character.' Certainly, if we consider it, Cleopatra must have had a way with her; Lady Macbeth, one would suppose, had a will of her own; Rosalind, one might conclude, was an attractive girl. Professor Trevelyan is speaking no more than the truth when he remarks that Shakespeare's women do not seem wanting in personality and character. Not being a historian, one might go even further and say that women have burnt like beacons in all the works of all the poets from the beginning of time—Clytemnestra, Antigone, Cleopatra, Lady Macbeth, Phèdre, Cressida, Rosalind, Desdemona, the Duchess of Malfi, among the dramatists; then among the prose writers: Millamant, Clarissa, Becky Sharp, Anna Karenina, Emma Bovary, Madame de Guermantes—the names flock to mind, nor do they recall women 'lacking in personality and character'. Indeed, if woman had no existence save in the fiction written by men, one would imagine her a person of the utmost importance; very various; heroic and mean; splendid and sordid; infinitely beautiful and hideous in the extreme; as great as a man, some think even greater.[1] But this is woman

[1] 'It remains a strange and almost inexplicable fact that in Athena's city, where women were kept in almost Oriental suppression as odalisques or drudges, the stage should yet have produced figures like Clytemnestra and Cassandra, Atossa and Antigone, Phèdre and Medea, and all the other heroines who dominate play after play of the "misogynist" Euripides. But the paradox of this world where in real life a respectable woman could hardly show her face alone in the

in fiction. In fact, as Professor Trevelyan points out, she was locked up, beaten and flung about the room.

A very queer, composite being thus emerges. Imaginatively she is of the highest importance; practically she is completely insignificant. She pervades poetry from cover to cover; she is all but absent from history. She dominates the lives of kings and conquerors in fiction; in fact she was the slave of any boy whose parents forced a ring upon her finger. Some of the most inspired words, some of the most profound thoughts in literature fall from her lips; in real life she could hardly read, could scarcely spell, and was the property of her husband.

It was certainly an odd monster that one made up by reading the historians first and the poets afterwards—a worm winged like an eagle; the spirit of life and beauty in a kitchen chopping up suet. But these monsters, however amusing to the imagination, have no existence in fact. What one must do to bring her

---

street, and yet on the stage woman equals or surpasses man, has never been satisfactorily explained. In modern tragedy the same predominance exists. At all events, a very cursory survey of Shakespeare's work (similarly with Webster, though not with Marlowe or Jonson) suffices to reveal how this dominance, this initiative of women, persists from Rosalind to Lady Macbeth. So too in Racine; six of his tragedies bear their heroines' names; and what male characters of his shall we set against Hermione and Andromaque, Bérénice and Roxane, Phèdre and Athalie? So again with Ibsen; what men shall we match with Solveig and Nora, Heda and Hilda Wangel and Rebecca West?'—F. L. LUCAS, *Tragedy* (1927), 114–15.

to life was to think poetically and prosaically at one
and the same moment, thus keeping in touch with
fact—that she is Mrs Martin, aged thirty-six, dressed
in blue, wearing a black hat and brown shoes; but not
losing sight of fiction either—that she is a vessel in
which all sorts of spirits and forces are coursing and
flashing perpetually. The moment, however, that one
tries this method with the Elizabethan woman, one
branch of illumination fails; one is held up by the
scarcity of facts. One knows nothing detailed,
nothing perfectly true and substantial about her.
History scarcely mentions her. And I turned to
Professor Trevelyan again to see what history meant
to him. I found by looking at his chapter headings
that it meant——

'The Manor Court and the Methods of Open-field
Agriculture . . . The Cistercians and Sheep-farming
. . . The Crusades . . . The University . . . The House
of Commons . . . The Hundred Years' War . . . The
Wars of the Roses . . . The Renaissance Scholars . . .
The Dissolution of the Monasteries . . . Agrarian and
Religious Strife . . . The Origin of English Sea-power
. . . The Armada . . .' and so on. Occasionally an
individual woman is mentioned, an Elizabeth, or a
Mary; a queen or a great lady. But by no possible
means could middle-class women with nothing but
brains and character at their command have taken
part in any one of the great movements which,
brought together, constitute the historian's view of

the past. Nor shall we find her in any collection of anecdotes. Aubrey* hardly mentions her. She never writes her own life and scarcely keeps a diary; there are only a handful of her letters in existence. She left no plays or poems by which we can judge her. What one wants, I thought—and why does not some brilliant student at Newnham or Girton supply it?— is a mass of information; at what age did she marry; how many children had she as a rule; what was her house like; had she a room to herself; did she do the cooking; would she be likely to have a servant? All these facts lie somewhere, presumably, in parish registers and account books; the life of the average Elizabethan woman must be scattered about somewhere, could one collect it and make a book of it. It would be ambitious beyond my daring, I thought, looking about the shelves for books that were not there, to suggest to the students of those famous colleges that they should rewrite history, though I own that it often seems a little queer as it is, unreal, lop-sided; but why should they not add a supplement to history? calling it, of course, by some inconspicuous name so that women might figure there without impropriety? For one often catches a glimpse of them in the lives of the great, whisking away into the background, concealing, I sometimes think, a wink, a laugh, perhaps a tear. And, after all, we have lives enough of Jane Austen; it scarcely seems necessary to consider again the influence of the tragedies of Joanna

Baillie* upon the poetry of Edgar Allan Poe; as for myself, I should not mind if the homes and haunts of Mary Russell Mitford were closed to the public for a century at least. But what I find deplorable, I continued, looking about the bookshelves again, is that nothing is known about women before the eighteenth century. I have no model in my mind to turn about this way and that. Here am I asking why women did not write poetry in the Elizabethan age, and I am not sure how they were educated; whether they were taught to write; whether they had sitting-rooms to themselves; how many women had children before they were twenty-one; what, in short, they did from eight in the morning till eight at night. They had no money evidently; according to Professor Trevelyan they were married whether they liked it or not before they were out of the nursery, at fifteen or sixteen very likely. It would have been extremely odd, even upon this showing, had one of them suddenly written the plays of Shakespeare, I concluded, and I thought of that old gentleman, who is dead now, but was a bishop, I think, who declared that it was impossible for any woman, past, present, or to come, to have the genius of Shakespeare. He wrote to the papers about it. He also told a lady who applied to him for information that cats do not as a matter of fact go to heaven, though they have, he added, souls of a sort. How much thinking those old gentlemen used to save one! How the borders of ignorance shrank back at their approach! Cats do not go to heaven. Women cannot write the plays of Shakespeare.

Be that as it may, I could not help thinking, as I looked at the works of Shakespeare on the shelf, that the bishop was right at least in this; it would have been impossible, completely and entirely, for any woman to have written the plays of Shakespeare in the age of Shakespeare. Let me imagine, since facts are so hard to come by, what would have happened had Shakespeare had a wonderfully gifted sister, called Judith, let us say. Shakespeare himself went, very probably,—his mother was an heiress—to the grammar school, where he may have learnt Latin— Ovid, Virgil and Horace—and the elements of grammar and logic. He was, it is well known, a wild boy who poached rabbits, perhaps shot a deer, and had, rather sooner than he should have done, to marry a woman in the neighbourhood, who bore him a child rather quicker than was right. That escapade sent him to seek his fortune in London. He had, it seemed, a taste for the theatre; he began by holding horses at the stage door. Very soon he got work in the theatre, became a successful actor, and lived at the hub of the universe, meeting everybody, knowing everybody, practising his art on the boards, exercising his wits in the streets, and even getting access to the palace of the queen. Meanwhile his extraordinarily gifted sister, let us suppose, remained at home. She was as adventurous, as imaginative, as agog to see the world as he was. But she was not sent to school. She had no chance of learning grammar and logic, let alone of reading Horace and Virgil. She picked up a book now and then, one of her brother's perhaps, and read a few pages. But then her parents came in and told her to mend the stockings or mind the stew and not moon about with books and papers. They would have spoken sharply but kindly, for they were substantial people who knew the conditions of life for a woman and loved their daughter—indeed, more likely than not she was the apple of her father's eye. Perhaps she scribbled some pages up in an apple loft on the sly, but was careful to hide them or set fire to them. Soon, however, before she was out of her teens, she was to be betrothed to the son of a neighbouring wool-stapler. She cried out that marriage was hateful to her, and for that she was severely beaten by her father. Then he ceased to scold her. He begged her instead not to hurt him, not to shame him in this matter of her marriage. He would give her a chain of beads or a fine petticoat, he said; and there were tears in his eyes. How could she disobey him? How could she break his heart? The force of her own gift alone drove her to it. She made up a small parcel of her belongings, let herself down by a rope one summer's night and took the road to London. She was not seventeen. The birds that sang in the hedge were not more musical than she was. She had the quickest fancy, a gift like her brother's, for the tune of words. Like him, she had a taste for the theatre. She stood at the stage door; she wanted to act, she said. Men laughed in her face. The manager—a fat, loose-lipped man—guffawed. He bellowed something about poodles dancing and women acting*—no woman, he said, could possibly be an actress. He hinted—you can imagine what. She could get no training in her craft. Could she even seek her dinner in a tavern or roam the streets at midnight? Yet her genius was for fiction and lusted to feed abundantly upon the lives of men and women and the study of their ways. At last—for she was very young, oddly like Shakespeare the poet in her face, with the same grey eyes and rounded brows—at last Nick Greene* the actor–manager took pity on her; she found herself with child by that gentleman and so—who shall measure the heat and violence of the poet's heart when caught and tangled in a woman's body?—killed herself one winter's night and lies buried at some cross-roads where the omnibuses now stop outside the Elephant and Castle.

That, more or less, is how the story would run, I think, if a woman in Shakespeare's day had had Shakespeare's genius. But for my part, I agree with the deceased bishop, if such he was—it is unthinkable that any woman in Shakespeare's day should have had Shakespeare's genius. For genius like Shakespeare's is not born among labouring, uneducated, servile people. It was not born in England among the Saxons and the Britons. It is not born today among the working classes. How, then, could it have been born among women whose work began, according to Professor Trevelyan, almost before they were out of the nursery, who were forced to it by their parents and held to it by all the power of law and custom? Yet genius of a sort must have existed among women as it must have existed among the working classes. Now and again an Emily Brontë or a Robert Burns blazes out and proves its presence. But certainly it never got itself on to paper. When, however, one reads of a witch being ducked, of a woman possessed by devils, of a wise woman selling herbs, or even of a very remarkable man who had a mother, then I think we are on the track of a lost novelist, a suppressed poet, of some mute and inglorious Jane Austen,* some Emily Brontë who dashed her brains out on the moor or mopped and mowed about the highways crazed with the torture that her gift had put her to. Indeed, I would venture to guess that Anon, who wrote so many poems without signing them, was often a woman. It was a woman Edward Fitzgerald, I think, suggested who made the ballads and the folk-songs, crooning them to her children, beguiling her spinning with them, or the length of the winter's night.

This may be true or it may be false—who can say?—but what is true in it, so it seemed to me, reviewing the story of Shakespeare's sister as I had made it, is that any woman born with a great gift in the sixteenth century would certainly have gone crazed, shot herself, or ended her days in some lonely cottage outside the village, half witch, half wizard, feared and mocked at. For it needs little skill in psychology to be sure that a highly gifted girl who had tried to use her gift for poetry would have been so thwarted and hindered by other people, so tortured and pulled asunder by her own contrary instincts, that she must have lost her health and sanity to a certainty. No girl could have walked to London and stood at a stage door and forced her way into the presence of actor-managers without doing herself a violence and suffering an anguish which may have been irrational—for chastity may be a fetish invented by certain societies for unknown reasons—but were none the less inevitable. Chastity had then, it has even now, a religious importance in a woman's life, and has so wrapped itself round with nerves and instincts that to cut it free and bring it to the light of day demands courage of the rarest. To have lived a free life in London in the sixteenth century would have meant for a woman who was poet and playwright a nervous stress and dilemma which might well have killed her. Had she survived, whatever she had written would have been twisted and deformed, issuing from a strained and morbid imagination. And undoubtedly, I thought, looking at the shelf where there are no plays by women, her work would have gone unsigned. That refuge she would have sought certainly. It was the relic of the sense of chastity that dictated anonymity to women even so late as the nineteenth century. Currer Bell,* George Eliot, George Sand, all the victims of inner strife as their writings prove, sought ineffectively to veil themselves by using the name of a man. Thus they did homage to the convention, which if not implanted by the other sex was liberally encouraged by them (the chief glory of a woman is not to be talked of, said Pericles,* himself a much-talked-of man) that publicity in women is detestable. Anonymity runs in their blood. The desire to be veiled still possesses them. They are not even now as concerned about the health of their fame as men are, and, speaking generally, will pass a tombstone or a signpost without feeling an irresistible desire to cut their names on it, as Alf, Bert or Chas. must do in obedience to their instinct, which murmurs if it sees a fine woman go by, or even a dog, Ce chien est à moi.* And, of course, it may not be a dog, I thought, remembering Parliament Square, the Sieges Allee* and other avenues; it may be a piece of land or a man with curly black hair. It is one of the great advantages of being a woman that one can pass even a very fine negress without wishing to make an Englishwoman of her.

That woman, then, who was born with a gift of poetry in the sixteenth century, was an unhappy woman, a woman at strife against herself. All the conditions of her life, all her own instincts, were hostile to the state of mind which is needed to set free whatever is in the brain. But what is the state of mind that is most propitious to the act of creation, I asked? Can one come by any notion of the state that furthers and makes possible that strange activity? Here I opened the volume containing the Tragedies of Shakespeare. What was Shakespeare's state of mind, for instance, when he wrote *Lear* and *Antony and Cleopatra*? It was certainly the state of mind most favourable to poetry that there has ever existed. But Shakespeare himself said nothing about it. We only know casually and by chance that he 'never blotted a line'.* Nothing indeed was ever said by the artist himself about his state of mind until the eighteenth century perhaps. Rousseau perhaps began it.* At any rate, by the nineteenth century self-consciousness had developed so far that it was the habit for men of letters to describe their minds in confessions and autobiographies. Their lives also were written, and their letters were printed after their deaths. Thus, though we do not know what Shakespeare went through when he wrote *Lear*, we do know what Carlyle went through when he wrote *The French Revolution*; what Flaubert went through when he wrote *Madame Bovary*; what Keats was going through when he tried to write poetry against the coming of death and the indifference of the world.

And one gathers from this enormous modern literature of confession and self-analysis that to write a work of genius is almost always a feat of prodigious difficulty. Everything is against the likelihood that it will come from the writer's mind whole and entire. Generally material circumstances are against it. Dogs will bark; people will interrupt; money must be made; health will break down. Further, accentuating all these difficulties and making them harder to bear is the world's notorious indifference. It does not ask people to write poems and novels and histories; it does not need them. It does not care whether Flaubert finds the right word or whether Carlyle scrupulously verifies this or that fact. Naturally, it will not pay for what it does not want. And so the writer, Keats, Flaubert, Carlyle, suffers, especially in the creative years of youth, every form of distraction and discouragement. A curse, a cry of agony, rises from those books of analysis and confession. 'Mighty poets in their misery dead'*—that is the burden of their song. If anything comes through in spite of all this, it is a miracle, and probably no book is born entire and uncrippled as it was conceived.

But for women, I thought, looking at the empty shelves, these difficulties were infinitely more formidable. In the first place, to have a room of her own, let alone a quiet room or a sound-proof room, was out of the question, unless her parents were exceptionally rich or very noble, even up to the beginning of the nineteenth century. Since her pin money, which depended on the goodwill of her father, was only enough to keep her clothed, she was debarred from such alleviations as came even to Keats or Tennyson or Carlyle, all poor men, from a walking tour, a little journey to France, from the separate lodging which, even if it were miserable enough, sheltered them from the claims and tyrannies of their families. Such material difficulties were formidable; but much worse were the immaterial. The indifference of the world which Keats and Flaubert and other men of genius have found so hard to bear was in her case not indifference but hostility. The world did not say to her as it said to them, Write if you choose; it makes no difference to me. The world said with a guffaw, Write? What's the good of your writing? Here the psychologists of Newnham and Girton might come to our help, I thought, looking again at the blank spaces on the shelves. For surely it is time that the effect of discouragement upon the mind of the artist should be measured, as I have seen a dairy company measure the effect of ordinary milk and Grade A milk upon the body of the rat. They set two rats in cages side by side, and of the two one was furtive, timid and small, and the other was glossy, bold and big. Now what food do we feed women as artists upon? I asked, remembering, I suppose, that dinner of prunes and custard. To answer that question I had only to open the evening paper and to read that Lord Birkenhead is of opinion—but really I am not going to trouble to copy out Lord Birkenhead's opinion* upon the writing of women. What Dean Inge* says I will leave in peace. The Harley Street specialist may be allowed to rouse the echoes of Harley Street with his vociferations without raising a hair on my head. I will quote, however, Mr Oscar Browning,* because Mr Oscar Browning was a great figure in Cambridge at one time, and used to examine the students at Girton and Newnham. Mr Oscar Browning was wont to declare 'that the impression left on his mind, after looking over any set of examination papers, was that, irrespective of the marks he might give, the best woman was intellectually the inferior of the worst man'. After saying that Mr Browning went back to his rooms—and it is this sequel that endears him and makes him a human figure of some bulk and majesty—he went back to his rooms and found a stable-boy lying on the sofa—'a mere skeleton, his cheeks were cavernous and sallow, his teeth were black, and he did not appear to have the full use of his limbs. . . . "That's Arthur" [said Mr Browning]. "He's a dear boy really and most high-minded."'* The two pictures always seem to me to complete each other. And happily in this age of biography the two pictures often do complete each other, so that we are able to interpret the opinions of great men not only by what they say, but by what they do.

But though this is possible now, such opinions coming from the lips of important people must have been formidable enough even fifty years ago. Let us suppose that a father from the highest motives did not wish his daughter to leave home and become writer, painter or scholar. 'See what Mr Oscar Browning says,' he would say; and there was not only Mr Oscar Browning; there was the *Saturday Review*; there was Mr Greg—the 'essentials of a woman's being', said Mr Greg emphatically, 'are that *they are supported by, and they minister to, men*'*— there was an enormous body of masculine opinion to the effect that nothing could be expected of women intellectually. Even if her father did not read out loud these opinions, any girl could read them for herself; and the reading, even in the nineteenth century, must have lowered her vitality, and told profoundly upon her work. There would always have been that assertion—you cannot do this, you are incapable of doing that—to protest against, to overcome. Probably for a novelist this germ is no longer of much effect; for there have been women novelists of merit. But for painters it must still have some sting in it; and for musicians, I imagine, is even now active and poisonous in the extreme. The woman composer stands where the actress stood in the time of Shakespeare. Nick Greene, I thought, remembering the story I had made about Shakespeare's sister, said that a woman acting put him in mind of a dog dancing. Johnson repeated the phrase two hundred years later of women preaching. And here, I said, opening a book about music, we have the very words used again in this year of grace, 1928, of women who try to write music. 'Of Mlle Germaine Tailleferre* one can only repeat Dr Johnson's dictum concerning a woman preacher, transposed into terms of music. "Sir, a woman's composing is like a dog's walking on his hind legs. It is not done well, but you are surprised to find it done at all." '[2] So accurately does history repeat itself.

Thus, I concluded, shutting Mr Oscar Browning's life and pushing away the rest, it is fairly evident that even in the nineteenth century a woman was not encouraged to be an artist. On the contrary, she was snubbed, slapped, lectured and exhorted. Her mind must have been strained and her vitality lowered by the need of opposing this, of disproving that. For here again we come within range of that very interesting and obscure masculine complex which has had so much influence upon the woman's movement; that deep-seated desire, not so much that *she* shall be inferior as that *he* shall be superior, which plants him wherever one looks, not only in front of the arts, but barring the way to politics too, even when the risk to himself seems infinitesimal and the suppliant humble and devoted. Even Lady Bessborough, I remembered, with all her passion for politics, must humbly bow herself and write to Lord Granville Leveson-Gower: '. . . notwithstanding all my violence in politicks and

[2] *A Survey of Contemporary Music*, Cecil Gray (1924), 246.

talking so much on that subject, I perfectly agree with you that no woman has any business to meddle with that or any other serious business, farther than giving her opinion (if she is ask'd).'* And so she goes on to spend her enthusiasm where it meets with no obstacle whatsoever, upon that immensely important subject, Lord Granville's maiden speech in the House of Commons. The spectacle is certainly a strange one, I thought. The history of men's opposition to women's emancipation is more interesting perhaps than the story of that emancipation itself. An amusing book might be made of it if some young student at Girton or Newnham would collect examples and deduce a theory,—but she would need thick gloves on her hands, and bars to protect her of solid gold.

But what is amusing now, I recollected, shutting Lady Bessborough, had to be taken in desperate earnest once. Opinions that one now pastes in a book labelled cock-a-doodle-dum and keeps for reading to select audiences on summer nights once drew tears, I can assure you. Among your grandmothers and great-grandmothers there were many that wept their eyes out. Florence Nightingale shrieked aloud in her agony.[3] Moreover, it is all very well for you, who have got yourselves to college and enjoy sitting-rooms—or is it only bed-sitting-rooms?—of your

---

[3] See *Cassandra*, by Florence Nightingale, printed in *The Cause*, by R. Strachey (1928).

own to say that genius should disregard such opinions; that genius should be above caring what is said of it. Unfortunately, it is precisely the men or women of genius who mind most what is said of them. Remember Keats. Remember the words he had cut on his tombstone.* Think of Tennyson; think—but I need hardly multiply instances of the undeniable, if very fortunate, fact that it is the nature of the artist to mind excessively what is said about him. Literature is strewn with the wreckage of men who have minded beyond reason the opinions of others.

And this susceptibility of theirs is doubly unfortunate, I thought, returning again to my original enquiry into what state of mind is most propitious for creative work, because the mind of an artist, in order to achieve the prodigious effort of freeing whole and entire the work that is in him, must be incandescent, like Shakespeare's mind, I conjectured, looking at the book which lay open at *Antony and Cleopatra*. There must be no obstacle in it, no foreign matter unconsumed.

For though we say that we know nothing about Shakespeare's state of mind, even as we say that, we are saying something about Shakespeare's state of mind. The reason perhaps why we know so little of Shakespeare—compared with Donne or Ben Jonson or Milton—is that his grudges and spites and antipathies are hidden from us. We are not held up by some 'revelation' which reminds us of the writer. All desire to protest, to preach, to proclaim an injury, to pay off a score, to make the world the witness of some hardship or grievance was fired out of him and consumed. Therefore his poetry flows from him free and unimpeded. If ever a human being got his work expressed completely, it was Shakespeare. If ever a mind was incandescent, unimpeded, I thought, turning again to the bookcase, it was Shakespeare's mind.

CHAPTER IV

THAT one would find any woman in that state of mind in the sixteenth century was obviously impossible. One has only to think of the Elizabethan tombstones with all those children kneeling with clasped hands; and their early deaths; and to see their houses with their dark, cramped rooms, to realize that no woman could have written poetry then. What one would expect to find would be that rather later perhaps some great lady would take advantage of her comparative freedom and comfort to publish something with her name to it and risk being thought a monster. Men, of course, are not snobs, I continued, carefully eschewing 'the arrant feminism' of Miss Rebecca West; but they appreciate with sympathy for the most part the efforts of a countess to write verse. One would expect to find a lady of title meeting with far greater encouragement than an unknown Miss Austen or a Miss Brontë at that time would have met with. But one would also expect to find that her mind was disturbed by alien emotions like fear and hatred and that her poems showed traces of that disturbance. Here is Lady Winchilsea, for example, I thought, taking down her poems. She was born in the year 1661; she was noble both by birth and by marriage; she was childless; she wrote poetry, and one has only to open her poetry to find her bursting out in indignation against the position of women:

> How we are fallen! fallen by mistaken rules,
> And Education's more than Nature's fools;
> Debarred from all improvements of the mind,
> And to be dull, expected and designed;
> And if someone would soar above the rest,
> With warmer fancy, and ambition pressed,
> So strong the opposing faction still appears,
> The hopes to thrive can ne'er outweigh the fears.*

Clearly her mind has by no means 'consumed all impediments and become incandescent'. On the contrary, it is harassed and distracted with hates and grievances. The human race is split up for her into two parties. Men are the 'opposing faction'; men are hated and feared, because they have the power to bar her way to what she wants to do—which is to write.

> Alas! a woman that attempts the pen,
> Such a presumptuous creature is esteemed,
> The fault can by no virtue be redeemed.
> They tell us we mistake our sex and way;
> Good breeding, fashion, dancing, dressing, play,
> Are the accomplishments we should desire;
> To write, or read, or think, or to enquire,
> Would cloud our beauty, and exhaust our time,
> And interrupt the conquests of our prime,
> Whilst the dull manage of a servile house
> Is held by some our utmost art and use.

Indeed she has to encourage herself to write by supposing that what she writes will never be published; to soothe herself with the sad chant:

> To some few friends, and to thy sorrows sing,
> For groves of laurel thou wert never meant;
> Be dark enough thy shades, and be thou there content.

Yet it is clear that could she have freed her mind from hate and fear and not heaped it with bitterness and resentment, the fire was hot within her. Now and again words issue of pure poetry:

> Nor will in fading silks compose,
> Faintly the inimitable rose.*

—they are rightly praised by Mr Murry, and Pope, it is thought, remembered and appropriated those others:*

> Now the jonquille o'ercomes the feeble brain;
> We faint beneath the aromatic pain.

It was a thousand pities that the woman who could write like that, whose mind was tuned to nature and reflection, should have been forced to anger and bitterness. But how could she have helped herself? I asked, imagining the sneers and the laughter, the adulation of the toadies, the scepticism of the professional poet. She must have shut herself up in a room in the country to write, and been torn asunder by bitterness and scruples perhaps, though her husband was of the kindest, and their married life perfection. She 'must have', I say, because when one comes to seek out the facts about Lady Winchilsea, one finds, as usual, that almost nothing is known about her. She suffered terribly from melancholy, which we can explain at least to some extent when we find her telling us how in the grip of it she would imagine:

> My lines decried, and my employment thought
> An useless folly or presumptuous fault:

The employment, which was thus censured, was, as far as one can see, the harmless one of rambling about the fields and dreaming:

> My hand delights to trace unusual things,
> And deviates from the known and common way,
> Nor will in fading silks compose,
> Faintly the inimitable rose.

Naturally, if that was her habit and that was her delight, she could only expect to be laughed at; and, accordingly, Pope or Gay is said to have satirized her 'as a blue-stocking with an itch for scribbling'. Also it is thought that she offended Gay by laughing at him. She said that his *Trivia* showed that 'he was more proper to walk before a chair than to ride in one'. But this is all 'dubious gossip' and, says Mr Murry,* 'uninteresting'. But there I do not agree with him, for I should have liked to have had more even of dubious gossip so that I might have found out or made up some image of this melancholy lady, who loved wandering in the fields and thinking about unusual things and scorned, so rashly, so unwisely, 'the dull manage of a servile house'. But she became diffuse, Mr Murry says. Her gift is all grown about with weeds and bound with briars. It had no chance of showing itself for the fine distinguished gift it was. And so, putting her back on the shelf, I turned to the other great lady, the Duchess whom Lamb loved, hare-brained, fantastical Margaret of Newcastle,* her elder, but her contemporary. They were very different, but alike in this that both were noble and both childless, and both were married to the best of husbands. In both burnt the same passion for poetry and both are disfigured and deformed by the same causes. Open the Duchess and one finds the same outburst of rage, 'Women live like Bats or Owls, labour like Beasts, and die like Worms . . .' Margaret too might have been a poet; in our day all that activity would have turned a wheel of some sort. As it was, what could bind, tame or civilize for human use that wild, generous, untutored intelligence? It poured itself out, higgledy-piggledy, in torrents of rhyme and prose, poetry and philosophy which stand congealed in quartos and folios that nobody ever reads. She should have had a microscope put in her hand. She should have been taught to look at the stars and reason scientifically. Her wits were turned with solitude and freedom. No one checked her. No one taught her. The professors fawned on her. At Court they jeered at her. Sir Egerton Brydges* complained of her coarseness—'as flowing from a female of high rank brought up in the Courts'. She shut herself up at Welbeck alone.

What a vision of loneliness and riot the thought of Margaret Cavendish brings to mind! as if some giant cucumber had spread itself over all the roses and carnations in the garden and choked them to death. What a waste that the woman who wrote 'the best bred women are those whose mind are civilest' should have frittered her time away scribbling nonsense and plunging ever deeper into obscurity and folly till the people crowded round her coach when she issued out. Evidently the crazy Duchess became a bogey to frighten clever girls with. Here, I remembered, putting away the Duchess and opening Dorothy Osborne's letters, is Dorothy writing to Temple about the Duchess's new book. 'Sure the poore woman is a little distracted, shee could never bee soe rediculous else as to venture at writeing book's and in verse too, if I should not sleep this fortnight I should not come to that.'

And so, since no woman of sense and modesty could write books, Dorothy, who was sensitive and melancholy, the very opposite of the Duchess in temper, wrote nothing. Letters did not count. A woman might write letters while she was sitting by her father's sick-bed. She could write them by the fire whilst the men talked without disturbing them. The strange thing is, I thought, turning over the pages of Dorothy's letters, what a gift that untaught and solitary girl had for the framing of a sentence, for the fashioning of a scene. Listen to her running on:

'After dinner wee sitt and talk till Mr. B. com's in question and then I am gon. the heat of the day is spent in reading or working and about six or seven a Clock, I walke out into a Common that lyes hard by the house where a great many young wenches keep Sheep and Cow's and sitt in the shades singing of Ballads; I goe to them and compare their voyces and Beauty's to some Ancient Shepherdesses that I have read of and finde a vaste difference there, but trust mee I think these are as innocent as those could bee. I talke to them, and finde they want nothing to make them the happiest People in the world, but the knoledge that they are soe. most commonly when we are in the middest of our discourse one looks aboute her and spyes her Cow's goeing into the Corne and then away they all run, as if they had wing's at theire heels. I that am not soe nimble stay behinde, and when I see them driveing home theire Cattle I think tis time for mee to retyre too. when I have supped I goe into the Garden and soe to the syde of a small River that runs by it where I sitt downe and wish you with mee . . .'*

One could have sworn that she had the makings of a writer in her. But 'if I should not sleep this fortnight

I should not come to that'—one can measure the opposition that was in the air to a woman writing when one finds that even a woman with a great turn for writing has brought herself to believe that to write a book was to be ridiculous, even to show oneself distracted. And so we come, I continued, replacing the single short volume of Dorothy Osborne's letters upon the shelf, to Mrs Behn.*

And with Mrs Behn we turn a very important corner on the road. We leave behind, shut up in their parks among their folios, those solitary great ladies who wrote without audience or criticism, for their own delight alone. We come to town and rub shoulders with ordinary people in the streets. Mrs Behn was a middle-class woman with all the plebeian virtues of humour, vitality and courage; a woman forced by the death of her husband and some unfortunate adventures of her own to make her living by her wits. She had to work on equal terms with men. She made, by working very hard, enough to live on. The importance of that fact outweighs anything that she actually wrote, even the splendid 'A Thousand Martyrs I have made', or 'Love in Fantastic Triumph sat', for here begins the freedom of the mind, or rather the possibility that in the course of time the mind will be free to write what it likes. For now that Aphra Behn had done it, girls could go to their parents and say, You need not give me an allowance; I can make money by my pen. Of course the answer for many years to come was, Yes, by living the life of Aphra Behn! Death would be better! and the door was slammed faster than ever. That profoundly interesting subject, the value that men set upon women's chastity and its effect upon their education, here suggests itself for discussion, and might provide an interesting book if any student at Girton or Newnham cared to go into the matter. Lady Dudley, sitting in diamonds among the midges of a Scottish moor, might serve for frontispiece. Lord Dudley, *The Times* said* when Lady Dudley died the other day, 'a man of cultivated taste and many accomplishments, was benevolent and bountiful, but whimsically despotic. He insisted upon his wife's wearing full dress, even at the remotest shooting-lodge in the Highlands; he loaded her with gorgeous jewels', and so on, 'he gave her everything—always excepting any measure of responsibility'. Then Lord Dudley had a stroke and she nursed him and ruled his estates with supreme competence for ever after. That whimsical despotism was in the nineteenth century too.

But to return. Aphra Behn proved that money could be made by writing at the sacrifice, perhaps, of certain agreeable qualities; and so by degrees writing became not merely a sign of folly and a distracted mind, but was of practical importance. A husband might die, or some disaster overtake the family. Hundreds of women began as the eighteenth century drew on to add to their pin money, or to come to the

rescue of their families by making translations or
writing the innumerable bad novels which have ceased
to be recorded even in text-books, but are to be
picked up in the fourpenny boxes in the Charing
Cross Road. The extreme activity of mind which
showed itself in the later eighteenth century among
women—the talking, and the meeting, the writing of
essays on Shakespeare, the translating of the classics—
was founded on the solid fact that women could make
money by writing. Money dignifies what is frivolous
if unpaid for. It might still be well to sneer at 'blue
stockings with an itch for scribbling', but it could not
be denied that they could put money in their purses.
Thus, towards the end of the eighteenth century a
change came about which, if I were rewriting history,
I should describe more fully and think of greater
importance than the Crusades or the Wars of the
Roses. The middle-class woman began to write. For
if *Pride and Prejudice* matters, and *Middlemarch* and
*Villette* and *Wuthering Heights* matter, then it matters
far more than I can prove in an hour's discourse that
women generally, and not merely the lonely aristocrat
shut up in her country house among her folios and
her flatterers, took to writing. Without those forerunners, Jane Austen and the Brontës and George Eliot
could no more have written than Shakespeare could
have written without Marlowe, or Marlowe without
Chaucer, or Chaucer without those forgotten poets
who paved the ways and tamed the natural savagery

of the tongue. For masterpieces are not single and solitary births; they are the outcome of many years of thinking in common, of thinking by the body of the people, so that the experience of the mass is behind the single voice. Jane Austen should have laid a wreath upon the grave of Fanny Burney, and George Eliot done homage to the robust shade of Eliza Carter*—the valiant old woman who tied a bell to her bedstead in order that she might wake early and learn Greek. All women together ought to let flowers fall upon the tomb of Aphra Behn, which is, most scandalously but rather appropriately, in Westminster Abbey, for it was she who earned them the right to speak their minds. It is she—shady and amorous as she was—who makes it not quite fantastic for me to say to you tonight: Earn five hundred a year by your wits.

Here, then, one had reached the early nineteenth century. And here, for the first time, I found several shelves given up entirely to the works of women. But why, I could not help asking, as I ran my eyes over them, were they, with very few exceptions, all novels? The original impulse was to poetry. The 'supreme head of song'* was a poetess. Both in France and in England the women poets precede the women novelists. Moreover, I thought, looking at the four famous names, what had George Eliot in common with Emily Brontë? Did not Charlotte Brontë fail entirely to understand Jane Austen? Save for the possibly relev-

[ 85 ]

ant fact that not one of them had a child, four more incongruous characters could not have met together in a room—so much so that it is tempting to invent a meeting and a dialogue between them. Yet by some strange force they were all compelled when they wrote, to write novels. Had it something to do with being born of the middle class, I asked; and with the fact, which Miss Emily Davies a little later was so strikingly to demonstrate, that the middle-class family in the early nineteenth century was possessed only of a single sitting-room between them?* If a woman wrote, she would have to write in the common sitting-room. And, as Miss Nightingale was so vehemently to complain,—'women never have an half hour ... that they can call their own'—she was always interrupted.* Still it would be easier to write prose and fiction there than to write poetry or a play. Less concentration is required. Jane Austen wrote like that to the end of her days. 'How she was able to effect all this', her nephew writes in his Memoir, 'is surprising, for she had no separate study to repair to, and most of the work must have been done in the general sitting-room, subject to all kinds of casual interruptions. She was careful that her occupation should not be suspected by servants or visitors or any persons beyond her own family party.'[1] Jane Austen

[1] *Memoir of Jane Austen*, by her nephew, James Edward Austen-Leigh (1870), 128–9.

hid her manuscripts or covered them with a piece of blotting-paper. Then, again, all the literary training that a woman had in the early nineteenth century was training in the observation of character, in the analysis of emotion. Her sensibility had been educated for centuries by the influences of the common sitting-room. People's feelings were impressed on her; personal relations were always before her eyes. Therefore, when the middle-class woman took to writing, she naturally wrote novels, even though, as seems evident enough, two of the four famous women here named were not by nature novelists. Emily Brontë should have written poetic plays; the overflow of George Eliot's capacious mind should have spread itself when the creative impulse was spent upon history or biography. They wrote novels, however; one may even go further, I said, taking *Pride and Prejudice* from the shelf, and say that they wrote good novels. Without boasting or giving pain to the opposite sex, one may say that *Pride and Prejudice* is a good book. At any rate, one would not have been ashamed to have been caught in the act of writing *Pride and Prejudice*. Yet Jane Austen was glad that a hinge creaked, so that she might hide her manuscript before anyone came in. To Jane Austen there was something discreditable in writing *Pride and Prejudice*. And, I wondered, would *Pride and Prejudice* have been a better novel if Jane Austen had not thought it necessary to hide her manuscript from visitors? I read a page or two to see; but I could not find any signs that her circumstances had harmed her work in the slightest. That, perhaps, was the chief miracle about it. Here was a woman about the year 1800 writing without hate, without bitterness, without fear, without protest, without preaching. That was how Shakespeare wrote, I thought, looking at *Antony and Cleopatra*; and when people compare Shakespeare and Jane Austen, they may mean that the minds of both had consumed all impediments; and for that reason we do not know Jane Austen and we do not know Shakespeare, and for that reason Jane Austen pervades every word that she wrote, and so does Shakespeare. If Jane Austen suffered in any way from her circumstances it was in the narrowness of life that was imposed upon her. It was impossible for a woman to go about alone. She never travelled; she never drove through London in an omnibus or had luncheon in a shop by herself. But perhaps it was the nature of Jane Austen not to want what she had not. Her gift and her circumstances matched each other completely. But I doubt whether that was true of Charlotte Brontë, I said, opening *Jane Eyre* and laying it beside *Pride and Prejudice*.

I opened it at chapter twelve and my eye was caught by the phrase 'Anybody may blame me who likes'. What were they blaming Charlotte Brontë for? I wondered. And I read how Jane Eyre used to go up on to the roof when Mrs Fairfax was making jellies and looked over the fields at the distant view. And then she longed—and it was for this that they blamed her—that 'then I longed for a power of vision which might overpass that limit; which might reach the busy world, towns, regions full of life I had heard of but never seen: that then I desired more of practical experience than I possessed; more of intercourse with my kind, of acquaintance with variety of character than was here within my reach. I valued what was good in Mrs Fairfax, and what was good in Adèle; but I believed in the existence of other and more vivid kinds of goodness, and what I believed in I wished to behold.

'Who blames me? Many, no doubt, and I shall be called discontented. I could not help it: the restlessness was in my nature; it agitated me to pain sometimes. . . .

'It is vain to say human beings ought to be satisfied with tranquillity: they must have action; and they will make it if they cannot find it. Millions are condemned to a stiller doom than mine, and millions are in silent revolt against their lot. Nobody knows how many rebellions ferment in the masses of life which people earth. Women are supposed to be very calm generally: but women feel just as men feel; they need exercise for their faculties and a field for their efforts as much as their brothers do; they suffer from too rigid a restraint, too absolute a stagnation, precisely as men would suffer; and it is narrow-minded in their more privileged fellow-creatures to say that they ought to confine themselves to making puddings and knitting stockings, to playing on the piano and embroidering bags. It is thoughtless to condemn them, or laugh at them, if they seek to do more or learn more than custom has pronounced necessary for their sex.

'When thus alone I not unfrequently heard Grace Poole's laugh . . .'

That is an awkward break, I thought. It is upsetting to come upon Grace Poole all of a sudden. The continuity is disturbed. One might say, I continued, laying the book down beside *Pride and Prejudice*, that the woman who wrote those pages had more genius in her than Jane Austen; but if one reads them over and marks that jerk in them, that indignation, one sees that she will never get her genius expressed whole and entire. Her books will be deformed and twisted. She will write in a rage where she should write calmly. She will write foolishly where she should write wisely. She will write of herself where she should write of her characters. She is at war with her lot. How could she help but die young, cramped and thwarted?

One could not but play for a moment with the thought of what might have happened if Charlotte Brontë had possessed say three hundred a year—but the foolish woman sold the copyright of her novels outright for fifteen hundred pounds; had somehow possessed more knowledge of the busy world, and towns and regions full of life; more practical experience, and intercourse with her kind and acquaintance with a variety of character. In those words she puts her finger exactly not only upon her own defects as a novelist but upon those of her sex at that time. She knew, no one better, how enormously her genius would have profited if it had not spent itself in solitary visions over distant fields; if experience and intercourse and travel had been granted her. But they were not granted; they were withheld; and we must accept the fact that all those good novels, *Villette*, *Emma*, *Wuthering Heights*, *Middlemarch*, were written by women without more experience of life than could enter the house of a respectable clergyman; written too in the common sitting-room of that respectable house and by women so poor that they could not afford to buy more than a few quires of paper at a time upon which to write *Wuthering Heights* or *Jane Eyre*. One of them, it is true, George Eliot, escaped after much tribulation, but only to a secluded villa in St John's Wood. And there she settled down in the shadow of the world's disapproval. 'I wish it to be understood', she wrote, 'that I should never invite anyone to come and see me who did not ask for the invitation';* for was she not living in sin with a married man and might not the sight of her damage the chastity of Mrs Smith or whoever it might be that chanced to call? One must submit to the social convention, and be 'cut off from what is called the world'. At the same time, on the other side of Europe, there was a young man living freely with this gypsy or with that great lady; going to the wars; picking up unhindered and uncensored all that varied experience of human life which served him so splendidly later when he came to write his books. Had Tolstoi lived at the Priory in seclusion with a married lady 'cut off from what is called the world', however edifying the moral lesson, he could scarcely, I thought, have written *War and Peace*.

But one could perhaps go a little deeper into the question of novel-writing and the effect of sex upon the novelist. If one shuts one's eyes and thinks of the novel as a whole, it would seem to be a creation owning a certain looking-glass likeness to life, though of course with simplifications and distortions innumerable. At any rate, it is a structure leaving a shape on the mind's eye, built now in squares, now pagoda shaped, now throwing out wings and arcades, now solidly compact and domed like the Cathedral of Saint Sofia at Constantinople. This shape, I thought, thinking back over certain famous novels, starts in one the kind of emotion that is appropriate to it. But that emotion at once blends itself with others, for the 'shape' is not made by the relation of stone to stone, but by the relation of human being to human being. Thus a novel starts in us all sorts of antagonistic and opposed emotions. Life conflicts with something that is not life. Hence the difficulty of coming to any agreement about novels, and the immense sway that our private prejudices have upon us. On the one hand, we feel You—John the hero—must live, or I shall be in the depths of despair. On the other, we feel, Alas, John, you must die, because the shape of the book requires it. Life conflicts with something that is not life. Then since life it is in part, we judge it as life. James is the sort of man I most detest, one says. Or, This is a farrago of absurdity. I could never feel anything of the sort myself. The whole structure, it is obvious, thinking back on any famous novel, is one of infinite complexity, because it is thus made up of so many different judgements, of so many different kinds of emotion. The wonder is that any book so composed holds together for more than a year or two, or can possibly mean to the English reader what it means for the Russian or the Chinese. But they do hold together occasionally very remarkably. And what holds them together in these rare instances of survival (I was thinking of *War and Peace*) is something that one calls integrity, though it has nothing to do with paying one's bills or behaving honourably in an emergency. What one means by integrity, in the case of the novelist, is the conviction that he gives one that this is the truth. Yes, one feels, I should never have thought that this could be so; I have never known people behaving like that. But you have convinced me that so it is, so it happens. One holds every phrase, every scene to the light as one reads—for Nature seems, very oddly, to have provided us with an inner light by which to judge of the novelist's integrity or disintegrity. Or perhaps it is rather that Nature, in her most irrational mood, has traced in invisible ink on the walls of the mind a premonition which these great artists confirm; a sketch which only needs to be held to the fire of genius to become visible. When one so exposes it and sees it come to life one exclaims in rapture, But this is what I have always felt and known and desired! And one boils over with excitement, and, shutting the book even with a kind of reverence as if it were something very precious, a stand-by to return to as long as one lives, one puts it back on the shelf, I said, taking *War and Peace* and putting it back in its place. If, on the other hand, these poor sentences that one takes and tests rouse first a quick and eager response with their bright colouring and their dashing gestures but there they stop: something seems to check them in their development: or if they bring to light only a faint scribble in that corner and a blot over there, and nothing appears whole and entire, then one heaves a sigh of disappointment and says, Another failure. This novel has come to grief somewhere.

And for the most part, of course, novels do come to grief somewhere. The imagination falters under the enormous strain. The insight is confused; it can no longer distinguish between the true and the false; it has no longer the strength to go on with the vast labour that calls at every moment for the use of so many different faculties. But how would all this be affected by the sex of the novelist, I wondered, looking at *Jane Eyre* and the others. Would the fact of her sex in any way interfere with the integrity of a woman novelist—that integrity which I take to be the backbone of the writer? Now, in the passages I have quoted from *Jane Eyre*, it is clear that anger was tampering with the integrity of Charlotte Brontë the novelist. She left her story, to which her entire devotion was due, to attend to some personal grievance. She remembered that she had been starved of her proper due of experience—she had been made to stagnate in a parsonage mending stockings when she wanted to wander free over the world. Her imagination swerved from indignation and we feel it swerve. But there were many more influences than anger tugging at her imagination and deflecting it from its path. Ignorance, for instance. The portrait of Rochester* is drawn in the dark. We feel the influence of fear in it; just as we constantly feel an acidity which is the result of oppression, a buried suffering smouldering beneath her passion, a rancour which contracts those books, splendid as they are, with a spasm of pain.

And since a novel has this correspondence to real life, its values are to some extent those of real life. But it is obvious that the values of women differ very often from the values which have been made by the other sex; naturally, this is so. Yet it is the masculine values that prevail. Speaking crudely, football and sport are 'important'; the worship of fashion, the buying of clothes 'trivial'. And these values are inevitably transferred from life to fiction. This is an important book, the critic assumes, because it deals with war. This is an insignificant book because it deals with the feelings of women in a drawing-room. A scene in a battle-field is more important than a scene in a shop—everywhere and much more subtly the difference of value persists. The whole structure, therefore, of the early nineteenth-century novel was raised, if one was a woman, by a mind which was slightly pulled from the straight, and made to alter its clear vision in deference to external authority. One has only to skim those old forgotten novels and listen to the tone of voice in which they are written to divine that the writer was meeting criticism; she was saying this by way of aggression, or that by way of conciliation. She was admitting that she was 'only a woman', or protesting that she was 'as good as a man'. She met that criticism as her temperament dictated, with docility and diffidence, or with anger and emphasis. It does not matter which it was; she was thinking of something other than the thing itself. Down comes her book upon our heads. There was a flaw in the centre of it. And I thought of all the women's novels that lie scattered, like small pockmarked apples in an orchard, about the second-hand book shops of London. It was the flaw in the centre that had rotted them. She had altered her values in deference to the opinion of others.

But how impossible it must have been for them not to budge either to the right or to the left. What genius, what integrity it must have required in face of all that criticism, in the midst of that purely patriarchal society, to hold fast to the thing as they saw it without shrinking. Only Jane Austen did it and Emily Brontë. It is another feather, perhaps the finest, in their caps. They wrote as women write, not as men write. Of all the thousand women who wrote novels then, they alone entirely ignored the perpetual admonitions of the eternal pedagogue—write this, think that. They alone were deaf to that persistent voice, now grumbling, now patronizing, now domineering, now grieved, now shocked, now angry, now avuncular, that voice which cannot let women alone, but must be at them, like some too conscientious governess, adjuring them, like Sir Egerton Brydges, to be refined; dragging even into the criticism of poetry criticism of sex;[2] admonishing them, if they would be good and win, as I suppose, some shiny prize, to keep

[2] '[She] has a metaphysical purpose, and that is a dangerous obsession, especially with a woman, for women rarely possess men's healthy love of rhetoric. It is a strange lack in the sex which is in other things more primitive and more materialistic.'—*New Criterion*, June 1928, p. 160.

within certain limits which the gentleman in question thinks suitable—'. . . female novelists should only aspire to excellence by courageously acknowledging the limitations of their sex'.[3] That puts the matter in a nutshell, and when I tell you, rather to your surprise, that this sentence was written not in August 1828 but in August 1928, you will agree, I think, that however delightful it is to us now, it represents a vast body of opinion—I am not going to stir those old pools; I take only what chance has floated to my feet—that was far more vigorous and far more vocal a century ago. It would have needed a very stalwart young woman in 1828 to disregard all those snubs and chidings and promises of prizes. One must have been something of a firebrand to say to oneself, Oh, but they can't buy literature too. Literature is open to everybody. I refuse to allow you, Beadle though you are, to turn me off the grass. Lock up your libraries if you like; but there is no gate, no lock, no bolt that you can set upon the freedom of my mind.

But whatever effect discouragement and criticism had upon their writing—and I believe that they had a very great effect—that was unimportant compared with the other difficulty which faced them (I was still

[3] 'If, like the reporter, you believe that female novelists should only aspire to excellence by courageously acknowledging the limitations of their sex (Jane Austen [has] demonstrated how gracefully this gesture can be accomplished . . .'—*Life and Letters*, August 1928, pp. 121–2.

considering those early nineteenth-century novelists) when they came to set their thoughts on paper—that is that they had no tradition behind them, or one so short and partial that it was of little help. For we think back through our mothers if we are women. It is useless to go to the great men writers for help, however much one may go to them for pleasure. Lamb, Browne, Thackeray, Newman, Sterne, Dickens, De Quincey—whoever it may be—never helped a woman yet, though she may have learnt a few tricks of them and adapted them to her use. The weight, the pace, the stride of a man's mind are too unlike her own for her to lift anything substantial from him successfully. The ape is too distant to be sedulous.* Perhaps the first thing she would find, setting pen to paper, was that there was no common sentence ready for her use. All the great novelists like Thackeray and Dickens and Balzac have written a natural prose, swift but not slovenly, expressive but not precious, taking their own tint without ceasing to be common property. They have based it on the sentence that was current at the time. The sentence that was current at the beginning of the nineteenth century ran something like this perhaps: 'The grandeur of their works was an argument with them, not to stop short, but to proceed. They could have no higher excitement or satisfaction than in the exercise of their art and endless generations of truth and beauty. Success prompts to exertion; and habit facilitates success.' That is a man's

sentence; behind it one can see Johnson, Gibbon*
and the rest. It was a sentence that was unsuited for a
woman's use. Charlotte Brontë, with all her splendid
gift for prose, stumbled and fell with that clumsy
weapon in her hands. George Eliot committed atrocities with it that beggar description. Jane Austen
looked at it and laughed at it and devised a perfectly
natural, shapely sentence proper for her own use and
never departed from it. Thus, with less genius for
writing than Charlotte Brontë, she got infinitely more
said. Indeed, since freedom and fullness of expression
are of the essence of the art, such a lack of tradition,
such a scarcity and inadequacy of tools, must have
told enormously upon the writing of women. Moreover, a book is not made of sentences laid end to end,
but of sentences built, if an image helps, into arcades
or domes. And this shape too has been made by men
out of their own needs for their own uses. There is
no reason to think that the form of the epic or of the
poetic play suit a woman any more than the sentence
suits her. But all the older forms of literature were
hardened and set by the time she became a writer.
The novel alone was young enough to be soft in her
hands—another reason, perhaps, why she wrote
novels. Yet who shall say that even now 'the novel' (I
give it inverted commas to mark my sense of the
words' inadequacy), who shall say that even this most
pliable of all forms is rightly shaped for her use? No
doubt we shall find her knocking that into shape for

herself when she has the free use of her limbs; and providing some new vehicle, not necessarily in verse, for the poetry in her. For it is the poetry that is still denied outlet. And I went on to ponder how a woman nowadays would write a poetic tragedy in five acts. Would she use verse?—would she not use prose rather?

But these are difficult questions which lie in the twilight of the future. I must leave them, if only because they stimulate me to wander from my subject into trackless forests where I shall be lost and, very likely, devoured by wild beasts. I do not want, and I am sure that you do not want me, to broach that very dismal subject, the future of fiction, so that I will only pause here one moment to draw your attention to the great part which must be played in that future so far as women are concerned by physical conditions. The book has somehow to be adapted to the body, and at a venture one would say that women's books should be shorter, more concentrated, than those of men, and framed so that they do not need long hours of steady and uninterrupted work. For interruptions there will always be. Again, the nerves that feed the brain would seem to differ in men and women, and if you are going to make them work their best and hardest, you must find out what treatment suits them—whether these hours of lectures, for instance, which the monks devised, presumably, hundreds of years ago, suit them—what alternations of work and rest they need, interpreting rest not as doing nothing but as doing something but something that is different; and what should that difference be? All this should be discussed and discovered; all this is part of the question of women and fiction. And yet, I continued, approaching the bookcase again, where shall I find that elaborate study of the psychology of women by a woman? If through their incapacity to play football women are not going to be allowed to practise medicine——

Happily my thoughts were now given another turn.

CHAPTER V

I HAD come at last, in the course of this rambling, to
the shelves which hold books by the living; by
women and by men; for there are almost as many
books written by women now as by men. Or if that
is not yet quite true, if the male is still the voluble
sex, it is certainly true that women no longer write
novels solely. There are Jane Harrison's books on
Greek archaeology; Vernon Lee's books on aesthetics;* Gertrude Bell's books on Persia.* There are
books on all sorts of subjects which a generation ago
no woman could have touched. There are poems and
plays and criticism; there are histories and biographies, books of travel and books of scholarship and
research; there are even a few philosophies and books
about science and economics. And though novels
predominate, novels themselves may very well have
changed from association with books of a different
feather. The natural simplicity, the epic age of
women's writing, may have gone. Reading and criticism may have given her a wider range, a greater
subtlety. The impulse towards autobiography may be
spent. She may be beginning to use writing as an art,
not as a method of self-expression. Among these new
novels one might find an answer to several such
questions.

I took down one of them at random. It stood at the

very end of the shelf, was called *Life's Adventure*, or some such title, by Mary Carmichael,* and was published in this very month of October. It seems to be her first book, I said to myself, but one must read it as if it were the last volume in a fairly long series, continuing all those other books that I have been glancing at—Lady Winchilsea's poems and Aphra Behn's plays and the novels of the four great novelists. For books continue each other, in spite of our habit of judging them separately. And I must also consider her—this unknown woman—as the descendant of all those other women whose circumstances I have been glancing at and see what she inherits of their characteristics and restrictions. So, with a sigh, because novels so often provide an anodyne and not an antidote, glide one into torpid slumbers instead of rousing one with a burning brand, I settled down with a notebook and a pencil to make what I could of Mary Carmichael's first novel, *Life's Adventure*.

To begin with, I ran my eye up and down the page. I am going to get the hang of her sentences first, I said, before I load my memory with blue eyes and brown and the relationship that there may be between Chloe and Roger. There will be time for that when I have decided whether she has a pen in her hand or a pickaxe. So I tried a sentence or two on my tongue. Soon it was obvious that something was not quite in order. The smooth gliding of sentence after sentence was interrupted. Something tore, something scratched; a single word here and there flashed its torch in my eyes. She was 'unhanding' herself as they say in the old plays. She is like a person striking a match that will not light, I thought. But why, I asked her as if she were present, are Jane Austen's sentences not of the right shape for you? Must they all be scrapped because Emma and Mr Woodhouse* are dead? Alas, I sighed, that it should be so. For while Jane Austen breaks from melody to melody as Mozart from song to song, to read this writing was like being out at sea in an open boat. Up one went, down one sank. This terseness, this short-windedness, might mean that she was afraid of something; afraid of being called 'sentimental' perhaps; or she remembers that women's writing has been called flowery and so provides a superfluity of thorns; but until I have read a scene with some care, I cannot be sure whether she is being herself or someone else. At any rate, she does not lower one's vitality, I thought, reading more carefully. But she is heaping up too many facts. She will not be able to use half of them in a book of this size. (It was about half the length of *Jane Eyre*.) However, by some means or other she succeeded in getting us all—Roger, Chloe, Olivia, Tony and Mr Bigham—in a canoe up the river. Wait a moment, I said, leaning back in my chair, I must consider the whole thing more carefully before I go any further.

I am almost sure, I said to myself, that Mary

Carmichael is playing a trick on us. For I feel as one feels on a switchback railway when the car, instead of sinking, as one has been led to expect, swerves up again. Mary is tampering with the expected sequence. First she broke the sentence; now she has broken the sequence. Very well, she has every right to do both these things if she does them not for the sake of breaking, but for the sake of creating. Which of the two it is I cannot be sure until she has faced herself with a situation. I will give her every liberty, I said, to choose what that situation shall be; she shall make it of tin cans and old kettles if she likes; but she must convince me that she believes it to be a situation; and then when she has made it she must face it. She must jump. And, determined to do my duty by her as reader if she would do her duty by me as writer, I turned the page and read . . . I am sorry to break off so abruptly. Are there no men present? Do you promise me that behind that red curtain over there the figure of Sir Chartres Biron* is not concealed? We are all women you assure me? Then I may tell you that the very next words I read were these— 'Chloe liked Olivia . . .' Do not start. Do not blush. Let us admit in the privacy of our own society that these things sometimes happen. Sometimes women do like women.

'Chloe liked Olivia,' I read. And then it struck me how immense a change was there. Chloe liked Olivia perhaps for the first time in literature. Cleopatra did not like Octavia. And how completely *Antony and Cleopatra* would have been altered had she done so! As it is, I thought, letting my mind, I am afraid, wander a little from *Life's Adventure*, the whole thing is simplified, conventionalized, if one dared say it, absurdly. Cleopatra's only feeling about Octavia is one of jealousy. Is she taller than I am? How does she do her hair? The play, perhaps, required no more. But how interesting it would have been if the relationship between the two women had been more complicated. All these relationships between women, I thought, rapidly recalling the splendid gallery of fictitious women, are too simple. So much has been left out, unattempted. And I tried to remember any case in the course of my reading where two women are represented as friends. There is an attempt at it in *Diana of the Crossways*.* They are confidantes, of course, in Racine and the Greek tragedies. They are now and then mothers and daughters. But almost without exception they are shown in their relation to men. It was strange to think that all the great women of fiction were, until Jane Austen's day, not only seen by the other sex, but seen only in relation to the other sex. And how small a part of a woman's life is that; and how little can a man know even of that when he observes it through the black or rosy spectacles which sex puts upon his nose. Hence, perhaps, the peculiar nature of women in fiction; the astonishing extremes of her beauty and horror; her alternations between heavenly goodness and hellish depravity—for so a lover would see her as his love rose or sank, was prosperous or unhappy. This is not so true of the nineteenth-century novelists, of course. Woman becomes much more various and complicated there. Indeed it was the desire to write about women perhaps that led men by degrees to abandon the poetic drama which, with its violence, could make so little use of them, and to devise the novel as a more fitting receptacle. Even so it remains obvious, even in the writing of Proust, that a man is terribly hampered and partial in his knowledge of women, as a woman in her knowledge of men.

Also, I continued, looking down at the page again, it is becoming evident that women, like men, have other interests besides the perennial interests of domesticity. 'Chloe liked Olivia. They shared a laboratory together . . .' I read on and discovered that these two young women were engaged in mincing liver, which is, it seems, a cure for pernicious anæmia; although one of them was married and had—I think I am right in stating—two small children. Now all that, of course, has had to be left out, and thus the splendid portrait of the fictitious woman is much too simple and much too monotonous. Suppose, for instance, that men were only represented in literature as the lovers of women, and were never the friends of men, soldiers, thinkers, dreamers; how few parts in the plays of Shakespeare could be allotted to them;

how literature would suffer! We might perhaps have most of Othello; and a good deal of Antony; but no Caesar, no Brutus, no Hamlet, no Lear, no Jaques— literature would be incredibly impoverished, as indeed literature is impoverished beyond our counting by the doors that have been shut upon women. Married against their will, kept in one room, and to one occupation, how could a dramatist give a full or interesting or truthful account of them? Love was the only possible interpreter. The poet was forced to be passionate or bitter, unless indeed he chose to 'hate women', which meant more often than not that he was unattractive to them.

Now if Chloe likes Olivia and they share a laboratory, which of itself will make their friendship more varied and lasting because it will be less personal; if Mary Carmichael knows how to write, and I was beginning to enjoy some quality in her style; if she has a room to herself, of which I am not quite sure; if she has five hundred a year of her own—but that remains to be proved—then I think that something of great importance has happened.

For if Chloe likes Olivia and Mary Carmichael knows how to express it she will light a torch in that vast chamber where nobody has yet been. It is all half lights and profound shadows like those serpentine caves where one goes with a candle peering up and down, not knowing where one is stepping. And I began to read the book again, and read how Chloe watched Olivia put a jar on a shelf and say how it was time to go home to her children. That is a sight that has never been seen since the world began, I exclaimed. And I watched too, very curiously. For I wanted to see how Mary Carmichael set to work to catch those unrecorded gestures, those unsaid or half-said words, which form themselves, no more palpably than the shadows of moths on the ceiling, when women are alone, unlit by the capricious and coloured light of the other sex. She will need to hold her breath, I said, reading on, if she is to do it; for women are so suspicious of any interest that has not some obvious motive behind it, so terribly accustomed to concealment and suppression, that they are off at the flicker of an eye turned observingly in their direction. The only way for you to do it, I thought, addressing Mary Carmichael as if she were there, would be to talk of something else, looking steadily out of the window, and thus note, not with a pencil in a notebook, but in the shortest of shorthand, in words that are hardly syllabled yet, what happens when Olivia—this organism that has been under the shadow of the rock these million years—feels the light fall on it, and sees coming her way a piece of strange food—knowledge, adventure, art. And she reaches out for it, I thought, again raising my eyes from the page, and has to devise some entirely new combination of her resources, so highly developed for other purposes, so as to absorb the new into the old without disturbing the infinitely intricate and elaborate balance of the whole.

But, alas, I had done what I had determined not to do; I had slipped unthinkingly into praise of my own sex. 'Highly developed'—'infinitely intricate'—such are undeniably terms of praise, and to praise one's own sex is always suspect, often silly; moreover, in this case, how could one justify it? One could not go to the map and say Columbus discovered America and Columbus was a woman; or take an apple and remark, Newton discovered the laws of gravitation and Newton was a woman; or look into the sky and say aeroplanes are flying overhead and aeroplanes were invented by women. There is no mark on the wall to measure the precise height of women. There are no yard measures, neatly divided into the fractions of an inch, that one can lay against the qualities of a good mother or the devotion of a daughter, or the fidelity of a sister, or the capacity of a housekeeper. Few women even now have been graded at the universities; the great trials of the professions, army and navy, trade, politics and diplomacy have hardly tested them. They remain even at this moment almost unclassified. But if I want to know all that a human being can tell me about Sir Hawley Butts, for instance, I have only to open Burke or Debrett* and I shall find that he took such and such a degree; owns a hall; has an heir; was Secretary to a Board; represented Great Britain in Canada; and has received a certain number of degrees, offices, medals and other distinctions by which his merits are stamped upon him indelibly. Only Providence can know more about Sir Hawley Butts than that.

When, therefore, I say 'highly developed', 'infinitely intricate' of women, I am unable to verify my words either in Whitaker, Debrett or the University Calendar. In this predicament what can I do? And I looked at the bookcase again. There were the biographies: Johnson and Goethe and Carlyle and Sterne and Cowper and Shelley and Voltaire and Browning and many others. And I began thinking of all those great men who have for one reason or another admired, sought out, lived with, confided in, made love to, written of, trusted in, and shown what can only be described as some need of and dependence upon certain persons of the opposite sex. That all these relationships were absolutely Platonic I would not affirm, and Sir William Joynson Hicks* would probably deny. But we should wrong these illustrious men very greatly if we insisted that they got nothing from these alliances but comfort, flattery and the pleasures of the body. What they got, it is obvious, was something that their own sex was unable to supply; and it would not be rash, perhaps, to define it further, without quoting the doubtless rhapsodical words of the poets, as some stimulus, some renewal of creative power which is in the gift only of the opposite sex to bestow. He would open the door of drawing-room or nursery, I thought, and find her among her children perhaps, or with a piece of embroidery on her knee—at any rate, the centre of some different order and system of life, and the contrast between this world and his own, which might be the law courts or the House of Commons, would at once refresh and invigorate; and there would follow, even in the simplest talk, such a natural difference of opinion that the dried ideas in him would be fertilized anew; and the sight of her creating in a different medium from his own would so quicken his creative power that insensibly his sterile mind would begin to plot again, and he would find the phrase or the scene which was lacking when he put on his hat to visit her. Every Johnson has his Thrale,* and holds fast to her for some such reasons as these, and when the Thrale marries her Italian music master Johnson goes half mad with rage and disgust, not merely that he will miss his pleasant evenings at Streatham, but that the light of his life will be 'as if gone out'.

And without being Dr Johnson or Goethe or Carlyle or Voltaire, one may feel, though very differently from these great men, the nature of this intricacy and the power of this highly developed creative faculty among women. One goes into the room—but the resources of the English language would be much put to the stretch, and whole flights of words would need to wing their way illegitimately into existence before a woman could say what happens when she goes into a room. The rooms differ so completely; they are calm or thunderous; open on to the sea, or, on the contrary, give on to a prison yard; are hung with washing; or alive with opals and silks; are hard as horsehair or soft as feathers—one has only to go into any room in any street for the whole of that extremely complex force of femininity to fly in one's face. How should it be otherwise? For women have sat indoors all these millions of years, so that by this time the very walls are permeated by their creative force, which has, indeed, so overcharged the capacity of bricks and mortar that it must needs harness itself to pens and brushes and business and politics. But this creative power differs greatly from the creative power of men. And one must conclude that it would be a thousand pities if it were hindered or wasted, for it was won by centuries of the most drastic discipline, and there is nothing to take its place. It would be a thousand pities if women wrote like men, or lived like men, or looked like men, for if two sexes are quite inadequate, considering the vastness and variety of the world, how should we manage with one only? Ought not education to bring out and fortify the differences rather than the similarities? For we have too much likeness as it is, and if an explorer should come back and bring word of other sexes looking through the branches of other trees at other skies, nothing would be of greater service to humanity; and we should have the immense pleasure into the bargain of watching Professor X rush for his measuring-rods to prove himself 'superior'.

Mary Carmichael, I thought, still hovering at a little distance above the page, will have her work cut out for her merely as an observer. I am afraid indeed that she will be tempted to become, what I think the less interesting branch of the species—the naturalist–novelist, and not the contemplative. There are so many new facts for her to observe. She will not need to limit herself any longer to the respectable houses of the upper middle classes. She will go without kindness or condescension, but in the spirit of fellowship, into those small, scented rooms where sit the courtesan, the harlot and the lady with the pug dog. There they still sit in the rough and ready-made clothes that the male writer has had perforce to clap upon their shoulders. But Mary Carmichael will have out her scissors and fit them close to every hollow and angle. It will be a curious sight, when it comes, to see these women as they are, but we must wait a little, for Mary Carmichael will still be encumbered with that self-consciousness in the presence of 'sin' which is the legacy of our sexual barbarity. She will still wear the shoddy old fetters of class on her feet.

However, the majority of women are neither harlots nor courtesans; nor do they sit clasping pug dogs to dusty velvet all through the summer afternoon.

But what do they do then? and there came to my mind's eye one of those long streets somewhere south of the river whose infinite rows are innumerably populated. With the eye of the imagination I saw a very ancient lady crossing the street on the arm of a middle-aged woman, her daughter, perhaps, both so respectably booted and furred that their dressing in the afternoon must be a ritual, and the clothes themselves put away in cupboards with camphor, year after year, throughout the summer months. They cross the road when the lamps are being lit (for the dusk is their favourite hour), as they must have done year after year. The elder is close on eighty; but if one asked her what her life has meant to her, she would say that she remembered the streets lit for the battle of Balaclava,* or had heard the guns fire in Hyde Park for the birth of King Edward the Seventh.* And if one asked her, longing to pin down the moment with date and season, but what were you doing on the fifth of April 1868, or the second of November 1875, she would look vague and say that she could remember nothing. For all the dinners are cooked; the plates and cups washed; the children sent to school and gone out into the world. Nothing remains of it all. All has vanished. No biography or history has a word to say about it. And the novels, without meaning to, inevitably lie.

All these infinitely obscure lives remain to be recorded, I said, addressing Mary Carmichael as if she were present; and went on in thought through the streets of London feeling in imagination the pressure of dumbness, the accumulation of unrecorded life, whether from the women at the street corners with their arms akimbo, and the rings embedded in their fat swollen fingers, talking with a gesticulation like the swing of Shakespeare's words; or from the violet-sellers and match-sellers and old crones stationed under doorways; or from drifting girls whose faces, like waves in sun and cloud, signal the coming of men and women and the flickering lights of shop windows. All that you will have to explore, I said to Mary Carmichael, holding your torch firm in your hand. Above all, you must illumine your own soul with its profundities and its shallows, and its vanities and its generosities, and say what your beauty means to you or your plainness, and what is your relation to the everchanging and turning world of gloves and shoes and stuffs swaying up and down among the faint scents that come through chemists' bottles down arcades of dress material over a floor of pseudo-marble. For in imagination I had gone into a shop; it was laid with black and white paving; it was hung, astonishingly beautifully, with coloured ribbons. Mary Carmichael might well have a look at that in passing, I thought, for it is a sight that would lend itself to the pen as fittingly as any snowy peak or rocky gorge in the Andes. And there is the girl behind the counter too—I would as soon have her true history as the hundred and fiftieth life of Napoleon or seventieth study of Keats and his use of Miltonic inversion which old Professor Z and his like are now inditing. And then I went on very warily, on the very tips of my toes (so cowardly am I, so afraid of the lash that was once almost laid on my own shoulders), to murmur that she should also learn to laugh, without bitterness, at the vanities—say rather at the peculiarities, for it is a less offensive word—of the other sex. For there is a spot the size of a shilling at the back of the head which one can never see for oneself. It is one of the good offices that sex can discharge for sex—to describe that spot the size of a shilling at the back of the head. Think how much women have profited by the comments of Juvenal; by the criticism of Strindberg. Think with what humanity and brilliancy men, from the earliest ages, have pointed out to women that dark place at the back of the head! And if Mary were very brave and very honest, she would go behind the other sex and tell us what she found there. A true picture of man as a whole can never be painted until a woman has described that spot the size of a shilling. Mr Woodhouse and Mr Casaubon* are spots of that size and nature. Not of course that anyone in their senses would counsel her to hold up to scorn and ridicule of set purpose—literature shows the futility of what is written in that spirit. Be truthful, one would say, and the result is bound to be amazingly interesting.

Comedy is bound to be enriched. New facts are bound to be discovered.

However, it was high time to lower my eyes to the page again. It would be better, instead of speculating what Mary Carmichael might write and should write, to see what in fact Mary Carmichael did write. So I began to read again. I remembered that I had certain grievances against her. She had broken up Jane Austen's sentence, and thus given me no chance of pluming myself upon my impeccable taste, my fastidious ear. For it was useless to say, 'Yes, yes, this is very nice; but Jane Austen wrote much better than you do', when I had to admit that there was no point of likeness between them. Then she had gone further and broken the sequence—the expected order. Perhaps she had done this unconsciously, merely giving things their natural order, as a woman would, if she wrote like a woman. But the effect was somehow baffling; one could not see a wave heaping itself, a crisis coming round the next corner. Therefore I could not plume myself either upon the depths of my feelings and my profound knowledge of the human heart. For whenever I was about to feel the usual things in the usual places, about love, about death, the annoying creature twitched me away, as if the important point were just a little further on. And thus she made it impossible for me to roll out my sonorous phrases about 'elemental feelings', the 'common stuff of humanity', 'the depths of the human heart', and all those other phrases which support us in our belief that, however clever we may be on top, we are very serious, very profound and very humane underneath. She made me feel, on the contrary, that instead of being serious and profound and humane, one might be—and the thought was far less seductive—merely lazy minded and conventional into the bargain.

But I read on, and noted certain other facts. She was no 'genius'—that was evident. She had nothing like the love of Nature, the fiery imagination, the wild poetry, the brilliant wit, the brooding wisdom of her great predecessors, Lady Winchilsea, Charlotte Brontë, Emily Brontë, Jane Austen and George Eliot; she could not write with the melody and the dignity of Dorothy Osborne—indeed she was no more than a clever girl whose books will no doubt be pulped by the publishers in ten years' time. But, nevertheless, she had certain advantages which women of far greater gift lacked even half a century ago. Men were no longer to her 'the opposing faction'; she need not waste her time railing against them; she need not climb on to the roof and ruin her peace of mind longing for travel, experience and a knowledge of the world and character that were denied her. Fear and hatred were almost gone, or traces of them showed only in a slight exaggeration of the joy of freedom, a tendency to the caustic and satirical, rather than to the romantic, in her treatment of the other sex. Then there could be no doubt that as a novelist she enjoyed some natural advantages of a high order. She had a sensibility that was very wide, eager and free. It responded to an almost imperceptible touch on it. It feasted like a plant newly stood in the air on every sight and sound that came its way. It ranged, too, very subtly and curiously, among almost unknown or unrecorded things; it lighted on small things and showed that perhaps they were not small after all. It brought buried things to light and made one wonder what need there had been to bury them. Awkward though she was and without the unconscious bearing of long descent which makes the least turn of the pen of a Thackeray or a Lamb delightful to the ear, she had—I began to think—mastered the first great lesson: she wrote as a woman, but as a woman who has forgotten that she is a woman, so that her pages were full of that curious sexual quality which comes only when sex is unconscious of itself.

All this was to the good. But no abundance of sensation or fineness of perception would avail unless she could build up out of the fleeting and the personal the lasting edifice which remains unthrown. I had said that I would wait until she faced herself with 'a situation'. And I meant by that until she proved by summoning, beckoning and getting together that she was not a skimmer of surfaces merely, but had looked beneath into the depths. Now is the time, she would say to herself at a certain moment, when without doing anything violent I can show the meaning of all this. And she would begin—how unmistakable that quickening is!—beckoning and summoning, and there would rise up in memory, half forgotten, perhaps quite trivial things in other chapters dropped by the way. And she would make their presence felt while someone sewed or smoked a pipe as naturally as possible, and one would feel, as she went on writing, as if one had gone to the top of the world and seen it laid out, very majestically, beneath.

At any rate, she was making the attempt. And as I watched her lengthening out for the test, I saw, but hoped that she did not see, the bishops and the deans, the doctors and the professors, the patriarchs and the pedagogues all at her shouting warning and advice. You can't do this and you shan't do that! Fellows and scholars only allowed on the grass! Ladies not admitted without a letter of introduction! Aspiring and graceful female novelists this way! So they kept at her like the crowd at a fence on the race-course, and it was her trial to take her fence without looking to right or to left. If you stop to curse you are lost, I said to her; equally, if you stop to laugh. Hesitate or fumble and you are done for. Think only of the jump, I implored her, as if I had put the whole of my money on her back; and she went over it like a bird. But there was a fence beyond that and a fence beyond that. Whether she had the staying power I was doubtful, for the clapping and the crying were fraying to the nerves. But she did her best. Considering that

Mary Carmichael was no genius, but an unknown girl writing her first novel in a bed-sitting-room, without enough of those desirable things, time, money and idleness, she did not do so badly, I thought.

Give her another hundred years, I concluded, reading the last chapter—people's noses and bare shoulders showed naked against a starry sky, for someone had twitched the curtain in the drawing-room—give her a room of her own and five hundred a year, let her speak her mind and leave out half that she now puts in, and she will write a better book one of these days. She will be a poet, I said, putting *Life's Adventure*, by Mary Carmichael, at the end of the shelf, in another hundred years' time.

## CHAPTER VI

NEXT day the light of the October morning was
falling in dusty shafts through the uncurtained windows, and the hum of traffic rose from the street.
London then was winding itself up again; the factory
was astir; the machines were beginning. It was tempting, after all this reading, to look out of the window
and see what London was doing on the morning of
the 26th of October 1928. And what was London
doing? Nobody, it seemed, was reading *Antony and
Cleopatra*. London was wholly indifferent, it
appeared, to Shakespeare's plays. Nobody cared a
straw—and I do not blame them—for the future of
fiction, the death of poetry or the development by
the average woman of a prose style completely
expressive of her mind. If opinions upon any of these
matters had been chalked on the pavement, nobody
would have stooped to read them. The nonchalance
of the hurrying feet would have rubbed them out in
half an hour. Here came an errand-boy; here a woman
with a dog on a lead. The fascination of the London
street is that no two people are ever alike; each seems
bound on some private affair of his own. There were
the business-like, with their little bags; there were the
drifters rattling sticks upon area railings; there were
affable characters to whom the streets serve for club-
room, hailing men in carts and giving information

without being asked for it. Also there were funerals to which men, thus suddenly reminded of the passing of their own bodies, lifted their hats. And then a very distinguished gentleman came slowly down a door-step and paused to avoid collision with a bustling lady who had, by some means or other, acquired a splen-did fur coat and a bunch of Parma violets. They all seemed separate, self-absorbed, on business of their own.

At this moment, as so often happens in London, there was a complete lull and suspension of traffic. Nothing came down the street; nobody passed. A single leaf detached itself from the plane tree at the end of the street, and in that pause and suspension fell. Somehow it was like a signal falling, a signal pointing to a force in things which one had over-looked. It seemed to point to a river, which flowed past, invisibly, round the corner, down the street, and took people and eddied them along, as the stream at Oxbridge had taken the undergraduate in his boat and the dead leaves. Now it was bringing from one side of the street to the other diagonally a girl in patent leather boots, and then a young man in a maroon overcoat; it was also bringing a taxi-cab; and it brought all three together at a point directly beneath my window; where the taxi stopped; and the girl and the young man stopped; and they got into the taxi; and then the cab glided off as if it were swept on by the current elsewhere.

The sight was ordinary enough; what was strange was the rhythmical order with which my imagination had invested it; and the fact that the ordinary sight of two people getting into a cab had the power to communicate something of their own seeming satisfaction. The sight of two people coming down the street and meeting at the corner seems to ease the mind of some strain, I thought, watching the taxi turn and make off. Perhaps to think, as I had been thinking these two days, of one sex as distinct from the other is an effort. It interferes with the unity of the mind. Now that effort had ceased and that unity had been restored by seeing two people come together and get into a taxi-cab. The mind is certainly a very mysterious organ, I reflected, drawing my head in from the window, about which nothing whatever is known, though we depend upon it so completely. Why do I feel that there are severances and oppositions in the mind, as there are strains from obvious causes on the body? What does one mean by 'the unity of the mind'? I pondered, for clearly the mind has so great a power of concentrating at any point at any moment that it seems to have no single state of being. It can separate itself from the people in the street, for example, and think of itself as apart from them, at an upper window looking down on them. Or it can think with other people spontaneously, as, for instance, in a crowd waiting to hear some piece of news read out. It can think back through its fathers or through its mothers, as I have said that a woman writing thinks back through her mothers. Again if one is a woman one is often surprised by a sudden splitting off of consciousness, say in walking down Whitehall, when from being the natural inheritor of that civilization, she becomes, on the contrary, outside of it, alien and critical. Clearly the mind is always altering its focus, and bringing the world into different perspectives. But some of these states of mind seem, even if adopted spontaneously, to be less comfortable than others. In order to keep oneself continuing in them one is unconsciously holding something back, and gradually the repression becomes an effort. But there may be some state of mind in which one could continue without effort because nothing is required to be held back. And this perhaps, I thought, coming in from the window, is one of them. For certainly when I saw the couple get into the taxi-cab the mind felt as if, after being divided, it had come together again in a natural fusion. The obvious reason would be that it is natural for the sexes to co-operate. One has a profound, if irrational, instinct in favour of the theory that the union of man and woman makes for the greatest satisfaction, the most complete happiness. But the sight of the two people getting into the taxi and the satisfaction it gave me made me also ask whether there are two sexes in the mind corresponding to the two sexes in the body, and whether they also require to be united in order to get complete

satisfaction and happiness? And I went on amateurishly to sketch a plan of the soul so that in each of us
two powers preside, one male, one female; and in the
man's brain the man predominates over the woman,
and in the woman's brain the woman predominates
over the man. The normal and comfortable state of
being is that when the two live in harmony together,
spiritually co-operating. If one is a man, still the
woman part of the brain must have effect; and a
woman also must have intercourse with the man in
her. Coleridge perhaps meant this when he said that a
great mind is androgynous.* It is when this fusion
takes place that the mind is fully fertilized and uses
all its faculties. Perhaps a mind that is purely masculine cannot create, any more than a mind that is
purely feminine, I thought. But it would be well to
test what one meant by man-womanly, and con-
versely by woman-manly, by pausing and looking at
a book or two.

Coleridge certainly did not mean, when he said
that a great mind is androgynous, that it is a mind
that has any special sympathy with women; a mind
that takes up their cause or devotes itself to their
interpretation. Perhaps the androgynous mind is less
apt to make these distinctions than the single-sexed
mind. He meant, perhaps, that the androgynous
mind is resonant and porous; that it transmits emotion without impediment; that it is naturally creative,
incandescent and undivided. In fact one goes back to

Shakespeare's mind as the type of the androgynous, of the man-womanly mind, though it would be impossible to say what Shakespeare thought of women. And if it be true that it is one of the tokens of the fully developed mind that it does not think specially or separately of sex, how much harder it is to attain that condition now than ever before. Here I came to the books by living writers, and there paused and wondered if this fact were not at the root of something that had long puzzled me. No age can ever have been as stridently sex-conscious as our own; those innumerable books by men about women in the British Museum are a proof of it. The Suffrage campaign was no doubt to blame. It must have roused in men an extraordinary desire for self-assertion; it must have made them lay an emphasis upon their own sex and its characteristics which they would not have troubled to think about had they not been challenged. And when one is challenged, even by a few women in black bonnets, one retaliates, if one has never been challenged before, rather excessively. That perhaps accounts for some of the characteristics that I remember to have found here, I thought, taking down a new novel by Mr A, who is in the prime of life and very well thought of, apparently, by the reviewers. I opened it. Indeed, it was delightful to read a man's writing again. It was so direct, so straightforward after the writing of women. It indicated such freedom of mind, such liberty of person, such confidence in himself. One had a sense of physical well-being in the presence of this well-nourished, well-educated, free mind, which had never been thwarted or opposed, but had had full liberty from birth to stretch itself in whatever way it liked. All this was admirable. But after reading a chapter or two a shadow seemed to lie across the page. It was a straight dark bar, a shadow shaped something like the letter 'I'. One began dodging this way and that to catch a glimpse of the landscape behind it. Whether that was indeed a tree or a woman walking I was not quite sure. Back one was always hailed to the letter 'I'. One began to be tired of 'I'. Not but what this 'I' was a most respectable 'I'; honest and logical; as hard as a nut, and polished for centuries by good teaching and good feeding. I respect and admire that 'I' from the bottom of my heart. But—here I turned a page or two, looking for something or other—the worst of it is that in the shadow of the letter 'I' all is shapeless as mist. Is that a tree? No, it is a woman. But . . . she has not a bone in her body, I thought, watching Phoebe, for that was her name, coming across the beach. Then Alan got up and the shadow of Alan at once obliterated Phoebe. For Alan had views and Phoebe was quenched in the flood of his views. And then Alan, I thought, has passions; and here I turned page after page very fast, feeling that the crisis was approaching, and so it was. It took place on the beach under the

sun. It was done very openly. It was done very
vigorously. Nothing could have been more indecent.
But . . . I had said 'but' too often. One cannot go on
saying 'but'. One must finish the sentence somehow,
I rebuked myself. Shall I finish it, 'But—I am bored!'
But why was I bored? Partly because of the dominance of the letter 'I' and the aridity, which, like the
giant beech tree, it casts within its shade. Nothing
will grow there. And partly for some more obscure
reason. There seemed to be some obstacle, some
impediment in Mr A's mind which blocked the
fountain of creative energy and shored it within
narrow limits. And remembering the lunch party at
Oxbridge, and the cigarette ash and the Manx cat and
Tennyson and Christina Rossetti all in a bunch, it
seemed possible that the impediment lay there. As he
no longer hums under his breath, 'There has fallen a
splendid tear from the passion-flower at the gate',
when Phoebe crosses the beach, and she no longer
replies, 'My heart is like a singing bird whose nest is
in a water'd shoot', when Alan approaches what can
he do? Being honest as the day and logical as the sun,
there is only one thing he can do. And that he does,
to do him justice, over and over (I said turning the
pages) and over again. And that, I added, aware of
the awful nature of the confession, seems somehow
dull. Shakespeare's indecency uproots a thousand
other things in one's mind, and is far from being
dull. But Shakespeare does it for pleasure; Mr A, as

the nurses say, does it on purpose. He does it in protest. He is protesting against the equality of the other sex by asserting his own superiority. He is therefore impeded and inhibited and self-conscious as Shakespeare might have been if he too had known Miss Clough and Miss Davies.* Doubtless Elizabethan literature would have been very different from what it is if the women's movement had begun in the sixteenth century and not in the nineteenth.

What, then, it amounts to, if this theory of the two sides of the mind holds good, is that virility has now become self-conscious—men, that is to say, are now writing only with the male side of their brains. It is a mistake for a woman to read them, for she will inevitably look for something that she will not find. It is the power of suggestion that one most misses, I thought, taking Mr B the critic in my hand and reading, very carefully and very dutifully, his remarks upon the art of poetry. Very able they were, acute and full of learning; but the trouble was that his feelings no longer communicated; his mind seemed separated into different chambers; not a sound carried from one to the other. Thus, when one takes a sentence of Mr B into the mind it falls plump to the ground—dead; but when one takes a sentence of Coleridge into the mind, it explodes and gives birth to all kinds of other ideas, and that is the only sort of writing of which one can say that it has the secret of perpetual life.

But whatever the reason may be, it is a fact that one must deplore. For it means—here I had come to rows of books by Mr Galsworthy and Mr Kipling— that some of the finest works of our greatest living writers fall upon deaf ears. Do what she will a woman cannot find in them that fountain of perpetual life which the critics assure her is there. It is not only that they celebrate male virtues, enforce male values and describe the world of men; it is that the emotion with which these books are permeated is to a woman incomprehensible. It is coming, it is gathering, it is about to burst on one's head, one begins saying long before the end. That picture will fall on old Jolyon's head;* he will die of the shock; the old clerk will speak over him two or three obituary words; and all the swans on the Thames will simultaneously burst out singing. But one will rush away before that happens and hide in the gooseberry bushes, for the emotion which is so deep, so subtle, so symbolical to a man moves a woman to wonder. So with Mr Kipling's officers who turn their backs; and his Sowers who sow the Seed; and his Men who are alone with their Work; and the Flag— one blushes at all these capital letters as if one had been caught eavesdropping at some purely masculine orgy. The fact is that neither Mr Galsworthy nor Mr Kipling has a spark of the woman in him. Thus all their qualities seem to a woman, if one may generalize, crude and immature. They lack suggestive power. And when a book lacks suggestive power, however hard it hits the surface of the mind it cannot penetrate within.

And in that restless mood in which one takes books out and puts them back again without looking at them I began to envisage an age to come of pure, of self-assertive virility, such as the letters of professors (take Sir Walter Raleigh's* letters, for instance) seem to forebode, and the rulers of Italy have already brought into being. For one can hardly fail to be impressed in Rome by the sense of unmitigated masculinity; and whatever the value of unmitigated masculinity upon the state, one may question the effect of it upon the art of poetry. At any rate, according to the newspapers, there is a certain anxiety about fiction in Italy. There has been a meeting of academicians whose object it is 'to develop the Italian novel'. 'Men famous by birth, or in finance, industry or the Fascist corporations' came together the other day and discussed the matter, and a telegram was sent to the Duce expressing the hope 'that the Fascist era would soon give birth to a poet worthy of it'. We may all join in that pious hope, but it is doubtful whether poetry can come out of an incubator. Poetry ought to have a mother as well as a father. The Fascist poem, one may fear, will be a horrid little abortion such as one sees in a glass jar in the museum of some county town. Such monsters never live long, it is said; one has never seen a prodigy of that sort cropping grass in a field. Two heads on one body do not make for length of life.

However, the blame for all this, if one is anxious to lay blame, rests no more upon one sex than upon the other. All seducers and reformers are responsible: Lady Bessborough when she lied to Lord Granville; Miss Davies when she told the truth to Mr Greg. All who have brought about a state of sex-consciousness are to blame, and it is they who drive me, when I want to stretch my faculties on a book, to seek it in that happy age, before Miss Davies and Miss Clough were born, when the writer used both sides of his mind equally. One must turn back to Shakespeare then, for Shakespeare was androgynous; and so were Keats and Sterne and Cowper and Lamb and Coleridge. Shelley perhaps was sexless. Milton and Ben Jonson had a dash too much of the male in them. So had Wordsworth and Tolstoi. In our time Proust was wholly androgynous, if not perhaps a little too much of a woman. But that failing is too rare for one to complain of it, since without some mixture of the kind the intellect seems to predominate and the other faculties of the mind harden and become barren. However, I consoled myself with the reflection that this is perhaps a passing phase; much of what I have said in obedience to my promise to give you the course of my thoughts will seem out of date; much of what flames in my eyes will seem dubious to you who have not yet come of age.

Even so, the very first sentence that I would write here, I said, crossing over to the writing-table and taking up the page headed Women and Fiction, is that it is fatal for anyone who writes to think of their sex. It is fatal to be a man or woman pure and simple; one must be woman-manly or man-womanly. It is fatal for a woman to lay the least stress on any grievance; to plead even with justice any cause; in any way to speak consciously as a woman. And fatal is no figure of speech; for anything written with that conscious bias is doomed to death. It ceases to be fertilized. Brilliant and effective, powerful and masterly, as it may appear for a day or two, it must wither at nightfall; it cannot grow in the minds of others. Some collaboration has to take place in the mind between the woman and the man before the art of creation can be accomplished. Some marriage of opposites has to be consummated. The whole of the mind must lie wide open if we are to get the sense that the writer is communicating his experience with perfect fullness. There must be freedom and there must be peace. Not a wheel must grate, not a light glimmer. The curtains must be close drawn. The writer, I thought, once his experience is over, must lie back and let his mind celebrate its nuptials in darkness. He must not look or question what is being done. Rather, he must pluck the petals from a rose or watch the swans float calmly down the river. And I saw again the current which took the boat and the undergraduate and the dead leaves; and the taxi took the man and the woman, I thought, seeing them come together across the street, and the current swept them away, I thought, hearing far off the roar of London's traffic, into that tremendous stream.

Here, then, Mary Beton ceases to speak. She has told you how she reached the conclusion—the prosaic conclusion—that it is necessary to have five hundred a year and a room with a lock on the door if you are to write fiction or poetry. She has tried to lay bare the thoughts and impressions that led her to think this. She has asked you to follow her flying into the arms of a Beadle, lunching here, dining there, drawing pictures in the British Museum, taking books from the shelf, looking out of the window. While she has been doing all these things, you no doubt have been observing her failings and foibles and deciding what effect they have had on her opinions. You have been contradicting her and making whatever additions and deductions seem good to you. That is all as it should be, for in a question like this truth is only to be had by laying together many varieties of error. And I will end now in my own person by anticipating two criticisms, so obvious that you can hardly fail to make them.

No opinion has been expressed, you may say, upon the comparative merits of the sexes even as writers. That was done purposely, because, even if the time had come for such a valuation—and it is far more important at the moment to know how much money women had and how many rooms than to theorize about their capacities—even if the time had come I do not believe that gifts, whether of mind or character, can be weighed like sugar and butter, not even in Cambridge, where they are so adept at putting people into classes and fixing caps on their heads and letters after their names. I do not believe that even the Table of Precedency which you will find in Whitaker's *Almanac* represents a final order of values, or that there is any sound reason to suppose that a Commander of the Bath will ultimately walk in to dinner behind a Master in Lunacy. All this pitting of sex against sex, of quality against quality; all this claiming of superiority and imputing of inferiority, belong to the private-school stage of human existence where there are 'sides', and it is necessary for one side to beat another side, and of the utmost importance to walk up to a platform and receive from the hands of the Headmaster himself a highly ornamental pot. As people mature they cease to believe in sides or in Headmasters or in highly ornamental pots. At any rate, where books are concerned, it is notoriously difficult to fix labels of merit in such a way that they do not come off. Are not reviews of current literature a perpetual illustration of the difficulty of judgement? 'This great book', 'this worthless book', the same book is called by both names. Praise and blame alike mean nothing. No, delightful as the pastime of measuring may be, it is the most futile of all occupations, and to submit to the decrees of the measurers the most servile of attitudes. So long as you write what you wish to write, that is all that matters; and whether it matters for ages or only for hours, nobody can say. But to sacrifice a hair of the head of your vision, a shade of its colour, in deference to some Headmaster with a silver pot in his hand or to some professor with a measuring-rod up his sleeve, is the most abject treachery, and the sacrifice of wealth and chastity which used to be said to be the greatest of human disasters, a mere flea-bite in comparison.

Next I think that you may object that in all this I have made too much of the importance of material things. Even allowing a generous margin for symbolism, that five hundred a year stands for the power to contemplate, that a lock on the door means the power to think for oneself, still you may say that the mind should rise above such things; and that great poets have often been poor men. Let me then quote to you the words of your own Professor of Literature, who knows better than I do what goes to the making of a poet. Sir Arthur Quiller-Couch writes:[1]

'What are the great poetical names of the last hundred years or so? Coleridge, Wordsworth, Byron, Shelley, Landor, Keats, Tennyson, Browning,

---

[1] Sir Arthur Quiller-Couch, *On the Art of Writing* (1916), 38–9.

Arnold, Morris, Rossetti, Swinburne—we may stop there. Of these, all but Keats, Browning, Rossetti were University men, and of these three, Keats, who died young, cut off in his prime, was the only one not fairly well to do. It may seem a brutal thing to say, and it is a sad thing to say: but, as a matter of hard fact, the theory that poetical genius bloweth where it listeth, and equally in poor and rich, holds little truth. As a matter of hard fact, nine out of those twelve were University men: which means that somehow or other they procured the means to get the best education England can give. As a matter of hard fact, of the remaining three you know that Browning was well to do, and I challenge you that, if he had not been well to do, he would no more have attained to write *Saul* or *The Ring and the Book* than Ruskin would have attained to writing *Modern Painters* if his father had not dealt prosperously in business. Rossetti had a small private income; and, moreover, he painted. There remains but Keats; whom Atropos slew young, as she slew John Clare in a mad-house, and James Thomson by the laudanum he took to drug disappointment. These are dreadful facts, but let us face them. It is—however dishonouring to us as a nation—certain that, by some fault in our commonwealth, the poor poet has not in these days, nor has had for two hundred years, a dog's chance. Believe me—and I have spent a great part of ten years in watching some three hundred and twenty elementary schools,—we may prate of democracy, but actually, a poor child in England has little more hope than had the son of an Athenian slave to be emancipated into that intellectual freedom of which great writings are born.'

Nobody could put the point more plainly. 'The poor poet has not in these days, nor has had for two hundred years, a dog's chance . . . a poor child in England has little more hope than had the son of an Athenian slave to be emancipated into that intellectual freedom of which great writings are born.' That is it. Intellectual freedom depends upon material things. Poetry depends upon intellectual freedom. And women have always been poor, not for two hundred years merely, but from the beginning of time. Women have had less intellectual freedom than the sons of Athenian slaves. Women, then, have not had a dog's chance of writing poetry. That is why I have laid so much stress on money and a room of one's own. However, thanks to the toils of those obscure women in the past, of whom I wish we knew more, thanks, curiously enough to two wars, the Crimean which let Florence Nightingale out of her drawing-room, and the European War which opened the doors to the average woman some sixty years later, these evils are in the way to be bettered. Otherwise you would not be here tonight, and your chance of earning five hundred pounds a year, precarious as I am afraid that it still is, would be minute in the extreme.

[ 141 ]

Still, you may object, why do you attach so much importance to this writing of books by women when, according to you, it requires so much effort, leads perhaps to the murder of one's aunts, will make one almost certainly late for luncheon, and may bring one into very grave disputes with certain very good fellows? My motives, let me admit, are partly selfish. Like most uneducated Englishwomen, I like reading—I like reading books in the bulk. Lately my diet has become a trifle monotonous; history is too much about wars; biography too much about great men; poetry has shown, I think, a tendency to sterility, and fiction—but I have sufficiently exposed my disabilities as a critic of modern fiction and will say no more about it. Therefore I would ask you to write all kinds of books, hesitating at no subject however trivial or however vast. By hook or by crook, I hope that you will possess yourselves of money enough to travel and to idle, to contemplate the future or the past of the world, to dream over books and loiter at street corners and let the line of thought dip deep into the stream. For I am by no means confining you to fiction. If you would please me—and there are thousands like me—you would write books of travel and adventure, and research and scholarship, and history and biography, and criticism and philosophy and science. By so doing you will certainly profit the art of fiction. For books have a way of influencing each other. Fiction will be much the better for standing

cheek by jowl with poetry and philosophy. Moreover, if you consider any great figure of the past, like
Sappho, like the Lady Murasaki,* like Emily Brontë,
you will find that she is an inheritor as well as an
originator, and has come into existence because
women have come to have the habit of writing
naturally; so that even as a prelude to poetry such
activity on your part would be invaluable.

But when I look back through these notes and
criticize my own train of thought as I made them, I
find that my motives were not altogether selfish.
There runs through these comments and discursions
the conviction—or is it the instinct?—that good
books are desirable and that good writers, even if
they show every variety of human depravity, are still
good human beings. Thus when I ask you to write
more books I am urging you to do what will be for
your good and for the good of the world at large.
How to justify this instinct or belief I do not know,
for philosophic words, if one has not been educated
at a university, are apt to play one false. What is
meant by 'reality'? It would seem to be something
very erratic, very undependable—now to be found in
a dusty road, now in a scrap of newspaper in the
street, now a daffodil in the sun. It lights up a group
in a room and stamps some casual saying. It over-
whelms one walking home beneath the stars and
makes the silent world more real than the world of
speech—and then there it is again in an omnibus in

the uproar of Piccadilly. Sometimes, too, it seems to dwell in shapes too far away for us to discern what their nature is. But whatever it touches, it fixes and makes permanent. That is what remains over when the skin of the day has been cast into the hedge; that is what is left of past time and of our loves and hates. Now the writer, as I think, has the chance to live more than other people in the presence of this reality. It is his business to find it and collect it and communicate it to the rest of us. So at least I infer from reading *Lear* or *Emma* or *A la recherche du temps perdu*. For the reading of these books seems to perform a curious couching operation on the senses; one sees more intensely afterwards; the world seems bared of its covering and given an intenser life. Those are the enviable people who live at enmity with unreality; and those are the pitiable who are knocked on the head by the thing done without knowing or caring. So that when I ask you to earn money and have a room of your own, I am asking you to live in the presence of reality, an invigorating life, it would appear, whether one can impart it or not.

Here I would stop, but the pressure of convention decrees that every speech must end with a peroration. And a peroration addressed to women should have something, you will agree, particularly exalting and ennobling about it. I should implore you to remember your responsibilities, to be higher, more spiritual; I should remind you how much depends upon you, and what an influence you can exert upon the future. But those exhortations can safely, I think, be left to the other sex, who will put them, and indeed have put them, with far greater eloquence than I can compass. When I rummage in my own mind I find no noble sentiments about being companions and equals and influencing the world to higher ends. I find myself saying briefly and prosaically that it is much more important to be oneself than anything else. Do not dream of influencing other people, I would say, if I knew how to make it sound exalted. Think of things in themselves.

And again I am reminded by dipping into newspapers and novels and biographies that when a woman speaks to women she should have something very unpleasant up her sleeve. Women are hard on women. Women dislike women. Women—but are you not sick to death of the word? I can assure you that I am. Let us agree, then, that a paper read by a woman to women should end with something particularly disagreeable.

But how does it go? What can I think of? The truth is, I often like women. I like their unconventionality. I like their completeness. I like their anonymity. I like—but I must not run on in this way. That cupboard there,—you say it holds clean table-napkins only; but what if Sir Archibald Bodkin* were concealed among them? Let me then adopt a sterner tone. Have I, in the preceding words, conveyed to you sufficiently the warnings and reprobation of mankind? I have told you the very low opinion in which you were held by Mr Oscar Browning. I have indicated what Napoleon once thought of you and what Mussolini thinks now. Then, in case any of you aspire to fiction, I have copied out for your benefit the advice of the critic about courageously acknowledging the limitations of your sex. I have referred to Professor X and given prominence to his statement that women are intellectually, morally and physically inferior to men. I have handed on all that has come my way without going in search of it, and here is a final warning—from Mr John Langdon Davies.[2] Mr John Langdon Davies warns women 'that when children cease to be altogether desirable, women cease to be altogether necessary'.* I hope you will make a note of it.

How can I further encourage you to go about the business of life? Young women, I would say, and please attend, for the peroration is beginning, you are, in my opinion, disgracefully ignorant. You have never made a discovery of any sort of importance. You have never shaken an empire or led an army into battle. The plays of Shakespeare are not by you, and you have never introduced a barbarous race to the blessings of civilization. What is your excuse? It is all very well for you to say, pointing to the streets and

[2] *A Short History of Women*, by John Langdon-Davies (1928).

[ 146 ]

squares and forests of the globe swarming with black and white and coffee-coloured inhabitants, all busily engaged in traffic and enterprise and love-making, we have had other work on our hands. Without our doing, those seas would be unsailed and those fertile lands a desert. We have borne and bred and washed and taught, perhaps to the age of six or seven years, the one thousand six hundred and twenty-three million human beings who are, according to statistics, at present in existence, and that, allowing that some had help, takes time.

There is truth in what you say—I will not deny it. But at the same time may I remind you that there have been at least two colleges for women in existence in England since the year 1866; that after the year 1880 a married woman was allowed by law to possess her own property; and that in 1919—which is a whole nine years ago—she was given a vote? May I also remind you that most of the professions have been open to you for close on ten years now? When you reflect upon these immense privileges and the length of time during which they have been enjoyed, and the fact that there must be at this moment some two thousand women capable of earning over five hundred a year in one way or another, you will agree that the excuse of lack of opportunity, training, encouragement, leisure and money no longer holds good. Moreover, the economists are telling us that Mrs Seton has had too many children. You must, of course, go on bearing children, but, so they say, in twos and threes, not in tens and twelves.

Thus, with some time on your hands and with some book learning in your brains—you have had enough of the other kind, and are sent to college partly, I suspect, to be un-educated—surely you should embark upon another stage of your very long, very laborious and highly obscure career. A thousand pens are ready to suggest what you should do and what effect you will have. My own suggestion is a little fantastic, I admit; I prefer, therefore, to put it in the form of fiction.

I told you in the course of this paper that Shakespeare had a sister; but do not look for her in Sir Sidney Lee's life of the poet. She died young—alas, she never wrote a word. She lies buried where the omnibuses now stop, opposite the Elephant and Castle. Now my belief is that this poet who never wrote a word and was buried at the cross-roads still lives. She lives in you and in me, and in many other women who are not here tonight, for they are washing up the dishes and putting the children to bed. But she lives; for great poets do not die; they are continuing presences; they need only the opportunity to walk among us in the flesh. This opportunity, as I think, it is now coming within your power to give her. For my belief is that if we live another century or so—I am talking of the common life which is the real life and not of the little separate lives which we live as individuals—and have five hundred a year each of us and rooms of our own; if we have the habit of freedom and the courage to write exactly what we think; if we escape a little from the common sitting-room and see human beings not always in their relation to each other but in relation to reality; and the sky, too, and the trees or whatever it may be in themselves; if we look past Milton's bogey, for no human being should shut out the view; if we face the fact, for it is a fact, that there is no arm to cling to, but that we go alone and that our relation is to the world of reality and not only to the world of men and women, then the opportunity will come and the dead poet who was Shakespeare's sister will put on the body which she has so often laid down. Drawing her life from the lives of the unknown who were her forerunners, as her brother did before her, she will be born. As for her coming without that preparation, without that effort on our part, without that deter-mination that when she is born again she shall find it possible to live and write her poetry, that we cannot expect, for that would be impossible. But I maintain that she would come if we worked for her, and that so to work, even in poverty and obscurity, is worth while.

# THREE GUINEAS

# LIST OF ILLUSTRATIONS

## ONE

THREE years is a long time to leave a letter unanswered, and your letter has been lying without an answer even longer than that. I had hoped that it would answer itself, or that other people would answer it for me. But there it is with its question— How in your opinion are we to prevent war?—still unanswered.

It is true that many answers have suggested themselves, but none that would not need explanation, and explanations take time. In this case, too, there are reasons why it is particularly difficult to avoid misunderstanding. A whole page could be filled with excuses and apologies; declarations of unfitness, incompetence, lack of knowledge, and experience: and they would be true. But even when they were said there would still remain some difficulties so fundamental that it may well prove impossible for you to understand or for us to explain. But one does not like to leave so remarkable a letter as yours—a letter perhaps unique in the history of human correspondence, since when before has an educated man asked a woman how in her opinion war can be prevented?—unanswered. Therefore let us make the attempt; even if it is doomed to failure.

In the first place let us draw what all letter-writers instinctively draw, a sketch of the person to whom the letter is addressed. Without someone warm and breathing on the other side of the page, letters are worthless. You, then, who ask the question, are a little grey on the temples; the hair is no longer thick on the top of your head. You have reached the middle years of life not without effort, at the Bar; but on the whole your journey has been prosperous. There is nothing parched, mean or dissatisfied in your expression. And without wishing to flatter you, your prosperity—wife, children, house—has been deserved. You have never sunk into the contented apathy of middle life, for, as your letter from an office in the heart of London shows, instead of turning on your pillow and prodding your pigs, pruning your pear trees—you have a few acres in Norfolk—you are writing letters, attending meetings, presiding over this and that, asking questions, with the sound of the guns in your ears. For the rest, you began your education at one of the great public schools and finished it at the university.

It is now that the first difficulty of communication between us appears. Let us rapidly indicate the reason. We both come of what, in this hybrid age when, though birth is mixed, classes still remain fixed, it is convenient to call the educated class. When we meet in the flesh we speak with the same accent; use knives and forks in the same way; expect maids to cook dinner and wash up after dinner; and can talk during dinner without much difficulty about politics and people; war and peace; barbarism and civilization—all the questions indeed suggested by your letter. Moreover, we both earn our livings. But . . . those three dots mark a precipice, a gulf so deeply cut between us that for three years and more I have been sitting on my side of it wondering whether it is any use to try to speak across it. Let us then ask someone else—it is Mary Kingsley—to speak for us. 'I don't know if I ever revealed to you the fact that being allowed to learn German was *all* the paid-for education I ever had. Two thousand pounds was spent on my brother's, I still hope not in vain.'[1] Mary Kingsley is not speaking for herself alone; she is speaking, still, for many of the daughters of educated men. And she is not merely speaking for them; she is also pointing to a very important fact about them, a fact that must profoundly influence all that follows: the fact of Arthur's Education Fund.* You, who have read *Pendennis*, will remember how the mysterious letters A.E.F. figured in the household ledgers. Ever since the thirteenth century English families have been paying money into that account. From the Pastons* to the Pendennises, all educated families from the thirteenth century to the present moment have paid money into that account. It is a voracious receptacle. Where there were many sons to educate it required a great effort on the part of the family to keep it full. For your education was not merely in book-learning; games educated your body; friends taught you more than

[ 155 ]

books or games. Talk with them broadened your outlook and enriched your mind. In the holidays you travelled; acquired a taste for art; a knowledge of foreign politics; and then, before you could earn your own living, your father made you an allowance upon which it was possible for you to live while you learnt the profession which now entitles you to add the letters K.C. to your name. All this came out of Arthur's Education Fund. And to this your sisters, as Mary Kingsley indicates, made their contribution. Not only did their own education, save for such small sums as paid the German teacher, go into it; but many of those luxuries and trimmings which are, after all, an essential part of education—travel, society, solitude, a lodging apart from the family house—they were paid into it too. It was a voracious receptacle, a solid fact—Arthur's Education Fund—a fact so solid indeed that it cast a shadow over the entire landscape. And the result is that though we look at the same things, we see them differently. What is that congregation of buildings there, with a semi-monastic look, with chapels and halls and green playing-fields? To you it is your old school; Eton or Harrow; your old university, Oxford or Cambridge; the source of memories and of traditions innumerable. But to us, who see it through the shadow of Arthur's Education Fund, it is a schoolroom table; an omnibus going to a class; a little woman with a red nose who is not well educated herself but has an invalid mother to support; an allowance of £50 a year with which to buy clothes, give presents and take journeys on coming to maturity. Such is the effect that Arthur's Education Fund has had upon us. So magically does it change the landscape that the noble courts and quadrangles of Oxford and Cambridge often appear to educated men's daughters[2] like petticoats with holes in them, cold legs of mutton, and the boat train starting for abroad while the guard slams the door in their faces.

The fact that Arthur's Education Fund changes the landscape—the halls, the playing grounds, the sacred edifices—is an important one; but that aspect must be left for future discussion. Here we are only concerned with the obvious fact, when it comes to considering this important question—how we are to help you prevent war—that education makes a difference. Some knowledge of politics, of international relations, of economics, is obviously necessary in order to understand the causes which lead to war. Philosophy, theology even, might come in usefully. Now you the uneducated, you with an untrained mind, could not possibly deal with such questions satisfactorily. War, as the result of impersonal forces, is you will agree beyond the grasp of the untrained mind. But war as the result of human nature is another thing. Had you not believed that human nature, the reasons, the emotions of the ordinary man and woman, lead to war, you would not have written asking for our help. You must have argued, men and women, here and now, are able to exert their wills; they are not pawns and puppets dancing on a string held by invisible hands. They can act, and think for themselves. Perhaps even they can influence other people's thoughts and actions. Some such reasoning must have led you to apply to us; and with justification. For happily there is one branch of education which comes under the heading 'unpaid-for education'—that understanding of human beings and their motives which, if the word is rid of its scientific associations, might be called psychology. Marriage, the one great profession open to our class since the dawn of time until the year 1919;* marriage, the art of choosing the human being with whom to live life successfully, should have taught us some skill in that. But here again another difficulty confronts us. For though many instincts are held more or less in common by both sexes, to fight has always been the man's habit, not the woman's. Law and practice have developed that difference, whether innate or accidental. Scarcely a human being in the course of history has fallen to a woman's rifle; the vast majority of birds and beasts have been killed by you, not by us; and it is difficult to judge what we do not share.[3]

How then are we to understand your problem, and if we cannot, how can we answer your question, how to prevent war? The answer based upon our experience and our psychology—Why fight?—is not an answer of any value. Obviously there is for you some glory, some necessity, some satisfaction in fighting which we have never felt or enjoyed. Complete understanding could only be achieved by blood transfusion and memory transfusion—a miracle still beyond the reach of science. But we who live now have a substitute for blood transfusion and memory transfusion which must serve at a pinch. There is that marvellous, perpetually renewed, and as yet largely untapped aid to the understanding of human motives which is provided in our age by biography and autobiography. Also there is the daily paper, history in the raw. There is thus no longer any reason to be confined to the minute span of actual experience which is still, for us, so narrow, so circumscribed. We can supplement it by looking at the picture of the lives of others. It is of course only a picture at present, but as such it must serve. It is to biography then that we will turn first, quickly and briefly, in order to attempt to understand what war means to you. Let us extract a few sentences from a biography.

First, this from a soldier's life:

I have had the happiest possible life, and have always been working for war, and have now got into the biggest in the prime of life for a soldier . . . Thank God, we are off in an hour. Such a magnificent regiment! Such men, such horses! Within ten days I hope Francis and I will be riding side by side straight at the Germans.[4]

To which the biographer adds:

From the first hour he has been supremely happy, for he had found his true calling.

To that let us add this from an airman's life:

We talked of the League of Nations and the prospects of peace and disarmament. On this subject he was not so much militarist as martial. The difficulty to which he could find no answer was that if permanent peace were ever achieved, and armies and navies ceased to exist, there would be no outlet for the manly qualities which fighting developed, and that human physique and human character would deteriorate.[5]

Here, immediately, are three reasons which lead your sex to fight; war is a profession; a source of happiness and excitement; and it is also an outlet for manly qualities, without which men would deteriorate. But that these feelings and opinions are by no means universally held by your sex is proved by the following extract from another biography, the life of a poet who was killed in the European war: Wilfred Owen.

Already I have comprehended a light which never will filter into the dogma of any national church: namely, that one of Christ's essential commands was: Passivity at any price! Suffer dishonour and disgrace, but never resort to arms. Be bullied, be outraged, be killed; but do not kill . . . Thus you see how pure Christianity will not fit in with pure patriotism.

And among some notes for poems that he did not live to write are these:

The unnaturalness of weapons ... Inhumanity of war
... The insupportability of war ... Horrible beastliness of
war ... Foolishness of war.[6]

From these quotations it is obvious that the same sex
holds very different opinions about the same thing.
But also it is obvious, from today's newspaper, that
however many dissentients there are, the great majority of your sex are today in favour of war. The
Scarborough Conference of educated men, the
Bournemouth Conference of working men* are both
agreed that to spend £300,000,000 annually upon arms
is a necessity. They are of opinion that Wilfred Owen
was wrong; that it is better to kill than to be killed.
Yet since biography shows that differences of opinion
are many, it is plain that there must be some one
reason which prevails in order to bring about this
overpowering unanimity. Shall we call it, for the sake
of brevity, 'patriotism'? What then, we must ask next,
is this 'patriotism' which leads you to go to war? Let
the Lord Chief Justice of England interpret it for us:

Englishmen are proud of England. For those who have
been trained in English schools and universities, and who
have done the work of their lives in England, there are few
loves stronger than the love we have for our country.
When we consider other nations, when we judge the merits
of the policy of this country or of that, it is the standard of
our own country that we apply. ... Liberty has made her
abode in England. England is the home of democratic
institutions ... It is true that in our midst there are many

[ 161 ]

enemies of liberty—some of them, perhaps, in rather unexpected quarters. But we are standing firm. It has been said that an Englishman's Home is his Castle. The home of Liberty is in England. And it is a castle indeed—a castle that will be defended to the last . . . Yes, we are greatly blessed, we Englishmen.[7]

That is a fair general statement of what patriotism means to an educated man and what duties it imposes upon him. But the educated man's sister—what does 'patriotism' mean to her? Has she the same reasons for being proud of England, for loving England, for defending England? Has she been 'greatly blessed' in England? History and biography when questioned would seem to show that her position in the home of freedom has been different from her brother's; and psychology would seem to hint that history is not without its effect upon mind and body. Therefore her interpretation of the word 'patriotism' may well differ from his. And that difference may make it extremely difficult for her to understand his definition of patriotism and the duties it imposes. If then our answer to your question, 'How in your opinion are we to prevent war?' depends upon understanding the reasons, the emotions, the loyalties which lead men to go to war, this letter had better be torn across and thrown into the waste-paper basket. For it seems plain that we cannot understand each other because of these differences. It seems plain that we think differently according as we are born differently; there is a

Grenfell point of view; a Knebworth point of view; a Wilfred Owen point of view; a Lord Chief Justice's point of view and the point of view of an educated man's daughter. All differ. But is there no absolute point of view? Can we not find somewhere written up in letters of fire or gold, 'This is right. This wrong'?—a moral judgement which we must all, whatever our differences, accept? Let us then refer the question of the rightness or wrongness of war to those who make morality their profession—the clergy. Surely if we ask the clergy the simple question: 'Is war right or is war wrong?' they will give us a plain answer which we cannot deny. But no—the Church of England, which might be supposed able to abstract the question from its worldly confusions, is of two minds also. The bishops themselves are at loggerheads. The Bishop of London maintained that 'the real danger to the peace of the world today were the pacifists. Bad as war was dishonour was far worse.'[8] On the other hand, the Bishop of Birmingham[9] described himself as an 'extreme pacifist . . . I cannot see myself that war can be regarded as consonant with the spirit of Christ.' So the Church itself gives us divided counsel—in some circumstances it is right to fight; in no circumstances is it right to fight. It is distressing, baffling, confusing, but the fact must be faced; there is no certainty in heaven above or on earth below. Indeed the more lives we read, the more speeches we listen to, the more opinions we consult, the greater the confusion becomes and the less possible it seems, since we cannot understand the impulses, the motives, or the morality which leads you to go to war, to make any suggestion that will help you to prevent war.

But besides these pictures of other people's lives and minds—these biographies and histories—there are also other pictures—pictures of actual facts; photographs. Photographs, of course, are not arguments addressed to the reason; they are simply statements of fact addressed to the eye. But in that very simplicity there may be some help. Let us see then whether when we look at the same photographs we feel the same things. Here then on the table before us are photographs. The Spanish Government sends them with patient pertinacity about twice a week.† They are not pleasant photographs to look upon. They are photographs of dead bodies for the most part.* This morning's collection contains the photograph of what might be a man's body, or a woman's; it is so mutilated that it might, on the other hand, be the body of a pig. But those certainly are dead children, and that undoubtedly is the section of a house. A bomb has torn open the side; there is still a birdcage hanging in what was presumably the sitting-room, but the rest of the house looks like nothing so much as a bunch of spillikins suspended in mid-air.

† Written in the winter of 1936–7.

[ 164 ]

Those photographs are not an argument; they are simply a crude statement of fact addressed to the eye. But the eye is connected with the brain; the brain with the nervous system. That system sends its messages in a flash through every past memory and present feeling. When we look at those photographs some fusion takes place within us; however different the education, the traditions behind us, our sensations are the same; and they are violent. You, Sir, call them 'horror and disgust'. We also call them horror and disgust. And the same words rise to our lips. War, you say, is an abomination; a barbarity; war must be stopped at whatever cost. And we echo your words. War is an abomination; a barbarity; war must be stopped. For now at last we are looking at the same picture; we are seeing with you the same dead bodies, the same ruined houses.

Let us then give up, for the moment, the effort to answer your question, how we can help you to prevent war, by discussing the political, the patriotic or the psychological reasons which lead you to go to war. The emotion is too positive to suffer patient analysis. Let us concentrate upon the practical suggestions which you bring forward for our consideration. There are three of them. The first is to sign a letter to the newspapers; the second is to join a certain society; the third is to subscribe to its funds. Nothing on the face of it could sound simpler. To scribble a name on a sheet of paper is easy; to attend a meeting where pacific opinions are more or less rhetorically reiterated to people who already believe in them is also easy; and to write a cheque in support of those vaguely acceptable opinions, though not so easy, is a cheap way of quieting what may conveniently be called one's conscience. Yet there are reasons which make us hesitate; reasons into which we must enter, less superficially, later on. Here it is enough to say that though the three measures you suggest seem plausible, yet it also seems that, if we did what you ask, the emotion caused by the photographs would still remain unappeased. That emotion, that very positive emotion, demands something more positive than a name written on a sheet of paper; an hour spent listening to speeches; a cheque written for whatever sum we can afford—say one guinea. Some more energetic, some more active method of expressing our belief that war is barbarous, that war is inhuman, that war, as Wilfred Owen put it, is insupportable, horrible and beastly seems to be required. But, rhetoric apart, what active method is open to us? Let us consider and compare. You, of course, could once more take up arms—in Spain, as before in France*—in defence of peace. But that presumably is a method that having tried you have rejected. At any rate that method is not open to us; both the Army and the Navy are closed to our sex. We are not allowed to fight. Nor again are we allowed to be members of the Stock Exchange. Thus we can use neither the pressure of force nor the pressure of money. The less direct but still effective weapons which our brothers, as educated men, possess in the diplomatic service, in the Church, are also denied to us. We cannot preach sermons or negotiate treaties. Then again although it is true that we can write articles or send letters to the Press, the control of the Press—the decision what to print, what not to print—is entirely in the hands of your sex. It is true that for the past twenty years we have been admitted to the Civil Service and to the Bar; but our position there is still very precarious and our authority of the slightest. Thus all the weapons with which an educated man can enforce his opinion are either beyond our grasp or so nearly beyond it that even if we used them we could scarcely inflict one scratch. If the men in your profession were to unite in any demand and were to say: 'If it is not granted we will stop work,' the laws of England would cease to be administered. If the women in your profession said the same thing it would make no difference to the laws of England whatever. Not only are we incomparably weaker than the men of our own class; we are weaker than the women of the working class. If the working women of the country were to say: 'If you go to war, we will refuse to make munitions or to help in the production of goods,' the difficulty of war-making would be seriously increased. But if all the daughters of educated men were to down tools tomorrow, nothing essential either to the life or to the war-making of the community would be embarrassed. Our class is the weakest of all the classes in the state. We have no weapon with which to enforce our will.[10]

The answer to that is so familiar that we can easily anticipate it. The daughters of educated men have no direct influence, it is true; but they possess the greatest power of all; that is, the influence that they can exert upon educated men. If this is true, if, that is, influence is still the strongest of our weapons and the only one that can be effective in helping you to prevent war, let us, before we sign your manifesto or join your society, consider what the influence amounts to. Clearly it is of such immense importance that it deserves profound and prolonged scrutiny. Ours cannot be profound; nor can it be prolonged; it must be rapid and imperfect—still, let us attempt it.

What influence then have we had in the past upon the profession that is most clearly connected with war—upon politics? There again are the innumerable, the invaluable biographies, but it would puzzle an alchemist to extract from the massed lives of politicians that particular strain which is the influence upon them of women. Our analysis can only be slight and superficial; still if we narrow our inquiry to manageable limits, and run over the memoirs of a century and a half we can hardly deny that there have been women who have influenced politics. The famous Duchess of Devonshire, Lady Palmerston, Lady Melbourne, Madame de Lieven, Lady Holland, Lady Ashburton*—to skip from one famous name to another—were all undoubtedly possessed of great political influence. Their famous houses and the parties that met in them play so large a part in the political memoirs of the time that we can hardly deny that English politics, even perhaps English wars, would have been different had those houses and those parties never existed. But there is one characteristic that all those memoirs possess in common; the names of the great political leaders—Pitt, Fox, Burke, Sheridan, Peel, Canning, Palmerston, Disraeli, Gladstone*—are sprinkled on every page; but you will not find either at the head of the stairs receiving the guests, or in the more private apartments of the house, any daughter of an educated man. It may be that they were deficient in charm, in wit, in rank, or in clothing. Whatever the reason, you may turn page after page, volume after volume, and though you will find their brothers and husbands—Sheridan at Devonshire House, Macaulay* at Holland House, Matthew Arnold at Lansdowne House, Carlyle* even at Bath House, the names of Jane Austen, Charlotte Brontë, and George Eliot do not occur; and though Mrs Carlyle went, Mrs Carlyle seems on her own showing to have found herself ill at ease.

But, as you will point out, the daughters of educated men may have possessed another kind of influence—one that was independent of wealth and rank, of wine, food, dress and all the other amenities that make the great houses of the great ladies so seductive. Here indeed we are on firmer ground, for there was of course one political cause which the daughters of educated men had much at heart during the past 150 years: the franchise. But when we consider how long it took them to win that cause, and what labour, we can only conclude that influence has to be combined with wealth in order to be effective as a political weapon, and that influence of the kind that can be exerted by the daughters of educated men is very low in power, very slow in action, and very painful in use.[11] Certainly the one great political achievement of the educated man's daughter cost her over a century of the most exhausting and menial labour; kept her trudging in processions, working in offices, speaking at street corners; finally, because she used force, sent her to prison, and would very likely still keep her there, had it not been, paradoxically enough, that the help she gave her brothers when they used force at last gave her the right to call herself, if not a full daughter, still a stepdaughter of England.[12]

Influence then when put to the test would seem to be only fully effective when combined with rank, wealth and great houses. The influential are the daughters of noblemen, not the daughters of educated men. And that influence is of the kind described by a distinguished member of your own profession, the late Sir Ernest Wild.

He claimed that the great influence which women exerted over men always had been, and always ought to be, an indirect influence. Man liked to think he was doing his job himself when, in fact, he was doing just what the woman wanted, but the wise woman always let him think he was running the show when he was not. Any woman who chose to take an interest in politics had an immensely greater power without the vote than with it, because she could influence many voters. His feeling was that it was not right to bring women down to the level of men. He looked up to women, and wanted to continue to do so. He desired that the age of chivalry should not pass, because every man who had a woman to care about him liked to shine in her eyes.[13]

And so on.

If such is the real nature of our influence, and we all recognize the description and have noted the effects, it is either beyond our reach, for many of us are plain, poor and old; or beneath our contempt, for many of us would prefer to call ourselves prostitutes simply and to take our stand openly under the lamps of Piccadilly Circus rather than use it. If such is the real nature, the indirect nature, of this celebrated weapon, we must do without it; add our pigmy impetus to your more substantial forces, and have recourse, as you suggest, to letter signing, society joining and the drawing of an occasional exiguous cheque. Such would seem to be the inevitable, though depressing, conclusion of our inquiry into the nature of influence, were it not that for some reason, never satisfactorily explained, the right to vote,[14] in itself by no means negligible, was mysteriously connected with another right of such immense value to the daughters of educated men that almost every word in the dictionary has been changed by it, including the word 'influence'. You will not think these words exaggerated if we explain that they refer to the right to earn one's living.

That, Sir, was the right that was conferred upon us less than twenty years ago, in the year 1919, by an Act which unbarred the professions. The door of the private house was thrown open. In every purse there was, or might be, one bright new sixpence in whose light every thought, every sight, every action looked different. Twenty years is not, as time goes, a long time; nor is a sixpenny bit a very important coin; nor can we yet draw upon biography to supply us with a picture of the lives and minds of the new-sixpenny owners. But in imagination perhaps we can see the educated man's daughter, as she issues from the shadow of the private house, and stands on the bridge which lies between the old world and the new, and asks, as she twirls the sacred coin in her hand, 'What shall I do with it? What do I see with it?' Through that light we may guess everything she saw looked different—men and women, cars and churches. The moon even, scarred as it is in fact with forgotten craters, seemed to her a white sixpence, a chaste

[ 172 ]

sixpence, an altar upon which she vowed never to side with the servile, the signers-on, since it was hers to do what she liked with—the sacred sixpence that she had earned with her own hands herself. And if checking imagination with prosaic good sense, you object that to depend upon a profession is only another form of slavery, you will admit from your own experience that to depend upon a profession is a less odious form of slavery than to depend upon a father. Recall the joy with which you received your first guinea for your first brief, and the deep breath of freedom that you drew when you realized that your days of dependence upon Arthur's Education Fund were over. From that guinea, as from one of the magic pellets to which children set fire and a tree rises, all that you most value—wife, children, home— and above all that influence which now enables you to influence other men, have sprung. What would that influence be if you were still drawing £40 a year from the family purse, and for any addition to that income were dependent even upon the most bene- volent of fathers? But it is needless to expatiate. Whatever the reason, whether pride, or love of free- dom, or hatred of hypocrisy, you will understand the excitement with which in 1919 your sisters began to earn not a guinea but a sixpenny bit, and will not scorn that pride, or deny that it was justly based, since it meant that they need no longer use the influence described by Sir Ernest Wild.

The word 'influence' then has changed. The educated man's daughter has now at her disposal an influence which is different from any influence that she has possessed before. It is not the influence which the great lady, the Siren, possesses; nor is it the influence which the educated man's daughter possessed when she had no vote; nor is it the influence which she possessed when she had a vote but was debarred from the right to earn her living. It differs, because it is an influence from which the charm element has been removed; it is an influence from which the money element has been removed. She need no longer use her charm to procure money from her father or brother. Since it is beyond the power of her family to punish her financially she can express her own opinions. In place of the admirations and antipathies which were often unconsciously dictated by the need of money she can declare her genuine likes and dislikes. In short, she need not acquiesce; she can criticize. At last she is in possession of an influence that is disinterested.

Such in rough and rapid outlines is the nature of our new weapon, the influence which the educated man's daughter can exert now that she is able to earn her own living. The question that has next to be discussed, therefore, is how can she use this new weapon to help you to prevent war? And it is immediately plain that if there is no difference between men who earn their livings in the professions and women who earn their livings, then this letter can end; for if our point of view is the same as yours then we must add our sixpence to your guinea; follow your methods and repeat your words. But, whether fortunately or unfortunately, that is not true. The two classes still differ enormously. And to prove this, we need not have recourse to the dangerous and uncertain theories of psychologists and biologists; we can appeal to facts. Take the fact of education. Your class has been educated at public school and universities for five or six hundred years, ours for sixty. Take the fact of property.[15] Your class possesses in its own right and not through marriage practically all the capital, all the land, all the valuables, and all the patronage in England. Our class possesses in its own right and not through marriage practically none of the capital, none of the land, none of the valuables, and none of the patronage in England. That such differences make for very considerable differences in mind and body, no psychologist or biologist would deny. It would seem to follow then as an indisputable fact that 'we'—meaning by 'we' a whole made up of body, brain and spirit, influenced by memory and tradition—must still differ in some essential respects from 'you', whose body, brain and spirit have been so differently trained and are so differently influenced by memory and tradition. Though we see the same world, we see it through different eyes. Any help we can give you must be different from that you can give yourselves, and perhaps the value of that help may lie in the fact of that difference. Therefore before we agree to sign your manifesto or join your society, it might be well to discover where the difference lies, because then we may discover where the help lies also. Let us then by way of a very elementary beginning lay before you a photograph—a crudely coloured photograph—of your world as it appears to us who see it from the threshold of the private house; through the shadow of the veil that St Paul still lays upon our eyes;* from the bridge which connects the private house with the world of public life.

Your world, then, the world of professional, of public life, seen from this angle undoubtedly looks queer. At first sight it is enormously impressive. Within quite a small space are crowded together St Paul's, the Bank of England, the Mansion House, the massive if funereal battlements of the Law Courts; and on the other side, Westminster Abbey and the Houses of Parliament. There, we say to ourselves, pausing, in this moment of transition on the bridge, our fathers and brothers have spent their lives. All these hundreds of years they have been mounting those steps, passing in and out of those doors, ascending those pulpits, preaching, money-making, administering justice. It is from this world that the private house (somewhere, roughly speaking, in the West End) has derived its creeds, its laws, its clothes and carpets, its beef and mutton. And then, as is now permissible, cautiously pushing aside the swing doors of one of these temples, we enter on tiptoe and survey the scene in greater detail. The first sensation of colossal size, of majestic masonry is broken up into a myriad points of amazement mixed with interrogation. Your clothes in the first place make us gape with astonishment.[16] How many, how splendid, how extremely ornate they are—the clothes worn by the educated man in his public capacity! Now you dress in violet; a jewelled crucifix swings on your breast; now your shoulders are covered with lace; now furred with ermine; now slung with many linked chains set with precious stones. Now you wear wigs on your heads; rows of graduated curls descend to your necks. Now your hats are boat-shaped, or cocked; now they mount in cones of black fur; now they are made of brass and scuttle shaped; now plumes of red, now of blue hair surmount them. Sometimes gowns cover your legs; sometimes gaiters. Tabards embroidered with lions and unicorns swing from your shoulders; metal objects cut in star shapes or in circles glitter and twinkle upon your breasts. Ribbons of all colours— blue, purple, crimson—cross from shoulder to shoulder. After the comparative simplicity of your dress at home, the splendour of your public attire is dazzling.

But far stranger are two other facts that gradually reveal themselves when our eyes have recovered from their first amazement. Not only are whole bodies of men dressed alike summer and winter—a strange

[ 177 ]

characteristic to a sex which changes its clothes according to the season, and for reasons of private taste and comfort—but every button, rosette and stripe seems to have some symbolic meaning. Some have the right to wear plain buttons only; others rosettes; some may wear a single stripe; others three, four, five or six. And each curl or stripe is sewn on at precisely the right distance apart; it may be one inch for one man, one inch and a quarter for another. Rules again regulate the gold wire on the shoulders, the braid on the trousers, the cockades on the hats— but no single pair of eyes can observe all these distinctions, let alone account for them accurately.

Even stranger, however, than the symbolic splendour of your clothes are the ceremonies that take place when you wear them. Here you kneel; there you bow; here you advance in procession behind a man carrying a silver poker; here you mount a carved chair; here you appear to do homage to a piece of painted wood; here you abase yourselves before tables covered with richly worked tapestry. And whatever these ceremonies may mean you perform them always together, always in step, always in the uniform proper to the man and the occasion.

Apart from the ceremonies such decorative apparel appears to us at first sight strange in the extreme. For dress, as we use it, is comparatively simple. Besides the prime function of covering the body, it has two other offices—that it creates beauty for the eye, and

[ 178 ]

—

that it attracts the admiration of your sex. Since marriage until the year 1919—less than twenty years ago—was the only profession open to us, the enormous importance of dress to a woman can hardly be exaggerated. It was to her what clients are to you— dress was her chief, perhaps her only, method of becoming Lord Chancellor. But your dress in its immense elaboration has obviously another function. It not only covers nakedness, gratifies vanity, and creates pleasure for the eye, but it serves to advertise the social, professional, or intellectual standing of the wearer. If you will excuse the humble illustration, your dress fulfils the same function as the tickets in a grocer's shop. But, here, instead of saying 'This is margarine; this pure butter; this is the finest butter in the market,' it says, 'This man is a clever man—he is Master of Arts; this man is a very clever man—he is Doctor of Letters; this man is a most clever man—he is a Member of the Order of Merit.' It is this function—the advertisement function—of your dress that seems to us most singular. In the opinion of St Paul, such advertisement, at any rate for our sex, was unbecoming and immodest; until a very few years ago we were denied the use of it. And still the tradition, or belief, lingers among us that to express worth of any kind, whether intellectual or moral, by wearing pieces of metal, or ribbon, coloured hoods or gowns, is a barbarity which deserves the ridicule which we bestow upon the rites of savages. A woman who advertised her motherhood by a tuft of horsehair on the left shoulder would scarcely, you will agree, be a venerable object.

But what light does our difference here throw upon the problem before us? What connection is there between the sartorial splendours of the educated man and the photograph of ruined houses and dead bodies? Obviously the connection between dress and war is not far to seek; your finest clothes are those that you wear as soldiers. Since the red and the gold, the brass and the feathers are discarded upon active service, it is plain that their expensive and not, one might suppose, hygienic splendour is invented partly in order to impress the beholder with the majesty of the military office, partly in order through their vanity to induce young men to become soldiers. Here, then, our influence and our difference might have some effect; we, who are forbidden to wear such clothes ourselves, can express the opinion that the wearer is not to us a pleasing or an impressive spectacle. He is on the contrary a ridiculous, a barbarous, a displeasing spectacle. But as the daughters of educated men we can use our influence more effectively in another direction, upon our own class—the class of educated men. For there, in courts and universities, we find the same love of dress. There, too, are velvet and silk, fur and ermine. We can say that for educated men to emphasize their superiority over other people, either in birth or intellect, by dressing differently, or by adding titles before, or letters after their names are acts that rouse competition and jealousy—emotions which, as we need scarcely draw upon biography to prove, nor ask psychology to show, have their share in encouraging a disposition towards war. If then we express the opinion that such distinctions make those who possess them ridiculous and learning contemptible we should do something, indirectly, to discourage the feelings that lead to war. Happily we can now do more than express an opinion; we can refuse all such distinctions* and all such uniforms for ourselves. This would be a slight but definite contribution to the problem before us—how to prevent war; and one that a different training and a different tradition puts more easily within our reach than within yours.[17]

But our bird's-eye view of the outside of things is not altogther encouraging. The coloured photograph that we have been looking at presents some remarkable features, it is true; but it serves to remind us that there are many inner and secret chambers that we cannot enter. What real influence can we bring to bear upon law or business, religion or politics—we to whom many doors are still locked, or at best ajar, we who have neither capital nor force behind us? It seems as if our influence must stop short at the surface. When we have expressed an opinion upon the surface we have done all that we can do. It is true that the surface may have some connection with the depths, but if we are to help you to prevent war we must try to penetrate deeper beneath the skin. Let us then look in another direction—in a direction natural to educated men's daughters, in the direction of education itself.

Here, fortunately, the year, the sacred year 1919, comes to our help. Since that year put it into the power of educated men's daughters to earn their livings they have at last some real influence upon education. They have money. They have money to subscribe to causes. Honorary treasurers invoke their help. To prove it, here, opportunely, cheek by jowl with your letter, is a letter from one such treasurer asking for money with which to rebuild a women's college.* And when honorary treasurers invoke help, it stands to reason that they can be bargained with. We have the right to say to her, 'You shall only have our guinea with which to help you rebuild your college if you will help this gentleman whose letter also lies before us to prevent war.' We can say to her, 'You must educate the young to hate war. You must teach them to feel the inhumanity, the beastliness, the insupportability of war.' But what kind of education shall we bargain for? What sort of education will teach the young to hate war?

That is a question that is difficult enough in itself; and may well seem unanswerable by those who are of Mary Kingsley's persuasion—those who have had no direct experience of university education themselves.

Yet the part that education plays in human life is so important, and the part that it might play in answering your question is so considerable that to shirk any attempt to see how we can influence the young through education against war would be craven. Let us therefore turn from our station on the bridge across the Thames to another bridge over another river, this time in one of the great universities; for both have rivers, and both have bridges, too, for us to stand upon. Once more, how strange it looks, this world of domes and spires, of lecture rooms and laboratories, from our vantage point! How different it looks to us from what it must look to you! To those who behold it from Mary Kingsley's angle— 'being allowed to learn German was *all* the paid education I ever had'—it may well appear a world so remote, so formidable, so intricate in its ceremonies and traditions that any criticism or comment may well seem futile. Here, too, we marvel at the brilliance of your clothes; here, too, we watch maces erect themselves and processions form, and note with eyes too dazzled to record the differences, let alone to explain them, the subtle distinctions of hats and hoods, of purples and crimsons, of velvet and cloth, of cap and gown. It is a solemn spectacle. The words of Arthur's song in *Pendennis* rise to our lips:

> Although I enter not,
> Yet round about the spot
> Sometimes I hover,

And at the sacred gate,
With longing eyes I wait,
Expectant . . .

and again,

I will not enter there,
To sully your pure prayer
With thoughts unruly.

But suffer me to pace
Round the forbidden place,
 Lingering a minute,
Like outcast spirits, who wait
And see through Heaven's gate
Angels within it.*

But, since both you, Sir, and the honorary treasurer
of the college rebuilding fund are waiting for answers
to your letters we must cease to hang over old bridges
humming old songs; we must attempt to deal with
the question of education, however imperfectly.

What, then, is this 'university education' of which
Mary Kingsley's sisterhood have heard so much and
to which they have contributed so painfully? What is
this mysterious process that takes about three years
to accomplish, costs a round sum in hard cash, and
turns the crude and raw human being into the finished
product—an educated man or woman? There can be
no doubt in the first place of its supreme value. The
witness of biography—that witness which anyone

who can read English can consult on the shelves of any public library—is unanimous upon this point; the value of education is among the greatest of all human values. Biography proves this in two ways. First, there is the fact that the great majority of the men who have ruled England for the past 500 years, who are now ruling England in Parliament and the Civil Service, have received a university education. Second, there is the fact which is even more impressive if you consider what toil, what privation it implies—and of this, too, there is ample proof in biography—the fact of the immense sum of money that has been spent upon education in the past 500 years. The income of Oxford University is £435,656 (1933–4), the income of Cambridge University is £212,000 (1930). In addition to the university income each college has its own separate income, which, judging only from the gifts and bequests announced from time to time in the newspapers, must in some cases be of fabulous proportions.[18] If we add further the incomes enjoyed by the great public schools— Eton, Harrow, Winchester, Rugby, to name the largest only—so huge a sum of money is reached that there can be no doubt of the enormous value that human beings place upon education. And the study of biography—the lives of the poor, of the obscure, of the uneducated—proves that they will make any effort, any sacrifice to procure an education at one of the great universities.[19]

But perhaps the greatest testimony to the value of education with which biography provides us is the fact that the sisters of educated men not only made the sacrifices of comfort and pleasure, which were needed in order to educate their brothers, but actually desired to be educated themselves. When we consider the ruling of the Church on this subject, a ruling which we learn from biography was in force only a few years ago—'. . . I was told that desire for learning in women was against the will of God, . . .'[20]—we must allow that their desire must have been strong. And if we reflect that all the professions for which a university education fitted her brothers were closed to her, her belief in the value of education must appear still stronger, since she must have believed in education for itself. And if we reflect further that the one profession that was open to her—marriage—was held to need no education, and indeed was of such a nature that education unfitted women to practise it, then it would have been no surprise to find that she had renounced any wish or attempt to be educated herself, but had contented herself with providing education for her brothers—the vast majority of women, the nameless, the poor, by cutting down household expenses; the minute minority, the titled, the rich, by founding or endowing colleges for men. This indeed they did. But so innate in human nature is the desire for education that you will find, if you consult biography, that the same desire, in spite of all the impediments that tradition, poverty and ridicule could put in its way, existed too among women. To prove this let us examine one life only—the life of Mary Astell.[21] Little is known about her, but enough to show that almost 250 years ago this obstinate and perhaps irreligious desire was alive in her; she actually proposed to found a college for women. What is almost as remarkable, the Princess Anne was ready to give her £10,000—a very considerable sum then, and, indeed, now, for any woman to have at her disposal—towards the expenses. And then—then we meet with a fact which is of extreme interest, both historically and psychologically: the Church intervened. Bishop Burnet* was of opinion that to educate the sisters of educated men would be to encourage the wrong branch, that is to say, the Roman Catholic branch, of the Christian faith. The money went elsewhere; the college was never founded.

But these facts, as facts so often do, prove double-faced; for though they establish the value of education, they also prove that education is by no means a positive value; it is not good in all circumstances, and good for all people; it is only good for some people and for some purposes. It is good if it produces a belief in the Church of England; bad if it produces a belief in the Church of Rome; it is good for one sex and for some professions, but bad for another sex and for another profession.

Such at least would seem to be the answer of

biography—the oracle is not dumb,* but it is dubious. As, however, it is of great importance that we should use our influence through education to affect the young against war we must not be baffled by the evasions of biography or seduced by its charm. We must try to see what kind of education an educated man's sister receives at present, in order that we may do our utmost to use our influence in the universities where it properly belongs, and where it will have most chance of penetrating beneath the skin. Now happily we need no longer depend upon biography, which inevitably, since it is concerned with the private life, bristles with innumerable conflicts of private opinion. We have now to help us that record of the public life which is history. Even outsiders can consult the annals of those public bodies which record not the day-to-day opinions of private people, but use a larger accent and convey through the mouths of Parliaments and Senates the considered opinions of bodies of educated men.

History at once informs us that there are now, and have been since about 1870, colleges for the sisters of educated men both at Oxford and at Cambridge.* But history also informs us of facts of such a nature about those colleges that all attempt to influence the young against war through the education they receive there must be abandoned. In face of them it is mere waste of time and breath to talk of 'influencing the young'; useless to lay down terms, before allowing the honorary treasurer to have her guinea; better to take the first train to London than to haunt the sacred gates. But, you will interpose, what are these facts? these historical but deplorable facts? Therefore let us place them before you, warning you that they are taken only from such records as are available to an outsider and from the annals of the university which is not your own—Cambridge. Your judgement, therefore, will be undistorted by loyalty to old ties, or gratitude for benefits received, but it will be impartial and disinterested.

To begin then where we left off: Queen Anne died and Bishop Burnet died and Mary Astell died; but the desire to found a college for her own sex did not die. Indeed, it became stronger and stronger. By the middle of the nineteenth century it became so strong that a house was taken at Cambridge to lodge the students. It was not a nice house; it was a house without a garden in the middle of a noisy street.* Then a second house was taken, a better house this time, though it is true that the water rushed through the dining-room in stormy weather and there was no playground. But that house was not sufficient; the desire for education was so urgent that more rooms were needed, a garden to walk in, a playground to play in. Therefore another house was needed. Now history tells us that in order to build this house, money was needed. You will not question that fact but you may well question the next—that the money was borrowed. It will seem to you more probable that the money was given. The other colleges, you will say, were rich; all derived their incomes indirectly, some directly, from their sisters. There is Gray's *Ode** to prove it. And you will quote the song with which he hails the benefactors: the Countess of Pembroke who founded Pembroke; the Countess of Clare who founded Clare; Margaret of Anjou who founded Queens'; the Countess of Richmond and Derby who founded St John's and Christ's.

> What is grandeur, what is power?
> Heavier toil, superior pain.
> What the bright reward we gain?
> The grateful memory of the good.
> Sweet is the breath of vernal shower,
> The bee's collected treasures sweet,
> Sweet music's melting fall, but sweeter yet
> The still small voice of gratitude.[22]

Here, you will say in sober prose, was an opportunity to repay the debt. For what sum was needed? A beggarly £10,000—the very sum that the bishop intercepted about two centuries previously. That £10,000 surely was disgorged by the Church that had swallowed it? But churches do not easily disgorge what they have swallowed. Then the colleges, you will say, which had benefited, they must have given it gladly in memory of their noble benefactresses? What could £10,000 mean to St John's or Clare or Christ's?

And the land belonged to St John's. But the land, history says, was leased; and the £10,000 was not given; it was collected laboriously from private purses. Among them one lady must be for ever remembered because she gave £1,000;* and Anon. must receive whatever thanks Anon. will consent to receive, because she gave sums ranging from £20 to £100. And another lady was able, owing to a legacy from her mother, to give her services as mistress without salary. And the students themselves subscribed—so far as students can—by making beds and washing dishes, by forgoing amenities and living on simple fare. Ten thousand pounds is not at all a beggarly sum when it has to be collected from the purses of the poor, from the bodies of the young. It takes time, energy, brains, to collect it, sacrifice to give it. Of course, several educated men were very kind; they lectured to their sisters; others were not so kind; they refused to lecture to their sisters. Some educated men were very kind and encouraged their sisters; others were not so kind, they discouraged their sisters.[23] Nevertheless, by hook or by crook, the day came at last, history tells us, when somebody passed an examination. And then the mistresses, principals or whatever they called themselves—for the title that should be worn by a woman who will not take a salary must be a matter of doubt—asked the Chancellors and the Masters about whose titles there need by no doubt, at any rate upon that score, whether the girls who had passed examinations might advertise the fact as those gentlemen themselves did by putting letters after their names. This was advisable, because, as the present Master of Trinity, Sir J. J. Thompson, OM, FRS, after poking a little justifiable fun at the 'pardonable vanity' of those who put letters after their names, informs us, 'the general public who have not taken a degree themselves attach much more importance to BA after a person's name than those who have. Head mistresses of schools therefore prefer a belettered staff, so that students of Newnham and Girton, since they could not put BA after their names, were at a disadvantage in obtaining appointments.' And in Heaven's name, we may both ask, what conceivable reason could there be for preventing them from putting the letters BA after their names if it helped them to obtain appointments? To that question history supplies no answer; we must look for it in psychology, in biography; but history supplies us with the fact. 'The proposal, however,' the Master of Trinity continues—the proposal, that is, that those who had passed examinations might call themselves BA—'met with the most determined opposition . . . On the day of the voting there was a great influx of non-residents and the proposal was thrown out by the crushing majority of 1707 to 661. I believe the number of voters has never been equalled . . . The behaviour of some of the undergraduates after the poll was declared in the Senate House was exceptionally deplorable and disgraceful. A large band of them left the Senate House, proceeded to Newnham and damaged the bronze gates which had been put up as a memorial to Miss Clough, the first Principal.'[24]

Is that not enough? Need we collect more facts from history and biography to prove our statement that all attempt to influence the young against war through the education they receive at the universities must be abandoned? For do they not prove that education, the finest education in the world, does not teach people to hate force, but to use it? Do they not prove that education, far from teaching the educated generosity and magnanimity, makes them on the contrary so anxious to keep their possessions, that 'grandeur and power' of which the poet speaks, in their own hands, that they will use not force but much subtler methods than force when they are asked to share them? And are not force and possessiveness very closely connected with war? Of what use then is a university education in influencing people to prevent war? But history goes on of course; year succeeds to year. The years change things; slightly but imperceptibly they change them. And history tells us that at last, after spending time and strength whose value is immeasurable in repeatedly soliciting the authorities with the humility expected of our sex and proper to suppliants the right to impress head mistresses by putting the letters BA after the name was granted. But that right, history tells us, was only a titular right. At Cambridge, in the year 1937, the women's colleges—you will scarcely believe it, Sir, but once more it is the voice of fact that is speaking, not of fiction—the women's colleges are not allowed to be members of the university;[25] and the number of educated men's daughters who are allowed to receive a university education is still strictly limited; though both sexes contribute to the university funds.[26] As for poverty, *The Times* newspaper supplies us with figures; any ironmonger will provide us with a foot-rule; if we measure the money available for scholarships at the men's colleges with the money available for their sisters at the women's colleges, we shall save ourselves the trouble of adding up; and come to the conclusion that the colleges for the sisters of educated men are, compared with their brothers' colleges, unbelievably and shamefully poor.[27]

Proof of that last fact comes pat to hand in the honorary treasurer's letter, asking for money with which to rebuild her college. She has been asking for some time; she is still asking, it seems. But there is nothing, after what has been said above, that need puzzle us, either in the fact that she is poor, or in the fact that her college needs rebuilding. What is puzzling, and has become still more puzzling, in view of the facts give above, is this: What answer ought we to make her when she asks us to help her to rebuild her college? History, biography, and the daily paper between them make it difficult either to answer her letter or to dictate terms. For between them they have raised many questions. In the first place, what reason is there to think that a university education makes the educated against war? Again, if we help an educated man's daughter to go to Cambridge are we not forcing her to think not about education but about war?— not how she can learn, but how she can fight in order that she may win the same advantages as her brothers? Further, since the daughters of educated men are not members of Cambridge University they have no say in that education, therefore how can they alter that education even if we ask them to? And then, of course, other questions arise—questions of a practical nature, which will easily be understood by a busy man, an honorary treasurer, like yourself, Sir. You will be the first to agree that to ask people who are so largely occupied in raising funds with which to rebuild a college to consider the nature of education and what effect it can have upon war is to heap another straw upon an already overburdened back. From an outsider, moreover, who has no right to speak, such a request may well deserve, and perhaps receive, a reply too forcible to be quoted. But we have sworn that we will do all we can to help you to prevent war by using our influence—our earned money influence. And education is the obvious way. Since she is poor, since she is asking for money, and since the giver of money is entitled to dictate terms, let us risk it and draft a letter to her, laying down the terms upon which she shall have our money to help rebuild her college. Here, then, is an attempt:

'Your letter, Madam, has been waiting some time without an answer. But certain doubts and questions have arisen. May we put them to you, ignorantly as an outsider must, but frankly as an outsider should when asked to contribute money? You say, then, that you are asking for £100,000 with which to rebuild your college. But how can you be so foolish? Or are you so secluded among the nightingales and the willows, or so busy with profound questions of caps and gowns, and which is to walk first into the Provost's drawing-room—the Master's pug or the Mistress's pom—that you have no time to read the daily papers? Or are you so harassed with the problem of drawing £100,000 gracefully from an indifferent public that you can only think of appeals and committees, bazaars and ices, strawberries and cream?

'Let us then inform you: we are spending three hundred million annually upon the army and navy; for, according to a letter that lies cheek by jowl with your own, there is grave danger of war. How then can you seriously ask us to provide you with money with which to rebuild your college? If you reply that the college was built on the cheap, and that the college needs rebuilding, that may be true. But when you go on to say that the public is generous, and that the public is still capable of providing large sums for rebuilding colleges, let us draw your attention to a significant passage in the Master of Trinity's memoirs. It is this: "Fortunately, however, soon after the beginning of this century the University began to receive a succession of very handsome bequests and donations, and these, aided by a liberal grant from the Government, have put the finances of the University in such a good position that it has been quite unnecessary to ask for any increase in the contribution from the Colleges. The income of the University from all sources has increased from about £60,000 in 1900 to £212,000 in 1930. It is not a very wild hypothesis to suppose that this has been to a large extent due to the important and very interesting discoveries which have been made in the University, and Cambridge may be quoted as an example of the practical results which come from Research for its own sake."

'Consider only that last sentence. ". . . Cambridge may be quoted as an example of the practical results which come from Research for its own sake." What has your college done to stimulate great manufacturers to endow it? Have you taken a leading part in the invention of the implements of war? How far have your students succeeded in business as capitalists? How then can you expect "very handsome bequests and donations" to come your way? Again, are you a member of Cambridge University? You are not. How then can you fairly ask for any say in their distribution? You can not. Therefore, Madam, it is plain that you must stand at the door, cap in hand, giving parties, spending your strength and time in soliciting subscriptions. That is plain. But it is also plain that outsiders who find you thus occupied must ask themselves, when they receive a request for a contribution towards rebuilding your college, Shall I send it or shan't I? If I send it, what shall I ask them to do with it? Shall I ask them to rebuild the college on the old lines? Or shall I ask them to rebuild it, but differently? Or shall I ask them to buy rags and petrol and Bryant & May's matches and burn the college to the ground?

'These are the questions, Madam, that have kept your letter so long unanswered. They are questions of great difficulty and perhaps they are useless questions. But can we leave them unasked in view of this gentleman's questions? He is asking how can we help him to prevent war? He is asking us how we can help him to defend liberty; to defend culture? Also consider these photographs: they are pictures of dead bodies and ruined houses. Surely in view of these questions and pictures you must consider very carefully before you begin to rebuild your college what is the aim of education, what kind of society, what kind of human being it should seek to produce. At any rate I will only send you a guinea with which to rebuild your college if you can satisfy me that you will use it to produce the kind of society, the kind of people that will help to prevent war.

'Let us then discuss as quickly as we can the sort of education that is needed. Now since history and biography—the only evidence available to an outsider—seem to prove that the old education of the old colleges breeds neither a particular respect for liberty nor a particular hatred of war it is clear that you must rebuild your college differently. It is young and poor; let it therefore take advantage of those qualities and be founded on poverty and youth. Obviously, then, it must be an experimental college, an adventurous college. Let it be built on lines of its own. It must be built not of carved stone and stained glass, but of some cheap, easily combustible material which does not hoard dust and perpetrate traditions. Do not have chapels.[28] Do not have museums and libraries with chained books and first editions under glass cases. Let the pictures and the books be new and always changing. Let it be decorated afresh by each generation with their own hands cheaply. The work of the living is cheap; often they will give it for the sake of being allowed to do it. Next, what should be taught in the new college, the poor college? Not the arts of dominating other people; not the arts of ruling, of killing, of acquiring land and capital. They require too many overhead expenses; salaries and uniforms and ceremonies. The poor college must teach only the arts that can be taught cheaply and practised by poor people; such as medicine, mathematics, music, painting and literature. It should teach the arts of human intercourse; the art of understanding other people's lives and minds, and the little arts of talk, of dress, of cookery that are allied with them. The aim of the new college, the cheap college, should be not to segregate and specialize, but to combine. It should explore the ways in which mind and body can be made to co-operate; discover what new combinations make good wholes in human life. The teachers should be drawn from the good livers as well as from the good thinkers. There should be no difficulty in attracting them. For there would be none of the barriers of wealth and ceremony, of advertisements and competition which now make the old and rich universities such uneasy dwelling-places—cities of strife, cities where this is locked up and that is chained down; where nobody can walk freely or talk freely for fear of transgressing some chalk mark, of displeasing some dignitary. But if the college were poor it would have nothing to offer; competition would be abolished. Life would be open and easy. People who love learning for itself would gladly come there. Musicians, painters, writers, would teach there, because they would learn. What could be of greater help to a writer than to discuss the art of writing with people who were thinking not of examinations or degrees or of what honour or profit they could make literature give them but of the art itself?

'And so with the other arts and artists. They would come to the poor college and practise their arts there because it would be a place where society was free; not parcelled out into the miserable distinctions of rich and poor, of clever and stupid; but where all the different degrees and kinds of mind, body and soul merit co-operated. Let us then found this new college; this poor college; in which learning is sought for itself; where advertisement is abolished; and there are no degrees; and lectures are not given, and sermons are not preached, and the old poisoned vanities and parades which breed competition and jealousy . . .'

The letter broke off there. It was not from lack of things to say; the peroration indeed was only just beginning. It was because the face on the other side of the page—the face that a letter-writer always sees—appeared to be fixed with a certain melancholy, upon a passage in the book from which quotation has already been made. 'Head mistresses of schools therefore prefer a belettered staff, so that students of Newnham and Girton, since they could not put BA after their name, were at a disadvantage in obtaining appointments.' The honorary treasurer of the Rebuilding Fund had her eyes fixed on that. 'What is the use of thinking how a college can be different,' she seemed to say, 'when it must be a place where students are taught to obtain appointments?' 'Dream your dreams,' she seemed to add, turning, rather wearily, to the table which she was arranging for some festival, a bazaar presumably, 'but we have to face realities.'

That then was the 'reality' on which her eyes were fixed; students must be taught to earn their livings. And since that reality meant that she must rebuild her college on the same lines as the others, it followed that the college for the daughters of educated men must also make Research produce practical results which will induce bequests and donations from rich men; it must encourage competition; it must accept degrees and coloured hoods; it must accumulate great wealth; it must exclude other people from a share of its wealth; and, therefore, in 500 years or so, that college, too, must ask the same question that you, Sir, are asking now: 'How in your opinion are we to prevent war?'

An undesirable result that seemed; why then sub-scribe a guinea to procure it? That question at any rate was answered. No guinea of earned money should go to rebuilding the college on the old plan; just as certainly none could be spent upon building a college upon a new plan; therefore the guinea should be earmarked 'Rags. Petrol. Matches.' And this note should be attached to it. 'Take this guinea and with it burn the college to the ground. Set fire to the old hypocrisies. Let the light of the burning building scare the nightingales and incarnadine the willows. And let the daughters of educated men dance round the fire and heap armful upon armful of dead leaves upon the flames. And let their mothers lean from the upper windows and cry "Let it blaze! Let it blaze! For we have done with this 'education'!"'

That passage, Sir, is not empty rhetoric, for it is based upon the respectable opinion of the late headmaster of Eton, the present Dean of Durham.[29] Nevertheless, there is something hollow about it, as is shown by a moment's conflict with fact. We have said that the only influence which the daughters of educated men can at present exert against war is the disinterested influence that they possess through earning their livings. If there were no means of training them to earn their livings, there would be an end of that influence. They could not obtain appointments. If they could not obtain appointments they would again be dependent upon their fathers and brothers; and if they were again dependent upon their fathers and brothers they would again be consciously and unconsciously in favour of war. History would seem to put that beyond doubt. Therefore we must send a guinea to the honorary treasurer of the college rebuilding fund, and let her do what she can with it. It is useless as things are to attach conditions as to the way in which that guinea is to be spent.

Such then is the rather lame and depressing answer to our question whether we can ask the authorities of the colleges for the daughters of educated men to use their influence through education to prevent war. It appears that we can ask them to do nothing; they must follow the old road to the old end; our own influence as outsiders can only be of the most indirect sort. If we are asked to teach, we can examine very carefully into the aim of such teaching, and refuse to teach any art or science that encourages war. Further, we can pour mild scorn upon chapels, upon degrees, and upon the value of examinations. We can intimate that a prize poem can still have merit in spite of the fact that it has won a prize; and maintain that a book may still be worth reading in spite of the fact that its author took a first class with honours in the English tripos.* If we are asked to lecture we can refuse to bolster up the vain and vicious system of lecturing by refusing to lecture.[30] And, of course, if we are offered offices and honours for ourselves we can refuse them—how, indeed, in view of the facts, could we possibly do otherwise? But there is no blinking the fact that in the present state of things the most effective way in which we can help you through education to prevent war is to subscribe as generously as possible to the colleges for the daughters of educated men. For, to repeat, if those daughters are not going to be educated they are not going to earn their livings, if they are not going to earn their livings, they are going once more to be restricted to the education of the private house; and if they are going to be restricted to the education of the private house they are going, once more, to exert all their influence both consciously and unconsciously in favour of war. Of that there can be little doubt. Should you doubt it, should you ask proof, let us once more consult biography. Its testimony upon this point is so conclusive, but so voluminous, that we must try to condense many volumes into one story. Here, then, is the narrative of the life of an educated man's daughter who was dependent upon father and brother in the private house of the nineteenth century.

The day was hot, but she could not go out. 'How many a long dull summer's day have I passed immured indoors because there was no room for me in the family carriage and no lady's maid who had time to walk out with me.' The sun set; and out she went at last, dressed as well as could be managed upon an allowance of from £40 to £100 a year.[31] But 'to any sort of entertainment she must be accompanied by father or mother or by some married woman'. Whom did she meet at those entertainments thus dressed, thus accompanied? Educated men—'cabinet ministers, ambassadors, famous soldiers and the like, all splendidly dressed, wearing decorations'. What did they talk about? Whatever refreshed the minds of busy men who wanted to forget their own work—'the gossip of the dancing world' did very well. The days passed. Saturday came. On Saturday 'MPs and other busy men had leisure to enjoy society'; they came to tea and they came to dinner. Next day was Sunday. On Sundays 'the great majority of us went as a matter of course to morning church.'

The seasons changed. It was summer. In the summer they entertained visitors, 'mostly relatives' in the country. Now it was winter. In the winter 'they studied history and literature and music, and tried to draw and paint. If they did not produce anything remarkable they learnt much in the process.' And so with some visiting the sick and teaching the poor, the years passed. And what was the great end and aim of these years, of that education? Marriage, of course '. . . it was not a question of *whether* we should marry, but simply of *whom* we should marry,' says one of them. It was with a view to marriage that her mind was taught. It was with a view to marriage that she tinkled on the piano, but was not allowed to join an orchestra; sketched innocent domestic scenes, but was not allowed to study from the nude; read this book, but was not allowed to read that, charmed, and talked. It was with a view to marriage that her body was educated; a maid was provided for her; that the streets were shut to her; that the fields were shut to her; that solitude was denied her—all this was enforced upon her in order that she might preserve her body intact for her husband. In short, the thought of marriage influenced what she said, what she thought, what she did. How could it be otherwise? Marriage was the only profession open to her.[32]

The sight is so curious for what it shows of the educated man as well as of his daughter that it is tempting to linger. The influence of the pheasant upon love alone deserves a chapter to itself.[33] But we are not asking now the interesting question, what was the effect of that education upon the race? We are asking why did such an education make the person so educated consciously and unconsciously in favour of war? Because consciously, it is obvious, she was forced to use whatever influence she possessed to bolster up the system which provided her with maids; with carriages; with fine clothes; with fine parties—it was by these means that she achieved marriage. Consciously she must use whatever charm or beauty she possessed to flatter and cajole the busy men, the soldiers, the lawyers, the ambassadors, the cabinet ministers who wanted recreation after their day's work. Consciously she must accept their views, and fall in with their decrees because it was only so that she could wheedle them into giving her the means to marry or marriage itself.[34] In short, all her conscious effort must be in favour of what Lady Lovelace called 'our splendid Empire' . . . 'the price of which,' she added, 'is mainly paid by women.' And who can doubt her, or that the price was heavy?

But her unconscious influence was even more strongly perhaps in favour of war. How else can we explain that amazing outburst in August 1914, when the daughters of educated men who had been educated thus rushed into hospitals, some still attended by their maids, drove lorries, worked in fields and munition factories, and used all their immense stores of charm, of sympathy, to persuade young men that to fight was heroic, and that the wounded in battle deserved all her care and all her praise? The reason lies in that same education. So profound was her unconscious loathing for the education of the private house with its cruelty, its poverty, its hypocrisy, its immorality, its inanity that she would undertake any task however menial, exercise any fascination however fatal that enabled her to escape. Thus consciously she desired 'our splendid Empire'; unconsciously she desired our splendid war.

So, Sir, if you want us to help you to prevent war the conclusion seems to be inevitable; we must help to rebuild the college which, imperfect as it may be, is the only alternative to the education of the private house. We must hope that in time that education may be altered. That guinea must be given before we give you the guinea that you ask for your own society. But it is contributing to the same cause—the prevention of war. Guineas are rare; guineas are valuable, but let us send one without any condition attached to the honorary treasurer of the building fund, because by so doing we are making a positive contribution to the prevention of war.

## TWO

Now that we have given one guinea towards rebuilding a college we must consider whether there is not more that we can do to help you to prevent war. And it is at once obvious, if what we have said about influence is true, that we must turn to the professions, because if we could persuade those who can earn their livings, and thus actually hold in their hands this new weapon, our only weapon, the weapon of independent opinion based upon independent income, to use that weapon against war, we should do more to help you than by appealing to those who must teach the young to earn their livings; or by lingering, however long, round the forbidden places and sacred gates of the universities where they are thus taught. This, therefore, is a more important question than the other.

Let us then lay your letter asking for help to prevent war, before the independent, the mature, those who are earning their livings in the professions. There is no need of rhetoric; hardly, one would suppose, of argument. 'Here is a man,' one has only to say, 'whom we all have reason to respect; he tells us that war is possible; perhaps probable; he asks us, who can earn our livings, to help him in any way we can to prevent war.' That surely will be enough without pointing to the photographs that are all this time piling up on the table—photographs of more dead bodies, of more ruined houses, to call forth an answer, and an answer that will give you, Sir, the very help that you require. But ... it seems that there is some hesitation, some doubt—not certainly that war is horrible, that war is beastly, that war is insupportable and that war is inhuman, as Wilfred Owen said, or that we wish to do all we can to help you to prevent war. Nevertheless, doubts and hesitations there are; and the quickest way to understand them is to place before you another letter, a letter as genuine as your own, a letter that happens to lie beside it on the table.[1]

It is a letter from another honorary treasurer, and it is again asking for money. 'Will you,' she writes, 'send a subscription to' [a society to help the daughters of educated men to obtain employment in the professions]* 'in order to help us to earn our livings? Failing money,' she goes on, 'any gift will be acceptable—books, fruit or cast-off clothing that can be sold in a bazaar.' Now that letter has so much bearing upon the doubts and hesitations referred to above, and upon the help we can give you, that it seems impossible either to send her a guinea or to send you a guinea until we have considered the questions which it raises.

The first question is obviously, Why is she asking for money? Why is she so poor, this representative of professional women, that she must beg for cast-off clothing for a bazaar? That is the first point to clear up, because if she is as poor as this letter indicates, then the weapon of independent opinion upon which we have been counting to help you to prevent war is not, to put it mildly, a very powerful weapon. On the other hand, poverty has its advantages; for if she is poor, as poor as she pretends to be, then we can bargain with her, as we bargained with her sister at Cambridge, and exercise the right of potential givers to impose terms. Let us then question her about her financial position and certain other facts before we give her a guinea, or lay down the terms upon which she is to have it. Here is the draft of such a letter:

'Accept a thousand apologies, Madam, for keeping you waiting so long for an answer to your letter. The fact is, certain questions have arisen, to which we must ask you to reply before we send you a subscription. In the first place you are asking for money— money with which to pay your rent. But how can it be, how can it possibly be, my dear Madam, that you are so terribly poor? The professions have been open to the daughters of educated men for almost 20 years. Therefore, how can it be, that you, whom we take to be their representative, are standing, like your sister at Cambridge, hat in hand, pleading for money, or failing money, for fruit, books, or cast-off clothing to sell at a bazaar? How can it be, we repeat? Surely there must be some very grave defect, of common humanity, of common justice, or of common sense.

Or can it simply be that you are pulling a long face and telling a tall story like the beggar at the street corner who has a stocking full of guineas safely hoarded under her bed at home? In any case, this perpetual asking for money and pleading of poverty is laying you open to very grave rebukes, not only from indolent outsiders who dislike thinking about practical affairs almost as much as they dislike signing cheques, but from educated men. You are drawing upon yourselves the censure and contempt of men of established reputation as philosophers and novelists— of men like Mr Joad and Mr Wells. Not only do they deny your poverty, but they accuse you of apathy and indifference. Let me draw your attention to the charges that they bring against you. Listen, in the first place, to what Mr C. E. M. Joad has to say of you. He says: "I doubt whether at any time during the last fifty years young women have been more politically apathetic, more socially indifferent than at the present time." That is how he begins. And he goes on to say, very rightly, that it is not his business to tell you what you ought to do; but he adds, very kindly, that he will give you an example of what you might do. You might imitate your sisters in America. You might found "a society for the advertisement of peace". He gives an example. This society explained, "I know not with what truth, that the number of pounds spent by the world on armaments in the current year was exactly equal to the number of minutes (or was it seconds?) which had elapsed since the death of Christ, who taught that war is unchristian . . ." Now why should not you, too, follow their example and create such a society in England? It would need money, of course; but—and this is the point that I wish particularly to emphasize—there can be no doubt that you have the money. Mr Joad provides the proof. "Before the war money poured into the coffers of the WSPU* in order that women might win the vote which, it was hoped, would enable them to make war a thing of the past. The vote is won," Mr Joad continues, "but war is very far from being a thing of the past." That I can corroborate myself— witness this letter from a gentleman asking for help to prevent war, and there are certain photographs of dead bodies and ruined houses—but let Mr Joad continue. "Is it unreasonable", he goes on, "to ask that contemporary women should be prepared to give as much energy and money, to suffer as much oblo-quy and insult in the cause of peace, as their mothers gave and suffered in the cause of equality?" And again, I cannot help but echo, is it unreasonable to ask women to go on, from generation to generation, suffering obloquy and insult first from their brothers and then for their brothers? Is it not both perfectly reasonable and on the whole for their physical, moral and spiritual welfare? But let us not interrupt Mr Joad. "If it is, then the sooner they give up the pretence of playing with public affairs and return to

[ 213 ]

private life the better. If they cannot make a job of the House of Commons, let them at least make something of their own houses. If they cannot learn to save men from the destruction which incurable male mischievousness bids fair to bring upon them, let women at least learn to feed them, before they destroy themselves."² Let us not pause to ask how even with a vote they can cure what Mr Joad himself admits to be incurable, for the point is how, in the fact of that statement, you have the effrontery to ask me for a guinea towards your rent? According to Mr Joad you are not only extremely rich; you are also extremely idle; and so given over to the eating of peanuts and ice cream that you have not learnt how to cook him a dinner before he destroys himself, let alone how to prevent that fatal act. But more serious charges are to follow. Your lethargy is such that you will not fight even to protect the freedom which your mothers won for you. That charge is made against you by the most famous of living English novelists— Mr H. G. Wells. Mr H. G. Wells says, "There has been no perceptible woman's movement to resist the practical obliteration of their freedom by Fascists or Nazis."³ Rich, idle, greedy and lethargic as you are, how have you the effrontery to ask me to subscribe to a society which helps the daughters of educated men to make their livings in the professions? For as these gentlemen prove in spite of the vote and the wealth which that vote must have brought with it, you have not ended war; in spite of the vote and power which that vote must have brought with it, you have not resisted the practical obliteration of your freedom by Fascists or Nazis. What other conclusion then can one come to but that the whole of what you called "the woman's movement" has proved itself a failure; and the guinea which I am sending you herewith is to be devoted not to paying your rent but to burning your building. And when that is burnt, retire once more to the kitchen, Madam, and learn, if you can, to cook the dinner which you may not share . . .'[4]

There, Sir, the letter stopped; for on the face at the other side of the letter—the face that a letter-writer always sees—was an expression, of boredom was it, or was it of fatigue? The honorary treasurer's glance seemed to rest upon a little scrap of paper upon which were written two dull little facts which, since they have some bearing upon the question we are discussing, how the daughters of educated men who are earning their livings in the professions can help you to prevent war, may be copied here. The first fact that was the income of the WSPU upon which Mr Joad has based his estimate of their wealth was (in the year 1912 at the height of their activity) £42,000.[5]* The second fact was that: 'To earn £250 a year is quite an achievement even for a highly qualified woman with years of experience.'[6] The date of that statement is 1934.

[ 215 ]

Both facts are interesting; and since both have a direct bearing upon the question before us, let us examine them. To take the first fact first—that is interesting because it shows that one of the greatest political changes of our times was accomplished upon the incredibly minute income of £42,000 a year. 'Incredibly minute' is, of course, a comparative term; it is incredibly minute, that is to say, compared with the income which the Conservative party, or the Liberal party—the parties to which the educated woman's brother belonged—had at their disposal for their political causes. It is considerably less than the income which the Labour party—the party to which the working woman's brother belongs—has at their disposal.[7] It is incredibly minute compared with the sums that a society like the Society for the Abolition of Slavery for example had at its disposal for the abolition of that slavery. It is incredibly minute compared with the sums which the educated man spends annually, not upon political causes, but upon sports and pleasure. But our amazement, whether at the poverty of educated men's daughters or at their economy, is a decidedly unpleasant emotion in this case, for it forces us to suspect that the honorary treasurer is telling the sober truth; she is poor; and it forces us to ask once more how, if £42,000 was all that the daughters of educated men could collect after many years of indefatigable labour for their own cause, they can help you to win yours? How much peace will £42,000 a year buy at the present moment when we are spending £300,000,000 annually upon arms?

But the second fact is the more startling and the more depressing of the two—the fact that now, almost 20 years, that is, after they have been admitted to the money-making professions 'to earn £250 a year is quite an achievement even for a highly qualified woman with years of experience.' Indeed, that fact, if it is a fact, is so startling and has so much bearing upon the question before us that we must pause for a moment to examine it. It is so important that it must be examined, moreover, by the white light of facts, not by the coloured light of biography. Let us have recourse then to some impersonal and impartial authority who has no more axe to grind or dinner to cook than Cleopatra's Needle*—Whitaker's Almanack,* for example.

Whitaker, needless to say, is not only one of the most dispassionate of authors, but one of the most methodical. There, in his Almanack he has collected all the facts about all, or almost all, of the professions that have been opened to the daughters of educated men. In a section called 'Government and Public Offices' he provides us with a plain statement of whom the Government employs professionally, and of what the Government pays those whom it employs. Since Whitaker adopts the alphabetical system, let us follow his lead and examine the first six letters of the alphabet. Under A there are the Admiralty, the Air Ministry, and Ministry of Agriculture. Under B there is the British Broadcasting Corporation; under C the Colonial Office and the Charity Commissioners; under D the Dominions Office and Development Commission; under E there are the Ecclesiastical Commissioners and the Board of Education; and so we come to the sixth letter F under which we find the Ministry of Fisheries, the Foreign Office, the Friendly Societies and the Fine Arts. These then are some of the professions which are now, as we are frequently reminded, open to both men and women equally. And the salaries paid to those employed in them come out of public money which is supplied by both sexes equally. And the income tax which supplies those salaries (among other things) now stands at about five shillings in the pound. We have all, therefore, an interest in asking how that money is spent, and upon whom. Let us look at the salary list of the Board of Education, since that is the class to which we both, Sir, though in very different degrees, have the honour to belong. The President, Whitaker says, of the Board of Education, gets £2,000; his principal Private Secretary gets from £847 to £1,058; his Assistant Private Secretary gets from £277 to £634. Then there is the Permanent Secretary of the Board of Education. He gets £3,000; his Private Secretary gets from £277 to £634. The Parliamentary Secretary gets £1,200; his Private Secretary gets from

£277 to £634. The Deputy Secretary gets £2,200. The Permanent Secretary of the Welsh Department gets £1,650. And then there are Principal Assistant Secretaries and Assistant Secretaries, there are Directors of Establishments, Accountants-General, principal Finance Officers, Finance Officers, Legal Advisers, Assistant Legal Advisers—all these ladies and gentlemen, the impeccable and impartial Whitaker informs us, get incomes which run into four figures or over. Now an income which is over or about a thousand a year is a nice round sum when it is paid yearly and paid punctually; but when we consider that the work is a wholetime job and a skilled job we shall not grudge these ladies and gentlemen their salaries, even though our income tax does stand at five shillings in the pound, and our incomes are by no means paid punctually or paid annually. Men and women who spend every day and all day in an office from the age of about 23 to the age of 60 or so deserve every penny they get. Only, the reflection will intrude itself, if these ladies are drawing £1,000, £2,000 and £3,000 a year, not only in the Board of Education, but in all the other boards and offices which are now open to them, from the Admiralty at the beginning of the alphabet to the Board of Works at the end, the statement that '£250 is quite an achievement, even for a highly qualified woman with years of experience' must be, to put it plainly, an unmitigated lie. Why, we have only to walk down Whitehall; consider how

[ 219 ]

many boards and offices are housed there; reflect that each is staffed and officered by a flock of secretaries and under-secretaries so many and so nicely graded that their very names make our heads spin; and remember that each has his or her own sufficient salary, to exclaim that the statement is impossible, inexplicable. How can we explain it? Only by putting on a stronger pair of glasses. Let us read down the list, further and further and further down. At last we come to a name to which the prefix 'Miss' is attached. Can it be that all the names on top of hers, all the names to which the big salaries are attached, are the names of gentlemen? It seems so. So then it is not the salaries that are lacking; it is the daughters of educated men.

Now three good reasons for this curious deficiency or disparity lie upon the surface. Dr Robson supplies us with the first—'The Administrative Class, which occupies all the controlling positions in the Home Civil Service, consists to an overwhelming extent of the fortunate few who can manage to get to Oxford and Cambridge; and the entrance examination has always been expressly designed for that purpose.'[8] The fortunate few in our class, the daughters of educated men class, are very, very few. Oxford and Cambridge, as we have seen, strictly limit the number of educated men's daughters who are allowed to receive a university education. Secondly, many more daughters stay at home to look after old mothers than sons stay at home to look after old fathers. The private house, we must remember, is still a going concern. Hence fewer daughters than sons enter for the Civil Service Examination. In the third place, we may fairly assume that 60 years of examination passing are not so effective as 500. The Civil Service Examination is a stiff one; we may reasonably expect more sons to pass it than daughters. We have nevertheless to explain the curious fact that though a certain number of daughters enter for the examination and pass the examination those to whose names the word 'Miss' is attached do not seem to enter the four-figure zone. The sex distinction seems, according to Whitaker, possessed of a curious leaden quality, liable to keep any name to which it is fastened circling in the lower spheres. Plainly the reason for this may lie not upon the surface, but within. It may be, to speak bluntly, that the daughters are in themselves deficient; that they have proved themselves untrustworthy; unsatisfactory; so lacking in the necessary ability that it is to the public interest to keep them to the lower grades where, if they are paid less, they have less chance of impeding the transaction of public business. This solution would be easy but, unfortunately, it is denied to us. It is denied to us by the Prime Minister himself. Women in the Civil Service are not untrustworthy, Mr Baldwin† informed us the other day.

† Since these words were written Mr Baldwin has ceased to be Prime Minister and become an Earl.

'Many of them,' he said, 'are in positions in the course of their daily work to amass secret information. Secret information has a way of leaking very often, as we politicians know to our cost. I have never known a case of such a leakage being due to a woman, and I have known cases of leakage coming from men who should have known a great deal better.' So they are not so loose-lipped and fond of gossip as the tradition would have it? A useful contribution in its way to psychology and a hint to novelists; but still there may be other objections to women's employment as Civil Servants.

Intellectually, they may not be so able as their brothers. But here again the Prime Minister will not help us out. 'He was not prepared to say that any conclusion had been formed—or was even necessary—whether women were as good as, or better than, men, but he believed that women had worked in the Civil Service to their own content, and certainly to the complete satisfaction of everybody who had anything to do with them.' Finally, as if to cap what must necessarily be an inconclusive statement by expression a personal opinion which might rightly be more positive he said, 'I should like to pay my personal tribute to the industry, capacity, ability and loyalty of the women I have come across in Civil Service positions.' And he went on to express the hope that business men would make more use of those very valuable qualities.[9]

[ 222 ]

Now if anyone is in a position to know the facts it is the Prime Minister; and if anyone is able to speak the truth about them it is the same gentleman. Yet Mr Baldwin says one thing; Mr Whitaker says another. If Mr Baldwin is well informed, so is Mr Whitaker. Nevertheless, they contradict each other. The issue is joined; Mr Baldwin says that women are first-class civil servants; Mr Whitaker says that they are third-class civil servants. It is, in short, a case of *Baldwin* v. *Whitaker*, and since it is a very important case, for upon it depends the answer to many questions which puzzle us, not only about the poverty of educated men's daughters but about the psychology of educated men's sons, let us try the case of the *Prime Minister* v. *the Almanack*.

For such a trial you, Sir, have definite qualifications; as a barrister you have first-hand knowledge of one profession, and as an educated man second-hand knowledge of many more. And if it is true that the daughters of educated men who are of Mary Kingsley's persuasion have no direct knowledge, still through fathers and uncles, cousins and brothers they may claim some indirect knowledge of professional life—it is a photograph they have often looked upon—and this indirect knowledge they can improve, if they have a mind, by peeping through doors, taking notes, and asking questions discreetly. If, then, we pool our first-hand, second-hand, direct and indirect knowledge of the professions with a view to trying the important case of *Baldwin* v. *Whitaker* we shall agree at the outset that professions are very queer things. It by no means follows that a clever man gets to the top or that a stupid man stays at the bottom. This rising and falling is by no means a cut-and-dried clear-cut rational process, we shall both agree. After all, as we both have reason to know, Judges are fathers; and Permanent Secretaries have sons. Judges require marshals; Permanent Secretaries, private secretaries. What is more natural than that a nephew should be a marshal or the son of an old school friend a private secretary? To have such perquisites in their gift is as much the due of the public servant as a cigar now and then or a cast-off dress here and there are perquisites of the private servant. But the giving of such perquisites, the exercise of such influence, queers the professions. Success is easier for some, harder for others, however equal the brain power may be so that some rise unexpectedly; some fall unexpectedly; some remain strangely stationary; with the result that the professions are queered. Often indeed it is the public advantage that they should be queered. Since nobody, from the Master of Trinity downwards (bating, presumably, a few Head Mistresses), believes in the infallability of examiners, a certain degree of elasticity is to the public advantage; since the impersonal is fallible, it is well that it should be supplemented by the personal. Happily for us all, therefore, we may conclude, a board is not made literally of oak, nor a

division of iron.* Both boards and divisions transmit
human sympathies, and reflect human antipathies
with the result that the imperfections of the examination system are rectified; the public interest is served;
and the ties of blood and friendship are recognized.
Thus it is quite possible that the name 'Miss' transmits
through the board or division some vibration which
is not registered in the examination room. 'Miss'
transmits sex; and sex may carry with it an aroma.
'Miss' may carry with it the swish of petticoats, the
savour of scent or other odour perceptible to the nose
on the further side of the partition and obnoxious to
it. What charms and consoles in the private house
may distract and exacerbate in the public office. The
Archbishops' Commission assures us that this is so in
the pulpit.[10] Whitehall may be equally susceptible. At
any rate since Miss is a woman, Miss was not educated
at Eton or Christ Church. Since Miss is a woman,
Miss is not a son or a nephew. We are hazarding our
way among imponderables. We can scarcely proceed
too much on tiptoe. We are trying, remember, to
discover what flavour attaches itself to sex in a public
office; we are sniffing most delicately not facts but
savours. And therefore it would be well not to depend
on our own private noses, but to call in evidence from
outside. Let us turn to the public press and see if we
can discover from the opinions aired there any hint
that will guide us in our attempt to decide the delicate
and difficult question as to the aroma, the atmosphere

that surrounds the word 'Miss' in Whitehall. We will consult the newspapers.

First:

I think your correspondent . . . correctly sums up this discussion in the observation that woman has too much liberty. It is probable that this so-called liberty came with the war, when women assumed responsibilities so far unknown to them. They did splendid service during those days. Unfortunately, they were praised and petted out of all proportion to the value of their performances.[11]

That does very well for a beginning. But let us proceed:

I am of the opinion that a considerable amount of the distress which is prevalent in this section of the community [the clerical] could be relieved by the policy of employing men instead of women, wherever possible. There are today in Government offices, post offices, insurance companies, banks and other offices, thousands of women doing work which men could do. At the same time there are thousands of qualified men, young and middle-aged, who cannot get a job of any sort. There is a large demand for woman labour in the domestic arts, and in the process of regrading a large number of women who have drifted into clerical service would become available for domestic service.[12]

The odour thickens, you will agree.

Then once more:

I am certain I voice the opinion of thousands of young men when I say that if men were doing the work that thousands of young women are now doing the men would be able to keep those same women in decent homes. Homes are the real places of the women who are now compelling men to be idle. It is time the Government insisted upon employers giving work to more men, thus enabling them to marry the women they cannot now approach.[13]

There! There can be no doubt of the odour now. The cat is out of the bag; and it is a Tom.

After considering the evidence contained in those three quotations, you will agree that there is good reason to think that the word 'Miss', however delicious its scent in the private house, has a certain odour attached to it in Whitehall which is disagreeable to the noses on the other side of the partition; and that it is likely that a name to which 'Miss' is attached will, because of this odour, circle in the lower spheres where the salaries are small rather than mount to the higher spheres where the salaries are substantial. As for 'Mrs', it is a contaminated word; an obscene word. The less said about that word the better. Such is the smell of it, so rank does it stink in the nostrils of Whitehall, that Whitehall excludes it entirely. In Whitehall as in heaven, there is neither marrying nor giving in marriage.[14]*

Odour then—or shall we call it 'atmosphere'?—is a very important element in professional life; in spite of the fact that like other important elements it is impalpable. It can escape the noses of examiners in examination rooms, yet penetrate boards and divisions and affect the senses of those within. Its bearing upon the case before us is undeniable. For it allows us to decide in the case of *Baldwin* v. *Whitaker* that both the Prime Minister and the Almanack are telling the truth. It is true that women civil servants deserve to be paid as much as men. The discrepancy is due to atmosphere.

Atmosphere plainly is a very mighty power. Atmosphere not only changes the sizes and shapes of things; it affects solid bodies, like salaries, which might have been thought impervious to atmosphere. An epic poem might be written about atmosphere, or a novel in ten or fifteen volumes. But since this is only a letter, and you are pressed for time, let us confine ourselves to the plain statement that atmosphere is one of the most powerful, partly because it is one of the most impalpable, of the enemies with which the daughters of educated men have to fight. If you think that statement exaggerated, look once more at the samples of atmosphere contained in those three quotations. We shall find there not only the reason why the pay of the professional woman is still so small, but something more dangerous, something which, if it spreads, may poison both sexes equally. There, in those quotations, is the egg of the very same worm that we know under other names in other countries. There we have in embryo the creature, Dictator as we call him when he is Italian or German, who believes that he has the right whether given by

God, Nature, sex or race is immaterial, to dictate to other human beings how they shall live; what they shall do. Let us quote again: 'Homes are the real places of the women who are now compelling men to be idle. It is time the Government insisted upon employers giving work to more men, thus enabling them to marry the women they cannot now approach.' Place beside it another quotation: 'There are two worlds in the life of the nation, the world of men and the world of women. Nature has done well to entrust the man with the care of his family and the nation. The woman's world is her family, her husband, her children, and her home.'* One is written in English, the other in German. But where is the difference? Are they not both saying the same thing? Are they not both the voices of Dictators, whether they speak English or German, and are we not all agreed that the dictator when we meet him abroad is a very dangerous as well as a very ugly animal? And he is here among us, raising his ugly head, spitting his poison, small still, curled up like a caterpillar on a leaf,* but in the heart of England. Is it not from this egg, to quote Mr Wells again, that 'the practical obliteration of [our] freedom by Fascists or Nazis' will spring? And is not the woman who has to breathe that poison and to fight that insect, secretly and without arms, in her office, fighting the Fascist or the Nazi as surely as those who fight him with arms in the limelight of publicity? And must not that fight wear down her strength and exhaust her spirit? Should we not help her to crush him in our own country before we ask her to help us to crush him abroad? And what right have we, Sir, to trumpet our ideals of freedom and justice to other countries when we can shake out from our most respectable newspapers any day of the week eggs like these?

Here, rightly, you will check what has all the symptoms of becoming a peroration by pointing out that though the opinions expressed in these letters are not altogether agreeable to our national self-esteem they are the natural expression of fear and a jealousy which we must understand before we condemn them. It is true, you will say, that these gentlemen seem a little unduly concerned with their own salaries and their own security, but that is comprehensible, given the traditions of their sex, and even compatible with a genuine love of freedom and a genuine hatred of dictatorship. For these gentlemen are, or wish to become, husbands and fathers, and in that case the support of the family will depend upon them. In other words, sir, I take you to mean that the world as it is at present is divided into two services; one the public and the other the private. In one world the sons of educated men work as civil servants, judges, soldiers and are paid for that work; in the other world, the daughters of educated men work as wives, mothers, daughters—but are they not paid for that work? Is the work of a mother, of a wife, of a daughter, worth nothing to the nation in solid cash? That fact, if it be a fact, is so astonishing that we must confirm it by appealing once more to the impeccable Whitaker. Let us turn to his pages again. We may turn them, and turn them again. It seems incredible, yet it seems undeniable. Among all those offices there is no such office as a mother's; among all those salaries there is no such salary as a mother's. The work of an archbishop is worth £15,000 a year to the State; the work of a judge is worth £5,000 a year; the work of a permanent secretary is worth £3,000 a year; the work of an army captain, of a sea captain, of a sergeant of dragoons, of a policeman, of a postman— all these works are worth paying out of the taxes, but wives and mothers and daughters who work all day and every day, without whose work the State would collapse and fall to pieces, without whose work your sons, sir, would cease to exist, are paid nothing whatever. Can it be possible? Or have we convicted Whitaker, the impeccable, of errata?

Ah, you will interpose, here is another misunder-standing. Husband and wife are not only one flesh; they are also one purse. The wife's salary is half the husband's income. The man is paid more than the woman for that very reason—because he has a wife to support. The bachelor then is paid at the same rate as the unmarried woman? It appears not—another queer effect of atmosphere, no doubt; but let it pass. Your statement that the wife's salary is half the

husband's income seems to be an equitable arrange-
ment, and no doubt, since it is equitable, it is confirmed by law. Your reply that the law leaves these
private matters to be decided privately is less satisfactory, for it means that the wife's half-share of the
common income is not paid legally into her hands, but
into her husband's. But still a spiritual right may be
as binding as a legal right; and if the wife of an
educated men has a spiritual right to half her husband's income, then we may assume that the wife of
an educated man has as much money to spend, once
the common household bills are met, upon any cause
that appeals to her as her husband. Now her husband,
witness Whitaker, witness the wills in the daily paper,
is often not merely well paid by his profession, but is
master of a very considerable capital sum. Therefore
this lady who asserts that £250 a year is all that a
woman can earn today in the professions is evading
the question; for the profession of marriage in the
educated class is a highly paid one, since she has a
right, a spiritual right, to half her husband's salary.
The puzzle deepens; the mystery thickens. For if the
wives of rich men are themselves rich women, how
does it come about that the income of the WSPU was
only £42,000 a year; how does it come about that the
honorary treasurer of the college rebuilding fund is
still asking for £100,000; how does it come about that
the treasurer of a society for helping professional
women to obtain employment is asking not merely

for money to pay her rent but will be grateful for books, fruit or cast-off clothing? It stands to reason that if the wife has a spiritual right to half her husband's income because her own work as his wife is unpaid, then she must have as much money to spend upon such causes as appeal to her as he has. And since those causes are standing hat in hand a-begging we are forced to conclude that they are causes that do not take the fancy of the educated man's wife. The charge against her is a very serious one. For consider—there is the money—that surplus fund that can be devoted to education, to pleasure, to phil-anthropy when the household dues are met; she can spend her share as freely as her husband can spend his. She can spend it upon whatever causes she likes; and yet she will not spend it upon the causes that are dear to her own sex. There they are, hat in hand a-begging. That is a terrible charge to bring against her.

But let us pause for a moment before we decide that charge against her. Let us ask what are the causes, the pleasures, the philanthropies upon which the educated man's wife does in fact spend her share of the common surplus fund. And here we are con-fronted with facts which, whether we like them or not, we must face. The fact is that the tastes of the married woman in our class are markedly virile. She spends vast sums annually upon party funds; upon sport; upon grouse moors; upon cricket and football.

She lavishes money upon clubs—Brooks', White's, the Travellers', the Reform, the Athenaeum—to mention only the most prominent. Her expenditure upon these causes, pleasures and philanthropies must run into many millions every year. And yet by far the greater part of this sum is spent upon pleasures which she does not share. She lays out thousands and thousands of pounds upon clubs to which her own sex is not admitted;[15] upon racecourses where she may not ride; upon colleges from which her own sex is excluded. She pays a huge bill annually for wine which she does not drink and for cigars which she does not smoke. In short, there are only two conclusions to which we can come about the educated man's wife—the first is that she is the most altruistic of beings who prefers to spend her share of the common fund upon his pleasures and causes; the second, and more probable, if less creditable, is not that she is the most altruistic of beings, but that her spiritual right to a share of half her husband's income peters out in practice to an actual right to board, lodging and a small annual allowance for pocket money and dress. Either of these conclusions is possible; the evidence of public institutions and subscription lists puts any other out of the question. For consider how nobly the educated man supports his old school, his old college; how splendidly he subscribes to party funds; how munificently he contributes to all those institutions and sports by which he and his sons educate their minds and develop their bodies—the daily papers bear daily witness to those indisputable facts. But the absence of her name from subscription lists, and the poverty of the insitutions which educate her mind and her body seem to prove that there is something in the atmosphere of the private house which deflects the wife's spiritual share of the common income impalpably but irresistibly towards those causes which her husband approves and those pleasures which he enjoys. Whether creditable or discreditable, that is the fact. And that is the reason why those other causes stand a-begging.

With Whitaker's facts and the facts of the subscription lists before us, we seem to have arrived at three facts which are indisputable and must have great influence upon our inquiry how we can help you to prevent war. The first is that the daughters of educated men are paid very little from the public funds for their public services; the second is that they are paid nothing at all from the public funds for their private services; and the third is that their share of the husband's income is not a flesh-and-blood share but a spiritual or nominal share, which means that when both are clothed and fed the surplus fund that can be devoted to causes, pleasures or philanthropies gravitates mysteriously but indisputably towards those causes, pleasures and philanthropies which the husband enjoys, and of which the husband approves. It seems that the person to whom the salary is actually paid is the person who has the actual right to decide how that salary shall be spent.

These facts then bring us back in a chastened mood and with rather altered views to our starting point. For we were going, you may remember, to lay your appeal for help in the prevention of war before the women who earn their livings in the professions. It is to them, we said, to whom we must appeal, because it is they who have our new weapon, the influence of an independent opinion based upon an independent income, in their possession. But the facts once more are depressing. They make it clear in the first place that we must rule out, as possible helpers, that large group to whom marriage is a profession, because it is an unpaid profession, and because the spiritual share of half the husband's salary is not, facts seem to show, an actual share. Therefore, her disinterested influence founded upon an independent income is nil. If he is in favour of force, she too will be in favour of force. In the second place, facts seem to prove that the statement 'To earn £250 a year is quite an achievement even for a highly qualified woman with years of experience' is not an unmitigated lie but a highly probable truth. Therefore, the influence which the daughters of educated men have at present from their money-earning power cannot be rated very highly. Yet since it has become more than ever obvious that it is to them that we must look for help, for they alone can help us, it is to them that we must appeal.

This conclusion then brings us back to the letter from which we quoted above—the honorary treasurer's letter, the letter asking for a subscription to the society for helping the daughters of educated men to obtain employment in the professions. You will agree, sir, that we have strong selfish motives for helping her—there can be no doubt about that. For to help women to earn their livings in the professions is to help them to possess that weapon of independent opinion which is still their most powerful weapon. It is to help them to have a mind of their own and a will of their own with which to help you to prevent war. But ... —here again, in those dots, doubts and hesitations assert themselves—can we, considering the facts given above, send her our guinea without laying down very stringent terms as to how that guinea shall be spent?

For the facts which we have discovered in checking her statement as to her financial position have raised questions which make us wonder whether we are wise to encourage people to enter the professions if we wish to prevent war. You will remember that we are using our psychological insight (for that is our only qualification) to decide what kind of qualities in human nature are likely to lead to war. And the facts disclosed above are of a kind to make us ask, before we write our cheque, whether if we encourage the daughters of educated men to enter the professions we shall not be encouraging the very qualities that we wish to prevent? Shall we not be doing our guinea's worth to ensure that in two or three centuries not only the educated men in the professions but the educated women in the professions will be asking—oh, of whom? as the poet says*—the very question that you are asking us now: How can we prevent war? If we encourage the daughters to enter the professions without making any conditions as to the way in which the professions are to be practised shall we not be doing our best to stereotype the old tune which human nature, like a gramophone whose needle has stuck, is now grinding out with such disastrous unanimity? 'Here we go round the mulberry tree, the mulberry tree, the mulberry tree.* Give it all to me, give it all to me, all to me. Three hundred millions spent upon war.' With that song, or something like it, ringing in our ears we cannot send our guinea to the honorary treasurer without warning her that she shall only have it on condition that she shall swear that the professions in future shall be practised so that they shall lead to a different song and a different conclusion. She shall only have it if she can satisfy us that our guinea shall be spent in the cause of peace. It is difficult to formulate such conditions; in our present psychological ignorance perhaps impossible. But the matter is so serious, war is so insupportable, so horrible, so inhuman, that an attempt must be made. Here then is another letter to the same lady.

'Your letter, Madam, has waited a long time for an answer, but we have been examining into certain charges made against you and making certain inquiries. We have acquitted you, Madam, you will be relieved to learn, of telling lies. It would seem to be true that you are poor. We have acquitted you further, of idleness, apathy and greed. The number of causes that you are championing, however secretly and ineffectively, is in your favour. If you prefer ice creams and peanuts to roast beef and beer the reason would seem to be economic rather than gustatory. It would seem probable that you have not much money to spend upon food or much leisure to spend upon eating it in view of the circulars and leaflets you issue, the meetings you arrange, the bazaars you organize. Indeed, you would appear to be working, without a salary too, rather longer hours than the Home Office would approve. But though we are willing to deplore your poverty and to commend your industry we are not going to send you a guinea to help you to help women to enter the professions unless you can assure us that they will practise those professions in such a way as to prevent war. That, you will say, is a vague statement, an impossible condition. Still, since guineas are rare and guineas are valuable you will listen to the terms we wish to impose if, you intimate, they can be stated briefly. Well then, Madam, since you are pressed for time, what with the Pensions Bill,* what with shepherding the Peers into the House of Lords

[ 239 ]

so that they may vote on it as instructed by you, what with reading Hansard* and the newspapers—though that should not take much time; you will find no mention of your activities there;[16] a conspiracy of silence seems to be the rule; what with plotting still for equal pay for equal work in the Civil Service, while at the same time you are arranging hares and old coffee-pots so as to seduce people into paying more for them than they are strictly worth at a bazaar—since, in one word, it is obvious that you are busy, let us be quick; make a rapid survey; discuss a few passages in the books in your library; in the papers on your table, and then see if we can make the statement less vague, the conditions more clear.

'Let us then begin by looking at the outside of things, at the general aspect. Things have outsides let us remember as well as insides. Close at hand is a bridge over the Thames, an admirable vantage ground for such a survey. The river flows beneath; barges pass, laden with timber, bursting with corn; there on one side are the domes and spires of the city; on the other, Westminster and the Houses of Parliament. It is a place to stand on by the hour, dreaming. But not now. Now we are pressed for time. Now we are here to consider facts; now we must fix our eyes upon the procession—the procession of the sons of educated men.

'There they go, our brothers who have been educated at public schools and universities, mounting those steps, passing in and out of those doors, ascending those pulpits, preaching, teaching, administering justice, practising medicine, transacting business, making money. It is a solemn sight always—a procession, like a caravanserai crossing a desert. Great-grandfathers, grandfather, fathers, uncles—they all went that way, wearing their gowns, wearing their wigs, some with ribbons across their breasts, others without. One was a bishop. Another a judge. One was an admiral. Another a general. One was a professor. Another a doctor. And some left the procession and were last heard of doing nothing in Tasmania; were seen, rather shabbily dressed, selling newspapers at Charing Cross. But most of them kept in step, walked according to rule, and by hook or by crook made enough to keep the family house, somewhere, roughly speaking, in the West End, supplied with beef and mutton for all, and with education for Arthur. It is a solemn sight, this procession, a sight that has often caused us, you may remember, looking at it sidelong from an upper window, to ask ourselves certain questions. But now, for the past twenty years or so, it is no longer a sight merely, a photograph, or fresco scrawled upon the walls of time, at which we can look with merely an aesthetic appreciation. For there, trapesing along at the tail end of the procession, we go ourselves. And that makes a difference. We who have looked so long at the pageant in books, or from a curtained window watched educated men leaving the house at about nine-thirty to go to an office, returning to the house at about six-thirty from an office, need look passively no longer. We too can leave the house, can mount those steps, pass in and out of those doors, wear wigs and gowns, make money, administer justice. Think—one of these days, you may wear a judge's wig on your head, an ermine cape on your shoulders; sit under the lion and the unicorn;* draw a salary of five thousand a year with a pension on retiring. We who now agitate these humble pens may in another century or two speak from a pulpit. Nobody will dare contradict us then; we shall be the mouthpieces of the divine spirit—a solemn thought, is it not? Who can say whether, as time goes on, we may not dress in military uniform, with gold lace on our breasts, swords at our sides, and something like the old family coal-scuttle on our heads, save that that venerable object was never decorated with plumes of white horsehair. You laugh—indeed the shadow of the private house still makes those dresses look a little queer. We have worn private clothes so long—the veil that St Paul recommended. But we have not come here to laugh, or to talk of fashions—men's and women's. We are here, on the bridge, to ask ourselves certain questions. And they are very important questions; and we have very little time in which to answer them. The questions that we have to ask and to answer about that procession during this moment of transition are so important that they may well change the lives of all men and women for ever. For we have to ask ourselves, here and now, do we wish to join that procession, or don't we? On what terms shall we join that procession? Above all, where is it leading us, the procession of educated men? The moment is short; it may last five years; ten years, or perhaps only a matter of a few months longer. But the questions must be answered; and they are so important that if all the daughters of educated men did nothing, from morning to night, but consider that procession from every angle, if they did nothing but ponder it and analyse it, and think about it and read about it and pool their thinking and reading, and what they see and what they guess, their time would be better spent than in any other activity now open to them. But, you will object, you have no time to think; you have your battles to fight, your rent to pay, your bazaars to organize. That excuse shall not serve you, Madam. As you know from your own experience, and there are facts that prove it, the daughters of educated men have always done their thinking from hand to mouth; not under green lamps at study tables in the cloisters of secluded colleges. They have thought while they stirred the pot, while they rocked the cradle. It was thus that they won us the right to our brand-new sixpence. It falls to us now to go on thinking; how are we to spend that sixpence? Think we must. Let us think in offices; in omnibuses; while we are standing in the crowd watching Coronations and Lord Mayor's Shows; let us think as we pass the Cenotaph; and in Whitehall; in the gallery of the House of Commons; in the Law Courts; let us think at baptisms and marriages and funerals. Let us never cease from thinking—what is this "civilization" in which we find ourselves? What are these ceremonies and why should we take part in them? What are these professions and why should we make money out of them? Where in short is it leading us, the procession of the sons of educated men?

'But you are busy; let us return to facts. Come indoors then, and open the books on your library shelves. For you have a library, and a good one. A working library, a living library; a library where nothing is chained down and nothing is locked up; a library where the songs of the singers rise naturally from the lives of the livers. There are the poems, here the biographies. And what light do they throw upon the professions, these biographies? How far do they encourage us to think that if we help the daughters to become professional women we shall discourage war? The answer to that question is scattered all about these volumes; and is legible to anyone who can read plain English. And the answer, one must admit, is extremely queer. For almost every biography we read of professional men in the nineteenth century, to limit ourselves to that not distant and fully documented age, is large concerned with war. They were great fighters, it seems, the professional men in the age of

Queen Victoria. There was the battle of Westminster. There was the battle of the universities. There was the battle of Whitehall.* There was the battle of Harley Street.* There was the battle of the Royal Academy.* Some of these battles, as you can testify, are still in progress. In fact the only profession which does not seem to have fought a fierce battle during the nineteenth century is the profession of literature. All the other professions, according to the testimony of biography, seem to be as bloodthirsty as the profession of arms itself. It is true that the combatants did not inflict flesh wounds;[17] chivalry forbade; but you will agree that a battle that wastes time is as deadly as a battle that wastes blood. You will agree that a battle that costs money is as deadly as a battle that costs a leg or an arm. You will agree that a battle that forces youth to spend its strength haggling in committee rooms, soliciting favours, assuming a mask of reverence to cloak its ridicule, inflicts wounds upon the human spirit which no surgery can heal. Even the battle of equal pay for equal work is not without its timeshed, its spiritshed, as you yourself, were you not unaccountably reticent on certain matters, might agree. Now the books in your library record so many of these battles that it is impossible to go into them all; but as they all seem to have been fought on much the same plan, and by the same combatants, that is by professional men *v.* their sisters and daughters, let us, since time presses, glance at one of these campaigns only and examine the battle of Harley Street, in order that we may understand what effect the professions have upon those who practise them.

'The campaign was opened in the year 1869 under the leadership of Sophia Jex-Blake. Her case is so typical an instance of the great Victorian fight between the victims of the patriarchal system and the patriarchs, of the daughters against the fathers, that it deserves a moment's examination. Sophia's father was an admirable specimen of the Victorian educated man, kindly, cultivated and well-to-do. He was a proctor of Doctors' Commons.* He could afford to keep six servants, horses and carriages, and could provide his daughter not only with food and lodging but with "handsome furniture" and "a cosy fire" in her bedroom. For salary, "for dress and private money", he gave her £40 a year. For some reason she found this sum insufficient. In 1859, in view of the fact that she had only nine shillings and ninepence left to last her till next quarter, she wished to earn money herself. And she was offered a tutorship with the pay of five shillings an hour. She told her father of the offer. He replied, "Dearest, I have only this moment heard that you contemplate being *paid* for the tutorship. It would be quite beneath you, darling, and *I cannot consent to it*." She argued: "Why should I not take it? You as a man did your work and received your payment, and no one thought it any degradation, but a fair exchange . . . Tom is doing on a large scale what

I am doing on a small one." He replied: "The cases you cite, darling, are not to the point ... T.W. ... feels bound as a *man* ... to support his wife and family, and his position is a high one, which can only be filled by a first-class man of character, and yielding him nearer two than one thousand a year ... How entirely different is my darling's case! You want for nothing, and know that (humanly speaking) you will want for nothing. If you married tomorrow—to my liking—and I don't believe you would ever marry otherwise—I should give you a good fortune." Upon which her comment, in a private diary, was: "Like a fool I have consented to give up the fees for this term only—though I am miserably poor. It was foolish. It only defers the struggle."[18]

'There she was right. The struggle with her own father was over. But the struggle with fathers in general, with the patriarchy itself, was deferred to another place and another time. The second fight was at Edinburgh in 1869. She had applied for admission to the Royal College of Surgeons. Here is a newspaper account of the first skirmish. "A disturbance of a very unbecoming nature took place yesterday afternoon in front of the Royal College of Surgeons ... Shortly before four o'clock ... nearly 200 students assembled in front of the gate leading to the building ..." The medical students howled and sang songs. "The gate was closed in their [the women's] faces ... Dr Handyside found it utterly impossible to begin his demonstration . . . a pet sheep was introduced into the room" and so on. The methods were much the same as those that were employed at Cambridge during the battle of the Degree. And again, as on that occasion, the authorities deplored those downright methods and employed others, more astute and more effective, of their own. Nothing would induce the authorities encamped within the sacred gates to allow the women to enter. They said that God was on their side, Nature was on their side, Law was on their side, and Property was on their side. The college was founded for the benefit of men only; men only were entitled by law to benefit from its endowments. The usual committees were formed. The usual petitions were signed. The humble appeals were made. The usual bazaars were held. The usual questions of tactics were debated. As usual it was asked, ought we to attack now, or is it wiser to wait? Who are our friends and who are our enemies? There were the usual differences of opinion, the usual divisions among the counsellors. But why particularize? The whole proceeding is so familiar that the battle of Harley Street in the year 1869 might well be the battle of Cambridge University at the present moment. On both occasions there is the same waste of strength, waste of temper, waste of time, and waste of money. Almost the same daughters ask almost the same brothers for almost the same privileges. Almost the same gentlemen intone the same refusals for almost the same reasons. It seems as if there were no progress in the human race, but only repetition. We can almost hear them if we listen singing the same old song, "Here we go round the mulberry tree, the mulberry tree, the mulberry tree" and if we add, "of property, of property, of property," we shall fill in the rhyme without doing violence to the facts.

'But we are not here to sing old songs or to fill in missing rhymes. We are here to consider facts. And the facts which we have just extracted from biography seem to prove that the professions have a certain undeniable effect upon the professors. They make the people who practise them possessive, jealous of any infringement of their rights, and highly combative if anyone dares dispute them. Are we not right then in thinking that if we enter the same professions we shall acquire the same qualities? And do not such qualities lead to war? In another century or so if we practise the professions in the same way, shall we not be just as possessive, just as jealous, just as pugnacious, just as positive as to the verdict of God, Nature, Law and Property as these gentlemen are now? Therefore this guinea, which is to help you to help women to enter the professons, has this condition as a first condition attached to it. You shall swear that you will do all in your power to insist that any woman who enters any profession shall in no way hinder any other human being, whether man or woman, white or black, provided that he or she is qualified to enter that profession, from entering it; but shall do all in her power to help them.

'You are ready to put your hand to that, here and now, you say, and at the same time stretch out that hand for the guinea. But wait. Other conditions are attached to it before it is yours. for consider once more the procession of the sons of educated men; ask yourself once more, where is it leading us? One answer suggests itself instantly. To incomes, it is obvious, that seem, to us at least, extremely handsome. Whitaker puts that beyond a doubt. And besides the evidence of Whitaker, there is the evidence of the daily paper—the evidence of the wills, of the subscription lists that we have considered already. In one issue of one paper, for example, it is stated that three educated men died; and one left £1,193,251; another £1,010,288; another £1,404,132. These are large sums for private people to amass, you will admit. And why should we not amass them too in course of time? Now that the Civil Service is open to us we may well earn from one thousand to three thousand a year; now that the Bar is open to us we may well earn £5,000 a year as judges, and any sum up to forty or fifty thousand a year as barristers. When the Church is open to us we may draw salaries of fifteen thousand, five thousand, three thousand yearly, with palaces and deaneries attached. When the Stock Exchange is open to us we may die worth as many millions as Pierpont Morgan,* or as Rockefeller* himself. As doctors we may make anything from two thousand to fifty thousand a year. As editors even we may earn salaries that are by no means despicable. One has a thousand a year; another two thousand; it is rumoured that the editor of a great daily paper has a salary of five thousand yearly. All this wealth may in the course of time come our way if we follow the professions. In short, we may change our position from being the victims of the patriarchal system, paid on the truck system,* with £30 or £40 a year in cash and board and lodging thrown in, to being the champions of the capitalist system, with a yearly income in our own possession of many thousands which, by judicious investment, may leave us when we die possessed of a capital sum of more millions than we can count.

'It is a thought not without its glamour. Consider what it would mean if among us there were now a woman motor-car manufacturer who, with a stroke of the pen, could endow the women's colleges with two or three hundred thousand pounds apiece. The honorary treasurer of the rebuilding fund, your sister at Cambridge, would have her labours considerably lightened then. There would be no need of appeals and committees, of strawberries and cream and bazaars. And suppose that there were not merely one rich woman, but that rich women were as common as rich men. What could you not do? You could shut up your office at once. You could finance a woman's party in the House of Commons. You could run a daily newspaper committed to a conspiracy, not of silence, but of speech. You could get pensions for spinsters; those victims of the patriarchal system, whose allowance is insufficient and whose board and lodging are no longer thrown in. You could get equal pay for equal work. You could provide every mother with chloroform when her child is born;[19] bring down the maternal death-rate from four in every thousand to none at all, perhaps. In one session you could pass Bills that will now take you perhaps a hundred years of hard and continuous labour to get through the House of Commons. There seems at first sight nothing that you could not do, if you had the same capital at your disposal that your brothers have at theirs. Why not, then, you exclaim, help us to take the first step towards possessing it? The professions are the only way in which we can earn money. Money is the only means by which we can achieve objects that are immensely desirable. Yet here you are, you seem to protest, haggling and bargaining over conditions. But consider this letter from a professional man asking us to help him to prevent war. Look also at the photographs of dead bodies and ruined houses that the Spanish Government sends almost weekly. That is why it is necessary to haggle and to bargain over conditions.

'For the evidence of the letter and of the photographs when combined with the facts with which history and biography provide us about the professions seem together to throw a certain light, a red light, shall we say, upon those same professions. You make money in them; that is true; but how far is money in view of those facts in itself a desirable possession? A great authority upon human life, you will remember, held over two thousand years ago that great possessions were undesirable. To which you reply, and with some heat as if you suspected another excuse for keeping the purse-string tied, that Christ's words about the rich and the Kingdom of Heaven are no longer helpful to those who have to face different facts in a different world. You argue that as things are now in England extreme poverty is less desirable than extreme wealth. The poverty of the Christian who should give away all his possessions produces, as we have daily and abdundant proof, the crippled in body, the feeble in mind. The unemployed, to take the obvious example, are not a source of spiritual or intellectual wealth to their country. These are weighty arguments; but consider for a moment the life of Pierpont Morgan. Do you not agree with that evidence before us that extreme wealth is equally undesirable, and for the same reasons? If extreme wealth is undesirable and extreme poverty is undesirable, it is arguable that there is some mean between the two which is desirable. What then is that mean—how much money is needed to live upon in England today? How should that money be spent? What is

[ 253 ]

the kind of life, the kind of human being, you propose to aim at if you succeed in extracting this guinea? Those, Madam, are the questions that I am asking you to consider and you cannot deny that those are questions of the utmost importance. But alas, they are questions that would lead us far beyond the solid world of actual fact to which we are here confined. So let us shut the New Testament; Shakespeare, Shelley, Tolstoy and the rest, and face the fact that stares us in the face at this moment of transition—the fact of the procession; the fact that we are trapesing along somewhere in the rear and must consider that fact before we can fix our eyes upon the vision on the horizon.

'There it is then, before our eyes, the procession of the sons of educated men, ascending those pulpits, mounting those steps, passing in and out of those doors, preaching, teaching, administering justice, practising medicine, making money. And it is obvious that if you are going to make the same incomes from the same professions that those men make you will have to accept the same conditions that they accept. Even from an upper window and from books we know or can guess what those conditions are. You will have to leave the house at nine and come back to it at six. That leaves very little time for fathers to know their children. You will have to do this daily from the age of twenty-one or so to the age of about sixty-five. That leave very little time for friendship, travel or art. You will have to perform some duties that are very arduous, others that are very barbarous. You will have to wear certain uniforms and profess certain loyalties. If you succeed in your profession the words "For God and Empire" will very likely be written, like the address on a dog-collar, round your neck.[20] And if words have meaning, as words perhaps should have meaning, you will have to accept that meaning and do what you can to enforce it. In short, you will have to lead the same lives and profess the same loyalties that professional men have professed for many centuries. There can be no doubt of that.

'If you retaliate, what harm is there in that? Why should we hesitate to do what our fathers and grandfathers have done before us? let us go into greater detail and consult the facts which are nowadays open to the inspection of all who can read their mother tongue in biography. There they are, those innumerable and invaluable works upon the shelves of your own library. Let us glance again rapidly at the lives of professional men who have succeeded in their professions. Here is an extract from the life of a great lawyer. "He went to his chambers about half-past nine . . . He took briefs home with him . . . so that he was lucky if he got to bed about one or two o'clock in the morning."[21] That explains why most successful barristers are hardly worth sitting next at dinner— they yawn so. Next, here is a quotation from a

famous politician's speech. " . . . since 1914 I have
never seen the pageant of the blossom from the first
damson to the last apple—never once have I seen that
in Worcestershire since 1914, and if that is not a
sacrifice I do not know what is."[22] A sacrifice indeed,
and one that explains the perennial indifference of the
Government to art—why, these unfortunate gentlemen must be as blind as bats. Take the religious
profession next. Here is a quotation from the life of a
great bishop. "This is an awful mind- and soul-
destroying life. I really do not know how to live it.
The arrears of important work accumulate and
crush."[23] That bears out what so many people are
saying now about the Church and the nation. Our
bishops and deans seem to have no soul with which
to preach and no mind with which to write. Listen to
any sermon in any church; read the journalism of Dean
Alington or Dean Inge* in any newspaper. Take the
doctor's profession next. "I have taken a good deal
over £13,000 during the year, but this cannot possibly
be maintained, and while it lasts it is slavery. What I
feel most is being away from Eliza and the children
so frequently on Sundays, and again at Christmas."[24]
That is the complaint of a great doctor; and his
patient might well echo it, for what Harley Street
specialist has time to understand the body, let alone
the mind or both in combination, when he is a slave
to thirteen thousand a year? But is the life of a
professional writer any better? Here is a sample taken

from the life of a highly successful journalist. "On another day at this time he wrote a 1,600-words article on Nietzsche, a leader of equal length on the railway strike for the *Standard*, 600 words for the *Tribune* and in the evening was at Shoe Lane."[25] That explains among other things why the public reads its politics with cynicism, and authors read their reviews with foot-rules—it is the advertisement that counts; praise or blame have ceased to have any meaning. And with one more glance at the politician's life, for his profession after all is the most important practically, let us have done. "Lord Hugh *loitered in the lobby* ... The Bill [the Deceased Wife's Sister Bill] was in consequence dead, and the further chances of the cause were relegated to the chances and mischances of another year."[26] That not only serves to explain a certain prevalent distrust of politicians, but also reminds us that since you have the Pensions Bill to steer through the lobbies of so just and humane an institution as the House of Commons, we must not loiter too long ourselves among these delightful biographies, but must try to sum up the information which we have gained from them.

'What then do these quotations from the lives of successful professional men prove, you ask? They prove, as Whitaker proves things, nothing whatever. If Whitaker, that is, says that a bishop is paid five thousand a year, that is a fact; it can be checked and verified. But if Bishop Gore says that the life of a bishop is "an awful mind- and soul-destroying life" he is merely giving us his opinion; the next bishop on the bench may flatly contradict him. These quotations then prove nothing that can be checked and verified; they merely cause us to hold opinions. And those opinions cause us to doubt and criticize and question the value of professional life—not its cash value; that is great; but its spiritual, its moral, its intellectual value. They make us of the opinion that if people are highly successful in their professions they lose their senses. Sight goes. They have no time to look at pictures. Sound goes. They have no time to listen to music. Speech goes. They have no time for conversation. They lose their sense of proportion—the relations between one thing and another. Humanity goes. Money making becomes so important that they must work by night as well as by day. Health goes. And so competitive do they become that they will not share their work with others though they have more than they can do themselves. What then remains of a human being who has lost sight, and sound, and sense of proportion? Only a cripple in a cave.

'That of course is a figure, and fanciful; but that it has some connection with figures that are statistical and not fanciful—with the three hundred millions spent upon arms—seems possible. Such at any rate would seem to be the opinion of disinterested observers whose position gives them every opportunity for judging widely, and for judging fairly. Let us examine two such opinions only. The Marquess of Londonderry said:

[ 258 ]

We seem to hear a babel of voices among which direction and guidance are lacking, and the world appears to be marking time . . . During the last century gigantic forces of scientific discovery had been unloosed, while at the same time we could discern no corresponding advance in literary or scientific achievement . . . The question we are asking ourselves is whether man is capable of enjoying these new fruits of scientific knowledge and discovery, or whether by their misuse he will bring about the destruction of himself and the edifice of civilization.[27]

'Mr Churchill said:

Certain it is that while men are gathering knowledge and power with ever-increasing and measureless speed, their virtues and their wisdom have not shown any notable improvement as the centuries have rolled. The brain of a modern man does not differ in essentials from that of the human beings who fought and loved here millions of years ago. The nature of man has remained hitherto practically unchanged. Under sufficient stress—starvation, terror, warlike passion, or even cold intellectual frenzy, the modern man we know so well will do the most terrible deeds, and his modern woman will back him up.[28]

'Those are two quotations only from a great number to the same effect. And to them let us add another, from a less impressive source but worth your reading since it too bears upon our problem, from Mr Cyril Chaventre of North Wembley.

A woman's sense of values [he writes], is indisputably different from that of a man. Obviously therefore a woman is at a disadvantage and under suspicion when in competition in a man-created sphere of activity. More than ever today women have the opportunity to build a new and better world, but in this slavish imitation of men they are wasting their chance.[29]

'That opinion, too, is a representative opinion, one from a great number to the same effect provided by the daily papers. And the three quotations taken together are highly instructive. The two first seem to prove that the enormous professional competence of the educated man has not brought about an altogether desirable state of things in the civilized world; and the last, which calls upon professional women to use "their different sense of values" to "build a new and better world" not only implies that those who have built that world are dissatisfied with the results, but, by calling upon the other sex to remedy the evil imposes a great responsibility and implies a great compliment. For if Mr Chaventre and the gentlemen who agree with him believe that "at a disadvantage and under suspicion" as she is, with little or no political or professional training and upon a salary of about £250 a year, the professional woman can yet "build a new and better world", they must credit her with powers that might almost be called divine. They must agree with Goethe:

> The things that must pass
> Are only symbols;

Here shall all failure
Grow to achievement,
Here, the Untellable
Work all fulfilment,
The woman in woman
Lead forward for ever[30]

—another very great compliment, and from a very great poet you will agree.

'But you do not want compliments; you are pondering quotations. And since your expression is decidedly downcast, it seems as if these quotations about the nature of professional life have brought you to some melancholy conclusion. What can it be? Simply, you reply, that we, daughters of educated men, are between the devil and the deep sea. Behind us lies the patriarchal system; the private house, with its nullity, its immorality, its hypocrisy, its servility. Before us lies the public world, the professional system, with its possessiveness, its jealousy, its pugnacity, its greed. The one shuts us up like slaves in a harem; the other forces us to circle, like caterpillars head to tail, round and round the mulberry tree, the sacred tree, of property. It is a choice of evils. Each is bad. Had we not better plunge off the bridge into the river; give up the game; declare that the whole of human life is a mistake and so end it?

'But before you take that step, Madam, a decisive one, unless you share the opinion of the professors of the Church of England that death is the gate of life—

*Mors Janua Vitae* is written upon an arch in St Paul's—in which case there is, of course, much to recommend it, let us see if another answer is not possible.

'Another answer may be staring us in the face on the shelves of your own library, once more in the biographies. Is it not possible that by considering the experiments that the dead have made with their lives in the past we may find some help in answering the very difficult question that is now forced upon us? At any rate, let us try. The question that we will now put to biography is this: For reasons given above we are agreed that we must earn money in the professions. For reasons given above those professions seem to us highly undesirable. The questions we put to you, lives of the dead, is how can we enter the professions and yet remain civilized human beings; human beings, that is, who wish to prevent war?

'This time let us turn to the lives not of men but of women in the nineteenth century—to the lives of professional women. But there would seem to be a gap in your library, Madam. There are no lives of professional women in the nineteenth century. A Mrs Tomlinson, the wife of a Mr Tomlinson, FRS, FCS, explains the reason. This lady, who wrote a book "advocating the employment of young ladies as nurses for children", says: ". . . it seemed as if there were no way in which an unmarried lady could earn a living but by taking a situation as governess, for

which post she was often unfit by nature and education, or want of education."[31] That was written in
1859—less than 100 years ago. That explains the gap
on your shelves. There were no professional women,
except governesses, to have lives written of them.
And the lives of governesses, that is the written lives,
can be counted on the fingers of one hand. What then
can we learn about the lives of professional women
from studying the lives of governesses? Happily old
boxes are beginning to give up their old secrets. Out
the other day crept one such document written about
the year 1811. There was, it appears, an obscure Miss
Weeton, who used to scribble down her thoughts
upon professional life among other things when her
pupils were in bed. Here is one such thought. "Oh!
how I have burned to learn Latin, French, the Arts,
the Sciences, anything rather than the dog trot way of
sewing, teaching, writing copies, and washing dishes
every day . . . Why are not females permitted to study
physics, divinity, astronomy, etc., etc., with their
attendants, chemistry, botany, logic, mathematics,
&c.?"[32] That comment upon the lives of governesses,
that question from the lips of governesses, reaches us
from the darkness. It is illuminating, too. But let us
go on groping; let us pick up a hint here and a hint
there as to the professions as they were practised by
women in the nineteenth century. Next we find Anne
Clough, the sister of Arthur Clough, pupil of Dr
Arnold, Fellow of Oriel, who, though she served

without a salary, was the first principal of Newnham, and thus may be called a professional woman in embryo—we find her training for her profession by "doing much of the housework" . . . "earning money to pay off what had been lent by their friends", "pressing for leave to keep a small school", reading books her brother lent her, and exclaiming, "If I were a man, I would not work for riches, to make myself a name or to leave a wealthy family behind me. No, I think I would work for my country, and make its people my heirs."[33] The nineteenth-century women were not without ambition it seems. Next we find Josephine Butler, who, though not strictly speaking a professional woman, led the campaign against the Contagious Diseases Act* to victory, and then the campaign against the sale and purchase of children "for infamous purposes"—we find Josephine Butler refusing to have a life of herself written, and saying of the women who helped her in those campaigns: "The utter absence in them of any desire for recognition, of any vestige of egotism in any form, is worthy of remark. In the purity of their motives they shine out 'clear as crystal'."[34] That, then, was one of the qualities that the Victorian woman praised and practised—a negative one, it is true; not to be recognized; not to be egotistical; to do the work for the sake of doing the work.[35] An interesting contribution to psychology in its way. And then we come closer to our own time; we find Gertrude Bell, who, though the diplomatic service was and is shut to women, occupied a post in the East which almost entitled her to be called a pseudo-diplomat—we find rather to our surprise that "Gertrude could never go out in London without a female friend or, failing that, a maid[36] . . . when it seemed unavoidable for Gertrude to drive in a hansom with a young man from one tea party to another, she feels obliged to write and confess it to my mother."[37] So they were chaste, the women pseudo-dipolomats of the Victorian Age?[38] And not merely in body; in mind also. "Gertrude was not allowed to read Bourget's *The Disciple*"* for fear of contracting whatever disease that book may disseminate. Dissatisfied but ambitious, ambitious but austere, chaste yet adventurous—such are some of the qualities that we have discovered. But let us go on looking—if not at the lines, then between the lines of biography. And we find, between the lines of their husbands' biographies, so many women practising—but what are we to call the profession that consists in bringing nine or ten children into the world, the profession which consists in running a house, nursing an invalid, visiting the poor and the sick, tending here an old father, there an old mother?—there is no name and there is no pay for that profession; but we find so many mothers, sisters and daughters of educated men practising it in the nineteenth century that we must lump them and their lives together behind their husbands' and brothers', and leave them to deliver their message to those who have the time to extract it and the imagination with which to decipher it. Let us ourselves, who as you hint are pressed for time, sum up these random hints and reflections upon the professional life of women in the nineteenth century by quoting once more the highly significant words of a woman who was not a professional woman in the strict sense of the word, but had some nondescript reputation as a traveller nevertheless—Mary Kingsley:

I don't know if I ever revealed the fact to you that being allowed to learn German was *all* the paid-for education I ever had. £2,000 was spent on my brother's. I still hope not in vain.

'That statement is so suggestive that it may save us the bother of groping and searching between the lines of professional men's lives for the lives of their sisters. If we develop the suggestions we find in that statement, and connect it with the other hints and fragments that we have uncovered, we may arrive at some theory or point of view that may help us to answer the very difficult question, which now confronts us. For when Mary Kingsley says, " . . . being allowed to learn German was *all* the paid-for education I ever had", she suggests that she had an unpaid-for education. The other lives that we have been examining corroborate that suggestion. What then was the nature of that "unpaid-for education" which, whether for good or evil, has been ours for so many centuries? If we mass the lives of the obscure behind four lives that were not obscure, but were so successful and distinguished that they were actually written, the lives of Florence Nightingale, Miss Clough, Mary Kingsley and Gertrude Bell, it seems undeniable that they were all educated by the same teachers. And those teachers, biography indicates, obliquely, and indirectly, but emphatically and indisputably none the less, were poverty, chastity, derision, and—but what word covers "lack of rights and privileges"? Shall we press the old word "freedom" once more into service? "Freedom from unreal loyalties", then, was the fourth of their teachers; that freedom from loyalty to old schools, old colleges, old churches, old ceremonies, old countries which all those women enjoyed, and which, to a great extent, we still enjoy by the law and custom of England. We have no time to coin new words, greatly though the language is in need of them. Let "freedom from unreal loyalties" then stand as the fourth great teacher of the daughters of educated men.

'Biography thus provides us with the fact that the daughters of educated men received an unpaid-for education at the hands of poverty, chastity, derision and freedom from unreal loyalties. It was this unpaid-for education, biography informs us, that fitted them, aptly enough, for the unpaid-for professions. And biography also informs us that those unpaid-for professions had their laws, traditions, and labours no less certainly than the paid-for professions. Further, the student of biography cannot possibly doubt from the evidence of biography that this education and these professions were in many ways bad in the extreme, both for the unpaid themselves and for their descendants. The intensive childbirth of the unpaid wife, the intensive money-making of the paid husband in the Victorian age had terrible results, we cannot doubt, upon the mind and body of the present age. To prove it we need not quote once more the famous passage in which Florence Nightingale* denounced that education and its results; nor stress the natural delight with which she greeted the Crimean war; nor illustrate from other sources—they are, alas, innumerable—the inanity, the pettiness, the spite, the tyranny, the hypocrisy, the immorality which it engendered as the lives of both sexes so abundantly testify. Final proof of its harshness upon one sex at any rate can be found in the annals of our "great war", when hospitals, harvest fields and munition works were largely staffed by refugees flying from its horrors to their comparative amenity.

'But biography is many-sided; biography never returns a single and simple answer to any question that is asked of it. Thus the biographies of those who had biographies—say Florence Nightingale, Anne Clough, Emily Brontë, Christina Rossetti, Mary Kingsley—prove beyond a doubt that this same education, the unpaid for, must have had great virtues as well as great defects, for we cannot deny that these, if not educated, still were civilized women. We cannot, when we consider the lives of our uneducated mothers and grandmothers, judge education simply by its power to "obtain appointments", to win honour, to make money. We must if we are honest, admit that some who had no paid-for education, no salaries and no appointments were civilized human beings—whether or not they can rightly be called "English" women is matter for dispute; and thus admit that we should be extremely foolish if we threw away the results of that education or gave up the knowledge that we have obtained from it for any bribe or decoration whatsoever. Thus biography, when asked the question we have put to it—how can we enter the professions and yet remain civilized human beings, human beings who discourage war, would seem to reply: If you refuse to be separated from the four great teachers of the daughters of educated men—poverty, chastity, derision and freedom from unreal loyalties—but combine them with some wealth, some knowledge, and some service to real loyalties then you can enter the professions and escape the risks that make them undesirable.

'Such being the answer of the oracle, such are the conditions attached to this guinea. You shall have it, to recapitulate, on condition that you help all properly qualified people, of whatever sex, class or colour, to enter your profession; and further on condition that in the practice of your profession you refuse to be separated from poverty, chastity, derision and freedom from unreal loyalties. Is the statement now more positive, have the conditions been made more clear and do you agree to the terms? You hesitate. Some of the conditions, you seem to suggest, need further discussion. Let us take them, then, in order. By poverty is meant enough money to live upon. That is, you must earn enough to be independent of any other human being and to buy that modicum of health, leisure, knowledge and so on that is needed for the full development of body and mind. But no more. Not a penny more.

'By chastity is meant that when you have made enough to live on by your profession you must refuse to sell your brain for the sake of money. That is you must cease to practise your profession, or practise it for the sake of research and experiment; or, if you are an artist, for the sake of the art; or give the knowledge acquired professionally to those who need it for nothing. But directly the mulberry tree begins to make you circle, break off. Pelt the tree with laughter.

'By derision—a bad word, but once again the English language is much in need of new words—is meant that you must refuse all methods of advertising merit, and hold that ridicule, obscurity and censure are preferable, for psychological reasons, to fame and praise. Directly badges, orders, or degrees are offered you, fling them back in the giver's face.

'By freedom from unreal loyalties is meant that you must rid yourself of pride and nationality in the first place; also, of religious pride, college pride, school pride, family pride, sex pride and those unreal loyalties that spring from them. Directly the seducers come with their seductions to bribe you into captivity, tear up the parchments; refuse to fill up the forms.

'And if you still object that these definitions are both too arbitrary and too general, and ask how anybody can tell how much money and how much knowledge are needed for the full development of body and mind, and which are the real loyalties which we must serve and which the unreal which we must despise, I can only refer you—time presses—to two authorities. One is familiar enough. It is the psychometer that you carry on your wrist, the little instrument upon which you depend in all personal relationships. If it were visible it would look something like a thermometer. It has a vein of quicksilver in it which is affected by any body or soul, house or society in whose presence it is exposed. If you want to find out how much wealth is desirable, expose it in a rich man's presence; how much learning is desirable expose it in a learned man's presence. So with patriotism, religion and the rest. The conversation need not be interrupted while you consult it; nor its amenity disturbed. But if you object that this is too personal and fallible a method to employ without risk of mistake, witness the fact that the private psychometer has led to many unfortunate marriages and broken friendships, then there is the other authority now easily within the reach even of the poorest of the daughters of educated men. Go to the public galleries and look at pictures; turn on the wireless and rake down music from the air; enter any of the public libraries which are now free to all. There you will be able to consult the findings of the public psychometer for yourself. To take one example, since we are pressed for time. The *Antigone* of Sophocles* has been done into English prose or verse by a man whose name is immaterial.[39] Consider the character of Creon. There you have a most profound analysis by a poet, who is a psychologist in action, of the effect of power and wealth upon the soul. Consider Creon's claim to absolute rule over his subjects. That is a far more instructive analysis of tyranny than any our politicians can offer us. You want to know which are the unreal loyalties which we must despise, which are the real loyalties which we must honour? Consider Antigone's distinction between the laws and the Law. That is a far more profound statement of the duties of the individual to society than any our sociologists can offer us. Lame as the English rendering is, Antigone's five words are worth all the sermons of all the archbishops.[40] But to enlarge would be impertinent. Private judgement is still free in private and that freedom is the essence of freedom.

'For the rest, though the conditions may seem many and the guinea, alas, is single, they are not for the most part as things are at present very difficult of fulfilment. With the exception of the first—that we must earn enough money to live upon—they are largely ensured us by the laws of England. The law of England sees to it that we do not inherit great possessions; the law of England denies us, and let us hope will long continue to deny us, the full stigma of nationality. Then we can scarcely doubt that our brothers will provide us for many centuries to come, as they have done for many centuries past, with what is so essential for sanity, and so invaluable in preventing the great modern sins of vanity, egotism, megalomania—that is to say ridicule, censure and contempt.[41] And so long as the Church of England refuses our services—long may she exclude us!—and the ancient schools and colleges refuse to admit us to a share of their endowments and privileges we shall be immune without any trouble on our part from the particular loyalties and fealties which such endowments and privileges engender. Further, Madam, the traditions of the private house, that ancestral memory which lies behind the present moment, are there to help you. We have seen in the quotations given above how great a part chastity, bodily chastity, has played in the unpaid education of our sex. It should not be difficult to transmute the old ideal of bodily chastity into the new ideal of mental chastity—to hold that if it was wrong to sell the body for money it is much more wrong to sell the mind for money, since the mind, people say, is nobler than the body. Then again, are we not greatly fortified in resisting the seductions of the most powerful of all seducers—money—by those same traditions? For how many centuries have we not enjoyed the right of working all day and every day for £40 a year with board and lodging thrown in? And does not Whitaker prove that half the work of educated men's daughters is still unpaid-for work? Finally, honour, fame, consequence—is it not easy for us to resist that seduction, we who have worked for centuries without other honour than that which is reflected from the coronets and badges on our father's or husband's brows and breasts?

'Thus, with law on our side, and property on our side, and ancestral memory to guide us, there is no need of further argument; you will agree that the conditions upon which this guinea is yours are, with the exception of the first, comparatively easy to fulfil. They merely require that you should develop, modify and direct by the findings of the two psychometers the traditions and the education of the private house which have been in existence these 2,000 years. And if you will agree to do that, there can be an end of bargaining between us. Then the guinea with which to pay the rent of your house is yours—would that it were a thousand! For if you agree to these terms then you can join the professions and yet remain uncontaminated by them; you can rid them of their possessiveness, their jealousy, their pugnacity, their greed. You can use them to have a mind of your own and a will of your own. And you can use that mind and will to abolish the inhumanity, the beastliness, the horror, the folly of war. Take this guinea then and use it, not to burn the house down, but to make its windows blaze. And let the daughters of uneducated women dance round the new house, the poor house, the house that stands in a narrow street where omnibuses pass and the street hawkers cry their wares, and let them sing, "We have done with war! We have done with tyranny!" And their mothers will laugh from their graves, "It was for this that we suffered obloquy and contempt! Light up the windows of the new house, daughters! Let them blaze!"

'Those then are the terms upon which I give you this guinea with which to help the daughters of uneducated women to enter the professions. And by cutting short the peroration let us hope that you will be able to give the finishing touches to your bazaar, arrange the hare and the coffee-pot, and receive the Right Honourable Sir Sampson Legend, OM, KCB, LL D, DCL, PC, etc., with that air of smiling deference which befits the daughter of an educated man in the presence of her brother.'

[ 275 ]

Such then, Sir, was the letter finally sent to the honorary treasurer of the society for helping the daughters of educated men to enter the professions. Those are the conditions upon which she is to have her guinea. They have been framed, so far as possible, to ensure that she shall do all that a guinea can make her do to help you to prevent war. Whether the conditions have been rightly laid down, who shall say? But as you will see, it was necessary to answer her letter and the letter from the honorary treasurer of the college rebuilding fund, and to send them both guineas before answering your letter, because unless they are helped, first to educate the daughters of educated men, and then to earn their living in the professions, those daughters cannot possess an independent and disinterested influence with which to help you to prevent war. The causes it seems are connected. But having shown this to the best of our ability, let us return to your own letter and to your request for a subscription to your own society.

## THREE

HERE then is your own letter. In that, as we have seen, after asking for an opinion as to how to prevent war, you go on to suggest certain practical measures by which we can help you to prevent it. These are it appears that we should sign a manifesto, pledging ourselves 'to protect culture and intellectual liberty';[1]* that we should join a certain society, devoted to certain measures whose aim is to preserve peace; and, finally, that we should subscribe to that society which like the others is in need of funds.

First, then, let us consider how we can help you to prevent war by protecting culture and intellectual liberty, since you assure us that there is a connection between those rather abstract words and these very positive photographs—the photographs of dead bodies and ruined houses.

But if it was surprising to be asked for an opinion how to prevent war, it is still more surprising to be asked to help you in the rather abstract terms of your manifesto to protect culture and intellectual liberty. Consider, Sir, in the light of the facts given above, what this request of yours means. It means that in the year 1938 the sons of educated men are asking the daughters to help them to protect culture and intellectual liberty. And why, you may ask, is that so surprising? Suppose that the Duke of Devonshire, in

his star and garter, stepped down into the kitchen and
said to the maid who was peeling potatoes with a
smudge on her cheek: 'Stop your potato peeling,
Mary, and help me to construe this rather difficult
passage in Pindar,' would not Mary be surprised and
run screaming to Louisa the cook, 'Lawks, Louie,
Master must be mad!' That, or something like it, is
the cry that rises to our lips when the sons of educated
men ask us, their sisters, to protect intellectual liberty
and culture. But let us try to translate the kitchenmaid's cry into the language of educated people.

Once more we must beg you, Sir, to look from our
angle, from our point of view, at Arthur's Education
Fund. Try once more, difficult though it is to twist
your head in that direction, to understand what it has
meant to us to keep that receptacle filled all these
centuries so that some 10,000 of our brothers may be
educated every year at Oxford and Cambridge. It has
meant that we have already contributed to the cause
of culture and intellectual liberty more than any other
class in the community. For have not the daughters
of educated men paid into Arthur's Education Fund
from the year 1262 to the year 1870 all the money
that was needed to educate themselves, bating such
miserable sums as went to pay the governess, the
German teacher, and the dancing master? Have they
not paid with their own education for Eton and
Harrow, Oxford and Cambridge, and all the great
schools and universities on the continent—the Sor-

bonne and Heidelberg, Salamanca and Padua and Rome? Have they not paid so generously and lavishly if so indirectly, that when at last, in the nineteenth century, they won the right to some paid-for education for themselves, there was not a single woman who had received enough paid-for education to be able to teach them?[2] And now, out of the blue, just as they were hoping that they might filch not only a little of that same university education for themselves but some of the trimmings—travel, pleasure, liberty—for themselves, here is your letter informing them that the whole of that vast, that fabulous sum— for whether counted directly in cash, or indirectly in things done without, the sum of that filled Arthur's Education Fund is vast—has been wasted or wrongly applied. With what other purpose were the universities of Oxford and Cambridge founded, save to protect culture and intellectual liberty?* For what other object did your sisters go without teaching or travel or luxuries themselves except that with the money so saved their brothers should go to schools and universities and there learn to protect culture and intellectual liberty? But now since you proclaim them in danger and ask us to add our voice to yours, and our sixpence to your guinea, we must assume that the money so spent was wasted and that those societies have failed. Yet, the reflection must intrude, if the public schools and universities with their elaborate machinery for mind-training and body-training have

[ 279 ]

failed, what reason is there to think that your society, sponsored though it is by distinguished names, is going to succeed, or that your manifesto, signed though it is by still more distinguished names, is going to convert? Ought you not, before you lease an office, hire a secretary, elect a committee and appeal for funds, to consider why those schools and universities have failed?

That, however, is a question for you to answer. The question which concerns us is what possible help we can give you in protecting culture and intellectual liberty—we, who have been shut out from the universities so repeatedly, and are only now admitted so restrictedly; we who have received no paid-for education whatsoever, or so little that we can only read our own tongue and write our own language, we who are, in fact, members not of the intelligentsia but of the ignorantsia? To confirm us in our modest estimate of our own culture and to prove that you in fact share it there is Whitaker with his facts. Not a single educated man's daughter, Whitaker says, is thought capable of teaching the literature of her own language at either university. Nor is her opinion worth asking, Whitaker informs us, when it comes to buying a picture for the National Gallery, a portrait for the Portrait Gallery, or a mummy for the British Museum. How then can it be worth your while to ask us to protect culture and intellectual liberty when, as Whitaker proves with his cold facts, you have no belief that our advice is worth having when it comes to spending the money, to which we have contributed, in buying culture and intellectual liberty for the State? Do you wonder that the unexpected compliment takes us by surprise? Still, there is your letter. There are facts in that letter, too. In it you say that war is imminent; and you go on to say, in more languages than one—here is the French version:[3] *Seule la culture désintéressée peut garder le monde de sa ruine*\*—you go on to say that by protecting intellectual liberty and our inheritance of culture we can help you to prevent war. And since the first statement at least is indisputable and any kitchenmaid even if her French is defective can read and understand the meaning of 'Air Raid Precautions' when written in large letters upon a blank wall, we cannot ignore your request on the plea of ignorance or remain silent on the plea of modesty. Just as any kitchenmaid would attempt to construe a passage in Pindar if told that her life depended on it, so the daughters of educated men, however little their training qualifies them, must consider what they can do to protect culture and intellectual liberty if by so doing they can help you to prevent war. So let us by all means in our power examine this further method of helping you, and see, before we consider your request that we should join your society, whether we can sign this manifesto in favour of culture and intellectual liberty with some intention of keeping our word.

What, then, is the meaning of those rather abstract words? If we are to help you to protect them it would be well to define them in the first place. But like all honorary treasurers you are pressed for time, and to ramble through English literature in search of a definition, though a delightful pastime in its way, might well lead us far. Let us agree, then, for the present, that we know what they are, and concentrate upon the practical question how we can help you to protect them. Now the daily paper with its provision of facts lies on the table; and a single quotation from it may save time and limit our inquiry. 'It was decided yesterday at a conference of head masters that women were not fit teachers for boys over the age of fourteen.' That fact is of instant help to us here, for it proves that certain kinds of help are beyond our reach. For us to attempt to reform the education of our brothers at public schools and universities would be to invite a shower of dead cats, rotten eggs and broken gates from which only street scavengers and locksmiths would benefit, while the gentlemen in authority, history assures us, would survey the tumult from their study windows without taking the cigars from their lips or ceasing to sip, slowly as its bouquet deserves, their admirable claret.[4] The teaching of history, then, reinforced by the teaching of the daily paper, drives us to a more restricted position. We can only help you to defend culture and intellectual liberty by defending our own culture and our own

[ 282 ]

intellectual liberty. That is to say, we can hint, if the treasurer of one of the women's colleges asks us for a subscription, that some change might be made in that satellite body when it ceases to be satellite; or again, if the treasurer of some society for obtaining professional employment for women asks us for a subscription, suggest that some change might be desirable, in the interests of culture and intellectual liberty, in the practice of the professions. But as paid-for education is still raw and young, and as the number of those allowed to enjoy it at Oxford and Cambridge is still strictly limited, culture for the great majority of educated men's daughters must still be that which is acquired outside the sacred gates, in public libraries or in private libraries, whose doors by some unaccountable oversight have been left unlocked. It must still, in the year 1938, largely consist in reading and writing our own tongue. The question thus becomes more manageable. Shorn of its glory it is easier to deal with. What we have to do now, then, Sir, is to lay your request before the daughters of educated men and to ask them to help you to prevent war, not by advising their brothers how they shall protect culture and intellectual liberty, but simply by reading and writing their own tongue in such a way as to protect those rather abstract goddesses themselves.

This would seem, on the face of it, a simple matter, and one that needs neither argument nor rhetoric. But we are met at the outset by a new difficulty. We have already noted the fact that the profession of literature, to give it a simple name, is the only profession which did not fight a series of battles in the nineteenth century. There has been no battle of Grub Street.* That profession has never been shut to the the daughters of educated men. This was due of course to the extreme cheapness of its professional requirements. Books, pens and paper are so cheap, reading and writing have been, since the eighteenth century at least, so universally taught in our class, that it was impossible for any body of men to corner the necessary knowledge or to refuse admittance, except on their own terms, to those who wished to read books or to write them. But it follows, since the profession of literature is open to the daughters of educated men, that there is no honorary treasurer of the profession in such need of a guinea with which to prosecute her battle that she will listen to our terms, and promise to do what she can to observe them. This places us, you will agree, in an awkward predicament. For how then can we bring pressure upon them—what can we do to persuade them to help us? The profession of literature differs, it would seem, from all the other professions. There is no head of the profession; no Lord Chancellor as in your own case: no official body with the power to lay down rules and enforce them.[5] We cannot debar women from the use of libraries;[6] or forbid them to buy ink and paper; or rule that metaphors shall only be used by one sex, as the male only in art schools was allowed to study from the nude; or rule that rhyme shall be used by one sex only as the male only in Academies of music was allowed to play in orchestras. Such is the inconceivable licence of the profession of letters that any daughter of an educated man may use a man's name—say George Eliot or George Sand—with the result that an editor or a publisher, unlike the authorities in Whitehall, can detect no difference in the scent or savour of a manuscript, or even know for certain whether the writer is married or not.

Thus, since we have very little power over those who earn their livings by reading and writing, we must go to them humbly without bribes or penalties. We must go to them cap in hand, like beggars, and ask them of their goodness to spare time to listen to our request that they shall practise the profession of reading and writing in the interests of culture and intellectual liberty.

And now, clearly, some further definition of 'culture and intellectual liberty' would be useful. Fortunately, it need not be, for our purposes, exhaustive or elaborate. We need not consult Milton, Goethe, or Matthew Arnold; for their definition would apply to paid-for culture—the culture which, in Miss Weeton's definition, includes physics, divinity, astronomy, chemistry, botany, logic and mathematics, as well as Latin, Greek and French. We are appealing in the main to those whose culture is the unpaid-for culture, that which consists in being able to read and write their own tongue. Happily your manifesto is at hand to help us to define the terms further; 'disinterested' is the word you use. Therefore let us define culture for our purposes as the disinterested pursuit of reading and writing the English language. And intellectual liberty may be defined for our purposes as the right to say or write what you think in your own words, and in your own way. These are very crude definitions, but they must serve. Our appeal then might begin: 'Oh, daughters of educated men, this gentleman, whom we all respect, says that war is imminent; by protecting culture and intellectual liberty he says that we can help him to prevent war. We entreat you, therefore, who earn your livings by reading and writing . . .' But here the words falter on our lips, and the prayer peters out into three separate dots because of facts again—because of facts in books, facts in biographies, facts which make it difficult, perhaps impossible, to go on.

What are those facts then? Once more we must interrupt our appeal in order to examine them. And there is no difficulty in finding them. Here, for example, is an illuminating document before us, a most genuine and indeed moving piece of work, the autobiography of Mrs Oliphant, which is full of facts. She was an educated man's daughter who earned her living by reading and writing. She wrote books of all kinds. Novels, biographies, histories, handbooks of

Florence and Rome, reviews, newspaper articles innumerable came from her pen. With the proceeds she earned her living and educated her children. But how far did she protect culture and intellectual liberty? That you can judge for yourself by reading first a few of her novels: *The Duke's Daughter*, *Diana Trelawny*, *Harry Joscelyn*, say; continue with the lives of Sheridan and Cervantes; go on to the *Makers of Florence and Rome*; conclude by sousing yourself in the innumerable faded articles, reviews, sketches of one kind and another which she contributed to literary papers. When you have done, examine the state of your own mind, and ask yourself whether that reading has led you to respect disinterested culture and intellectual liberty. Has it not on the contrary smeared your mind and dejected your imagination, and led you to deplore the fact that Mrs Oliphant sold her brain, her very admirable brain, prostituted her culture and enslaved her intellectual liberty in order that she might earn her living and educate her children?[7] Inevitably, considering the damage that poverty inflicts upon mind and body, the necessity that is laid upon those who have children to see that they are fed and clothed, nursed and educated, we have to applaud her choice and to admire her courage. But if we applaud the choice and admire the courage of those who do what she did, we can spare ourselves the trouble of addressing our appeal to them, for they will no more be able to protect disinterested culture and intellectual liberty than she was. To ask them to sign your manifesto would be to ask a publican to sign a manifesto in favour of temperance. He may himself be a total abstainer; but since his wife and children depend upon the sale of beer, he must continue to sell beer, and his signature to the manifesto would be of no value to the cause of temperance because directly he had signed it he must be at the counter inducing his customers to drink more beer. So to ask the daughters of educated men who have to earn their livings by reading and writing to sign your manifesto would be of no value to the cause of disinterested culture and intellectual liberty, because directly they had signed it they must be at the desk writing those books, lectures and articles by which culture is prostituted and intellectual liberty is sold into slavery. As an expression of opinion it may have value; but if what you need is not merely an expression of opinion but positive help, you must frame your request rather differently. Then you will have to ask them to pledge themselves not to write anything that defiles culture, or to sign any contract that infringes intellectual liberty. And to that the answer given us by biography would be short but sufficient: Have I not to earn my living?

Thus, Sir, it becomes clear that we must make our appeal only to those daughters of educated men who have enough to live upon. To them we might address ourselves in this wise: 'Daughters of educated men who have enough to live upon ...' But again the voice falters: again the prayer peters out into separate dots. For how many of them are there? Dare we assume in the face of Whitaker, of the laws of property, of the wills in the newspapers, of facts in short, that 1,000, 500, or even 250 will answer when thus addressed? However that may be, let the plural stand and continue: 'Daughters of educated men who have enough to live upon, and read and write your own language for your own pleasure, may we very humbly entreat you to sign this gentleman's manifesto with some intention of putting your promise into practice?'

Here, if indeed they consent to listen, they might very reasonably ask us to be more explicit—not indeed to define culture and intellectual liberty, for they have books and leisure and can define the words for themselves. But what, they may well ask, is meant by this gentleman's 'disinterested' culture, and how are we to protect that and intellectual liberty in practice? Now as they are daughters, not sons, we may begin by reminding them of a compliment once paid them by a great historian. 'Mary's conduct,' says Macaulay, 'was really a signal instance of that perfect disinterestedness and self-devotion of which man seems to be incapable, but which is sometimes found in women.'[8] Compliments, when you are asking a favour, never come amiss. Next let us refer them to the tradition which has long been honoured in the private house—the tradition of chastity. 'Just as for many centuries, Madam,' we might plead, 'it was thought vile for a woman to sell her body without love, but right to give it to the husband whom she loved, so it is wrong, you will agree, to sell your mind without love, but right to give it to the art which you love.' 'But what,' she may ask, 'is meant by "selling your mind without love"?' 'Briefly,' we might reply, 'to write at the command of another person what you do not want to write for the sake of money. But to sell a brain is worse than to sell a body, for when the body seller has sold her momentary pleasure she takes good care that the matter shall end there. But when a brain seller has sold her brain, its anaemic, vicious and diseased progeny are let loose upon the world to infect and corrupt and sow the seeds of disease in others. Thus we are asking you, Madam, to pledge yourself not to commit adultery of the brain because it is a much more serious offence than the other.' 'Adultery of the brain,' she may reply, 'means writing what I do not want to write for the sake of money. Therefore you ask me to refuse all publishers, editors, lecture agents and so on who bribe me to write or to speak what I do not want to write or to speak for the sake of money?' 'That is so, Madam; and we further ask that if you should receive proposals for such sales you will resent them and expose them as you would resent and expose such proposals for selling your body, both for your own

[ 290 ]

—

sake and for the sake of others. But we would have you observe that the verb "to adulterate" means, according to the dictionary, "to falsify by admixture of baser ingredients". Money is not the only baser ingredient. Advertisement and publicity are also adulterers. Thus, culture mixed with personal charm, or culture mixed with advertisement and publicity, are also adulterated forms of culture. We must ask you to abjure them; not to appear on public platforms; not to lecture; not to allow your private face to be published, or details of your private life; not to avail yourself, in short, of any of the forms of brain prostitution which are so insidiously suggested by the pimps and panders of the brain-selling trade; or to accept any of those baubles and labels by which brain merit is advertised and certified—medals, honours, degrees—we must ask you to refuse them absolutely, since they are all tokens that culture has been prostituted and intellectual liberty sold into captivity.'

Upon hearing this definition, mild and imperfect as it is, of what it means, not merely to sign your manifesto in favour of culture and intellectual liberty, but to put that opinion into practice, even those daughters of educated men who have enough to live upon may object that the terms are too hard for them to keep. For they would mean loss of money, which is desirable, loss of fame which is universally held to be agreeable, and censure and ridicule which are by no means negligible. Each would be the butt of all who have an interest to serve or money to make from the sale of brains. And for what reward? Only, in the rather abstract terms of your manifesto, that they would thus 'protect culture and intellectual liberty', not by their opinion but by their practice.

Since the terms are so hard, and there is no body in existence whose ruling they need respect or obey, let us consider what other method of persuasion is left to us. Only, it would seem, to point to the photographs—the photographs of dead bodies and ruined houses. Can we bring out the connection between them and prostituted culture and intellectual slavery and make it so clear that the one implies the other, that the daughters of educated men will prefer to refuse money and fame, and to be the objects of scorn and ridicule rather than suffer themselves, or allow others to suffer, the penalties there made visible? It is difficult in the short time at our disposal, and with the weak weapons in our possession, to make that connection clear, but if what you, Sir, say is true, and there is a connection and a very real one between them, we must try to prove it.

Let us then begin by summoning, if only from the world of imagination, some daughter of an educated man who has enough to live upon and can read and write for her own pleasure and, taking her to be the representative of what may in fact be no class at all, let us ask her to examine the products of that reading and writing which lie upon her own table. 'Look,

Madam,' we might begin, 'at the newspapers on your table. Why, may we ask, do you take in three dailies, and three weeklies?' 'Because,' she replies, 'I am interested in politics, and wish to know the facts.' 'An admirable desire, Madam. But why three? Do they differ then about facts, and if so, why?' To which she replies, with some irony, 'You call yourself an educated man's daughter, and yet pretend not to know the facts—roughly that each paper is financed by a board; that each board has a policy; that each board employs writers to expound that policy, and if the writers do not agree with that policy, the writers, as you may remember after a moment's reflection, find themselves unemployed in the street. Therefore if you want to know any fact about politics you must read at least three different papers, compare at least three different versions of the same fact, and come in the end to your own conclusion. Hence the three daily papers on my table.' Now that we have discussed, very briefly, what may be called the literature of fact, let us turn to what may be called the literature of fiction. 'There are such things, Madam,' we may remind her, 'as pictures, plays, music and books. Do you pursue the same rather extravagant policy there— glance at three daily papers and three weekly papers if you want to know the facts about pictures, plays, music and books, because those who write about art are in the pay of an editor, who is in the pay of a board, which has a policy to pursue, so that each paper takes a different view, so that it is only by comparing three different views that you can come to your own conclusion—what pictures to see, what play or concert to go to, which book to order from the library?' And to that she replies, 'Since I am an educated man's daughter, with a smattering of culture picked up from reading, I should no more dream, given the conditions of journalism at present, of taking my opinions of pictures, plays, music or books from the newspapers than I would take my opinion of politics from the newspapers. Compare the views, make allowance for the distortions, and then judge for yourself. That is the only way. Hence the many newspapers on my table.'⁹

So then the literature of fact and the literature of opinion, to make a crude distinction, are not pure fact, or pure opinion, but adulterated fact and adulterated opinion, that is fact and opinion 'adulterated by the admixture of baser ingredients' as the dictionary has it. In other words you have to strip each statement of its money motive, of its power motive, of its advertisement motive, of its publicity motive, of its vanity motive, let alone of all the other motives which, as an educated man's daughter, are familiar to you, before you make up your mind which fact about politics to believe, or even which opinion about art? 'That is so,' she agrees. But if you were told by somebody who had none of those motives for wrapping up truth that the fact was in his or her opinion this or that, you would believe him or her, always allowing of course for the fallibility of human judgement which, in judging works of art, must be considerable? 'Naturally,' she agrees. If such a person said that war was bad, you would believe him; or if such a person said that some picture, symphony, play or poem were good you would believe him? 'Allowing for human fallibility, yes.' Now suppose, Madam, that there were 250 or 50, or 25 such people in existence, people pledged not to commit adultery of the brain, so that it was unnecessary to strip what they said of its money motive, power motive, advertisement motive, publicity motive, vanity motive and so on, before we unwrapped the grain of truth, might not two very remarkable consequences follow? Is it not possible that if we knew the truth about war, the glory of war would be scotched and crushed where it lies curled up in the rotten cabbage leaves of our prostituted fact-purveyors; and if we knew the truth about art instead of shuffling and shambling through the smeared and dejected pages of those who must live by prostituting culture, the enjoyment and practice of art would become so desirable that by comparison the pursuit of war would be a tedious game for elderly dilettantes in seach of a mildly sanitary amusement—the tossing of bombs instead of balls over frontiers instead of nets? In short, if newspapers were written by people whose sole object in writing was to tell the truth about politics and the truth about art we should not believe in war, and we should believe in art.

Hence there is a very clear connection between culture and intellectual liberty and those photographs of dead bodies and ruined houses. And to ask the daughters of educated men who have enough to live upon not to commit adultery of the brain is to ask them to help in the most positive way now open to them—since the profession of literature is still that which stands widest open to them—to prevent war.

Thus, Sir, we might address this lady, crudely, briefly it is true; but time pases and we cannot define further. And to this appeal she might well reply, if indeed she exists: 'What you say is obvious; so obvious that every educated man's daughter already knows it for herself, or if she does not, has only to read the newspapers to be sure of it. But suppose she were well enough off not merely to sign this manifesto in favour of disinterested culture and intellectual liberty but to put her opinion into practice, how could she set about it? And do not,' she may reasonably add, 'dream dreams about ideal worlds behind the stars; consider actual facts in the actual world.' Indeed, the actual world is much more difficult to deal with than the dream world. Still, Madam, the private printing press is an actual fact, and not beyond the reach of a moderate income. Typewriters and duplicators are actual facts and even cheaper. By using these cheap and so far unforbidden instruments you can at once rid yourself of the pressure of boards, policies and editors. They will speak your own mind, in your own words, at your own time, at your own length, at your own bidding. And that, we are agreed, is our definition of 'intellectual liberty'. 'But,' she may say, '"the public"? How can that be reached without putting my own mind through the mincing machine and turning it into sausage?' '"The public", Madam,' we may assure her, 'is very like ourselves; it lives in rooms; it walks in streets, and is said moreover to be tired of sausage. Fling leaflets down basements; expose them on stalls; trundle them along streets on barrows to be sold for a penny or given away. Find out new ways of approaching "the public"; single it into separate people instead of massing it into one monster, gross in body, feeble in mind. And then reflect—since you have enough to live on, you have a room, not necessarily "cosy" or "handsome" but still silent, private; a room where safe from publicity and its poison you could, even asking a reasonable fee for the service, speak the truth to artists, about pictures, music, books, without fear of affecting their sales, which are exiguous, or wounding their vanity, which is prodigious.[10] Such at least was the criticism that Ben Jonson gave Shakespeare at the Mermaid* and there is no reason to suppose, with *Hamlet* as evidence, that literature suffered in consequence. Are not the best critics private people, and is not the only criticism worth having spoken criticism? Those then are some of the active ways in which you, as a writer of your own tongue, can put your opinion into practice. But if you are passive, a reader, not a writer, then you must adopt not active but passive methods of protecting culture and intellectual liberty.' 'And what may they be?' she will ask. 'To abstain, obviously. Not to subscribe to papers that encourage intellectual slavery; not to attend lectures that prostitute culture; for we are agreed that to write at the command of another what you do not want to write is to be enslaved, and to mix culture with personal charm or advertisement is to prostitute culture. By these active and passive measures you would do all in your power to break the ring, the vicious circle, the dance round and round the mulberry tree, the poison tree of intellectual harlotry. The ring once broken, the captives would be freed. For who can doubt that once writers had the chance of writing what they enjoy writing they would find it so much more pleasurable that they would refuse to write on any other terms; or that readers once they had the chance of reading what writers enjoy writing, would find it so much more nourishing than what is written for money that they would refuse to be palmed off with the stale substitute any longer? Thus the slaves who are now kept hard at work piling words into books, piling words into articles, as the old slaves piled stones into pyramids, would shake the manacles from their wrists and give up their loathsome labour. And "culture", that amorphous bundle, swaddled up as she now is in insincerity, emitting half truths from her timid lips, sweetening and diluting her message with whatever sugar or water serves to swell the writer's fame or his master's purse, would regain her shape and become, as Milton, Keats and other great writers assure us that she is in reality, muscular, adventurous, free. Whereas now, Madam, at the very mention of culture the head aches, the eyes close, the doors shut, the air thickens; we are in a lecture room, rank with the fumes of stale print, listening to a gentleman who is forced to lecture or to write every Wednesday, every Sunday, about Milton or about Keats, while the lilac shakes its branches in the garden free, and the gulls, swirling and swooping, suggest with wild laughter that such stale fish might with advantage be tossed to them. That is our plea to you, Madam; those are our reasons for urging it. Do not merely sign this manifesto in favour of culture and intellectual liberty; attempt at least to put your promise into practice.'

Whether the daughters of educated men who have enough to live upon and read and write their own tongue for their own pleasure will listen to this request or not, we cannot say, Sir. But if culture and intellectual liberty are to be protected, not by opinions merely but by practice, this would seem to be the way. It is not an easy way, it is true. Nevertheless, such as it is, there are reasons for thinking that the way is easier for them than for their brothers. They are immune, through no merit of their own, from certain compulsions. To protect culture and intellectual liberty in practice would mean, as we have said, ridicule and chastity, loss of publicity and poverty. But those, as we have seen, are their familiar teachers. Further, Whitaker with his facts is at hand to help them; for since he proves that all the fruits of professional culture—such as directorships of art galleries and museums, professorships and lectureships and editorships—are still beyond their reach, they should be able to take a more purely disinterested view of culture than their brothers, without for a moment claiming, as Macaulay asserts, that they are by nature more disinterested. Thus helped by tradition and by facts as they are, we have not only some right to ask them to help us to break the circle, the vicious circle of prostituted culture, but some hope that if such people exist they will help us. To return then to your manifesto: we will sign it if we can keep these terms; if we cannot keep them, we will not sign it.

Now that we have tried to see how we can help you to prevent war by attempting to define what is meant by protecting culture and intellectual liberty let us consider your next and inevitable request: that we should subscribe to the funds of your society. For you, too, are an honorary treasurer, and like the other honorary treasurers in need of money. Since you, too, are asking for money it might be possible to ask you, also, to define your aims, and to bargain and to impose terms as with the other honorary treasurers. What then are the aims of your society? To prevent war, of course. And by what means? Broadly speaking, by protecting the rights of the individual; by opposing dictatorship; by ensuring the democratic ideals of equal opportunity for all. Those are the chief means by which as you say, 'the lasting peace of the world can be assured.' Then, Sir, there is no need to bargain or to haggle. If those are your aims, and if, as it is impossible to doubt, you mean to do all in your power to achieve them, the guinea is yours—would that it were a million! The guinea is yours; and the guinea is a free gift, given freely.

But the word 'free' is used so often, and has come, like used words, to mean so little, that it may be well to explain exactly, even pedantically, what the word 'free' means in this context. It means here that no right or privilege is asked in return. The giver is not asking you to admit her to the priesthood of the Church of England; or to the Stock Exchange; or to the Diplomatic Service. The giver has no wish to be 'English' on the same terms that you yourself are 'English'. The giver does not claim in return for the gift admission to any profession; any honour, title, or medal; any professorship or lectureship; any seat upon any society, committee or board. The gift is free from all such conditions because the one right of paramount importance to all human beings is already won. You cannot take away her right to earn a living. Now then for the first time in English history an educated man's daughter can give her brother one guinea of her own making at his request for the purpose specified above without asking for anything in return. It is a free gift, given without fear, without flattery, and without conditions. That, Sir, is so momentous an occasion in the history of civilization that some celebration seems called for. But let us have done with the old ceremonies—the Lord Mayor, with turtles* and sheriffs in attendance, tapping nine times with his mace upon a stone while the Archbishop of Canterbury in full canonicals invokes a blessing. Let us invent a new ceremony for this new occasion. What more fitting than to destroy an old word, a vicious and corrupt word that has done much harm in its day and is now obsolete? The word 'femininist' is the word indicated. That word, according to the dictionary, means 'one who champions the rights of women'. Since the only right, the right to earn a living, has been won, the word no longer has a meaning. And a word without a meaning is a dead word, a corrupt word. Let us therefore celebrate this occasion by cremating the corpse. Let us write that word in large black letters on a sheet of foolscap; then solemnly apply a match to the paper. Look, how it burns! What a light dances over the world! Now let us bray the ashes in a mortar with a goose-feather pen, and declare in unison singing together that anyone who uses that word in future is a ring-the-bell-and-run-away-man,[11] a mischief maker, a groper among old bones, the proof of whose defilement is written in a smudge of dirty water upon his face. The smoke has died down; the word is destroyed. Observe, Sir, what has happened as the result of our celebration. The word 'feminist' is destroyed; the air is cleared; and in that clearer air what do we see? Men and women working together for the same cause. The cloud has lifted from the past too. What were they working for in the nineteenth century—those queer dead women in their poke bonnets and shawls? The very same cause for which we are working now. 'Our claim was no claim of women's rights only;'—it is Josephine Butler who speaks—'it was larger and deeper; it was a claim for the rights of all—all men and women—to the respect in their persons of the great principles of Justice and Equality and Liberty.' The words are the same as yours; the claim is the same as yours. The daughters of educated men who were called, to their resentment, 'feminists' were in fact the advance guard of your own movement. They were fighting the same enemy that you are fighting and for the same reasons. They were fighting the tyranny of the patriarchal state as you are fighting the tyranny of the Fascist state. Thus we are merely carrying on the same fight that our mothers and grandmothers fought; their words prove it; your words prove it. But now with your letter before us we have your assurance that you are fighting with us, not against us. That fact is so inspiring that another celebration seems called for. What could be more fitting than to write more dead words, more corrupt words, upon more sheets of paper and burn them— the words, Tyrant, Dictator, for example? But, alas, those words are not yet obsolete. We can still shake out eggs from newspapers; still smell a peculiar and unmistakable odour in the region of Whitehall and Westminster. And abroad the monster has come more openly to the surface. There is no mistaking him there. He has widened his scope. He is interfering now with your liberty; he is dictating how you shall live; he is making distinctions not merely between the sexes, but between the races. You are feeling in your own persons what your mothers felt when they were shut out, when they were shut up, because you are Jews, because you are democrats, because of race, because of religion. It is not a photograph that you look upon any longer; there you go, trapesing along in the procession yourselves. And that makes a difference. The whole iniquity of dictatorship, whether in Oxford or Cambridge, in Whitehall or Downing Street, against Jews or against women, in England, or in Germany, in Italy or in Spain is now apparent to you. But now we are fighting together. The daughters and sons of educated men are fighting side by side. That fact is so inspiring, even if no celebration is

[ 304 ]

possible, that if this one guinea could be multiplied a million times all those guineas should be at your service without any other conditions than those that you have imposed upon yourself. Take this one guinea then and use it to assert 'the rights of all—all men and women—to the respect in their persons of the great principles of Justice and Equality and Liberty'. Put this penny candle in the window of your new society, and may we live to see the day when in the blaze of our common freedom the words tyrant and dictator shall be burnt to ashes, because the words tyrant and dictator shall be obsolete.

That request then for a guinea answered, and the cheque signed, only one further request of yours remains to be considered—it is that we should fill up a form and become members of your society. On the face of it that seems a simple request, easily granted. For what can be simpler than to join the society to which this guinea has just been contributed? On the face of it, how easy, how simple; but in the depths, how difficult, how complicated ... What possible doubts, what possible hesitations can those dots stand for? What reason or what emotion can make us hesitate to become members of a society whose aims we approve, to whose funds we have contributed? It may be neither reason nor emotion, but something more profound and fundamental than either. It may be difference. Different we are, as facts have proved, both in sex and in education. And it is from that difference, as we have already said, that our help can come, if help we can, to protect liberty, to prevent war. But if we sign this form which implies a promise to become active members of your society, it would seem that we must lose that difference and therefore sacrifice that help. To explain why this is so is not easy, even though the gift of a guinea has made it possible (so we have boasted), to speak freely without fear or flattery. Let us then keep the form unsigned on the table before us while we discuss, so far as we are able, the reasons and the emotions which make us hesitate to sign it. For those reasons and emotions have their origin deep in the darkness of ancestral memory; they have grown together in some confusion; it is very difficult to untwist them in the light.

To begin with an elementary distinction: a society is a conglomeration of people joined together for certain aims; while you, who write in your own person with your own hand are single. You the individual are a man whom we have reason to respect; a man of the brotherhood, to which, as biography proves, many brothers have belonged. Thus Anne Clough, describing her brother, says: 'Arthur is my best friend and adviser . . . Arthur is the comfort and joy of my life; it is for him, and from him, that I am incited to seek after all that is lovely and of good report.' To which William Wordsworth, speaking of his sister but answering the other as if one nightingale called to another in the forests of the past, replies:

The Blessing of my later years
Was with me when a Boy:
She gave me eyes, she gave me ears;
And humble cares, and delicate fears;
A heart, the fountain of sweet tears;
And love, and thought, and joy.[12]

Such was, such perhaps still is, the relationship of many brothers and sisters in private, as individuals. They respect each other and help each other and have aims in common. Why then, if such can be their private relationship, as biography and poetry prove, should their public relationship, as law and history prove, be so very different? And here, since you are a lawyer, with a lawyer's memory, it is not necessary to remind you of certain decrees of English law from its first records to the year 1919 by way of proving that the public, the society relationship of brother and sister has been very different from the private. The very word 'society' sets tolling in memory the dismal bells of a harsh music: shall not, shall not, shall not. You shall not learn; you shall not earn; you shall not own; you shall not—such was the society relationship of brother to sister for many centuries. And though it is possible, and to the optimistic credible, that in time a new society may ring a carillon of splendid harmony, and your letter heralds it, that day is far distant. Inevitably we ask ourselves, is there not something in the conglomeration of people into societies that releases what is most selfish and violent,

least rational and humane in the individuals themselves? Inevitably we look upon society, so kind to
you, so harsh to us, as an ill-fitting form that distorts
the truth; deforms the mind; fetters the will. Inevitably we look upon societies as conspiracies that sink
the private brother, whom many of us have reason to
respect, and inflate in his stead a monstrous male,
loud of voice, hard of fist, childishly intent upon
scoring the floor of the earth with chalk marks, within
whose mystic boundaries human beings are penned,
rigidly, separately, artificially; where, daubed red and
gold, decorated like a savage with feathers he goes
through mystic rites and enjoys the dubious pleasures
of power and dominion while we, 'his' women, are
locked in the private house without share in the many
societies of which his society is composed. For such
reasons compact as they are of many memories and
emotions—for who shall analyse the complexity of a
mind that holds so deep a reservoir of time past
within it?—it seems both wrong for us rationally and
impossible for us emotionally to fill up your form
and join your society. For by so doing we should
merge our identity in yours; follow and repeat and
score still deeper the old worn ruts in which society,
like a gramophone whose needle has stuck, is grinding
out with intolerable unanimity 'Three hundred millions spent upon arms'. We should not give effect to
a view which our own experience of 'society' should
have helped us to envisage. Thus, Sir, while we respect

you as a private person and prove it by giving you a guinea to spend as you choose, we believe that we can help you most effectively by refusing to join your society; by working for our common ends—justice and equality and liberty for all men and women—outside your society, not within.

But this, you will say, if it means anything, can only mean that you, the daughters of educated men, who have promised us your positive help, refuse to join our society in order that you may make another of your own. And what sort of society do you propose to found outside ours, but in co-operation with it, so that we may both work together for our common ends? That is a question which you have every right to ask, and which we must try to answer in order to justify our refusal to sign the form you send. Let us then draw rapidly in outline the kind of society which the daughters of educated men might found and join outside your society but in co-operation with its ends. In the first place, this new society, you will be relieved to learn, would have no honorary treasurer, for it would need no funds. It would have no office, no committee, no secretary; it would call no meetings; it would hold no conferences. If name it must have, it could be called the Outsiders' Society. That is not a resonant name, but it has the advantage that it squares with facts—the facts of history, of law, of biography; even, it may be, with the still hidden facts of our still unknown psychology.

It would consist of educated men's daughters working in their own class—how indeed can they work in any other?[13]—and by their own methods for liberty, equality and peace. Their first duty, to which they would bind themselves not by oath, for oaths and ceremonies have no part in a society which must be anonymous and elastic before everything would be not to fight with arms. This is easy for them to observe, for in fact, as the papers inform us, 'the Army Council have no intention of opening recruiting for any women's corps.'[14] The country ensures it. Next they would refuse in the event of war to make munitions or nurse the wounded. Since in the last war both these activities were mainly discharged by the daughters of working men, the pressure upon them here too would be slight, though probably disagreeable. On the other hand the next duty to which they would pledge themselves is one of considerable difficulty, and calls not only for courage and initiative, but for the special knowledge of the educated man's daughter. It is, briefly, not to incite their brothers to fight, or to dissuade them, but to maintain an attitude of complete indifference. But the attitude expressed by the word 'indifference' is so complex and of such importance that it needs even here further definition. Indifference in the first place must be given a firm footing upon fact. As it is a fact that she cannot understand what instinct compels him, what glory, what interest, what manly satisfaction fighting pro-

vides for him—'without war there would be no outlet
for the manly qualities which fighting develops'—as
fighting thus is a sex characteristic which she cannot
share, the counterpart some claim of the maternal
instinct which he cannot share, so is it an instinct
which she cannot judge. The outsider therefore must
leave him free to deal with this instinct by himself,
because liberty of opinion must be respected, especially when it is based upon an instinct which is as
foreign to her as centuries of tradition and education
can make it.[15] This is a fundamental and instinctive
distinction upon which indifference may be based.
But the outsider will make it her duty not merely to
base her indifference upon instinct, but upon reason.
When he says, as history proves that he has said, and
may say again, 'I am fighting to protect our country'
and thus seeks to rouse her patriotic emotion, she will
ask herself, 'What does "our country" mean to me an
outsider?' To decide this she will analyse the meaning
of patriotism in her own case. She will inform herself
of the position of her sex and her class in the past.
She will inform herself of the amount of land, wealth
and property in the possession of her own sex and
class in the present—how much of 'England' in fact
belongs to her. From the same sources she will inform
herself of the legal protection which the law has given
her in the past and now gives her. And if he adds that
he is fighting to protect her body, she will reflect
upon the degree of physical protection that she now

enjoys when the words 'Air Raid Precaution'* are written on blank walls. And if he says that he is fighting to protect England from foreign rule, she will reflect that for her there are no 'foreigners', since by law she becomes a foreigner if she marries a foreigner. And she will do her best to make this a fact, not by forced fraternity, but by human sympathy. All these facts will convince her reason (to put it in a nutshell) that her sex and class has very little to thank England for in the past; not much to thank England for in the present; while the security of her person in the future is highly dubious. But probably she will have imbibed, even from the governess, some romantic notion that Englishmen, those fathers and grand-fathers whom she sees marching in the picture of history, are 'superior' to the men of other countries. This she will consider it her duty to check by comparing French historians with English; German with French; the testimony of the ruled—the Indians or the Irish, say—with the claims made by their rulers. Still some 'patriotic' emotion, some ingrained belief in the intellectual superiority of her own country over other countries may remain. Then she will compare English painting with French painting; English music with German music; English literature with Greek literature, for translations abound. When all these comparisons have been faithfully made by the use of reason, the outsider will find herself in possession of very good reasons for her indifference.

She will find that she has no good reason to ask her brother to fight on her behalf to protect 'our' country. '"Our country",' she will say, 'throughout the greater part of its history has treated me as a slave; it has denied me education or any share in its possessions. "Our" country still ceases to be mine if I marry a foreigner. "Our" country denies me the means of protecting myself, forces me to pay others a very large sum annually to protect me, and is so little able, even so, to protect me that Air Raid precautions are written on the wall. Therefore if you insist upon fighting to protect me, or "our" country, let it be understood, soberly and rationally between us, that you are fighting to gratify a sex instinct which I cannot share; to procure benefits which I have not shared and probably will not share; but not to gratify my instincts, or to protect either myself or my country. For,' the outsider will say, 'in fact, as a woman, I have no country. As a woman I want no country. As a woman my country is the whole world.' And if, when reason has said its say, still some obstinate emotion remains, some love of England dropped into a child's ears by the cawing of rooks in an elm tree, by the splash of waves on a beach, or by English voices murmuring nursery rhymes, this drop of pure, if irrational, emotion she will make serve her to give to England first what she desires of peace and freedom for the whole world.

Such then will be the nature of her 'indifference'

and from this indifference certain actions must follow. She will bind herself to take no share in patriotic demonstrations; to assent to no form of national self-praise; to make no part of any claque or audience that encourages war; to absent herself from military displays, tournaments, tattoos, prize-givings and all such ceremonies as encourage the desire to impose 'our' civilization or 'our' dominion upon other people. The psychology of private life, moreover, warrants the belief that this use of indifference by the daughters of educated men would help materially to prevent war. For psychology would seem to show that it is far harder for human beings to take action when other people are indifferent and allow them complete freedom of action, than when their actions are made the centre of excited emotion. The small boy struts and trumpets outside the window: implore him to stop; he goes on: say nothing; he stops. That the daughters of educated men then should give their brothers neither the white feather of cowardice nor the red feather of courage, but no feather at all; that they should shut the bright eyes that rain influence, or let those eyes look elsewhere when war is discussed— that is the duty to which outsiders will train themselves in peace before the threat of death inevitably makes reason powerless.

Such then are some of the methods by which the society, the anonymous and secret Society of Outsiders would help you, Sir, to prevent war and to ensure freedom. Whatever value you may attach to them you will agree that they are duties which your own sex would find it more difficult to carry out than ours; and duties moreover which are specially appropriate to the daughters of educated men. For they would need some acquaintance with the psychology of educated men, and the minds of educated men are more highly trained and their words subtler than those of working men.[16] There are other duties, of course—many have already been outlined in the letters to the other honorary treasurers. But at the risk of some repetition let us roughly and rapidly repeat them, so that they may form a basis for a society of outsiders to take its stand upon. First, they would bind themselves to earn their own livings. The importance of this as a method of ending war is obvious; sufficient stress has already been laid upon the superior cogency of an opinion based upon economic independence over an opinion based upon no income at all or upon a spiritual right to an income to make further proof unnecessary. It follows that an outsider must make it her business to press for a living wage in all the professions now open to her sex; further that she must create new professions in which she can earn the right to an independent opinion. Therefore she must bind herself to press for a money wage for the unpaid worker in her own class—the daughters and sisters of educated men who, as biographies have shown us, are now paid on the truck system, with food, lodging and a pittance of £40 a year. But above all she must press for a wage to be paid by the State legally to the mothers of educated men. The importance of this to our common fight is immeasurable; for it is the most effective way in which we can ensure that the large and very honourable class of married women shall have a mind and a will of their own, with which, if his mind and will are good in her eyes, to support her husband, if bad to resist him, in any case to cease to be 'his woman' and to be herself. You will agree, Sir, without any aspersion upon the lady who bears your name, that to depend upon her for your income would effect a most subtle and undesirable change in your psychology. Apart from that, this measure is of such importance directly to yourselves, in your own fight for liberty and equality and peace, that if any condition were to be attached to the guinea it would be this: that you should provide a wage to be paid by the State to those whose profession is marriage and motherhood. Consider, even at the risk of a digression, what effect this would have upon the birth-rate, in the very class where the birth-rate is falling, in the very class where births are desirable—the educated class. Just as the increase in the pay of soldiers has resulted, the papers say, in additional recruits to the force of arm-bearers, so the same inducement would serve to recruit the child-bearing force, which we can hardly deny to be as necessary and as honourable, but which, because of its poverty, and its hardships, is now failing to attract recruits. That method might succeed where the one in use at present—abuse and ridicule—has failed. But the point which, at the risk of further digression, the outsiders would press upon you is one that vitally concerns your own lives as educated men and the honour and vigour of your professions. For if your wife were paid for her work, the work of bearing and bringing up children, a real wage, a money wage, so that it became an attractive profession instead of being as it is now an unpaid profession, an unpensioned profession, and therefore a precarious and dishonoured profession, your own slavery would be lightened.[17] No longer need you go to the office at nine-thirty and stay there till six. Work could be equally distributed. Patients could be sent to the patientless. Briefs to the briefless. Articles could be left unwritten. Culture would thus be stimulated. You could see the fruit trees flower in spring. You could share the prime of life with your children. And after that prime was over no longer need you be thrown from the machine on to the scrap heap without any life left or interests surviving to parade the environs of Bath or Cheltenham in the care of some unfortunate slave. No longer would you be the Saturday caller, the albatross on the neck of society, the sympathy addict, the deflated work slave calling for replenishment; or, as Herr Hitler puts it, the hero requiring recreation, or, as Signor Mussolini puts it,

[ 317 ]

the wounded warrior requiring female dependants to bandage his wounds.[18] If the State paid your wife a living wage for her work which, sacred though it is, can scarcely be called more sacred than that of the clergyman, yet as his work is paid without derogation so may hers be—if this step which is even more essential to your freedom than to hers were taken the old mill in which the professional man now grinds out his round, often so wearily, with so little pleasure to himself or profit to his profession, would be broken; the opportunity of freedom would be yours; the most degrading of all servitudes, the intellectual servitude, would be ended; the half-man might become whole. But since three hundred millions or so have to be spent upon the arm-bearers, such expenditure is obviously, to use a convenient word supplied by the politicians, 'impracticable' and it is time to return to more feasible projects.

The outsiders then would bind themselves not only to earn their own livings, but to earn them so expertly that their refusal to earn them would be a matter of concern to the work master. They would bind themselves to obtain full knowledge of professional practices, and to reveal any instance of tyranny or abuse in their professions. And they would bind themselves not to continue to make money in any profession, but to cease all competition and to practise their profession experimentally, in the interests of research and for love of the work itself, when they had earned

enough to live upon. Also they would bind themselves to remain outside any profession hostile to
freedom, such as the making or the improvement of
the weapons of war. And they would bind themselves
to refuse to take office or honour from any society
which, while professing to respect liberty, restricts it,
like the universities of Oxford and Cambridge. And
they would consider it their duty to investigate the
claims of all public societies to which, like the Church
and the universities, they are forced to contribute as
taxpayers as carefully and fearlessly as they would
investigate the claims of private societies to which
they contribute voluntarily. They would make it their
business to scrutinize the endowments of the schools
and universities and the objects upon which that
money is spent. As with the educational, so with the
religious profession. By reading the New Testament
in the first place and next those divines and historians
whose works are all easily accessible to the daughters
of educated men, they would make it their business
to have some knowledge of the Christian religion and
its history. Further they would inform themselves of
the practice of that religion by attending Church
services, by analysing the spiritual and intellectual
value of sermons; by criticizing the opinions of men
whose profession is religion as freely as they would
criticize the opinions of any other body of men. Thus
they would be creative in their activities, not merely
critical. By criticizing education they would help to

create a civilized society which protects culture and intellectual liberty. By criticizing religion they would attempt to free the religious spirit from its present servitude and would help, if need be, to create a new religion based it might well be upon the New Testament, but, it might well be, very different from the religion now erected upon that basis. And in all this, and in much more than we have time to particularize, they would be helped, you will agree, by their position as outsiders, that freedom from unreal loyalties, that freedom from interested motives which are at present assured them by the State.

It would be easy to define in greater number and more exactly the duties of those who belong to the Society of Outsiders, but not profitable. Elasticity is essential; and some degree of secrecy, as will be shown later, is at present even more essential. But the description thus loosely and imperfectly given is enough to show you, Sir, that the Society of Outsiders has the same ends as your society—freedom, equality, peace; but that it seeks to achieve them by the means that a different sex, a different tradition, a different education, and the different values which result from those differences have placed within our reach. Broadly speaking, the main distinction between us who are outside society and you who are inside society must be that whereas you will make use of the means provided by your position—leagues, conferences, campaigns, great names, and all such public measures as your wealth and political influence place within your reach—we, remaining outside, will experiment not with public means in public but with private means in private. Those experiments will not be merely critical but creative. To take two obvious instances—the outsiders will dispense with pageantry not from any puritanical dislike of beauty. On the contrary, it will be one of their aims to increase private beauty; the beauty of spring, summer, autumn; the beauty of flowers, silks, clothes; the beauty which brims not only every field and wood but every barrow in Oxford Street; the scattered beauty which needs only to be combined by artists in order to become visible to all. But they will dispense with the dictated, regimented, official pageantry, in which only one sex takes an active part—those ceremonies, for example, which depend upon the deaths of kings, or their coronations to inspire them. Again, they will dispense with personal distinctions—medals, ribbons, badges, hoods, gowns—not from any dislike of personal adornment, but because of the obvious effect of such distinctions to constrict, to stereotype and to destroy. Here, as so often, the example of the Fascist States is at hand to instruct us—for if we have no example of what we wish to be, we have, what is perhaps equally valuable, a daily and illuminating example of what we do not wish to be. With the example then, that they give us of the power of medals, symbols, orders and even, it would seem, of decorated ink-pots[19] to hypnotize the human mind it must be our aim not to submit ourselves to such hypnotism. We must extinguish the coarse glare of advertisement and publicity, not merely because the limelight is apt to be held in incompetent hands, but because of the psychological effect of such illumination upon those who receive it. Consider next time you drive along a country road the attitude of a rabbit caught in the glare of a head-lamp—its glazed eyes, its rigid paws. Is there not good reason to think without going outside our own country, that the 'attitudes', the false and unreal positions taken by the human form in England as well as in Germany, are due to the limelight which paralyses the free action of the human faculties and inhibits the human power to change and create new wholes much as a strong head-lamp paralyses the little creatures who run out of the darkness into its beams? It is a guess; guessing is dangerous; yet we have some reason to guide us in the guess that ease and freedom, the power to change and the power to grow, can only be preserved by obscurity; and that if we wish to help the human mind to create, and to prevent it from scoring the same rut repeatedly, we must do what we can to shroud it in darkness.

But enough of guessing. To return to facts—what chance is there, you may ask, that such a Society of Outsiders without office, meetings, leaders or any hierarchy, without so much as a form to be filled up, or a secretary to be paid, can be brought into existence, let alone work to any purpose? Indeed it would have been waste of time to write even so rough a definition of the Outsiders' Society were it merely a bubble of words, a covert form of sex or class glorification, serving, as so many such expressions do, to relieve the writer's emotion, lay the blame elsewhere, and then burst. Happily there is a model in being, a model from which the above sketch has been taken, furtively it is true, for the model, far from sitting still to be painted, dodges and disappears. That model then, the evidence that such a body, whether named or unnamed, exists and works is provided not yet by history or biography, for the outsiders have only had a positive existence for twenty years—that is since the professions were opened to the daughters of educated men. But evidence of their existence is provided by history and biography in the raw—by the newspapers that is, sometimes openly in the lines, sometimes covertly between them. There, anyone who wishes to verify the existence of such a body, can find innumerable proofs. Many, it is obvious, are of dubious value. For example, the fact that an immense amount of work is done by the daughters of educated men without pay or for very little pay need not be taken as a proof that they are experimenting of their own free will in the psychological value of poverty. Nor need the fact that many daughters of educated men do not 'eat properly'[20] serve as a proof that they are experimenting in the physical value of undernourishment. Nor need the fact that a very small proportion of women compared with men accept honours be held to prove that they are experimenting in the virtues of obscurity. Many such experiments are forced experiments and therefore of no positive value. But others of a much more positive kind are coming daily to the surface of the Press. Let us examine three only, in order that we may prove our statement that the Society of Outsiders is in being. The first is straightforward enough.

Speaking at a bazaar last week at the Plumstead Common Baptist Church the Mayoress (of Woolwich) said: '. . . I myself would not even do as much as darn a sock to help in a war.' These remarks are resented by the majority of the Woolwich public, who hold that the Mayoress was, to say the least, rather tactless. Some 12,000 Woolwich electors are employed in Woolwich Arsenal on armament making.[21]

There is no need to comment upon the tactlessness of such a statement made publicly, in such circumstances; but the courage can scarcely fail to command our admiration, and the value of the experiment, from a practical point of view, should other mayoresses in other towns and other countries where the electors are employed in armament-making follow suit may well be immeasurable. At any rate, we shall agree that the Mayoress of Woolwich, Mrs Kathleen Rance, has made a courageous and effective experiment in the prevention of war by not knitting socks. For a second proof that the outsiders are at work let us choose another example from the daily paper, one that is less obvious, but still you will agree an outsider's experiment, a very original experiment, and one that may be of great value to the cause of peace.

Speaking of the work of the great voluntary associations for the playing of certain games, Miss Clarke [Miss E. R. Clarke of the Board of Education] referred to the women's organizations for hockey, lacrosse, netball, and cricket, and pointed out that under the rules there could be no cup or award of any kind to a successful team. The 'gates' for their matches might be a little smaller than for the men's games, but their players played the game for the love of it, and they seemed to be proving that cups and awards are not necessary to stimulate interest for each year the numbers of players steadily continued to increase.[22]

That, you will agree, is an extraordinarily interesting experiment, one that may well bring about a psychological change of great value in human nature, and a change that may be of real help in preventing war. It is further of interest because it is an experiment that outsiders, owing to their comparative freedom from certain inhibitions and persuasions, can carry out much more easily than those who are necessarily exposed to such influences inside. That statement is corroborated in a very interesting way by the following quotation:

Official football circles here [Wellingborough, Northants] regard with anxiety the growing popularity of girls' football. A secret meeting of the Northants Football Association's consultative committee was held here last night to discuss the playing of a girls' match on the Peterborough ground. Members of the Committee are reticent . . . One member, however, said today: 'The Northants Football Association is to forbid women's football. This popularity of girls' football comes when many men's clubs in the country are in a parlous state through lack of support. Another serious aspect is the possibility of grave injury to women players.[23]

There we have proof positive of those inhibitions and persuasions which make it harder for your sex to experiment freely in altering current values than for ours; and without spending time upon the delicacies of psychological analysis even a hasty glance at the reasons given by this Association for its decision will throw a valuable light upon the reasons which lead other and even more important associations to come to their decisions. But to return to the outsiders' experiments. For our third example let us choose what we may call an experiment in passivity.

A remarkable change in the attitude of young women to the Church was discussed by Canon F. A. Barry, vicar of St Mary the Virgin (the University Church), at Oxford last night . . . The task before the Church, he said, was nothing less than to make civilization moral, and this was a great cooperative task which demanded all that Christians could bring to it. It simply could not be carried through by men alone. For a century, or a couple of centuries, women had predominated in the congregations in roughly the ratio of 75 per cent to 25 per cent. The whole situation was now changing, and what the keen observer would notice in almost any church in England was the paucity of young women ... Among the student population the young women were, on the whole, farther away from the Church of England and the Christian faith than the young men.[24]

That again is an experiment of very great interest. It is, as we have said, a passive experiment. For while the first example was an outspoken refusal to knit socks in order to discourage war, and the second was an attempt to prove whether cups and awards are necessary to stimulate interest in games, the third is an attempt to discover what happens if the daughters of educated men absent themselves from church. Without being in itself more valuable than the others, it is of more practical interest because it is obviously the kind of experiment that great numbers of outsiders can practise with very little difficulty or danger. To absent yourself—that is easier than to speak aloud at a bazaar, or to draw up rules of an original kind for playing games. Therefore it is worth watching very carefully to see what effect the experiment of absenting oneself has had—if any. The results are positive and they are encouraging. There can be no doubt that the Church is becoming concerned about the attitude to the Church of educated men's daughters at the universities. The report of the Archbishops' Commission on the Ministry of Women is there to prove it. This document, which costs only one shilling and should be in the hands of all educated men's daughters, points out that 'one outstanding difference between men's colleges and women's colleges is the absence in the latter of a chaplain.' It reflects that 'It is natural that in this period of their lives they [the students] exercise to the full their critical faculties.' It deplores the fact that 'Very few women coming to the universities can now afford to offer continuous voluntary service either in social or in directly religious work.' And it concludes that 'There are many special spheres in which such services are particularly needed, and the time has clearly come when the functions and position of women within the Church require further determination.'[25] Whether this concern is due to the empty churches at Oxford, or whether the voices of the 'older schoolgirls' at Isleworth expressing 'very grave dissatisfaction at the way in which organized religion was carried on'[26] have somehow penetrated to those august spheres where their sex is not supposed to speak, or whether our incorrigible idealistic sex is at last beginning to take to heart Bishop Gore's warning, 'Men do not value ministrations which are gratuitous,'[27] and to express the opinion that a salary of £150 a year—the highest that the Church allows her daughters as deaconesses—is not enough—whatever the reason, considerable uneasiness at the attitude of educated men's daughters is apparent; and this experiment in passivity, whatever our belief in the value of the Church of England as a spiritual agency, is highly encouraging to us as outsiders. For it seems to show that to be passive is to be active; those also serve who remain outside.* By making their absence felt their presence becomes desirable. What light this throws upon the power of outsiders to abolish or modify other institutions of which they disapprove, whether public dinners, public speeches, Lord Mayors' banquets and other obsolete ceremonies are pervious to indifference and will yield to its pressure, are questions, frivolous questions, that may well amuse our leisure and stimulate our curiosity. But that is not now the object before us. We have tried to prove to you, Sir, by giving three different examples of three different kinds of experiment that the Society of Outsiders is in being and at work. When you consider that these examples have all come to the surface of the newspaper you will agree that they represent a far greater number of private and submerged experiments of which there is no public proof. Also you will agree that they substantiate the model of the society given above, and prove that it was no visionary sketch drawn at random but based upon a real body working by different means for the same ends that you have set before us in your own society. Keen observers, like Canon Barry, could, if they liked, discover many more proofs that experiments are being made not only in the empty churches of Oxford. Mr Wells even might be led to believe if he put his ear to the ground that a movement is going forward, not altogether imperceptibly, among educated men's daughters against the Nazi and the Fascist. But it is essential that the movement should escape the notice even of keen observers and of famous novelists.

Secrecy is essential. We must still hide what we are doing and thinking even though what we are doing and thinking is for our common cause. The necessity for this, in certain circumstances, is not hard to discover. When salaries are low, as Whitaker proves that they are, and jobs are hard to get and keep, as everybody knows them to be, it is, 'to say the least, rather tactless,' as the newspaper puts it, to criticize your master. Still, in country districts, as you yourself may be aware, farm labourers will not vote Labour. Economically, the educated man's daughter is much on a level with the farm labourer. But it is scarcely necessary for us to waste time in searching out what reason it is that inspires both his and her secrecy. Fear is a powerful reason; those who are economically dependent have strong reasons for fear. We need explore no further. But here you may remind us of a certain guinea, and draw our attention to the proud boast that our gift, small though it was, had made it possible not merely to burn a certain corrupt word, but to speak freely without fear or flattery. The boast it seems had an element of brag in it. Some fear, some ancestral memory prophesying war, still remains, it seems. There are still subjects that educated people, when they are of different sexes, even though financially independent, veil, or hint at in guarded terms and then pass on. You may have observed it in real life; you may have detected it in biography. Even when they meet privately and talk, as we have boasted, about 'politics and people, war and peace, barbarism and civilization', yet they evade and conceal. But it is so important to accustom ourselves to the duties of free speech, for without private there can be no public freedom, that we must try to uncover this fear and to face it. What then can be the nature of the fear that still makes concealment necessary between educated people and reduces our boasted freedom to a farce? . . . Again there are three dots; again they represent a gulf—of silence this time, of silence inspired by fear. And since we lack both the courage to explain it and the skill, let us lower the veil of St Paul between us, in other words take shelter behind an interpreter. Happily we have one at hand whose credentials are above suspicion. It is none other than the pamphlet from which quotation has already been made, the report of the Archbishops' Commission on the Ministry of Women—a document of the highest interest for many reasons. For not only does it throw light of a searching and scientific nature upon this fear, but it gives us an

[ 331 ]

opportunity to consider that profession which, since it is the highest of all may be taken as the type of all, the profession of religion, about which, purposely, very little has yet been said. And since it is the type of all it may throw light upon the other professions about which something has been said. You will pardon us therefore if we pause here to examine this report in some detail.

The Commission was appointed by the Archbishops of Canterbury and York 'in order to examine any theological or other relevant principles which have governed or ought to govern the Church in the development of the Ministry of Women'.[28] Now the profession of religion, for our purposes the Church of England, though it seems on the surface to resemble the others in certain respects—it enjoys, Whitaker says, a large income, owns much property, and has a hierarchy of officials drawing salaries and taking precedence one of the other—yet ranks above all the professions. The Archbishop of Canterbury precedes the Lord High Chancellor; the Archbishop of York precedes the Prime Minister. And it is the highest of all the professions because it is the profession of religion. But what, we may ask, is 'religion'? What the Christian religion is has been laid down once and for all by the founder of that religion in words that can be read by all in a translation of singular beauty; and whether or not we accept the interpretation that has been put on them we cannot deny them to be words of the most profound meaning. It can thus safely be said that whereas few people know what medicine is, or what law is, everyone who owns a copy of the New Testament knows what religion meant in the mind of its founder. Therefore, when in the year 1935 the daughters of educated men said that they wished to have the profession of religion opened to them, the priests of that profession, who correspond roughly to the doctors and barristers in the other professions, were forced not merely to consult some statute or charter which reserves the right to practise that profession professionally to the male sex; they were forced to consult the New Testament. They did so; and the result, as the Commissioners point out, was that they found that 'the Gospels show us that our Lord regarded men and women alike as members of the same spiritual kingdom, as children of God's family, and as possessors of the same spiritual capacities . . .' In proof of this they quote: 'There is neither male nor female: for ye are all one in Christ Jesus' (Gal. iii, 28). It would seem then that the founder of Christianity believed that neither training nor sex was needed for this profession. He chose his disciples from the working class from which he sprang himself. The prime qualification was some rare gift which in those early days was bestowed capriciously upon carpenters and fishermen, and upon women also. As the Commission points out there can be no doubt that in those early days there were prophetesses—women upon whom the divine gift had descended. Also they were allowed to preach. St Paul, for example, lays it down that women, when praying in public, should be veiled. 'The implication is that if veiled a woman might prophesy [i.e. preach] and lead in prayer.' How then can they be excluded from the priesthood since they were thought fit by the founder of the religion and by one of his apostles to preach? That was the question, and the Commission solved it by appealing not to the mind of the founder, but to the mind of the Church. That, of course, involved a distinction. For the mind of the Church had to be interpreted by another mind, and that mind was St Paul's mind; and St Paul, in interpreting that mind, changed his mind. For after summoning from the depths of the past certain venerable if obscure figures—Lydia and Chloe, Euodia and Syntyche, Tryphoena and Tryphosa and Persis,* debating their status, and deciding what was the difference between a prophetess and presbyteress, what the standing of a deaconess in the pre-Nicene Church and what in the post-Nicene Church, the Commissioners once more have recourse to St Paul, and say: 'In any case it is clear that the author of the Pastoral Epistles, be he St Paul or another, regarded woman as being debarred on the ground of her sex from the position of an official "teacher" in the Church, or from any office involving the exercise of a governmental authority over a man' (1 Tim. ii, 12).

That, it may frankly be said, is not so satisfactory as it might be; for we cannot altogether reconcile the ruling of St Paul, or another, with the ruling of Christ himself who 'regarded men and women alike as members of the same spiritual kingdom ... and as possessors of the same spiritual capacities'. But it is futile to quibble over the meaning of the words, when we are so soon in the presence of facts. Whatever Christ meant, or St Paul meant, the fact was that in the fourth or fifth century the profession of religion had become so highly organized that 'the deacon (unlike the deaconess) may, "after serving unto well-pleasing the ministry committed unto him", aspire to be appointed eventually to higher offices in the Church; whereas for the deaconess the Church prays simply that God "would grant unto her the Holy Spirit ... that she may worthily accomplish the work committed to her"'. In three or four centuries, it appears, the prophet or prophetess whose message was voluntary and untaught became extinct; and their places were taken by the three orders of bishops, priests and deacons, who are invariably men, and invariably, as Whitaker points out, paid men, for when the Church became a profession its professors were paid. Thus the profession of religion seems to have been originally much what the profession of literature is now.[29] It was originally open to anyone who had received the gift of prophecy. No training was needed; the professional requirements were simple in the extreme—a voice and a market-place, a pen and paper. Emily Brontë, for instance, who wrote

No coward soul is mine,
No trembler in the world's storm-troubled sphere;
I see Heaven's glories shine,
And faith shines equal, arming me from fear.

O God within my breast,
Almighty, ever-present Deity!
Life—that in me has rest,
As I—undying Life—have power in Thee!

though not worthy to be a priest in the Church of England, is the spiritual descendant of some ancient prophetess, who prophesied when prophecy was a voluntary and unpaid occupation. But when the Church became a profession, required special knowledge of its prophets and paid them for imparting it, one sex remained inside; the other was excluded. 'The deacons rose in dignity—partly no doubt from their close association with the bishops—and become subordinate ministers of worship and of the sacraments; but the deaconess shared only in the preliminary stages of this evolution.' How elementary that evolution has been is proved by the fact that in England in 1938 the salary of an archbishop is £15,000; the salary of a bishop is £10,000 and the salary of a dean is £3,000. But the salary of a deaconess is £150; and as for the 'parish worker', who 'is called upon to assist in almost every department of parish life', whose 'work is exacting and often solitary . . .' she is paid from £120 to £150 a year; nor is there anything to surprise us in the statement that 'prayer needs to be the very centre of her activities'. Thus we might even go further than the Commissioners and say that the evolution of the deaconess is not merely 'elementary', it is positively stunted; for though she is ordained, and 'ordination . . . conveys an indelible character, and involves the obligation of lifelong service', she must remain outside the Church; and rank beneath the humblest curate. Such is the decision of the Church. For the Commission, having consulted the mind and tradition of the Church, reported finally: 'While the Commission as a whole would not give their positive assent to the view that a woman is inherently incapable of receiving the grace of Order, and consequently to admission to any of the three Orders, we believe that the general mind of the Church is still in accord with the continuous tradition of a male priesthood.'

By thus showing that the highest of all the professions has many points of similarity with the other professions our interpreter, you will admit, has thrown further light upon the soul or essence of those professions. We must now ask him to help us, if he will, to analyse the nature of that fear which still, as we have admitted, makes it impossible for us to speak freely as free people should. Here again he is of service. Though identical in many respects, one very profound difference between the religious profession and other professions has been noted above: the Church being a spiritual profession has to give spiritual and not merely historical reasons for its actions; it has to consult the mind, not the law.[29] Therefore when the daughters of educated men wished to be admitted to the profession of the Church it seemed advisable to the Commissioners to give psychological and not merely historical reasons for their refusal to admit them. They therefore called in Professor Grensted, DD, the Nolloth Professor of the Philosophy of the Christian Religion in the University of Oxford, and asked him 'to summarize the relevant psychological and physiological material', and to indicate 'the grounds for the opinions and recommendations put forward by the Commission'. Now psychology is not theology; and the psychology of the sexes, as the Professor insisted, and 'its bearing upon human conduct, is still a matter for specialists . . . and . . . its interpretation remains controversial, in many respects obscure.' But he gave his evidence for what it was worth, and it is evidence that throws so much light upon the origin of the fear which we have admitted and deplored that we can do no better than follow his words exactly.

It was represented [he said] in evidence before the Commission that man has a natural precedence of woman. This view, in the sense intended, cannot be supported psychologically. Psychologists fully recognize the fact of male dominance, but this must not be confused with male superiority, still less with any type of precedence which could have a bearing upon questions as to the admissibility of one sex rather than the other to Holy Orders.

The psychologist, therefore, can only throw light upon certain facts. And this was the first fact he investigated.

It is clearly a fact of the very greatest practical importance that strong feeling is aroused by any suggestion that women should be admitted to the status and functions of the threefold Order of the Ministry. The evidence before the Commission went to show that this feeling is predominantly hostile to such proposals ... This strength of feeling, conjoined with a wide variety of rational explanations, is clear evidence of the presence of powerful and widespread subconscious motive. In the absence of detailed analytical material, of which there seems to be no record in this particular connection, it nevertheless remains clear that infantile fixation plays a predominant part in determining the strong emotion with which this whole subject is commonly approached.

The exact nature of this fixation must necessarily differ with different individuals, and suggestions which can be made as to its origin can only be general in character. But whatever be the exact value and interpretation of the material upon which theories of the 'Œdipus complex' and the 'castration complex' have been founded, it is clear that the general acceptance of male dominance, and still more of feminine inferiority, resting upon subconscious ideas of woman as 'man manqué', has its background in infantile conceptions of this type. These commonly, and even usually, survive in the adult, despite their irrationality, and betray their presence, below the level of conscious thought, by the strength of the emotions to which they give rise. It is strongly in support of this view that the admission of women to Holy Orders, and especially to the ministry of the sanctuary, is so commonly regarded as something shameful. This sense of shame cannot be regarded in any other light than as a non-rational sex-taboo.

Here we can take the Professor's word for it that he has sought, and found, 'ample evidence of these unconscious forces', both in Pagan religions and in the Old Testament, and so follow him to his conclusion:

At the same time it must not be forgotten that the Christian conception of the priesthood rests not upon these subconscious emotional factors, but upon the institution of Christ. It thus not only fulfils but supersedes the priesthoods of paganism and the Old Testament. So far as psychology is concerned there is no theoretical reason why this Christian priesthood should not be exercised by women as well as by men and in exactly the same sense. The difficulties which the psychologist foresees are emotional and practical only.[30]

With that conclusion we may leave him.

The Commissioners, you will agree, have performed the delicate and difficult task that we asked them to undertake. They have acted as interpreters between us. They have given us an admirable example of a profession in its purest state; and shown us how a profession bases itself upon mind and tradition. They have further explained why it is that educated people when they are of different sexes do not speak openly upon certain subjects. They have shown why the outsiders, even when there is no question of financial dependence, may still be afraid to speak freely or to experiment openly. And, finally, in words of scientific precision, they have revealed to us the nature of that fear. For as Professor Grensted gave his evidence, we, the daughters of educated men, seemed to be watching a surgeon at work—an impartial and scientific operator, who, as he dissected the human mind by human means laid bare for all to see what cause, what root lies at the bottom of our fear. It is an egg. Its scientific name is 'infantile fixation'. We, being unscientific, have named it wrongly. An egg we called it; a germ. We smelt it in the atmosphere; we detected its presence in Whitehall, in the universities, in the Church. Now undoubtedly the Professor has defined it and described it so accurately that no daughter of an educated man, however uneducated she may be, can miscall it or misinterpret it in future. Listen to the description. 'Strong feeling is aroused by any suggestion that women be admitted'—it matters not to which priesthood; the priesthood of medicine or the priesthood of science or the priesthood of the Church. Strong feeling, she can corroborate the Professor, is undoubtedly shown should she ask to be admitted. 'This strength of feeling is clear evidence of the presence of powerful and subconscious motive.' She will take the Professor's word for that, and even supply him with some motives that have escaped him. Let us draw attention to two only. There is the money motive for excluding her, to put it plainly. Are not salaries motives now, whatever they may have been in the time of Christ? The archbishop has £15,000, the deaconess £150; and the Church, so the Commissioners say, is poor. To pay women more would be to pay men less. Secondly, is there not a motive, a psychological motive, for excluding her, hidden beneath what the Commissioners call a 'practical consideration'? 'At present a married priest,' they tell us, 'is able to fulfil the requirements of the ordination service "to forsake and set aside all wordly cares and studies" largely because his wife can undertake the care of the household and the family . . .'31 To be able to set aside all wordly cares and studies and lay them upon another person is a motive, to some of great attractive force; for some undoubtedly wish to withdraw and study, as theology with its refinements, and scholarship with its subtleties, prove; to others, it is true, the motive is a bad motive, a vicious motive, the cause of that separation between the Church and the people; between literature and the people; between the husband and the wife which has had its part in putting the whole of our Commonwealth out of gear. But whatever the powerful and subconscious motives may be that lie behind the exclusion of women from the priesthoods, and plainly we cannot count them, let alone dig to the roots of them here, the educated man's daughter can testify from her own experience that they 'commonly, and even usually, survive in the adult and betray their presence, below the level of conscious thought, by the strength of the emotions to which they give rise'. And you will agree that to oppose strong emotion needs courage; and that when courage fails, silence and evasion are likely to manifest themselves.

But now that the interpreters have performed their task, it is time for us to raise the veil of St Paul and to attempt, face to face, a rough and clumsy analysis of that fear and of the anger which causes that fear; for they may have some bearing upon the question you put us, how we can help you to prevent war. Let us suppose, then, that in the course of that bi-sexual private conversation about politics and people, war and peace, barbarism and civilization, some question has cropped up, about admitting, shall we say, the daughters of educated men to the Church or the Stock Exchange or the diplomatic service. The question is adumbrated merely; but we on our side of the table become aware at once of some 'strong emotion' on your side 'arising from some motive below the

[ 343 ]

level of conscious thought' by the ringing of an alarm bell within us; a confused but tumultuous clamour: You shall not, shall not, shall not ... The physical symptoms are unmistakable. Nerves erect themselves; fingers automatically tighten upon spoon or cigarette; a glance at the private psychometer shows that the emotional temperature has risen from ten to twenty degrees above normal. Intellectually, there is a strong desire either to be silent; or to change the conversation; to drag in, for example, some old family servant, called Crosby, perhaps, whose dog Rover has died* ... and so evade the issue and lower the temperature.

But what analysis can we attempt of the emotions on the other side of the table—your side? Often, to be candid, while we are talking about Crosby, we are asking questions—hence a certain flatness in the dialogue—about you. What are the powerful and subconscious motives that are raising the hackles on your side of the table? Is the old savage who has killed a bison asking the other old savage to admire his prowess? Is the tired professional man demanding sympathy and resenting competition? Is the patriarch calling for the siren? Is dominance craving for submission? And, most persistent and difficult of all the questions that our silence covers, what possible satisfaction can dominance give to the dominator?[32] Now, since Professor Grensted has said that the psychology of the sexes is 'still a matter for specialists', while 'its interpretation remains controversial and in many respects obscure', it would be politic perhaps to leave these questions to be answered by specialists. But since, on the other hand, if common men and women are to be free they must learn to speak freely, we cannot leave the psychology of the sexes to the charge of specialists. There are two good reasons why we must try to analyse both our fear and your anger; first, because such fear and anger prevent real freedom in the private house; second, because such fear and anger may prevent real freedom in the public world: they may have a positive share in causing war. Let us then grope our way amateurishly enough among these very ancient and obscure emotions which we have known ever since the time of Antigone and Ismene* and Creon at least; which St Paul himself seems to have felt; but which the Professors have only lately brought to the surface and named 'infantile fixation', 'Œdipus complex', and the rest. We must try, however feebly, to analyse those emotions since you have asked us to help you in any way we can to protect liberty and to prevent war.

Let us then examine this 'infantile fixation', for such it seems is the proper name, in order that we may connect it with the question you have put to us. Once more, since we are generalists not specialists, we must rely upon such evidence as we can collect from history, biography, and from the daily paper— the only evidence that is available to the daughters of educated men. We will take our first example of infantile fixation from biography, and once more we will have recourse to Victorian biography because it is only in the Victorian age that biography becomes rich and representative. Now there are so many cases of infantile fixation as defined by Professor Grensted in Victorian biography that we scarcely know which to choose. The case of Mr Barrett of Wimpole Street is, perhaps, the most famous and the best authenticated. Indeed, it is so famous that the facts scarcely bear repetition. We all know the story of the father who would allow neither sons nor daughters to marry; we all know in greatest detail how his daughter Elizabeth was forced to conceal her lover from her father; how she fled with her lover from the house in Wimpole Street; and how her father never forgave her for that act of disobedience. We shall agree that Mr Barrett's emotions were strong in the extreme; and their strength makes it obvious that they had their origin in some dark place below the level of conscious thought. That is a typical, a classical case of infantile fixation which we can all bear in mind. But there are others less famous which a little investigation will bring to the surface and show to be of the same nature. There is the case of the Rev. Patrick Brontë. The Rev. Arthur Nicholls was in love with his daughter, Charlotte; 'What his words were,' she wrote, when Mr Nicholls proposed to her, 'you can't imagine; his manner you can hardly realize nor can I forget it . . . I asked if he had spoken to Papa. He said he dared not.' Why did he dare not? He was strong and young and passionately in love; the father was old. The reason is immediately apparent. 'He [the Rev. Patrick Brontë] always disapproved of marriages, and constantly talked against them. But he more than disapproved this time; he could not bear the idea of this attachment of Mr Nicholls to his daughter. Fearing the consequences . . . she made haste to give her father a promise that, on the morrow, Mr Nicholls should have a distinct refusal.'33 Mr Nicholls left Haworth; Charlotte remained with her father. Her married life—it was to be a short one—was shortened still further by her father's wish.

For a third example of infantile fixation let us choose one that is less simple, but for that reason more illuminating. There is the case of Mr Jex-Blake. Here we have the case of a father who is not confronted with his daughter's marriage but with his daughter's wish to earn her living. That wish also would seem to have aroused in the father a very strong emotion and an emotion which also seems to have its origin in the levels below conscious thought. Again with your leave we will call it a case of infantile fixation. The daughter, Sophia, was offered a small sum for teaching mathematics; and she asked her father's permission to take it. That permission was instantly and heatedly refused. 'Dearest, I have only this moment heard that you contemplate being *paid* for the tutorship. It would be quite beneath you,

darling, and I *cannot consent* to it.' [The italics are the
father's.] 'Take the post as one of honour and useful-
ness, and I shall be glad . . . But to be *paid* for the
work would be to alter the thing *completely*, and
would lower you sadly in the eyes of almost everybody.' That is a very interesting statement. Sophia,
indeed, was led to argue the matter. Why was it
beneath her, she asked, why should it lower her?
Taking money for work did not lower Tom in
anybody's eyes. That, Mr Jex-Blake explained, was
quite a different matter; Tom was a man; Tom 'feels
bound as a *man* . . . to support his wife and family';
Tom had therefore taken 'the *plain path* of duty'. Still
Sophia was not satisfied. She argued—not only was
she poor and wanted the money; but also she felt
strongly 'the honest, and I believe perfectly justifiable
pride of earning'. Thus pressed Mr Jex-Blake at last
gave, under a semi-transparent cover, the real reason
why he objected to her taking money. He offered to
give her the money himself if she would refuse to
take it from the College. It was plain, therefore, that
he did not object to her taking money; what he
objected to was her taking money from another man.
The curious nature of his proposal did not escape
Sophia's scrutiny. 'In that case,' she said, 'I must say
to the Dean, not, "I am willing to work without
payment," but "My Father prefers that I should
receive payment from *him*, not from the College,"
and I think the Dean would think us both ridiculous,

or at least foolish.' Whatever interpretation the Dean might have put upon Mr Jex-Blake's behaviour, we can have no doubt what emotion was at the root of it. He wished to keep his daughter in his own power. If she took money from him she remained in his power; if she took it from another man not only was she becoming independent of Mr Jex-Blake, she was becoming dependent upon another man. That he wished her to depend upon him, and felt obscurely that this desirable dependence could only be secured by financial dependence is proved indirectly by another of his veiled statements. 'If you married tomorrow to my liking—and I don't believe you would ever marry otherwise—I should give you a good fortune.'[34] If she became a wage-earner, she could dispense with the fortune and marry whom she liked. The case of Mr Jex-Blake is very easily diagnosed, but it is a very important case because it is a normal case, a typical case. Mr Jex-Blake was no monster of Wimpole Street; he was an ordinary father; he was doing what thousands of other Victorian fathers whose cases remain unpublished were doing daily. It is a case, therefore, that explains much that lies at the root of Victorian psychology—that psychology of the sexes which is still, Professor Grensted tells us, so obscure. The case of Mr Jex-Blake shows that the daughter must not on any account be allowed to make money because if she makes money she will be independent of her father and free to marry any man she chooses. Therefore the daughter's desire to earn her living rouses two different forms of jealousy. Each is strong separately; together they are very strong. It is further significant that in order to justify this very strong emotion which has its origin below the levels of conscious thought Mr Jex-Blake had recourse to one of the commonest of all evasions; the argument which is not an argument but an appeal to the emotions. He appealed to the very deep, ancient and complex emotion which we may, as amateurs, call the womanhood emotion. To take money was beneath her he said; if she took money she would lower herself in the eyes of almost everybody. Tom being a man would not be lowered; it was her sex that made the difference. He appealed to her womanhood.

Whenever a man makes that appeal to a woman he rouses in her, it is safe to say, a conflict of emotions of a very deep and primitive kind which it is extremely difficult for her to analyse or to reconcile. It may serve to transmit the feeling if we compare it with the confused conflict of manhood emotions that is roused in you, Sir, should a woman hand you a white feather.[35] It is interesting to see how Sophia, in the year 1859, tried to deal with this emotion. Her first instinct was to attack the most obvious form of womanhood, that which lay uppermost in her consciousness and seemed to be responsible for her father's attitude—her ladyhood. Like other educated

[ 350 ]

—

men's daughters Sophia Jex-Blake was what is called 'a lady'. It was the lady who could not earn money; therefore the lady must be killed. 'Do you honestly, father, think,' she asked, 'any lady lowered by the mere act of receiving money? Did you think the less of Mrs Teed because you paid her?' Then, as if aware that Mrs Teed, being a governess, was not on a par with herself who came of an upper middle-class family, 'whose lineage will be found in *Burke's Landed Gentry*', she quickly called in to help her to kill the lady 'Mary Jane Evans . . . one of the proudest families of our relations', and then Miss Wodehouse, 'whose family is better and older than mine'—they both thought her right in wishing to earn money. And not only did Miss Wodehouse think her right in wishing to earn money; Miss Wodehouse 'showed she agreed with my opinions by her actions. She sees no meanness in earning, but in those that think it mean. When accepting Maurice's school, she said to him, most nobly, I think, "If you think it better that I should work as a paid mistress, I will take any salary you please; if not, I am willing to do the work freely and for nothing."' The lady, sometimes, was a noble lady; and that lady it was hard to kill; but killed she must be, as Sophia realized, if Sophia were to enter that Paradise where 'lots of girls walk about London when and where they please', that 'Elysium upon earth', which is (or was), Queen's College, Harley Street,* where the daughters of educated men enjoy

[ 351 ]

the happiness not of ladies 'but of Queens—Work and independence!'[36] Thus Sophia's first instinct was to kill the lady;[37] but when the lady was killed the woman still remained. We can see her, concealing and excusing the disease of infantile fixation, more clearly in the other two cases. It was the woman, the human being whose sex made it her sacred duty to sacrifice herself to the father, whom Charlotte Brontë and Elizabeth Barrett had to kill. If it was difficult to kill the lady, it was even more difficult to kill the woman. Charlotte found it at first almost impossible. She refused her lover. '. . . thus thoughtfully for her father, and unselfishly for herself [she] put aside all consideration of how she should reply, excepting as he wished.' She loved Arthur Nicholls; but she refused him. '. . . she held herself simply passive, as far as words and actions went, while she suffered acute pain from the strong expressions which her father used in speaking of Mr Nicholls.' She waited; she suffered; until 'the great conqueror Time,' as Mrs Gaskell puts it, 'achieved his victory over strong prejudice and human resolve.' Her father consented. The great conqueror, however, had met his match in Mr Barrett; Elizabeth Barrett waited; Elizabeth suffered; at last Elizabeth fled.

The extreme force of the emotions to which the infantile fixation gives rise is proved by these three cases. It is remarkable, we may agree. It was a force that could quell not only Charlotte Brontë but Arthur

Nicholls; not only Elizabeth Barrett but Robert Browning. It was a force thus that could do battle with the strongest of human passions—the love of men and women; and could compel the most brilliant and the boldest of Victorian sons and daughters to quail before it; to cheat the father, to deceive the father, and then to fly from the father. But to what did it owe this amazing force? Partly as these cases make clear, to the fact that the infantile fixation was protected by society. Nature, law and property were all ready to excuse and conceal it. It was easy for Mr Barrett, Mr Jex-Blake and the Rev. Patrick Brontë to hide the real nature of their emotions from themselves. If they wished that their daughter should stay at home, society agreed that they were right. If the daughter protested, then nature came to their help. A daughter who left her father was an unnatural daughter; her womanhood was suspect. Should she persist further, then law came to his help. A daughter who left her father had no means of supporting herself. The lawful professions were shut to her. Finally, if she earned money in the one profession that was open to her, the oldest profession of all, she unsexed herself. There can be no question—the infantile fixation is powerful, even when a mother is infected. But when the father is infected it has a threefold power; he has nature to protect him; law to protect him; and property to protect him. Thus protected it was perfectly possible for the Rev. Patrick Brontë to cause 'acute pain' to his daughter Charlotte for several months, and to steal several months of her short married happiness without incurring any censure from the society in which he practised the profession of a priest of the Church of England; though had he tortured a dog, or stolen a watch, that same society would have unfrocked him and cast him forth. Society it seems was a father, and afflicted with the infantile fixation too.

Since society protected and indeed excused the victims of the infantile fixation in the nineteenth century, it is not surprising that the disease, though unnamed, was rampant. Whatever biography we open we find almost always the familiar symptoms—the father is opposed to his daughter's marriage; the father is opposed to his daughter's earning her living. Her wish either to marry, or to earn her living, rouses strong emotion in him; and he gives the same excuses for that strong emotion; the lady will debase her ladyhood; the daughter will outrage her womanhood. But now and again, very rarely, we find a father who was completely immune from the disease. The results are then extremely interesting. There is the case of Mr Leigh Smith.[38] This gentleman was contemporary with Mr Jex-Blake, and came of the same social caste. He, too, had property in Sussex; he, too, had horses and carriages; and he, too, had children. But there the resemblance ends. Mr Leigh Smith was devoted to his children; he objected to schools; he kept his children at home. It would be interesting to discuss Mr Leigh Smith's educational methods; how he had masters to teach them; how, in a large carriage built like an omnibus, he took them with him on long journeys yearly all over England. But like so many experimentalists, Mr Leigh Smith remains obscure; and we must content ourselves with the fact that he 'held the unusual opinion that daughters should have an equal provision with sons'. So completely immune was he from the infantile fixation that 'he did not adopt the ordinary plan of paying his daughters' bills and giving them an occasional present, but when Barbara came of age in 1848 he gave her an allowance of £300 a year.' The results of that immunity from the infantile fixation were remarkable. For 'treating her money as a power to do good, one of the first uses to which Barbara put it was educational.' She founded a school; a school that was open not only to different sexes and different classes, but to different creeds; Roman Catholics, Jews and 'pupils from families of advanced free thought' were received in it. 'It was a most unusual school,' an outsiders' school. But that was not all that she attempted upon three hundred a year. One thing led to another. A friend, with her help, started a co-operative evening class for ladies 'for drawing from an undraped model'. In 1858 only one life class in London was open to ladies. And then a petition was got up to the Royal Academy; its schools were actually, though as so often happens only nominally, opened to women in 1861;[39] next Barbara went into the question of the laws concerning women; so that actually in 1871 married women were allowed to own their property; and finally she helped Miss Davies to found Girton. When we reflect what one father who was immune from infantile fixation could do by allowing one daughter £300 a year we need not wonder that most fathers firmly refused to allow their daughters more than £40 a year with bed and board thrown in.

The infantile fixation in the fathers then was, it is clear, a strong force, and all the stronger because it was a concealed force. But the fathers were met, as the nineteenth century drew on, by a force which had become so strong in its turn that it is much to be hoped that the psychologists will find some name for it. The old names as we have seen are futile and false. 'Feminism', we have had to destroy. 'The emancipation of women' is equally inexpressive and corrupt. To say that the daughters were inspired prematurely by the principles of anti-Fascism is merely to repeat the fashionable and hideous jargon of the moment. To call them champions of intellectual liberty and culture is to cloud the air with the dust of lecture halls and the damp dowdiness of public meetings. Moreover, none of these tags and labels express the real emotions that inspired the daughters' opposition to the infantile fixation of the fathers, because, as biography shows, that force had behind it many

different emotions, and many that were contradictory. Tears were behind it, of course—tears, bitter
tears: the tears of those whose desire for knowledge
was frustrated. One daughter longed to learn chemistry; the books at home only taught her alchemy.
She 'cried bitterly at not being taught things'. Also
the desire for an open and rational love was behind it.
Again there were tears—angry tears.* 'She flung
herself on the bed in tears . . . "Oh," she said, "Harry
is on the roof." "Who's Harry?" said I; "which roof?
Why?" "Oh, don't be silly," she said; "he had to
go." '40 But again the desire not to love, to lead a
rational existence without love, was behind it. 'I make
the confession humbly . . . I know nothing myself of
love,'41 wrote one of them. An odd confession from
one of the class whose only profession for so many
centuries had been marriage; but significant. Others
wanted to travel; to explore Africa; to dig in Greece
and Palestine. Some wanted to learn music, not to
tinkle domestic airs, but to compose—operas, sym-
phonies, quartets. Others wanted to paint, not ivy-
clad cottages, but naked bodies. They all wanted—
but what one word can sum up the variety of the
things that they wanted, and had wanted, consciously
or subconsciously, for so long? Josephine Butler's
label*—Justice, Equality, Liberty—is a fine one; but
it is only a label, and in our age of innumerable labels,
of multi-coloured labels, we have become suspicious
of labels; they kill and constrict. Nor does the old

word 'freedom' serve, for it was not freedom in the sense of licence that they wanted; they wanted, like Antigone, not to break the laws, but to find the law.[42] Ignorant as we are of human motives and ill supplied with words, let us then admit that no one word expresses the force which in the nineteenth century opposed itself to the force of the fathers. All we can safely say about that force was that it was a force of tremendous power. It forced open the doors of the private house. It opened Bond Street and Piccadilly; it opened cricket grounds and football grounds; it shrivelled flounces and stays; it made the oldest profession in the world (but Whitaker supplies no figures) unprofitable. In fifty years, in short, that force made the life lived by Lady Lovelace and Gertrude Bell unlivable, and almost incredible. The fathers who had triumphed over the strongest emotions of strong men, had to yield.

If that full stop were the end of the story, the final slam of the door, we could turn at once to your letter, Sir, and to the form which you have asked us to fill up. But it was not the end; it was the beginning. Indeed though we have used the past, we shall soon find ourselves using the present tense. The fathers in private, it is true, yielded; but the fathers in public, massed together in societies, in professions, were even more subject to the fatal disease than the fathers in private. The disease had acquired a motive, had connected itself with a right, a conception, which made it still more virulent outside the house than within. The desire to support wife and children—what motive could be more powerful, or deeply rooted? For it was connected with manhood itself—a man who could not support his family failed in his own conception of manliness. And was not that conception as deep in him as the conception of womanhood in his daughter? It was those motives, those rights and conceptions that were now challenged. To protect them, and from women, gave, and gives, rise it can scarcely be doubted to an emotion perhaps below the level of conscious thought but certainly of the utmost violence. The infantile fixation develops, directly the priest's right to practise his profession is challenged, to an aggravated and exacerbated emotion to which the name sex-taboo is scientifically applied. Take two instances; one private, the other public. A scholar has 'to mark his disapproval of the admission of women to his university by refusing to enter his beloved college or city'.[43] A hospital has to decline an offer to endow a scholarship because it is made by a woman on behalf of women.[44] Can we doubt that both actions are inspired by that sense of shame which, as Professor Grensted says 'cannot be regarded in any other light than as a non-rational sex-taboo'? But since the emotion itself had increased in strength it became necessary to invoke the help of stronger allies to excuse and conceal it. Nature was called in; Nature it was claimed who is not only omniscient but unchanging, had made the brain of woman of the wrong shape or size. 'Anyone,' writes Bertrand Russell, 'who desires amusement may be advised to look up the tergiversations of eminent craniologists in their attempts to prove from brain measurements that women are stupider than men.'[45] Science, it would seem, is not sexless; she is a man, a father, and infected too. Science, thus infected, produced measurements to order: the brain was too small to be examined. Many years were spent waiting before the sacred gates of the universities and hospitals for permission to have the brains that the professors said that Nature had made incapable of passing examinations examined. When at last permission was granted the examinations were passed. A long and dreary list of those barren if necessary triumphs lies presumably along with other broken records[46] in college archives, and harassed head mistresses still consult them, it is said, when desiring official proof of impeccable mediocrity. Still Nature held out. The brain that could pass examinations was not the creative brain; the brain that can bear responsibility and earn the higher salaries. It was a practical brain, a pettifogging brain, a brain fitted for routine work under the command of a superior. And since the professions were shut, it was undeniable—the daughters had not ruled Empires, commanded fleets, or led armies to victory; only a few trivial books testified to their professional ability, for literature was the only profession that had been open to them. And, more-over, whatever the brain might do when the professions were opened to it, the body remained. Nature, the priests said, in her infinite wisdom, had laid down the unalterable law that man is the creator. He enjoys; she only passively endures. Pain was more beneficial than pleasure to the body that endures. 'The views of medical men on pregnancy, childbirth, and lactation were until fairly recently,' Bertrand Russell writes, 'impregnated with sadism. It required, for example, more evidence to persuade them that anaesthetics may be used in childbirth than it would have required to persuade them of the opposite.' So science argued, so the professors agreed. And when at last the daughters interposed, But are not brain and body affected by training? Does not the wild rabbit differ from the rabbit in the hutch? And must we not, and do we not change this unalterable nature? By setting a match to a fire frost is defied; Nature's decree of death is postponed. And the breakfast egg, they persisted, is it all the work of the cock? Without yolk, without white, how far would your breakfasts, oh priests and professors, be fertile? Then the priests and professors in solemn unison intoned: But childbirth itself, that burden you cannot deny, is laid upon woman alone. Nor could they deny it, nor wish to renounce it. Still they declared, consulting the statistics in books, the time occupied by woman in childbirth is under modern conditions—remember we are in the twentieth century now—only a fraction.[47] Did that fraction incapacitate us from working in Whitehall, in fields and factories, when our country was in danger? To which the fathers replied: The war is over; we are in England now.

And if, Sir, pausing in England now, we turn on the wireless of the daily press we shall hear what answer the fathers who are infected with infantile fixation now are making to those questions now. 'Homes are the real places of the women . . . Let them go back to their homes . . . The Government should give work to men . . . A strong protest is to be made by the Ministry of Labour . . . Women must not rule over men . . . There are two worlds, one for women, the other for men . . . Let them learn to cook our dinners . . . Women have failed . . . They have failed . . . They have failed . . .'

Even now the clamour, the uproar that infantile fixation is making even here is such that we can hardly hear ourselves speak; it takes the words out of our mouths; it makes us say what we have not said. As we listen to the voices we seem to hear an infant crying in the night, the black night that now covers Europe, and with no language but a cry, Ay, ay, ay, ay . . . But it is not a new cry, it is a very old cry. Let us shut off the wireless and listen to the past. We are in Greece now; Christ has not been born yet, nor St Paul either. But listen:

'Whomsoever the city may appoint, that man must

be obeyed, in little things and great, in just things and unjust . . . disobedience is the worst of evils . . . We must support the cause of order, and in no wise suffer a woman to worst us . . . They must be women, and not range at large. Servants, take them within.' That is the voice of Creon, the dictator. To whom Antigone, who was to have been his daughter, answered, 'Not such are the laws set among men by the justice who dwells with the gods below.' But she had neither capital nor force behind her. And Creon said: 'I will take her where the path is loneliest, and hide her, living, in a rocky vault.' And he shut her not in Holloway* or in a concentration camp, but in a tomb. And Creon we read brought ruin on his house, and scattered the land with the bodies of the dead. It seems, Sir, as we listen to the voices of the past, as if we were looking at the photographs again, at the picture of dead bodies and ruined houses that the Spanish Government sends us almost weekly. Things repeat themselves it seems. Pictures and voices are the same today as they were 2,000 years ago.

Such then is the conclusion to which our inquiry into the nature of fear has brought us—the fear which forbids freedom in the private house. That fear, small, insignificant and private as it is, is connected with the other fear, the public fear, which is neither small nor insignificant, the fear which has led you to ask us to help you to prevent war. Otherwise we should not be looking at the picture again. But it is not the same picture that caused us at the beginning of this letter to feel the same emotions—you called them 'horror and disgust'; we called them horror and disgust. For as this letter has gone on, adding fact to fact, another picture has imposed itself upon the foreground. It is the figure of a man; some say, others deny, that he is Man himself,[48] the quintessence of virility, the perfect type of which all the others are imperfect adumbrations. He is a man certainly. His eyes are glazed; his eyes glare. His body, which is braced in an unnatural position, is tightly cased in a uniform. Upon the breast of that uniform are sewn several medals and other mystic symbols. His hand is upon a sword. He is called in German and Italian Führer or Duce; in our own language Tyrant or Dictator. And behind him lie ruined houses and dead bodies—men, women and children. But we have not laid that picture before you in order to excite once more the sterile emotion of hate. On the contrary it is in order to release other emotions such as the human figure, even thus crudely in a coloured photograph, arouses in us who are human beings. For it suggests a connection and for us a very important connection. It suggests that the public and the private worlds are inseparably connected; that the tyrannies and servilities of the one are the tyrannies and servilities of the other. But the human figure even in a photograph suggests other and more complex emotions. It suggests that we cannot dissociate ourselves from that figure but are ourselves that figure. It suggests that we are not passive spectators doomed to unresisting obedience but by our thoughts and actions can ourselves change that figure. A common interest unites us; it is one world, one life. How essential it is that we should realize that unity the dead bodies, the ruined houses prove. For such will be our ruin if you, in the immensity of your public abstractions forget the private figure, or if we in the intensity of our private emotions forget the public world. Both houses will be ruined, the public and the private, the material and the spiritual, for they are inseparably connected. But with your letter before us we have reason to hope. For by asking our help you recognize that connection; and by reading your words we are reminded of other connections that lie far deeper than the facts on the surface. Even here, even now your letter tempts us to shut our ears to these little facts, these trivial details, to listen not to the bark of the guns and the bray of the gramophones but to the voices of the poets, answering each other, assuring us of a unity that rubs out divisions as if they were chalk marks only; to discuss with you the capacity of the human spirit to overflow boundaries and make unity out of multiplicity. But that would be to dream—to dream the recurring dream that has haunted the human mind since the beginning of time; the dream of peace, the dream of freedom. But, with the sound of the guns in your ears you have not asked us to dream. You have not asked us what peace is; you have asked us how to prevent war. Let us then leave it to the poets to tell us what the dream is; and fix our eyes upon the photograph again: the fact.

Whatever the verdict of others may be upon the man in uniform—and opinions differ—there is your letter to prove that to you the picture is the picture of evil. And though we look upon that picture from different angles our conclusion is the same as yours—it is evil. We are both determined to do what we can to destroy the evil which that picture represents, you by your methods, we by ours. And since we are different, our help must be different. What ours can be we have tried to show—how imperfectly, how superficially there is no need to say.[49] But as a result the answer to your question must be that we can best help you to prevent war not by repeating your words and following your methods but by finding new words and creating new methods. We can best help you to prevent war not by joining your society but by remaining outside your society but in co-operation with its aim. That aim is the same for us both. It is to assert 'the rights of all—all men and women—to the respect in their persons of the great principles of Justice and Equality and Liberty'. To elaborate further is unnecessary, for we have every confidence that you interpret those words as we do. And excuses are unnecessary, for we can trust you to make allowances for those deficiences which we foretold and which this letter has abundantly displayed.

To return then to the form that you have sent and ask us to fill up: for the reasons given we will leave it unsigned. But in order to prove as substantially as possible that our aims are the same as yours, here is the guinea, a free gift, given freely, without any other conditions than you choose to impose upon yourself. It is the third of three guineas; but the three guineas, you will observe, though given to three different treasurers are all given to the same cause, for the causes are the same and inseparable.

Now, since you are pressed for time, let me make an end; apologizing three times over to the three of you, first for the length of this letter, second for the smallness of the contribution, and thirdly for writing at all. The blame for that however rests upon you, for this letter would never have been written had you not asked for an answer to your own.

1. *The Life of Mary Kingsley*, by Stephen Gwynn, p. 15. It is difficult to get exact figures of the sums spent on the education of educated men's daughters. About £20 or £30 presumably covered the entire cost of Mary Kingsley's education (b. 1862; d. 1900). A sum of £100 may be taken as about the average in the nineteenth century and even later. The women thus educated often felt the lack of education very keenly. 'I always feel the defects of my education most painfully when I go out,' wrote Anne J. Clough, the first Principal of Newnham. (*Memoir of Anne J. Clough*, by B. A. Clough, p. 60.) Elizabeth Haldane, who came, like Miss Clough, of a highly literate family, but was educated in much the same way, says that when she grew up, 'My first conviction was that I was not educated, and I thought of how this could be put right. I should have loved going to college, but college in those days was unusual for girls, and the idea was not encouraged. It was also expensive. For an only daughter to leave a widowed mother was indeed considered to be out of the question, and no one made the plan seem feasible. There was in those days a new movement for carrying on correspondence classes . . .' (*From One Century to Another*, by Elizabeth Haldane, p. 73.) The efforts of such uneducated women to conceal their ignorance were often valiant, but not always successful. 'They talked agreeably on current topics, carefully avoiding controversial subjects. What impressed me was their ignorance and indifference concerning anything outside their own circle . . . no less a personage than the mother of the Speaker of the House of Commons believed that California belonged to us, part of our Empire!' (*Distant Fields*, by H. A. Vachell, p. 109.) That ignorance was often simulated in the nineteenth century owing to the current belief that educated men enjoyed it is shown by the energy with which Thomas Gisborne, in his instructive work *The Duties of the Female Sex* (p. 278), rebuked those who recommend women 'studiously to refrain from discovering

to their partners in marriage the full extent of their abilities and attainments'. 'This is not discretion but art. It is dissimulation, it is deliberate imposition ... It could scarcely be practised long without detection.'

But the educated man's daughter in the nineteenth century was even more ignorant of life than of books. One reason for that ignorance is suggested by the following quotation: 'It was supposed that most men were not "virtuous", that is, that nearly all would be capable of accosting and annoying—or worse—any unaccompanied young woman whom they met.' ('Society and the Season', by Mary, Countess of Lovelace, in *Fifty Years, 1882–1932*, p. 37.) She was therefore confined to a very narrow circle; and her 'ignorance and indifference' to anything outside it was excusable. The connection between that ignorance and the nineteenth-century conception of manhood, which—witness the Victorian hero—made 'virtue' and virility incompatible is obvious. In a well-known passage* Thackeray complains of the limitations which virtue and virility between them imposed upon his art.

2. Our ideology is still so inveterately anthropocentric that it has been necessary to coin this clumsy term—educated man's daughter—to describe the class whose fathers have been educated at public schools and universities. Obviously, if the term 'bourgeois' fits her brother, it is grossly incorrect to use it of one who differs so profoundly in the two prime characteristics of the bourgeoisie—capital and environment.

3. The number of animals killed in England for sport during the past century must be beyond computation. 1,212 head of game is given as the average for a day's shooting at Chatsworth in 1909. (*Men, Women and Things*, by the Duke of Portland, p. 251.) Little mention is made in sporting memoirs of women guns; and their appearance in the hunting field was the cause of much caustic comment. 'Skittles', the famous nineteenth-century horsewoman, was a lady of easy morals. It is highly probable that there was held to be some connection between sport and unchastity in women in the nineteenth century.

4. *Francis and Riversdale Grenfell*, by John Buchan, pp. 189, 205.

5. *Antony (Viscount Knebworth)*, by the Earl of Lytton, p. 355.

6. *The Poems of Wilfred Owen*, edited by Edmund Blunden, pp. 25, 41.

7. Lord Hewart, proposing the toast of 'England' at the banquet of the Society of St George at Cardiff.

8. and 9. The *Daily Telegraph*, 5 February 1937.

10. There is of course one essential that the educated woman can supply: children. And one method by which she can help to prevent war is to refuse to bear children. Thus Mrs Helena Normanton is of opinion that 'The only thing that women in any country can do to prevent war is to stop the supply of "cannon fodder".' (Report of the Annual Council for Equal Citizenship, *Daily Telegraph*, 5 March 1937.) Letters in the newspapers frequently support this view. 'I can tell Mr Harry Campbell why women refuse to have children in these times. When men have learnt how to run the lands they govern so that wars shall hit only those who make the quarrels, instead of mowing down those who do not, then women may again feel like having large families. Why should women bring children into such a world as this one is today?' (Edith Maturin-Porch, in the *Daily Telegraph*, 6 September 1937.) The fact that the birth rate in the educated class is falling would seem to show that educated women are taking Mrs Normanton's advice. It was offered them in very similar circumstances over two thousand years ago by Lysistrata.*

11. There are of course innumerable kinds of influence besides those specified in the text. It varies from the simple kind described in the following passage: 'Three years later . . . we find her writing to him as Cabinet Minister to solicit his interest on behalf of a favourite parson for a Crown living . . .' (*Henry Chaplin, a Memoir*, by Lady Londonderry, p. 57) to the very subtle kind exerted by Lady Macbeth upon her husband. Somewhere between the two lies the influence described by D. H. Lawrence: 'It is hopeless for me to try to do anything without I have a woman at the back of me . . . I daren't sit in the world without I have a woman behind me . . . But a woman that I love sort of keeps me in direct communication with the unknown, in which otherwise I am a bit lost' (*Letters of D. H. Lawrence*, pp. 93–4), with which

we may compare, though the collocation is strange, the famous and very similar definition given by the ex-King Edward VIII upon his abdication. Present political conditions abroad seem to favour a return to the use of interested influence. For example: 'A story serves to illustrate the present degree of women's influence in Vienna. During the past autumn a measure was planned to further diminish women's professional opportunities. Protests, pleas, letters, all were of no avail. Finally, in desperation, a group of well-known ladies of the city ... got together and planned. For the next fortnight, for a certain number of hours per day, several of these ladies got on to the telephone to the Ministers they knew personally, ostensibly to ask them to dinner at their homes. With all the charm of which the Viennese are capable, they kept the Ministers talking, asking about this and that, and finally mentioning the matter that distressed them so much. When the Ministers had been rung up by several ladies, all of whom they did not wish to offend, and kept from urgent State affairs by this manoeuvre, they decided on compromise—and so the measure was postponed.' (*Women Must Choose*, by Hilary Newitt, p. 129.) Similar use of influence was often deliberately made during the battle for the franchise. But women's influence is said to be impaired by the possession of a vote. Thus Marshal von Bieberstein was of opinion that 'Women led men always ... but he did not wish them to vote.' (*From One Century to Another*, by Elizabeth Haldane, p. 258.)

12. English women were much criticized for using force in the battle for the franchise. When in 1910 Mr Birrell had his hat 'reduced to pulp' and his shins kicked by suffragettes, Sir Almeric Fitzroy commented, 'an attack of this character upon a defenceless old man by an organized band of "janissaries" will, it is hoped, convince many people of the insane and anarchical spirit actuating the movement.' (*Memoirs of Sir Almeric Fitzroy*, vol. II, p. 425.) These remarks did not apply apparently to the force in the European war. The vote indeed was given to English women largely because of the help they gave to Englishmen in using force in that war. 'On 14 August [1916], Mr Asquith himself gave up his opposition [to the

franchise]. "It is true," he said, "[that women] cannot fight in the sense of going out with rifles and so forth, but . . . they have aided in the most effective way in the prosecution of the war."' (*The Cause*, by Ray Strachey, p. 354.) This raises the difficult question whether those who did not aid in the prosecution of the war, but did what they could to hinder the prosecution of the war, ought to use the vote to which they are entitled chiefly because others 'aided in the prosecution of the war'? That they are stepdaughters, not full daughters, of England is shown by the fact that they change nationality on marriage. A woman, whether or not she helped to beat the Germans, becomes a German if she marries a German. Her political views must then be entirely reversed, and her filial piety transferred.

13. *Sir Ernest Wild, K.C.*, by Robert J. Blackham, pp. 174–5.

14. That the right to vote has not proved negligible is shown by the facts published from time to time by the National Union of Societies for Equal Citizenship. 'This publication (*What the Vote has Done*) was originally a single-page leaflet; it has now (1927) grown to a six-page pamphlet, and has to be constantly enlarged.' (*Josephine Butler*, by M. G. Fawcett and E. M. Turner, note, p. 101.)

15. There are no figures available with which to check facts that must have a very important bearing upon the biology and psychology of the sexes. A beginning might be made in this essential but strangely neglected preliminary by chalking on a large-scale map of England property owned by men, red; by women, blue. Then the number of sheep and cattle consumed by each sex must be compared; the hogsheads of wine and beer; the barrels of tobacco; after which we must examine carefully their physical exercises; domestic employments; facilities for sexual intercourse, etc. Historians are of course mainly concerned with war and politics; but sometimes throw light upon human nature. Thus Macaulay dealing with the English country gentleman in the seventeenth century, says: 'His wife and daughter were in tastes and acquirements below a housekeeper or still-room maid of the present day. They stitched and spun, brewed gooseberry wine, cured marigolds, and made the crust for the venison pasty.'

Again, 'The ladies of the house, whose business it had commonly been to cook the repast, retired as soon as the dishes had been devoured, and left the gentlemen to their ale and tobacco.' (Macaulay, *History of England*, Chapter Three.) But the gentlemen were still drinking and the ladies were still withdrawing a great deal later. 'In my mother's young days before her marriage, the old hard-drinking habits of the Regency and of the eighteenth century still persisted. At Woburn Abbey it was the custom for the trusted old family butler to make his nightly report to my grandmother in the drawing-room. "The gentlemen have had a good deal tonight; it might be as well for the young ladies to retire," or, "The gentlemen have had very little tonight," was announced according to circumstances by this faithful family retainer. Should the young girls be packed off upstairs, they liked standing on an upper gallery of the staircase "to watch the shouting, riotous crowd issuing from the dining-room".' (*The Days Before Yesterday*, by Lord F. Hamilton, p. 322.) It must be left to the scientist of the future to tell us what effect drink and property have had upon chromosomes.

16. The fact that both sexes have a very marked though dissimilar love of dress seems to have escaped the notice of the dominant sex owing largely it must be supposed to the hypnotic power of dominance. Thus the late Mr Justice MacCardie, in summing up the case of Mrs Frankau, remarked: 'Women cannot be expected to renounce an essential feature of femininity or to abandon one of nature's solaces for a constant and insuperable physical handicap ... Dress, after all, is one of the chief methods of women's self-expression ... In matters of dress women often remain children to the end. The psychology of the matter must not be overlooked. But whilst bearing the above matters in mind the law has rightly laid it down that the rule of prudence and proportion must be observed.' The Judge who thus dictated was wearing a scarlet robe, an ermine cape, and a vast wig of artificial curls. Whether he was enjoying 'one of nature's solaces for a constant and insuperable physical handicap', whether again he was himself observing 'the rule of prudence and proportion' must be doubtful. But 'the psychology of the matter

must not be overlooked'; and the fact that the singularity of his own appearance together with that of Admirals, Generals, Heralds, Life Guards, Peers, Beefeaters, etc., was completely invisible to him so that he was able to lecture the lady without any consciousness of sharing her weakness, raises two questions: how often must an act be performed before it becomes tradition, and therefore venerable; and what degree of social prestige causes blindness to the remarkable nature of one's own clothes? Singularity of dress, when not associated with office, seldom escapes ridicule.

17. In the New Year's Honours List for 1937, 147 men accepted honours as against seven women. For obvious reasons this cannot be taken as a measure of their comparative desire for such advertisement. But that it should be easier, psychologically, for a woman to reject honours than for a man seems to be indisputable. For the fact that intellect (roughly speaking) is man's chief professional asset, and that stars and ribbons are his chief means of advertising intellect, suggests that stars and ribbons are identical with powder and paint, a woman's chief method of advertising her chief professional asset: beauty. It would therefore be as unreasonable to ask him to refuse a Knighthood as to ask her to refuse a dress. The sum paid for a Knighthood in 1901 would seem to provide a very tolerable dress allowance; '21 April (Sunday)—To see Meynell, who was as usual full of gossip. It appears that the King's debts have been paid off privately by his friends, one of whom is said to have lent £100,000, and satisfies himself with £25,000 in repayment plus a Knighthood.' (*My Diaries*, Wilfrid Scawen Blunt, Part II, p. 8.)

18. What the precise figures are it is difficult for an outsider to know. But that the incomes are substantial can be conjectured from a delightful review some years ago by Mr J. M. Keynes in the *Nation* of a history of Clare College, Cambridge. The book 'it is rumoured cost six thousand pounds to produce'. Rumour has it also that a band of students returning at dawn from some festivity about that time saw a cloud in the sky; which as they gazed assumed the shape of a woman; who, being supplicated for a sign, let fall in a shower of radiant hail the one word 'Rats'. This was interpreted to signify what

from another page of the same number of the *Nation* would seem to be the truth; that the students of one of the women's colleges suffered greatly from 'cold gloomy ground floor bedrooms overrun with mice'. The apparition, it was supposed, took this means of suggesting that if the gentlemen of Clare wished to do her honour a cheque for £6,000 payable to the Principal of —— would celebrate her better than a book even though 'clothed in the finest dress of paper and black buckram . . .' There is nothing mythical, however, about the fact recorded in the same number of the *Nation* that 'Somerville received with pathetic gratitude the £7,000 which went to it last year from the Jubilee gift and a private bequest.'*

19. A great historian has thus described the origin and character of the universities, in one of which he was edcuated: 'The schools of Oxford and Cambridge were founded in a dark age of false and barbarous science; and they are still tainted by the vices of their origin . . . The legal incorporation of these societies by the charters of popes and kings had given them a monopoly of public instruction; and the spirit of monopolists is narrow, lazy, and oppressive: their work is more costly and less productive than that of independent artists; and the new improvements so eagerly grasped by the competition of freedom, are admitted with slow and sullen reluctance in those proud corporations, above the fear of a rival, and below the confession of an error. We may scarcely hope that any reformation will be a voluntary act; and so deeply are they rooted in law and prejudice, that even the omnipotence of a parliament would shrink from an inquiry into the state and abuses of the two universities.' (Edward Gibbon, *Memoirs of My Life and Writings*.) 'The omnipotence of Parliament' did however institute an inquiry in the middle of the nineteenth century 'into the state of the University [of Oxford], its discipline, studies, and revenues. But there was so much passive resistance from the Colleges that the last item had to go by the board. It was ascertained however that out of 542 Fellowships in all the Colleges of Oxford only twenty-two were really open to competition without restrictive conditions of patronage, place or kin . . . The Commissioners . . . found that Gibbon's indictment had

been reasonable . . .' (*Herbert Warren of Magdalen*, by Laurie Magnus, pp. 47–9.) Nevertheless the prestige of a university education remained high; and Fellowships were considered highly desirable. When Pusey became a Fellow of Oriel, 'The bells of the parish church at Pusey expressed the satisfaction of his father and family.' Again, when Newman was elected a Fellow, 'all the bells of the three towers [were] set pealing— at Newman's expense.' (*Oxford Apostles*, by Geoffrey Faber, pp. 131, 69.) Yet both Pusey and Newman were men of a distinctly spiritual nature.

20. *The Crystal Cabinet*, by Mary Butts, p. 138. The sentence in full runs: 'For just as I was told that desire for learning in woman was against the will of God, so were many innocent freedoms, innocent delights, denied in the same Name'—a remark which makes it desirable that we should have a biography from the pen of an educated man's daughter of the Deity in whose Name such atrocities have been committed. The influence of religion upon women's education, one way or another, can scarcely be overestimated. 'If, for example,' says Thomas Gisborne, 'the uses of music are explained, let not its effect in heightening devotion be overlooked. If drawing is the subject of remark, let the student be taught habitually to contemplate in the works of creation the power, the wisdom and the goodness of their Author.' (*The Duties of the Female Sex*, by Thomas Gisborne, p. 85.) The fact that Mr Gisborne and his like—a numerous band—base their educational theories upon the teaching of St Paul would seem to hint that the female sex was to be 'taught habitually to contemplate in the works of creation, the power and wisdom and the goodness,' not so much of the Deity, but of Mr Gisborne. And from that we were led to conclude that a biography of the Deity would resolve itself into a Dictionary of Clerical Biography.

21. *Mary Astell*, by Florence M. Smith. 'Unfortunately, the opposition to so new an idea (a college for women) was greater than the interest in it, and came not only from the satirists of the day, who, like the wits of all ages, found the progressive woman a source of laughter and made Mary Astell the subject of stock jokes in comedies of the *Femmes*

*Savantes* type, but from the churchmen, who saw in the plan an attempt to bring back popery. The strongest opponent of the idea was a celebrated bishop, who, as Ballard asserts, prevented a prominent lady from subscribing £10,000 to the plan. Elizabeth Elstob gave to Ballard the name of this celebrated bishop in reply to an inquiry from him. "According to Elizabeth Elstob ... it was Bishop Burnet that prevented that good design by dissuading that lady from encouraging it."' (op. cit., pp. 21–2.) 'That lady' may have been Princess Anne, or Lady Elizabeth Hastings; but there seems reason to think that it was the Princess. That the Church swallowed the money is an assumption, but one perhaps justified by the history of the Church.

22. *Ode for Music*, performed in the Senate House at Cambridge, 1 July 1769.

23. 'I assure you I am not an enemy of women. I am very favourable to their employment as *labourers* or in other *menial* capacity. I have, however, doubts as to the likelihood of their succeeding in business as capitalists. I am sure the nerves of most women would break down under the anxiety, and that most of them are utterly destitute of the disciplined reticence necessary to every sort of cooperation. Two thousand years hence you may have changed it all, but the present women will only flirt with men, and quarrel with one another.' Extract from a letter from Walter Bagehot to Emily Davies, who had asked his help in founding Girton.

24. *Recollections and Reflections*, by Sir J. J. Thomson, pp. 86–8, 296–7.

25. 'Cambridge University still refuses to admit women to the full rights of membership; it grants them only titular degrees and they have therefore no share in the government of the University.' (*Memorandum on the Position of English Women in Relation to that of English Men*, by Philippa Strachey, 1935, p. 26.) Nevertheless, the Government makes a 'liberal grant' from public money to Cambridge University.

26. 'The total number of students at recognized institutions for the higher education of women who are receiving instruction in the University or working in the University laboratories or museums shall not at any time exceed five hundred.' (*The*

*Student's Handbook to Cambridge*, 1934–5, p. 616.) Whitaker informs us that the number of male students who were in residence at Cambridge in October 1935 was 5,328. Nor would there appear to be any limitation.

27. The men's scholarship list at Cambridge printed in *The Times* of 20 December 1937, measures roughly thirty-one inches; the women's scholarship list at Cambridge measures roughly five inches. There are, however, seventeen colleges for men and the list here measured includes only eleven. The thirty-one inches must therefore be increased. There are only two colleges for women; both are here measured.

28. Until the death of Lady Stanley of Alderley, there was no chapel at Girton. 'When it was proposed to build a chapel, she objected, on the ground that all the available funds should be spent on education. "So long as I live, there shall be no chapel at Girton," I heard her say. The present chapel was built immediately after her death.' (*The Amberley Papers*, Patricia and Betrand Russell, vol. I, p. 17.) Would that her ghost had possessed the same influence as her body! But ghosts, it is said, have no cheque books.

29. 'I have also a feeling that girls' schools have, on the whole, been content to take the general lines of their education from the older-established institutions for my own, the weaker sex. My own feeling is that the problem ought to be attacked by some original genius on quite different lines . . .' (*Things Ancient and Modern*, by C. A. Alington, pp. 216–17.) It scarcely needs genius or originality to see that 'the lines', in the first place, must be cheaper. But it would be interesting to know what meaning we are to attach to the word 'weaker' in the context. For since Dr Alington is a former Head Master of Eton he must be aware that his sex has not only acquired but retained the vast revenues of that ancient foundation—a proof, one would have thought, not of sexual weakness but of sexual strength. That Eton is not 'weak', at least from the material point of view, is shown by the following quotation from Dr Alington: 'Following out the suggestion of one of the Prime Minister's Committees on Education, the Provost and Fellows in my time decided that all scholarships at Eton should be of a fixed value, capable of

being liberally augmented in case of need. So liberal has been this augmentation that there are several boys in College whose parents pay nothing towards either their board or education.' One of the benefactors was the late Lord Rosebery. 'He was a generous benefactor to the school,' Dr Alington informs us, 'and endowed a history scholarship, in connection with which a characteristic episode occurred. He asked me whether the endowment was adequate and I suggested that a further £200 would provide for the payment to the examiner. He sent a cheque for £2,000: his attention was called to the discrepancy, and I have in my scrap book the reply in which he said that he thought a good round sum would be better than a fraction.' (op. cit., pp. 163, 186.) The entire sum spent at Cheltenham College for Girls in 1854 upon salaries and visiting teachers was £1,300; 'and the accounts in December showed a deficit of £400'. (*Dorothea Beale of Cheltenham*, by Elizabeth Raikes, p. 91.)

30. The words 'vain and vicious' require qualification. No one would maintain that all lecturers and lectures are 'vain and vicious'; many subjects can only be taught with diagrams and personal demonstration. The words in the text refer only to the sons and daughters of educated men who lecture their brothers and sisters upon English literature; and for the reasons that it is an obsolete practice dating from the Middle Ages when books were scarce; that it owes its survival to pecuniary motives; or to curiosity; that the publication in book form is sufficient proof of the evil effect of an audience upon the lecturer intellectually; and that psychologically eminence upon a platform encourages vanity and the desire to impose authority. Further, the reduction of English literature to an examination subject must be viewed with suspicion by all who have firsthand knowledge of the difficulty of the art, and therefore of the very superficial value of an examiner's approval or disapproval; and with profound regret by all who wish to keep one art at least out of the hands of middlemen and free, as long as may be, from all association with competition and money making. Again, the violence with which one school of literature is now opposed to another, the rapidity with which one school of taste succeeds

another, may not unreasonably be traced to the power which a mature mind lecturing immature minds has to infect them with strong, if passing, opinions, and to tinge those opinions with personal bias. Nor can it be maintained that the standard of critical or of creative writing has been raised. A lamentable proof of the mental docility to which the young are reduced by lecturers is that the demand for lectures upon English literature steadily increases (as every writer can bear witness) and from the very class which should have learnt to read at home—the educated. If, as is sometimes urged in excuse, what is desired by college literary societies is not knowledge of literature but acquaintance with writers, there are cocktails, and there is sherry; both better unmixed with Proust. None of this applies of course to those whose homes are deficient in books. If the working class finds it easier to assimilate English literature by word of mouth they have a perfect right to ask the educated class to help them thus. But for the sons and daughters of that class after the age of eighteen to continue to sip English literature through a straw, is a habit that seems to deserve the terms vain and vicious; which terms can justly be applied with greater force to those who pander to them.

31. It is difficult to procure exact figures of the sums allowed the daughters of educated men before marriage. Sophia Jex-Blake had an allowance of from £30 to £40 annually; her father was an upper-middle-class man. Lady Lascelles, whose father was an Earl, had, it seems, an allowance of about £100 in 1860; Mr Barrett, a rich merchant, allowed his daughter Elizabeth 'from forty to forty-five pounds . . . every three months, the income tax being first deducted'. But this seems to have been the interest upon £8,000, 'or more or less . . . it is difficult to ask about it', which she had 'in the funds', 'the money being in two different per cents', and apparently, though belonging to Elizabeth, under Mr Barrett's control. But these were unmarried women. Married women were not allowed to own property until the passing of the Married Women's Property Act in 1870. Lady St Helier records that since her marriage settlements had been drawn up in conformity with the old law, 'What money I had was settled on my husband, and no

part of it was reserved for my private use . . . I did not even possess a cheque book, nor was I able to get any money except by asking my husband. He was kind and generous but he acquiesced in the position then existing that a woman's property belonged to her husband . . . he paid all my bills, he kept my bank book, and gave me a small allowance for my personal expenses.' (*Memories of Fifty Years*, by Lady St Helier, p. 341.) But she does not say what the exact sum was. The sums allowed to the sons of educated men were considerably larger. An allowance of £200 was considered to be only just sufficient for an undergraduate at Balliol, 'which still had traditions of frugality', about 1880. On that allowance 'they could not hunt and they could not gamble . . . But with care, and with a home to fall back on in the vacations, they could make this do.' (*Anthony Hope and His Books*, by Sir C. Mallet, p. 38.) The sum that is now needed is considerably more. Gino Watkins 'never spent more than the £400 yearly allowance with which he paid all his college and vacation bills'. (*Gino Watkins*, by J. M. Scott, p. 59.) This was at Cambridge, a few years ago.

32. How incessantly women were ridiculed throughout the nineteenth century for attempting to enter their solitary profession, novel readers know, for those efforts provide half the stock-in-trade of fiction. But biography shows how natural it was, even in the present century, for the most enlightened of men to conceive of all women as spinsters, all desiring marriage. Thus: ' "Oh dear, what is to happen to them?" he [G. L. Dickinson] once murmured sadly as a stream of aspiring but uninspiring spinsters flowed round the front court of King's; "I don't know and they don't know." And then in still lower tones as if his bookshelves might overhear him, "Oh dear! What they want is a husband!" ' (*Goldsworthy Lowes Dickinson*, by E. M. Forster, p. 106.) 'What they wanted' might have been the Bar, the Stock Exchange or rooms in Gibb's Buildings,* had the choice been open to them. But it was not; and therefore Mr Dickinson's remark was a very natural one.

33. 'Now and then, at least in the larger houses, there would be a set party, selected and invited long beforehand, and over

these always one idol dominated—the pheasant. Shooting had to be used as a lure. At such times the father of the family was apt to assert himself. If his house was to be filled to bursting, his wines drunk in quantities, and his best shooting provided, then for that shooting he would have the best guns possible. What despair for the mother of daughters to be told that the one guest whom of all others she secretly desired to invite was a bad shot and totally inadmissible!' ('Society and the Season,' by Mary, Countess of Lovelace, in *Fifty Years, 1882–1932*, p. 29.)

34. Some idea of what men hoped that their wives might say and do, at least in the nineteenth century, may be gathered from the following hints in a letter 'addressed to a young lady for whom he had a great regard a short time before her marriage' by John Bowdler. 'Above all, avoid everything which has the *least tendency* to indelicacy or indecorum. Few women have any *idea* how much men are disgusted at the slightest approach to these in any female, and especially in one to whom they are attached. By attending the nursery, or the sick bed, women are too apt to acquire a habit of conversing on such subjects in language which men of delicacy are shocked at.' (*Life of John Bowdler*, p. 123.) But though delicacy was essential, it could, after marriage, be disguised. 'In the 'seventies of last century, Miss Jex-Blake and her associates were vigorously fighting the battle for admission of women to the medical profession, and the doctors were still more vigorously resisting their entry, alleging that it must be improper and demoralizing for a woman to have to study and deal with delicate and intimate medical questions. At that time Ernest Hart, the Editor of the *British Medical Journal*, told me that the majority of the contributions sent to him for publication in the *Journal* dealing with delicate and intimate medical questions were in the handwriting of the doctors' wives, to whom they had obviously been dictated. There were no typewriters or stenographers available in those days.' (*The Doctor's Second Thoughts*, by Sir J. Crichton-Browne, pp. 73, 74.)

The duplicity of delicacy was observed long before this, however. Thus Mandeville in *The Fable of the Bees* (1714) says: '. . . I would have it first consider'd that the Modesty of Woman is the result of Custom and Education, by which all unfashionable Denudations and filthy Expressions are render'd frightful and abominable to them, and that notwithstanding this, the most Virtuous Young Woman alive will often, in spite of her Teeth, have Thoughts and confus'd Ideas of Things arise in her Imagination, which she would not reveal to some People for a Thousand Worlds.'

## Notes and References: Two

1. To quote the exact words of one such appeal: 'This letter is to ask you to set aside for us garments for which you have no further use . . . Stockings, of every sort, no matter how worn, are also most acceptable . . . The Committee find that by offering these clothes at bargain prices . . . they are performing a really useful service to women whose professions require that they should have presentable day and evening dresses which they can ill afford to buy.' (Extract from a letter received from the London and National Society for Women's Service, 1938.)

2. *The Testament of Joad*, by C. E. M. Joad, pp. 210–11. Since the number of societies run directly or indirectly by Englishwomen in the cause of peace is too long to quote (see *The Story of the Disarmament Declaration*, p. 15, for a list of the peace activities of professional, business and working-class women) it is unnecessary to take Mr Joad's criticism seriously, however illuminating psychologically.

3. *Experiment in Autobiography*, by H. G. Wells, p. 486. The men's 'movement to resist the practical obliteration of their freedom by Nazis or Fascists' may have been more perceptible. But that it has been more successful is doubtful. Nazis now control the whole of Austria.' (Daily paper, 12 March 1938.)

4. 'Women, I think, ought not to sit down to table with men; their presence ruins conversation, tending to make it trivial and genteel, or at best merely clever.' (*Under the Fifth Rib*, by C. E. M. Joad, p. 58.) This is an admirably outspoken opinion, and if all who share Mr Joad's sentiments were to

express them as openly, the hostess's dilemma—whom to ask, whom not to ask—would be lightened and her labour saved. If those who prefer the society of their own sex at table would signify the fact, the men, say, by wearing a red, the women by wearing a white rosette, while those who prefer the sexes mixed wore parti-coloured buttonholes of red and white blended, not only would much inconvenience and misunderstanding be prevented, but it is possible that the honesty of the buttonhole would kill a certain form of social hypocrisy now all too prevalent. Meanwhile, Mr Joad's candour deserves the highest praise, and his wishes the most implicit observance.

5. According to Mrs H. M. Swanwick, the WSPU had 'an income from gifts, in the year 1912, of £42,000'. (*I Have Been Young*, by H. M. Swanwick, p. 189.) The total spent in 1912 by the Women's Freedom League was £26,772 12s. 9d. (*The Cause*, by Ray Strachey, p. 311.) Thus the joint income of the two societies was £68,772 12s. 9d. But the two societies were, of course, opposed.

6. 'But, exceptions apart, the general run of women's earnings is low, and £250 a year is quite an achievement, even for a highly qualified woman with years of experience.' (*Careers and Openings for Women*, by Ray Strachey, p. 70.) Nevertheless 'The numbers of women doing professional work have increased very fast in the last twenty years, and were about 400,000 in 1931, in addition to those doing secretarial work or employed in the Civil Service.' (op. cit., p. 44.)

7. The income of the Labour Party in 1936 was £50,153. (*Daily Telegraph*, September 1937.)

8. *The British Civil Servant*. 'The Public Service', by William A. Robson, p. 16.

Professor Ernest Barker suggests that there should be an alternative Civil Service Examination for 'men and women of an older growth' who have spent some years in social work and social service. 'Women candidates in particular might benefit. It is only a very small proportion of women students who succeed in the present open competition: indeed very few compete. On the alternative system here suggested it is possible, and indeed probable, that a much larger proportion of women would be candidates. Women have a genius and a capacity for social work and service. The alternative form of competition would give them a chance of showing that genius and that capacity. It might give them a new incentive to compete for entry into the administrative service of the state, in which their gifts and their presence are needed.' (*The British Civil Servant*. 'The Home Civil Service,' by Professor Ernest Barker, p. 41.) But while the home service remains as exacting as it is at present, it is difficult to see how an incentive can make women free to give 'their gifts and their presence' to the service of the state, unless the state will undertake the care of elderly parents; or make it a penal offence for elderly people of either sex to require the services of daughters at home.

9. Mr Baldwin, speaking at Downing Street, at a meeting on behalf of Newnham College Building Fund, 31 March 1936.

10. The effect of a woman in the pulpit is thus defined in *Women and the Ministry, Some Considerations on the Report of the Archbishops' Commission on the Ministry of Women* (1936), p. 24. 'But we maintain that the ministration of women . . . will tend to produce a lowering of the spiritual tone of Christian worship, such as is not produced by the ministrations of men before congregations largely or exclusively female. It is a tribute to the quality of Christian womanhood that it is possible to make this statement; but it would appear to be a simple matter of fact that in the thoughts and desires of that sex the natural is more easily made subordinate to the supernatural, the carnal to the spiritual than is the case with men; and that the ministrations of a male priesthood do not normally arouse that side of female human nature which should be quiescent during the times of the adoration of almighty God. We believe, on the other hand, that it would be impossible for the male members of the average Anglican congregation to be present at a service at which a woman ministered without becoming unduly conscious of her sex.'

In the opinion of the Commissioners, therefore, Christian women are more spiritually minded than Christian men—a remarkable, but no doubt adequate, reason for excluding them from the priesthood.

[ 385 ]

11. *Daily Telegraph*, 20 January 1936.
12. *Daily Telegraph*, 1936.
13. *Daily Telegraph*, 22 January 1936.
14. 'There are, so far as I know, no universal rules on this subject [i.e. sexual relations between civil servants]; but civil servants and municipal officers of both sexes are certainly expected to observe the conventional proprieties and to avoid conduct which might find its way into the newspapers and there be described as "scandalous". Until recently sexual relations between men and women officers of the Post Office were punishable with immediate dismissal of both parties . . . The problem of avoiding newspaper publicity is a fairly easy one to solve so far as court proceedings are concerned: but official restriction extends further so as to prevent women civil servants (who usually have to resign on marriage) from cohabiting openly with men if they desire to do so. The matter, therefore, takes on a different complexion.' (*The British Civil Servant*, 'The Public Service', by William A. Robson, pp. 14, 15.)
15. Most men's clubs confine women to a special room, or annexe, and exclude them from other apartments, whether on the principle observed at St Sofia that they are impure, or whether on the principle observed at Pompeii that they are too pure, is matter for speculation.
16. The power of the Press to burke discussion of any undesirable subject was, and still is, very formidable. It was one of the 'extraordinary obstacles' against which Josephine Butler had to fight in her campaign against the Contagious Diseases Act. 'Early in 1870 the London Press began to adopt that policy of silence with regard to the question, which lasted for many years, and called forth from the Ladies' Association the famous "Remonstrance against the Conspiracy of Silence", signed by Harriet Martineau and Josephine E. Butler, which concluded with the following words: "Surely, while such a conspiracy of silence is possible and practised among leading journalists, we English greatly exaggerate our privileges as a free people when we profess to encourage a free press, and to possess the right to hear both sides in a momentous question of morality and legislation."' (*Personal Reminiscences of a*

[ 386 ]

*Great Crusade*, by Josephine E. Butler, p. 49.) Again, during the battle for the vote the Press used the boycott with great effect. And so recently as July 1937 Miss Philippa Strachey in a letter headed 'A Conspiracy of Silence', printed (to its honour) by the *Spectator* almost repeats Mrs Butler's words: 'Many hundreds and thousands of men and women have been participating in an endeavour to induce the Government to abandon the provision in the new Contributory Pensions Bill for the black-coated workers which for the first time introduces a differential income limit for men and women entrants . . . In the course of the last month the Bill has been before the House of Lords, where this particular provision has met with strong and determined opposition from all sides of the Chamber . . . These are events one would have supposed to be of sufficient interest to be recorded in the daily Press. But they have been passed over in complete silence by the newspapers from *The Times* to the *Daily Herald* . . . The differential treatment of women under this Bill has aroused a feeling of resentment among them such as has not been witnessed since the granting of the franchise . . . How is one to account for this being completely concealed by the Press?'

17. Flesh wounds were of course inflicted during the battle of Westminster. Indeed the fight for the vote seems to have been more severe than is now recognized. Thus Flora Drummond says: 'Whether we won the vote by our agitation, as I believe, or whether we got it for other reasons, as some people say, I think many of the younger generation will find it hard to believe the fury and brutality aroused by our claim for votes for women less than thirty years ago.' (Flora Drummond in the *Listener*, 25 August 1937.) The younger generation is presumably so used to the fury and brutality that claims for liberty arouse that they have no emotion available for this particular instance. Moreover, that particular fight has not yet taken its place among the fights which have made England the home, and Englishmen the champions of, liberty. The fight for the vote is still generally referred to in terms of sour deprecation: '. . . and the women . . . had not begun that campaign of burning, whipping, and picture-slashing which was finally to prove to both Front Benches their eligibility

for the Franchise.' (*Reflections and Memories*, by Sir John Squire, p. 10.) The younger generation therefore can be excused if they believe that there was nothing heroic about a campaign in which only a few windows were smashed, shins broken, and Sargent's portrait of Henry James damaged, but not irreparably, with a knife. Burning, whipping and picture-slashing only it would seem become heroic when carried out on a large scale by men with machine-guns.

18. *The Life of Sophia Jex-Blake*, by Margaret Todd, MD, p. 72.

19. 'Much has lately been said and written of the achievements and accomplishments of Sir Stanley Baldwin during his Premierships and too much would be impossible. Might I be permitted to call attention to what Lady Baldwin has done? When I first joined the committee of this hospital in 1929, analgesics (pain deadeners) for normal maternity cases in the wards were almost unknown, now their use is ordinary routine and they are availed of in practically 100 per cent of cases, and what is true of this hospital is true virtually for all similar hospitals. This remarkable change in so short a time is due to the inspiration and the tireless efforts and encouragement of Mrs Stanley Baldwin, as she then was . . .' (Letter to *The Times* from C. S. Wentworth Stanley, Chairman House Committee, the City of London Maternity Hospital, 1937.) Since chloroform was first administered to Queen Victoria on the birth of Prince Leopold in April 1853 'normal maternity cases in the wards' have had to wait for seventy-six years and the advocacy of a Prime Minister's wife to obtain this relief.

20. According to *Debrett* the Knights and Dames of the Most Excellent Order of the British Empire wear a badge consisting of 'a cross patonce, enamelled pearl, fimbriated or, surmounted by a gold medallion with a representation of Britannia seated within a circle gules inscribed with the motto "For God and the Empire".' This is one of the few orders open to women, but their subordination is properly marked by the fact that the ribbon in their case is only two inches and one quarter in breadth; whereas the ribbon of the Knights is three inches and three quarters in breadth. The stars also differ in size. The motto, however, is the same for both sexes,

and must be held to imply that those who thus ticket themselves see some connection between the Deity and the Empire, and hold themselves prepared to defend them. What happens if Britannia seated within a circle gules is opposed (as is conceivable) to the other authority whose seat is not specified on the medallion, *Debrett* does not say, and the Knights and Dames must themselves decide.

21. *Life of Sir Ernest Wild, K.C.*, by R. J. Blackham, p. 91.
22. Lord Baldwin, speech reported in *The Times*, 20 April 1936.
23. *Life of Charles Gore*, by G. L. Prestige, DD, pp. 240–41.
24. *Life of Sir William Broadbent*, KCVO, FRS, edited by his daughter, M. E. Broadbent, p. 242.
25. *The Lost Historian, a Memoir of Sir Sidney Low*, by Desmond Chapman-Huston, p. 198.
26. *Thoughts and Adventures*, by the Rt Hon. Winston Churchill, p. 57.
27. Speech at Belfast by Lord Londonderry, reported in *The Times*, 11 July 1936,
28. *Thoughts and Adventures*, by the Rt Hon. Winston Churchill, p. 279.
29. *Daily Herald*, 12 February 1935.
30. Goethe's *Faust*, translated by Melian Stawell and G. L. Dickinson.
31. *The Life of Charles Tomlinson*, by his niece, Mary Tomlinson, p. 30.
32. *Miss Weeton, Journal of a Governess, 1807–1811*, edited by Edward Hall, pp. 14, xvii.
33. *A Memoir of Anne Jemima Clough*, by B. A. Clough, p. 32.
34. *Personal Reminiscences of a Great Crusade*, by Josephine Butler, p. 189.
35. 'You and I know that it matters little if we have to be the out-of-sight piers driven deep into the marsh, on which the visible ones are carried, that support the bridge. We do not mind if, hereafter, people forget that there *are* any low down at all; if some have to be used up in trying experiments, before the best way of building the bridge is discovered. We are quite willing to be among these. The bridge is what we care for, and not our place in it, and we believe that, to the end, it may be kept in remembrance that this is alone to be

our object.' (Letter from Octavia Hill to Mrs N. Senior, 20 September 1874. *The Life of Octavia Hill*, by C. Edmund Maurice, pp. 307–8.)

Octavia Hill (1838–1912) initiated the movement for 'securing better homes for the poor and open spaces for the public ... The "Octavia Hill System" has been adopted over the whole planned extension of [Amsterdam]. In January 1928 no less than 28,648 dwellings had been built.' (*Octavia Hill*, from letters edited by Emily S. Maurice, pp. 10–11.)

36. The maid played so important a part in English upper-class life from the earliest times until the year 1914, when the Hon. Monica Grenfell went to nurse wounded soldiers accompanied by a maid [*Bright Armour*, by Monica Salmond, p. 20], that some recognition of her services seems to be called for. Her duties were peculiar. Thus she had to escort her mistress down Piccadilly 'where a few club men might have looked at her out of a window', but was unnecessary in Whitechapel, 'where malefactors were possibly lurking round every corner'. But her office was undoubtedly arduous. Wilson's part in Elizabeth Barrett's private life is well known to readers of the famous letters. Later in the century (about 1889–92) Gertrude Bell 'went with Lizzie, her maid, to picture exhibitions; she was fetched by Lizzie from dinner parties; she went with Lizzie to see the Settlement in Whitechapel where Mary Talbot was working ...' (*Earlier Letters of Gertrude Bell*, edited by Lady Richmond.) We have only to consider the hours she waited in cloak rooms, the acres she toiled in picture galleries, the miles she trudged along West End pavements to conclude that if Lizzie's day is now almost over, it was in its day a long one. Let us hope that the thought that she was putting into practice the commands laid down by St Paul in his Letters to Titus and the Corinthians, was a support; and the knowledge that she was doing her utmost to deliver her mistress's body intact to her master a solace. Even so in the weakness of the flesh and in the darkness of the beetle-haunted basement she must sometimes have bitterly reproached St Paul on the one hand for his chastity, and the gentlemen of Piccadilly on the other for their lust. It is much to be regretted that no lives of maids,

from which a more fully documented account could be constructed, are to be found in the *Dictionary of National Biography*.

37. *Earlier Letters of Gertrude Bell*, collected and edited by Elsa Richmond, pp. 217–18.

38. The question of chastity, both of mind and body, is of the greatest interest and complexity. The Victorian, Edwardian and much of the Fifth Georgian conception of chastity was based, to go no further back, upon the words of St Paul. To understand their meaning we should have to understand his psychology and environment—no light task in view of his frequent obscurity and the lack of biographical material. From internal evidence, it seems clear that he was a poet and a prophet, but lacked logical power, and was without that psychological training which forces even the least poetic or prophetic nowadays to subject their personal emotions to scrutiny. Thus his famous pronouncement on the matter of veils, upon which the theory of women's chastity seems to be based, is susceptible to criticism from several angles. In the Letter to the Corinthians his argument that a woman must be veiled when she prays or prophesies is based upon the assumption that to be unveiled 'is one and the same thing as if she were shaven'. That assumption granted, we must ask next: What shame is there in being shaven? Instead of replying, St Paul proceeds to assert, 'For a man indeed ought not to have his head veiled, forasmuch as he is the image and glory of God': from which it appears that it is not being shaven in itself that is wrong; but to be a woman and to be shaven. It is wrong, it appears, for the woman because 'the woman is the glory of the man.' If St Paul had said openly that he liked the look of women's long hair many of us would have agreed with him, and thought the better of him for saying so. But other reasons appeared to him preferable, as appears from his next remark: 'For the man is not of the woman; but the woman of the man; for neither was the man created for the woman; but the woman for the man: for this cause ought the woman to have a sign of authority on her head, because of the angels.' What view the angels took of long hair we have no means of knowing; and St Paul himself

seems to have been doubtful of their support or he would not think it necessary to drag in the familiar accomplice nature. 'Doth not even nature itself teach you, that, if a man have long hair, it is a dishonour to him? But if a woman have long hair, it is a glory to her: for her hair is given her for a covering. But if any man seemeth to be contentious, we have no such custom, neither the churches of God.' The argument from nature may seem to us susceptible of amendment; nature, when allied with financial advantage, is seldom of divine origin; but if the basis of the argument is shifty, the conclusion is firm. 'Let the women keep silence in the churches: for it is not permitted unto them to speak; but let them be in subjection, as also saith the law.' Having thus invoked the familiar but always suspect trinity of accomplices, Angels, nature and law, to support his personal opinion, St Paul reaches the conclusion which has been looming unmistakably ahead of us: 'And if they would learn anything, let them ask their own husbands at home: for it is shameful for a woman to speak in the church.' The nature of that 'shame', which is closely connected with chastity has, as the letter proceeds, been considerably alloyed. For it is obviously compounded of certain sexual and personal prejudices. St Paul, it is obvious, was not only a bachelor (for his relations with Lydia see Renan, *Saint Paul*, p. 149. 'Est-il cependant absolument impossible que Paul ait contracté avec cette sœur une union plus intime? On ne saurait l'affirmer');* and, like many bachelors, suspicious of the other sex; but a poet and like many poets preferred to prophesy himself rather than to listen to the prophecies of others. Also he was of the virile or dominant type, so familiar at present in Germany, for whose gratification a subject race or sex is essential. Chastity then as defined by St Paul is seen to be a complex conception, based upon the love of long hair; the love of subjection; the love of an audience; the love of laying down the law, and, subconsciously, upon a very strong and natural desire that the woman's mind and body shall be reserved for the use of one man and one only. Such a conception when supported by the Angels, nature, law, custom and the Church, and enforced by a sex with a strong personal interest to enforce it, and the economic means, was of undoubted power. The grip of its white if skeleton fingers can be found upon whatever page of history we open from St Paul to Gertrude Bell. Chastity was invoked to prevent her from studying medicine; from painting from the nude; from reading Shakespeare; from playing in orchestras; from walking down Bond Street alone. In 1848 it was 'an unpardonable solecism' for the daughters of a gardener to drive down Regent Street in a hansom cab (*Paxton and the Bachelor Duke*, by Violet Markham, p. 288); that solecism became a crime, of what magnitude theologians must decide, if the flaps were left open. In the beginning of the present century the daughter of an ironmaster (for let us not flout distinctions said today to be of prime importance), Sir Hugh Bell, had 'reached the age of 27 and married without ever having walked alone down Piccadilly . . . Gertrude, of course, would never have dreamt of doing that . . .' The West End was the contaminated area. 'It was one's own class that was taboo; . . .' (*The Earlier Letters of Gertrude Bell*, collected and edited by Elsa Richmond, pp. 217–18.) But the complexities and inconsistencies of chastity were such that the same girl who had to be veiled, i.e. accompanied by a male or a maid, in Piccadilly, could visit Whitechapel, or Seven Dials, then haunts of vice and disease, alone and with her parents' approval. This anomaly did not altogether escape comment. Thus Charles Kingsley as a boy exclaimed: '. . . and the girls have their heads crammed full of schools, and district visiting, and baby linen, and penny clubs. Confound!!! and going about among the most abominable scenes of filth and wretchedness, and indecency to visit the poor and read the Bible to them. My own mother says that the places they go into are fit for no girl to see, and that they should not know such things exist.' (*Charles Kingsley*, by Margaret Farrand Thorp, p. 12.) Mrs Kingsley, however, was exceptional. Most of the daughters of educated men saw such 'abominable scenes', and knew that such things existed. That they concealed their knowledge, is probable; what effect that concealment had psychologically it is impossible here to inquire. But that chastity, whether real or imposed, was an immense

[ 393 ]

power, whether good or bad, it is impossible to doubt. Even today it is probable that a woman has to fight a psychological battle of some severity with the ghost of St Paul, before she can have intercourse with a man other than her husband. Not only was the social stigma strongly exerted on behalf of chastity, but the Bastardy Act did its utmost to impose chastity by financial pressure. Until women had the vote in 1918, 'the Bastardy Act of 1872 fixed the sum of 5s. a week as the maximum which a father, whatever his wealth, could be made to pay towards the maintenance of his child.' (*Josephine Butler*, by M. G. Fawcett and E. M. Turner, note, p. 101.) Now that St Paul and many of his apostles have been unveiled themselves by modern science chastity has undergone considerable revision. Yet there is said to be a reaction in favour of some degree of chastity for both sexes. This is partly due to economic causes; the protection of chastity by maids is an expensive item in the bourgeois budget. The psychological argument in favour of chastity is well expressed by Mr Upton Sinclair: 'Nowadays we hear a great deal about mental troubles caused by sex repression; it is the mood of the moment. We do not hear anything about the complexes which may be caused by sex indulgence. But my observation has been that those who permit themselves to follow every sexual impulse are quite as miserable as those who repress every sexual impulse. I remember a class-mate in College; I said to him: "Did it ever occur to you to stop and look at your own mind? Everything that comes to you is turned into sex." He looked surprised, and I saw that it was a new idea to him; he thought it over, and said: "I guess you are right."' (*Candid Reminiscences*, by Upton Sinclair, p. 63.) Further illustration is supplied by the following anecdote: 'In the splendid library of Columbia University were treasures of beauty, costly volumes of engravings, and in my usual greedy fashion I went at these, intending to learn all there was to know about Renaissance art in a week or two. But I found myself overwhelmed by this mass of nakedness; my senses reeled, and I had to quit.' (op. cit., pp. 62–3.)

39. The translation here used is by Sir Richard Jebb (*Sophocles, the Plays and Fragments*, with critical notes, commentary and

translation, in English prose). It is impossible to judge any book from a translation, yet even when thus read the *Antigone* is clearly one of the great masterpieces of dramatic literature. Nevertheless, it could undoubtedly be made, if necessary, into anti-Fascist propaganda. Antigone herself could be transformed either into Mrs Pankhurst, who broke a window and was imprisoned in Holloway; or into Frau Pommer, the wife of a Prussian mines official at Essen, who said: ' "The thorn of hatred has been driven deep enough into the people by the religious conflicts, and it is high time that the men of today disappeared." . . . She has been arrested and is to be tried on a charge of insulting and slandering the State and the Nazi movement.' (*The Times*, 12 August 1935.) Antigone's crime was of much the same nature and was punished in much the same way. Her words, 'See what I suffer, and from whom, because I feared to cast away the fear of heaven! . . . And what law of heaven have I transgressed? Why, hapless one, should I look to the gods any more—what ally should I invoke—when by piety I have earned the name of impious?' could be spoken either by Mrs Pankhurst, or by Frau Pommer; and are certainly topical. Creon, again, who 'thrust the children of the sunlight to the shades, and ruthlessly lodged a living soul in the grave'; who held that 'disobedience is the worst of evils', and that 'whomsoever the city may appoint, that man must be obeyed, in little things and great, in just things and unjust' is typical of certain politicans in the past, and of Herr Hitler and Signor Mussolini in the present. But though it is easy to squeeze these characters into up-do-date dress, it is impossible to keep them there. They suggest too much; when the curtain falls we sympathize, it may be noted, even with Creon himself. This result, to the propagandist undesirable, would seem to be due to the fact that Sophocles (even in a translation) uses freely all the faculties that can be possessed by a writer; and suggests, therefore, that if we use art to propagate political opinions, we must force the artist to clip and cabin his gift to do us a cheap and passing service. Literature will suffer the same mutilation that the mule has suffered; and there will be no more horses.

[ 395 ]

40. The five words of Antigone are: Οὔτοι συνέχθειν ἄλλα συμφιλφεῖν ἔφυν 'Tis not my nature to join in hating, but in loving. (*Antigone*, line 523, Jebb.) To which Creon replied: 'Pass, then, to the world of the dead, and, if thou must needs love, love them. While I live, no woman shall rule me.'

41. Even at a time of great political stress like the present it is remarkable how much criticism is still bestowed upon women. The announcement, 'A shrewd, witty and provocative study of modern woman', appears on an average three times yearly in publishers' lists. The author, often a doctor of letters, is invariably of the male sex; and 'to mere man', as the blurb puts it (see *Times Lit. Sup.*, 12 March 1938), 'this book will be an eye-opener'.

## NOTES AND REFERENCES: THREE

1. It is to be hoped that some methodical person has made a collection of the various manifestos and questionnaires issued and broadcast during the years 1936-7. Private people of no political training were invited to sign appeals asking their own and foreign governments to change their policy; artists were asked to fill up forms stating the proper relations of the artist to the State, to religion, to morality; pledges were required that the writer should use English grammatically and avoid vulgar expressions; and dreamers were invited to analyse their dreams. By way of inducement it was generally proposed to publish the results in the daily or weekly Press. What effect this inquisition has had upon governments it is for the politician to say. Upon literature, since the output of books is unstaunched, and grammar would seem to be neither better nor worse, the effect is problematical. But the inquisition is of great psychological and social interest. Presumably it originated in the state of mind suggested by Dean Inge (The Rickman Godlee Lecture, reported in *The Times*, 23 November 1937), 'whether in our own interests we were moving in the right direction. If we went on as we were doing now, would the man of the future be superior to us or not? . . . Thoughtful people were beginning to realize that before congratulating ourselves on moving fast we ought to

have some idea where we were moving to': a general self-dissatisfaction and desire 'to live differently'. It also points, indirectly, to the death of the Siren, that much ridiculed and often upper-class lady who by keeping open house for the aristocracy, plutocracy, intelligentsia, ignorantsia, etc., tried to provide all classes with a talking-ground or scratching-post where they could rub up minds, manners, and morals more privately, and perhaps as usefully. The part that the Siren played in promoting culture and intellectual liberty in the eighteenth century is held by historians to be of some importance. Even in our own day she had her uses. Witness W. B. Yeats—'How often I have wished that he [Synge] might live long enough to enjoy that communion with idle, charming, cultivated women which Balzac in one of his dedications calls "the chief consolation of genius"!' (*Dramatis Personae*, W. B. Yeats, p. 127.) Lady St Helier who, as Lady Jeune, preserved the eighteenth-century tradition, informs us, however, that 'Plovers' eggs at 2s. 6d. apiece, forced straw-berries, early asparagus, *petits poussins* . . . are now considered almost a necessity by anyone aspiring to give a good dinner' (1909); and her remark that the reception day was 'very fatiguing . . . how exhausted I felt when half-past seven came, and how gladly at eight o'clock I sat down to a peaceful *tête-à-tête* dinner with my husband!' (*Memories of Fifty Years*, by Lady St Helier, pp. 3, 5, 182) may explain why such houses are shut, why such hostesses are dead, and why therefore the intelligentsia, the ignorantsia, the aristocracy, the bureau-cracy, the bourgeoisie, etc., are driven (unless somebody will revive that society on an economic basis) to do their talking in public. But in view of the multitude of manifestos and questionnaires now in circulation it would be foolish to suggest another into the minds and motives of the Inquisitors.

2. 'He did begin however on 13 May (1844) to lecture weekly at Queen's College which Maurice and other professors at King's had established a year before, primarily for the examination and training of governesses. Kingsley was ready to share in this unpopular task because he believed in the higher education of women.' (*Charles Kingsley*, by Margaret Farrand Thorp, p. 65.)

[ 397 ]

3. The French, as the above quotation shows, are as active as the English in issuing manifestos. That the French, who refuse to allow the women of France to vote, and still inflict upon them laws whose almost medieval severity can be studied in *The Position of Women in Contemporary France*, by Frances Clark, should appeal to English women to help them to protect liberty and culture must cause surprise.

4. Strict accuracy, here slightly in conflict with rhythm and euphony, requires the word 'port'. A photograph in the daily Press of 'Dons in a Senior Common Room after dinner' (1937) showed 'a railed trolley in which the port decanter travels across a gap between diners at the fireplace, and thus continues its round without passing against the sun'. Another picture shows the 'sconce' cup in use. 'This old Oxford custom ordains that mention of certain subjects in Hall shall be punished by the offender drinking three pints of beer at one draught . . .' Such examples are by themselves enough to prove how impossible it is for a woman's pen to describe life at a man's college without committing some unpardonable solecism. But the gentlemen whose customs are often, it is to be feared, travestied, will extend their indulgence when they reflect that the female novelist, however reverent in intention, works under grave physical drawbacks. Should she wish, for example, to describe a Feast at Trinity, Cambridge, she has to 'listen through the peephole in the room of Mrs Butler (the Master's wife) to the speeches taking place at the Feast which was held in Trinity College'. Miss Haldane's observation was made in 1907, when she reflected that 'The whole surroundings seemed medieval.' (*From One Century to Another*, by E. Haldane, p. 235.)

5. According to Whitaker there is a Royal Society of Literature and also the British Academy, both presumably, since they have offices and officers, official bodies, but what their powers are it is impossible to say, since if Whitaker had not vouched for their existence it would scarcely have been suspected.

6. Women were apparently excluded from the British Museum Reading-Room in the eighteenth century. Thus: '*Miss Chudleigh* solicits permission to be received into the reading-room.

The only female student who as yet has honoured us was *Mrs Macaulay*: and your Lordship may recollect what an untoward event offended her delicacy.' (Daniel Wray to Lord Harwicke, 22 October 1768. Nichols, *Illustrations of the Literary History of the Eighteenth Century*, vol. I, p. 137.) The editor adds in a footnote: 'This alludes to the indelicacy of a gentleman there, in *Mrs Macaulay's* presence; of which the particulars will not bear to be repeated.'

7. *The Autobiography and Letters of Mrs M. O. W. Oliphant*, arranged and edited by Mrs Harry Coghill. Mrs Oliphant (1825–97) 'lived in perpetual embarrassment owing to her undertaking education and maintenance of her widowed brother's children in addition to her own two sons ...' (*Dictionary of National Biography*.)

8. Macaulay's *History of England*, vol. III, p. 278 (standard edition).

9. Mr Littlewood, until recently dramatic critic of the *Morning Post*, described the condition of Journalism at Present at a dinner given in his honour, 6 December 1937. Mr Littlewood said: 'that he had in season and out of season fought for more space for the theatre in the columns of the London daily papers. It was Fleet Street where, between eleven and half-past twelve, not to mention before and after, thousands of beautiful words and thoughts were systematically massacred. It had been his lot for at least two out of his four decades to return to that shambles every night with the sure and certain prospect of being told the paper was already full with important news, and that there was no room for any sanguinary stuff about the theatre. It had been his luck to wake up the next morning to find himself answerable for the mangled remains of what was once a good notice ... It was not the fault of the men in the office. Some of them put the blue pencil through with tears in their eyes. The real culprit was that huge public who knew nothing about the theatre and could not be expected to care.' (*The Times*, 6 December 1937.)

Mr Douglas Jerrold describes the treatment of politics in the Press. 'In those few brief years [between 1928–33] truth had fled from Fleet Street. You could never tell all the truth all the time. You never will be able to do so. But you used at least to be able to tell the truth about other countries. By 1933, you did it at your peril. In 1928 there was no direct political pressure from advertisers. Today it is not only direct but effective.'

Literary criticism would seem to be in much the same case and for the same reason: 'There are no critics in whom the public have any more confidence. They trust, if at all, to the different Book Societies, and the selections of individual newspapers, and on the whole they are wise ... The Book Societies are frankly book sellers, and the great national newspapers cannot afford to puzzle their readers. They must all choose books which have, at the prevailing level of public taste, a potentially large sale.' (*Georgian Adventure*, by Douglas Jerrold, pp. 282, 283, 298.)

10. While it is obvious that under the conditions of journalism at present the criticism of literature must be unsatisfactory, it is also obvious that no change can be made, without changing the economic structure of society and the psychological structure of the artist. Economically, it is necessary that the reviewer should herald the publication of a new book with his town-crier's shout 'O yez, O yez, O yez, such and such a book has been published: its subject is this, that or the other.' Psychologically, vanity and the desire for 'recognition' are still so strong among artists that to starve them of advertisement and to deny them frequent if contrasted shocks of praise and blame would be as rash as the introduction of rabbits into Australia: the balance of nature would be upset and the consequences might well be disastrous. The suggestion in the text is not to abolish public criticism; but to supplement it by a new service based on the example of the medical profession. A panel of critics recruited from reviewers (many of whom are potential critics of genuine taste and learning) would practise like doctors and in strictest privacy. Publicity removed, it follows that most of the distractions and corruptions which inevitably make contemporary criticism worthless to the writer would be abolished; all inducement to praise or blame for personal reasons would be destroyed; neither sales nor vanity would be affected; the author could attend to criticism without considering the

effect upon public or friends; the critic could criticize without considering the editor's blue pencil or the public taste. Since criticism is much desired by the living, as the constant demand for it proves, and since fresh books are as essential for the critic's mind as fresh meat for his body, each would gain; literature even might benefit. The advantages of the present system of public criticism are mainly economic; the evil effects psychologically are shown by the two famous *Quarterly* reviews of Keats and Tennyson. Keats was deeply wounded; and 'the effect . . . upon Tennyson himself was penetrating and prolonged. His first act was at once to withdraw from the press *The Lover's Tale* . . . We find him thinking of leaving England altogether, of living abroad.' (*Tennyson*, by Harold Nicolson, p. 118.) The effect of Mr Churton Collins upon Edmund Gosse was much the same: 'His self-confidence was undermined, his personality reduced . . . was not everyone watching his struggles regarding him as doomed? . . . His own account of his sensations was that he went about feeling that he had been flayed alive.' (*The Life and Letters of Sir Edmund Gosse*, by Evan Charteris, p. 196.)

11. 'A ring-the-bell-and-run-away-man.' This word has been coined in order to define those who make use of words with the desire to hurt but at the same time to escape detection. In a transitional age when many qualities are changing their value, new words to express new values are much to be desired. Vanity, for example, which would seem to lead to severe complications of cruelty and tyranny, judging from evidence supplied abroad, is still masked by a name with trivial associations. A supplement to the *Oxford English Dictionary* is indicated.

12. *Memoir of Anne J. Clough*, by B. A. Clough, pp. 38, 67. 'The Sparrow's Nest', by William Wordsworth.

13. In the nineteenth century much valuable work was done for the working class by educated men's daughters in the only way that was then open to them. But now that some of them at least have received an expensive education, it is arguable that they can work much more effectively by remaining in their own class and using the methods of that class to improve a class which stands much in need of improvement. If on the

other hand the educated (as so often happens) renounce the very qualities which education should have bought—reason, tolerance, knowledge—and play at belonging to the working class and adopting its cause, they merely expose that cause to the ridicule of the educated class, and do nothing to improve their own. But the number of books written by the educated about the working class would seem to show that the glamour of the working class and the emotional relief afforded by adopting its cause, are today as irresistible to the middle class as the glamour of the aristocracy was twenty years ago (see *A la recherche du temps perdu*). Meanwhile it would be interesting to know what the true-born working man or woman thinks of the playboys and playgirls of the educated class who adopt the working-class cause without sacrificing middle-class capital, or sharing working-class experience. 'The average housewife,' according to Mrs Murphy, Home Service Director of the British Commercial Gas Association, 'washed an acre of dirty dishes, a mile of glass and three miles of clothes and scrubbed five miles of floor yearly.' (*Daily Telegraph*, 29 September 1937.) For a more detailed account of working-class life, see *Life as We Have Known It*, by Co-operative working women, edited by Margaret Llewelyn Davies. The *Life of Joseph Wright* also gives a remarkable account of working-class life at first hand and not through pro-proletarian spectacles.

14. 'It was stated yesterday at the War Office that the Army Council have no intention of opening recruiting for any women's corps.' (*The Times*, 22 October 1937.) This marks a prime distinction between the sexes. Pacifism is enforced upon women. Men are still allowed liberty of choice.

15. The following quotation shows, however, that if sanctioned the fighting instinct easily develops. 'The eyes deeply sunk into the sockets, the features acute, the amazon keeps herself very straight on the stirrups at the head of her squadron . . . Five English parlementaries look at this woman with the respectful and a bit restless admiration one feels for a "fauve" of an unknown species . . .—Come nearer Amalia—orders the commandant. She pushes her horse towards us and salutes her chief with the sword.—Sergeant Amalia Bonilla—contin-

ues the chief of the squadron—how old are you?—Thirty-six—Where were you born?—In Granada—Why have you joined the army?—My two daughters were militiawomen. The younger has been killed in the Alto de Leon. I thought I had to supersede her and avenge her.—And how many enemies have you killed to avenge her?—You know it, commandant, five. The sixth is not sure.—No, but you have taken his horse. The amazon Amalia rides in fact a magnificent dapple-grey horse, with glossy hair, which flatters like a parade horse . . . This woman who has killed five men—but who feels not sure about the sixth—was for the envoys of the House of Commons an excellent introducer to the Spanish war.' (*The Martyrdom of Madrid*, Inedited Witnesses, by Louis Delaprée, pp. 34, 5, 6. Madrid, 1937.)

16. By way of proof, an attempt may be made to elucidate the reaons given by various Cabinet Ministers in various Parliaments from about 1870 to 1918 for opposing the Suffrage Bill. An able effort has been made by Mrs Oliver Strachey (see chapter 'The Deceitfulness of Politics' in her *The Cause*).

17. 'We have had women's civil and political status before the League only since 1935.' From reports sent in as to the position of the woman as wife, mother and home maker, 'the sorry fact was discovered that her economic position in many countries (including Great Britain) was unstable. She is entitled neither to salary nor wages and has definite duties to perform. In England, though she may have devoted her whole life to husband and children, her husband, no matter how wealthy, can leave her destitute at his death and she has no legal redress. We must alter this—by legislation . . .' (Linda P. Littlejohn, reported in the *Listener*, 10 November 1937.)

18. This particular definition of woman's task comes not from an Italian but from a German source. There are so many versions and all are so much alike that it seems unnecessary to verify each separately. But it is curious to find how easy it is to cap them from English sources. Mr Gerhardi for example writes: 'Never yet have I committed the error of looking on women writers as serious fellow artists. I enjoy them rather as spiritual helpers who, endowed with a sensitive capacity for

[ 403 ]

appreciation, may help the few of us afflicted with genius to bear our cross with good grace. Their true role, therefore, is rather to hold out the sponge to us, cool our brow, while we bleed. If their sympathetic understanding may indeed be put to a more romantic use, how we cherish them for it!' (*Memoirs of a Polyglot*, by William Gerhardi, pp. 320, 321.) This conception of woman's role tallies almost exactly with that quoted above.

19. To speak accurately, 'a large silver plaque in the form of the Reich eagle ... was created by President Hindenburg for scientists and other distinguished civilians ... It may not be worn. It is usually placed on the writing-desk of the recipient.' (Daily paper, 21 April 1936.)

20. 'It is a common thing to see the business girl contenting herself with a bun or a sandwich for her midday meal; and though there are theories that this is from choice ... the truth is that they often cannot afford to eat properly.' (*Careers and Openings for Women*, by Ray Strachey, p. 74.) Compare also Miss E. Turner: '... many offices had been wondering why they were unable to get through their work as smoothly as formerly. It had been found that junior typists were fagged out in the afternoons because they could afford only an apple and a sandwich for lunch. Employers should meet the increased cost of living by increased salaries.' (*The Times*, 28 March 1938.)

21. The Mayoress of Woolwich (Mrs Kathleen Rance) speaking at a bazaar, reported in *Evening Standard*, 20 December 1937.

22. Miss E. R. Clarke, reported in *The Times*, 24 September 1937.

23. Reported in *Daily Herald*, 15 August 1936.

24. Canon F. R. Barry, speaking at conference arranged by Anglican Group at Oxford, reported in *The Times*, 10 January 1933.

25. *The Ministry of Women. Report of the Archbishops' Commission*, VII. Secondary Schools and Universities, p. 65.

26. 'Miss D. Carruthers, Head Mistress of the Green School, Isleworth, said there was a "very grave dissatisfaction" among older schoolgirls at the way in which organized religion was

carried on. "The Churches seem somehow to be failing to supply the spiritual needs of young people," she said. "It is a fault that seems common to all churches." ' (*Sunday Times*, 21 November 1937.)

27. *Life of Charles Gore*, by G. L. Prestige, DD, p. 353.

28. *The Ministry of Women. Report of the Archbishops' Commission, passim.*

29. Whether or not the gift of prophecy and the gift of poetry were originally the same, a distinction has been made between those gifts and professions for many centuries. But the fact that the Song of Songs, the work of a poet, is included among the sacred books, and that propagandist poems and novels, the works of prophets, are included among the secular, points to some confusion. Lovers of English literature can scarcely be too thankful that Shakespeare lived too late to be canonized by the Church. Had the plays been ranked among the sacred books they must have received the same treatment as the Old and New Testaments; we should have had them doled out on Sundays from the mouths of priests in snatches; now a soliloquy from *Hamlet*; now a corrupt passage from the pen of some drowsy reporter; now a bawdy song; now half a page from *Antony and Cleopatra*, as the Old and New Testaments have been sliced up and interspersed with hymns in the Church of England service; and Shakespeare would have been as unreadable as the Bible. Yet those who have not been forced from childhood to hear it thus dismembered weekly assert that the Bible is a work of the greatest interest, much beauty, and deep meaning.

30. *The Ministry of Women*, Appendix I. 'Certain Psychological and Physiological Considerations', by Professor Grensted, DD, pp. 79–87.

31. 'At present a married priest is able to fulfil the requirements of the ordination service, "to forsake and set aside all worldly cares and studies", largely because his wife can undertake the care of the household and the family . . .' (*The Ministry of Women*, p. 32.)

   The Commissioners are here stating and approving a principle which is frequently stated and approved by the dictators. Herr Hitler and Signor Mussolini have both often in very similar words expressed the opinion that 'There are two worlds in the life of the nation, the world of men and the world of women'; and proceeded to much the same definition of the duties. The effect which this division has had upon the women; the petty and personal nature of her interests; her absorption in the practical; her apparent incapacity for the poetical and adventurous—all this has been made the staple of so many novels, the target for so much satire, has confirmed so many theorists in the theory that by the law of nature the woman is less spiritual than the man, that nothing more need be said to prove that she has carried out, willingly or unwillingly, her share of the contract. But very little attention has yet been paid to the intellectual and spiritual effect of this division of duties upon those who are enabled by it 'to forsake all worldly cares and studies'. Yet there can be no doubt that we owe to this segregation the immense elaboration of modern instruments and methods of war; the astonishing complexities of theology; the vast deposit of notes at the bottom of Greek, Latin and even English texts; the innumerable carvings, chasings and unnecessary ornamentations of our common furniture and crockery; the myriad distinctions of *Debrett* and *Burke*; and all those meaningless but highly ingenious turnings and twistings into which the intellect ties itself when rid of 'the cares of the household and the family'. The emphasis which both priests and dictators place upon the necessity for two worlds is enough to prove that it is essential to the domination.

32. Evidence of the complex nature of satisfaction of dominance is provided by the following quotation: 'My husband insists that I call him "Sir",' said a woman at the Bristol Police Court yesterday, when she applied for a maintenance order. 'To keep the peace I have complied with his request,' she added. 'I also have to clean his boots, fetch his razor when he shaves, and speak up promptly when he asks me questions.' In the same issue of the same paper Sir E. F. Fletcher is reported to have 'urged the House of Commons to stand up to dictators'. (*Daily Herald*, 1 August 1936.) This would seem to show that the common consciousness which includes husband, wife and House of Commons is feeling at one and

the same moment the desire to dominate, the need to comply in order to keep the peace, and the necessity of dominating the desire for dominance—a psychological conflict which serves to explain much that appears inconsistent and turbulent in contemporary opinion. The pleasure of dominance is of course further complicated by the fact that it is still, in the educated class, closely allied with the pleasures of wealth, social and professional prestige. Its distinction from the comparatively simple pleasures—e.g. the pleasure of a country walk—is proved by the fear of ridicule which great psychologists, like Sophocles, detect in the dominator; who is also peculiarly susceptible according to the same authority either to ridicule or defiance on the part of the female sex. An essential element in this pleasure therefore would seem to be derived not from the feeling itself but from the reflection of other people's feelings, and it would follow that it can be influenced by a change in those feelings. Laughter as an antidote to dominance is perhaps indicated.

33. *The Life of Charlotte Brontë*, by Mrs Gaskell.

34. *The Life of Sophia Jex-Blake*, by Margaret Todd, pp. 67–9, 70–71, 72.

35. External observation would suggest that a man still feels it a peculiar insult to be taunted with cowardice by a woman in much the same way that a woman feels it a peculiar insult to be taunted with unchastity by a man. The following quotation supports this view. Mr Bernard Shaw writes: 'I am not forgetting the gratification that war gives to the instinct of pugnacity and admiration of courage that are so strong in women . . . In England on the outbreak of war civilized young women rush about handing white feathers to all young men who are not in uniform. This,' he continues, 'like other survivals from savagery is quite natural,' and he points out that 'in old days a woman's life and that of her children depended on the courage and killing capacity of her mate.' Since vast numbers of young men did their work all through the war in offices without any such adornment, and the number of 'civilized young women' who stuck feathers in coats must have been infinitesimal compared with those who did nothing of the kind, Mr Shaw's exaggeration is sufficient

proof of the immense psychological impression that fifty or sixty feathers (no actual statistics are available) can still make. This would seem to show that the male still preserves an abnormal susceptibility to such taunts; therefore that courage and pugnacity are still among the prime attributes of manliness; therefore that he still wishes to be admired for possessing them; therefore that any derision of such qualities would have a proportionate effect. That 'the manhood emotion' is also connected with economic independence seems probable. 'We have never known a man who was not, openly or secretly, proud of being able to support women; whether they were his sisters or his mistresses. We have never known a woman who did not regard the change from economic independence on an employer to economic dependence on a man, as an honourable promotion. What is the good of men and women lying to each other about these things? It is not we that have made them'—(*A. H. Orage*, by Philip Mairet, vii)—an interesting statement, attributed by G. K. Chesterton to A. H. Orage.

36. Until the beginning of the eighties, according to Miss Haldane, the sister of R. B. Haldane, no lady could work. 'I should, of course, have liked to study for a profession, but that was an impossible idea unless one were in the sad position of "having to work for one's bread" and that would have been a terrible state of affairs. Even a brother wrote of the melancholy fact after he had been to see Mrs Langtry act. "She was a lady and acted like a lady, but what a sad thing it was that she should have to do so!"' (*From One Century to Another*, by Elizabeth Haldane, pp. 73–4.) Harriet Martineau earlier in the century was delighted when her family lost its money, for thus she lost her 'gentility' and was allowed to work.

37. *Life of Sophia Jex-Blake*, by Margaret Todd, pp. 69, 70.

38. For an account of Mr Leigh Smith, see *Emily Davies and Girton College*, by Barbara Stephen. Barbara Leigh Smith became Madame Bodichon.

39. How nominal that opening was is shown by the following account of the actual conditions under which women worked in the R.A. Schools about 1900. 'Why the female of the species

should never be given the same advantages as the male it is difficult to understand. At the R.A. Schools we women had to compete against men for all the prizes and medals that were given each year, and we were only allowed half the amount of tuition and less than half their opportunities for study . . . No nude model was allowed to be posed in the women's painting room at the R.A. Schools . . . The male students not only worked from nude models, both male and female, during the day, but they were given an evening class as well, at which they could make studies from the figure, the visiting R.A. instructing.' This seemed to the women students 'very unfair indeed'; Miss Collyer had the courage and the social standing necessary to beard first Mr Franklin Dicksee, who argued that since girls marry, money spent on their teaching is money wasted; next Lord Leighton; and at length the thin edge of the wedge, that is the undraped figure, was allowed. But 'the advantages of the night class we never did succeed in obtaining . . .' The women students therefore clubbed together and hired a photographer's studio in Baker Street. 'The money that we, as the committee, had to find, reduced our meals to near starvation diet.' (*Life of an Artist*, by Margaret Collyer, pp. 19–81, 82.) The same rule was in force at the Nottingham Art School in the twentieth century. 'Women were not allowed to draw from the nude. If the men worked from the living figure I had to go into the Antique Room . . . the hatred of those plaster figures stays with me till this day. I never got any benefit out of their study.' (*Oil Paint and Grease Paint*, by Dame Laura Knight, p. 47.) But the profession of art is not the only profession that is thus nominally open. The profession of medicine is 'open', but '. . . nearly all the Schools attached to London Hospitals are barred to women students, whose training in London is mainly carried on at the London School of Medicine.' (*Memorandum on the Position of English Women in Relation to that of English Men*, by Philippa Strachey, 1935, p. 26.) 'Some of the girl "medicals" at Cambridge University have formed themselves into a group to ventilate the grievance.' (*Evening News*, 25 March 1937.) In 1922 women students were admitted to the Royal Veterinary College, Camden Town. '. . .

since then the profession has attracted so many women that the number has recently been restricted to 50.' (*Daily Telegraph*, 1 October 1937.)

40. and 41. *The Life of Mary Kingsley*, by Stephen Gwynn, pp. 18, 26. In a fragment of a letter Mary Kingsley writes: 'I am useful occasionally, but that is all—very useful a few months ago when on calling on a friend she asked me to go up to her bedroom and see her new hat—a suggestion that staggered me, I knowing her opinion of mine in such matters.' 'The letter,' says Mr Gwynn, 'did not complete this adventure of an unauthorised *fiancé*, but I am sure she got him off the roof and enjoyed the experience riotously.'

42. According to Antigone there are two kinds of law, the written and the unwritten, and Mrs Drummond maintains that it may sometimes be necessary to improve the written law by breaking it. But the many and varied activities of the educated man's daughter in the nineteenth century were clearly not simply or even mainly directed towards breaking laws. They were, on the contrary, endeavours of an experimental kind to discover what are the unwritten laws; that is the private laws that should regulate certain instincts, passions, mental and physical desires. That such laws exist and are observed by civilized people, is fairly generally allowed; but it is beginning to be agreed that they were not laid down by 'God', who is now very generally held to be a conception, of patriarchial origin, valid only for certain races, at certain stages and times; nor by nature, who is now known to vary greatly in her commands and to be largely under control; but have to be discovered afresh by successive generations, largely by their own efforts of reason and imagination. Since, however, reason and imagination are to some extent the product of our bodies, and there are two kinds of body, male and female, and since these two bodies have been proved within the past few years to differ fundamentally, it is clear that the laws that they perceive and respect must be differently interpreted. Thus Professor Julian Huxley says: '. . . from the moment of fertilization onwards, man and woman differ in every cell of their body in regard to the number of their chromosomes— those bodies which, for all the world's unfamiliarity, have

been shown by the last decade's work to be the bearers of heredity, the determiners of our characters and qualities.' In spite of the fact, therefore, that 'the superstructure of intellectual and practical life is potentially the same in both sexes', and that 'The recent Board of Education Report of the Committee on the Differentiation of the Curriculum for Boys and Girls in Secondary Schools (London, 1923), has established that the intellectual differences between the sexes are very much slighter than popular belief allows' (*Essays in Popular Science*, by Julian Huxley, pp. 62–3), it is clear that the sexes now differ and will always differ. If it were possible not only for each sex to ascertain what laws hold good in its own case, and to respect each other's laws; but also to share the results of those discoveries, it might be possible for each sex to develop fully and improve in quality without surrendering its special characteristics. The old conception that one sex must 'dominate' another would then become not only obsolete, but so odious that if it were necessary for practical purposes that a dominant power should decide certain matters, the repulsive task of coercion and dominion would be relegated to an inferior and secret society, much as the flogging and execution of criminals is now carried out by masked beings in profound obscurity. But this is to anticipate.

43. From *The Times* obituary notice of H. W. Greene, fellow of Magdalen College, Oxford, familiarly called 'Grugger', 6 February 1933.

44. 'In 1747 the quarterly court (of the Middlesex Hospital) decided to set apart some of the beds for lying-in cases under rules which precluded any woman from acting as midwife. The exclusion of women has remained the traditional attitude. In 1861 Miss Garrett, afterwards Dr Garrett Anderson, obtained permisison to attend classes . . . and was permitted to visit the wards with the resident officers, but the students protested and the medical officers gave way. The Board declined an offer from her to endow a scholarship for women students.' (*The Times*, 17 May 1935.)

45. 'There is, in the modern world, a great body of well-attested knowledge . . . but as soon as any strong passion intervenes to warp the expert's judgment he becomes unreliable, what-

ever scientific equipment he may possess.' (*The Scientific Outlook*, by Bertrand Russell, p. 17.)

46. One of the record-breakers, however, gave a reason for record-breaking which must compel respect: 'Then, too, there was my belief that now and then women should do for themselves what men have already done—and occasionally what men have not done—thereby establishing themselves as persons, and perhaps encouraging other women towards greater independence of thought and action . . . When they fail, their failure must be a challenge to others.' (*The Last Flight*, by Amelia Earhart, pp. 21, 65.)

47. 'In point of fact this process [childbirth] actually disables women only for a very small fraction in most of their lives— even a woman who has six children is only necessarily laid up for twelve months out of her whole lifetime.' (*Careers and Openings for Women*, by Ray Strachey, pp. 47–8.) At present, however, she is necessarily occupied for much longer. The bold suggestion has been made that the occupation is not exclusively maternal, but could be shared by both parents to the common good.

48. The nature of manhood and the nature of womanhood are frequently defined both by Italian and German dictators. Both repeatedly insist that it is the nature of man and indeed the essence of manhood to fight. Hitler, for example, draws a distinction between 'a nation of pacifists and a nation of men'. Both repeatedly insist that it is the nature of womanhood to heal the wounds of the fighter. Nevertheless a very strong movement is on foot towards emancipating men from the old 'natural and eternal law' that man is essentially a fighter; witness the growth of pacifism among the male sex today. Compare further Lord Knebworth's statement 'that if permanent peace were ever achieved, and armies and navies ceased to exist, there would be no outlet for the manly qualities which fighting developed', with the following statement by another young man of the same social caste a few months ago: '. . . it is not true to say that every boy at heart longs for war. It is only other people who teach it us by giving us swords and guns, soldiers and uniforms to play with.' (*Conquest of the Past*, by Prince Hubertus Loewen-

stein, p. 215.) It is possible that the Fascist States by revealing to the younger generation at least the need for emancipation from the old conception of virility are doing for the male sex what the Crimean and the European wars did for their sisters. Professor Huxley, however, warns us that 'any considerable alteration of the hereditary constitution is an affair of millennia, not of decades.' On the other hand, as science also assures us that our life on earth is 'an affair of millennia, not of decades', some alteration in the hereditary constitution may be worth attempting.

49. Coleridge however expresses the views and aims of the outsiders with some accuracy in the following passage: 'Man must be *free* or to what purpose was he made a Spirit of Reason, and not a Machine of Instinct? Man must *obey*; or wherefore has he a conscience? The powers, which create this difficulty, contain its solution likewise; for *their* service is perfect freedom. And whatever law or system of law compels any other service, disennobles our nature, leagues itself with the animal against the godlike, kills in us the very principle of joyous well-doing, and fights against humanity ... If therefore society is to be under a *rightful* constitution of government, and one that can impose on rational Beings a true and moral obligation to obey it, it must be framed on such principles that every individual follows his own Reason, while he obeys the laws of the constitution, and performs the will of the state while he follows the dictates of his own Reason. This is expressly asserted by Rousseau, who states the problem of a perfect constitution of government in the following words: Trouver une forme d'Association—par laquelle chacun s'unissant à tous, n'obéisse pourtant qu'à lui même, et reste aussi libre qu'auparavant,* i.e. To find a form of society according to which each one uniting with the whole shall yet obey himself only and remain as free as before.' (*The Friend*, by S. T. Coleridge, vol. I, pp. 333, 334, 335, 1818 edition.) To which may be added a quotation from Walt Whitman:*

'Of Equality—as if it harm'd me, giving others the same chances and rights as myself—as if it were not indispensable to my own rights that others possess the same.'

And finally the words of a half-forgotten novelist, George Sand, are worth considering:

'Toutes les existences sont solidaires les unes des autres, et tout être humain qui présenterait la sienne isolément, sans la rattacher à celle de ses semblables, n'offrirait qu'une énigme à débrouiller ... Cette individualité n'a pas elle seule ni signification ni importance aucune. Elle ne prend un sens quelconque qu'en devenant une parcelle de la vie générale, en se fondant avec l'individualité de chacun de mes semblables, et c'est par là qu'elle devient de l'histoire.'* (*Histoire de ma Vie*, by George Sand, pp. 240–41.)

# EXPLANATORY NOTES TO
## *A ROOM OF ONE'S OWN*

3 *Haworth Parsonage*: Home of the Brontë family, in Yorkshire.

*Miss Mitford*: Mary Russell Mitford (1786–1855), sketch-writer, dramatist, and poet.

5 *call me Mary Beton . . . please*: VW is referring here to the 'Ballad of the Four Marys', which has the following refrain:

> Yestre'en the queen had four Marys;
> This night she'll hae but three;
> There was Mary Beaton and Mary Seaton
> Mary Carmichael and me.

The singer is Mary Hamilton, a lady-in-waiting, who is about to be killed as a punishment for her sexual relationship with the King. The song has been held to refer both to the Court of Mary Queen of Scots and the Court of Queen Catherine of Russia.

8 *some old essay about revisiting Oxbridge*: Charles Lamb, 'Oxford in the Vacation'.

*that famous library*: although VW insists that Oxbridge is an imaginary place, her reference here would seem to be quite precise: the *Lycidas* manuscript is in Trinity College, Cambridge.

10 *some had tufts of fur*: the Cambridge BA academic hood is fringed with fur.

15 *There has fallen . . . 'I wait'*: Alfred, Lord Tennyson, 'Maud', section XXII, stanza X.

16 *My heart is like . . . my love is come to me*: Christina Rossetti, 'A Birthday'.

21 *J—— H——*: Jane Harrison (1850–1928), classical scholar and anthropologist, who studied the role of female divinities in Greek religion.

25 *John Stuart Mill*: (1806–73), philosopher, author of *The Subjection of Women* (1869).

29 *the last forty-eight years*: VW's arithmetic is faulty here. The Married Women's Property Act, allowing married women to keep their own earnings, was actually passed in 1870. It was then amended in 1882, to allow women to retain a wider range of property after marriage.

34 *a wilderness of spiders*: the phrase echoes Shylock's use of the term 'a wilderness of monkeys' in *The Merchant of Venice*, Act III, sc. i.

37 *most women have no character at all*: Alexander Pope, 'Moral Essays: Epistle II—To a Lady', l. 2.

38 *les femmes . . . que les hommes*: 'women are extreme, they are better or worse than men' (La Bruyère, *Les Caractères*, 'Des femmes', 53).

40 *to adopt the Freudian theory*: VW does not seem to have any particular text by Freud in mind, but may be referring to the relations between trauma and fixation discussed in 'Three Essays on the Theory of Sexuality' (1905).

42 *Sir Austen Chamberlain*: (1863–1937), appointed Foreign Secretary in 1924.

43 *the power and the money and the influence*: VW suggests the disproportionate power involved by echoing the Lord's Prayer.

45 *Romney*: George Romney (1734–1802), painter, particularly well known for his portraits.

*The arrant feminist*: VW records Desmond MacCarthy's angry response to Rebecca West in her diary on 10 September 1928. MacCarthy is also the author of the phrase about women 'acknowledging the limitations of their sex', which Woolf addresses in Chapter IV.

48 *that one gift which it was death to hide*: cf. Milton's sonnet, 'On his Blindness': 'that one talent which is death to hide | Lodg'd with me useless, though my soul more bent | To serve therewith my Maker'.

49 *tearing the liver out*: Prometheus was tied to a rock where an eagle tore at his liver, as a punishment for defying Zeus by stealing fire.

50 *which Milton recommended for my perpetual adoration*: VW expresses anger at the patriarchal legacy of Milton's poetry on several occasions. In 1918 she referred to him in her diary as 'the first of the masculinists'.

54 *History of England*: VW cites from G. M. Trevelyan, *History of England* (London, 1926), 260–1.

55 *the Verneys and the Hutchinsons*: Frances Parthenope, Lady Verney (ed.), *Memoirs of the Verney Family during the Seventeenth Century* (1925) and Lucy Hutchinson, *Memoirs of the Life of Colonel Hutchinson . . . to which is Prefixed the Life of Mrs Hutchinson, Written by Herself* (1810).

58 *Aubrey*: John Aubrey (1626–97), author of *Brief Lives*.

59 *Joanna Baillie*: (1762–1851), poet and dramatist, who wrote a series of plays dealing with the passions.

62 *poodles dancing and women acting*: the allusion, to which Woolf returns later in the chapter, is to the remark by Samuel Johnson: 'Sir, a woman's preaching is like a dog's walking on his hind legs. It is not done well; but you are surprised to find it done at all' (Boswell, *Life of Johnson*, 31 July 1763).

*Nick Greene*: Nick Greene also appears in VW's *Orlando* (1928).

63 *mute and inglorious Jane Austen*: Thomas Gray, in 'Elegy Written in a Country Church-Yard', writes of communities in which genius is stunted by lack of education: 'Some mute inglorious Milton here may rest', l. 59.

65 *Currer Bell*: the pseudonym of Charlotte Brontë.

*Pericles*: Athenian statesman, born c.490 BC. For this remark about women see, 'Pericles' Funeral Oration', in Thucydides, *The Peloponnesian War*, Bk. II.

*ce chien est à moi*: 'this is my dog' (Blaise Pascal, *Pensées*, 64).

*Parliament Square, the Sieges Allee*: Parliament Square, a

favoured site for memorial statues, is in front of the Houses of Parliament, London; Sieges Allee (The Avenue of Victory) is in Berlin.

66 *never blotted a line*: the remark is made by Ben Jonson, 'Of Judging Poets and Poetry', in *Timber, or Discoveries*.

*Rousseau perhaps began it*: VW is thinking of Jean-Jacques Rousseau's *Confessions* (1782–9).

67 *Mighty poets in their misery dead*: Wordsworth, 'Resolution and Independence', l. 116.

68 *Lord Birkenhead's opinion*: Frederick Edwin Smith, Lord Birkenhead (1872–1930), Conservative politician and Lord Chancellor.

69 *Dean Inge*: Very Revd William Ralph Inge (1860–1954), Dean of St Paul's.

*Oscar Browning*: a Fellow of King's College, Cambridge. The details of his life are recorded in *Memories of Sixty Years* (1910).

*most high-minded*: the episode is described in H. E. Wortham, *Oscar Browning* (1927), pp. 246–7.

70 *they minister to, men*: W. R. Greg's remark, from 'Why are Women Redundant?', in *Social and Literary Judgments* (1868) is cited in Barbara Stephen, *Emily Davies and Girton College* (London, 1927), 7.

71 *Germaine Tailleferre*: French composer, b. 1892.

72 *(if she is ask'd)*: the letter is contained in Castalia, Countess Granville (ed.), *Lord Granville Leveson Gower: Private Correspondence 1781–1821* (2 vols.; London, 1916), i. 218.

73 *the words he had cut on his tombstone*: 'here lies one whose name was writ in water'.

76 *How we are fallen ... outweigh the fears*: extract from Anne Finch, Countess of Winchilsea, 'The Introduction'. The next two extracts are from the same poem.

77 *Nor will in fading silks ... the inimitable rose*: extract from Anne Finch, Countess of Winchilsea, 'The Spleen'. The next three extracts are from the same poem.

*appropriated those others*: Alexander Pope, 'Die of a rose in aromatic pain', in 'An Essay on Man: Epistle One', l. 22.

78 *says Mr Murry*: in his 'Introduction' to John Middleton Murry (ed.), *Poems by Anne, Countess of Winchilsea* (London, 1928).

79 *Margaret of Newcastle*: Margaret Cavendish, Duchess of Newcastle (1623–73), woman of letters. Her *Memoirs* were published in 1814, with a Preface by Sir Egerton Brydges.

80 *Sir Egerton Brydges*: (1762–1837), literary historian and genealogist.

81 *wish you with mee* ... : K. Hart (ed.), *The Letters of Dorothy Osborne to William Temple* (London, 1968), 53, 68.

82 *Mrs Behn*: Aphra Behn (1640–1689), dramatist, poet, and novelist. She worked at one time as a spy, was imprisoned for debt, and had a reputation for promiscuity.

83 The Times *said*: in the 'Obituary' of Georgina, Lady Dudley, 4 Feb. 1929, p. 17.

85 *Eliza Carter*: Elizabeth Carter (1717–1806), scholar, poet, and letter-writer.

*supreme head of song*: the phrase is from A. C. Swinburne, 'Ave Atque Vale', and refers to the Greek woman poet, Sappho.

86 *a single sitting-room between them*: Emily Davies remarks that 'It is usual for the whole family to congregate in one room, everyone carrying on her individual occupation in suspense ... liable at any moment to be called off from it' (Barbara Stephen, *Emily Davies and Girton College*, 30). The phrase is also found in R. Strachey, *The Cause* (1928), in a description of the early days of Newnham College: 'the students had but one room between them' (p. 161).

*she was always interrupted*: see Florence Nightingale, 'Cassandra', in R. Strachey, *The Cause* (1928), 395–418.

91 *for the invitation*: see J. W. Cross, *George Eliot's Life* (4 vols.; Leipzig, 1885), ii. 112.

95 *Rochester*: the hero in Charlotte Brontë's *Jane Eyre* (1847).

[ 419 ]

99  *too distant to be sedulous*: R. L. Stevenson describes his
literary apprenticeship as follows: 'I have played the sedulous
ape to Hazlitt, to Lamb, to Wordsworth . . .' ('A College
Magazine', in *Memories and Portraits* (London, 1887), 59).

100  *Gibbon*: Edward Gibbon (1737–94), historian, author of
*Decline and Fall of the Roman Empire* (1776–88).

103  *Vernon Lee's books on aesthetics*: Vernon Lee = Violet Paget
(1856–1935), novelist, critic, author of *Studies of the Eighteenth Century in Italy* (1880) and *The Handling of Words*
(1923).

*Gertrude Bell's books on Persia*: Gertrude Bell (1868–1926),
travel writer and stateswoman; her *Persian Pictures* was
reprinted in 1928.

104  *Mary Carmichael*: Marie Carmichael was the novelistic
pseudonym of the birth-control activist Marie Stopes. In
1928 she published a novel called *Love's Creation*.

105  *Emma and Mr Woodhouse*: characters in Jane Austen's
*Emma* (1816)

106  *Sir Chartres Biron*: Sir Chartres Biron was the Chief Magis-
trate in the trial against Radclyffe Hall's *The Well of
Loneliness*.

107  Diana of the Crossways: a novel by George Meredith (1885).

111  *Burke or Debrett*: works of reference, published annually
and dealing with the peerage and the landed gentry of Great
Britain.

112  *Sir William Joynson Hicks*: 1st Viscount Brentford
(1865–1932)

113  *Every Johnson has his Thrale*: Hester Lynch Thrale
(1741–1821), diarist and poet. She was an intimate friend of
Dr Johnson, but their friendship collapsed as a result of her
marriage to Gabriel Piozzi.

116  *battle of Balaclava*: a battle in the Crimean War, fought in
1854.

*birth of King Edward the Seventh*: in 1841.

118  *Mr Casaubon*: a character in George Eliot's *Middlemarch*
(1871–2).

128 *a great mind is androgynous*: S. T. Coleridge, 'Table Talk', 1 Sept. 1832.

132 *Miss Clough and Miss Davies*: Anne Jemima Clough (1820–92), educationalist, campaigner for women's education, Principal of Newnham College, Cambridge; Emily Davies (1830–1921), suffrage activist, campaigner for women's education, Mistress of Girton College, Cambridge.

133 *old Jolyon's head*: Old Jolyon is the patriarch of the Forsyte family in J. Galsworthy's *The Forsyte Saga* (1922).

134 *Sir Walter Raleigh*: Sir Walter Raleigh (1861–1922), critic and essayist.

143 *Lady Murasaki*: Shikibu Murasaki, *The Tale of the Genji*, trans. from the Japanese by A. Waley (London, 1925–33).

145 *Sir Archibald Bodkin*: Director of Public Prosecutions during the trial of Radclyffe Hall's *The Well of Loneliness*.

146 *that when children ... altogether necessary*: Langdon-Davies actually wrote: 'And if children cease to be altogether desirable, women cease to be altogether necessary' (*A Short History of Women* (London, 1928), 22).

# BIBLIOGRAPHY OF WORKS CITED
# IN *THREE GUINEAS*

VIRGINIA WOOLF develops her argument in *Three Guineas* through readings of a very wide range of biographies, memoirs, and literary texts. The following Bibliography gives full details of the texts cited by Woolf in this text.

ALINGTON, C. A., *Things Ancient and Modern* (London, 1936).

BARKER, E., 'The Home Civil Service', in W. A. Robson *et al.*, *The British Civil Servant* (London, 1937), 29–45.

BENTINCK, WILLIAM (6th Duke of Portland), *Men, Women and Things* (London, 1937).

BLACKHAM, ROBERT J., *Sir Ernest Wild K.C.* (London, 1935).

BLUNDEN, EDMUND (ed.), *The Poems of Wilfred Owen* (London, 1931).

BLUNT, WILFRID SCAWEN, *My Diaries* (London, 1919).

BOARD OF EDUCATION, *Report of the Consultative Committee on Differentiation of the Curriculum for Boys and Girls, in Secondary Schools* (London, 1923).

BOURGET, PAUL, *Le Disciple* (Paris, 1889).

BOWDLER, THOMAS, *Memoir of the Life of John Bowdler* (A. and R. Spottiswode, printed for private circulation; 1824).

BROADBENT, M. E. (ed.), *Life of Sir William Broadbent* (London, 1909).

BROWNING, Elizabeth Barrett and Robert, *Letters* (2 vols.; London, 1899).

BUCHAN, JOHN, *Francis and Riversdale Grenfell: A Memoir* (London, 1920).

BUTLER, JOSEPHINE A., *Personal Reminiscences of a Great Crusade* (London, 1896).

BUTTS, MARY, *The Crystal Cabinet, My Childhood at Salterns* (London, 1937).

CHAPMAN-HUSTON, D., *The Lost Historian: A Memoir of Sir Sidney Low* (London, 1936).

CHARTERIS, EVAN, *The Life and Letters of Sir Edmund Gosse* (London, 1931).

[ 422 ]

—

CHURCHILL, WINSTON, *Thoughts and Adventures* (London, 1932).

CLOUGH, B. A., *A Memoir of Anne Jemima Clough* (London, 1897).

COGHILL, ANNIE L. (ed.), *The Autobiography of Mrs M. O. W. Oliphant* (London, 1899).

COLERIDGE, S. T., *The Friend* (3 vols; London, 1818).

COLLYER, MARGARET, *Life of an Artist* (London, 1935).

CRIGHTON-BROWNE, Sir J. *The Doctor's Second Thoughts* (London, 1931).

DAVIES, MARGARET LLEWELLYN (ed.), *Life as We Have Known it, by Cooperative Working Women* (London, 1931).

DELAPRÉE, LOUIS, *Le Martyre de Madrid* (Madrid, 1937).

EARHART, AMELIA, *Last Flight* (London, 1938).

FABER, GEOFFREY, *Oxford Apostles* (London, 1933).

FAWCETT, M. G. and TURNER, E. M., *Josephine Butler* (London, 1928).

FITZROY, SIR ALMERIC, *Memoirs* (2 vols.; London, 1925).

FORSTER, E. M., *Goldsworthy Lowes Dickinson* (London, 1934).

GASKELL, ELIZABETH, *The Life of Charlotte Brontë* (London, 1901).

GERHARDI, WILLIAM, *Memoirs of a Polyglot* (London, 1931).

GIBBON, EDWARD, *Memoirs of my Life and Writings* (London, 1891).

GISBORNE, THOMAS, *An Enquiry into the Duties of the Female Sex* (London, 1797).

GWYNN, STEPHEN, *The Life of Mary Kingsley* (London, 1932).

HALDANE, ELIZABETH, *From One Century to Another* (London, 1937).

HALL, EDWARD (ed.), *Miss Weeton, Journal of a Governess* (London, 1936).

HAMILTON, LORD F., *The Days before Yesterday* (London, 1920).

HUXLEY, ALDOUS, (ed.), *The Letters of D. H. Lawrence* (London, 1932).

HUXLEY, JULIAN, *Essays in Popular Science* (London, 1926).

JEBB, SIR RICHARD, *Sophocles, the Plays and Fragments* (Cambridge, 1888).

JERROLD, DOUGLAS, *Georgian Adventure* (London, 1937).

JEUNE, MARY (Lady St Helier) *Memories of Fifty Years* (London, 1909).

JOAD, C. E. M., *The Testament of Joad* (London, 1937).

—— *Under the Fifth Rib: A Belligerent Autobiography* (London, 1932).

KNIGHT, LAURA, *Oil Paint and Grease Paint* (London, 1936).

LOEWENSTEIN, PRINCE HUBERTUS, *Conquest of the Past* (London, 1938).

LOVELACE, MARY, COUNTESS OF, 'Fifty Years: Society and the Seasons, the Chaperoned Age', *The Times*, 9 Mar. 1932, pp. 13–14.

LYTTON, EARL OF, *Antony (Viscount Knebworth)* (London, 1935).

MACAULAY, THOMAS BABINGTON, *History of England*, i (London, 1898).

MAGNUS, LAURIE, *Herbert Warren of Magdalen* (London, 1932).

MAIRET, PHILIP, *A. H. Orage* (London, 1936).

MALLET, SIR C., *Anthony Hope and his Books* (London, 1935).

MANDEVILLE, B., *The Fable of the Bees* (2 vols.; Oxford, 1924).

MARKHAM, VIOLET, *Paxton and the Bachelor Duke* (London, 1935).

MAURICE, C. EDMUND (ed.), *The Life of Octavia Hill* (London, 1913).

NEWITT, HILARY, *Women Must Choose* (London, 1937).

NICHOLS, JOHN (ed.), *Illustrations of the Literary History of the Eighteenth Century* (8 vols.; London, 1817).

NICOLSON, HAROLD, *Tennyson* (London, 1923).

PRESTIGE, G. L., *Life of Charles Gore* (London, 1935).

PROUST, MARCEL, *A la recherche du temps perdu* (8 vols.; 1914–27).

RAIKES, ELIZABETH, *Dorothea Beale of Cheltenham* (London, 1908).

RENAN, ERNEST, *Saint Paul* (Paris, 1905).

RICHMOND, ELSA (ed.), *Earlier Letters of Gertrude Bell* (London, 1937).

## EXPLANATORY NOTES

ROBSON, WILLIAM A., 'The Public Service', in W. A. Robson *et al.*, *The British Civil Servant* (London, 1937), 11–28.

RUSSELL, BERTRAND, *The Scientific Outlook* (London, 1931).

RUSSELL, PATRICIA and BERTRAND, *The Amberley Papers* (London, 1937).

SALMOND, MONICA, *Bright Armour* (London, 1935).

SAND, GEORGE, *Histoire de ma vie* (10 vols.; Paris, 1856).

SCOTT, J. M., *Gino Watkins* (London, 1935).

SINCLAIR, UPTON, *Candid Reminiscences* (London, 1932).

SMITH, FLORENCE M., *Mary Astell* (New York, 1916).

SQUIRE, SIR JOHN, *Reflections and Memories* (London, 1935).

STAWELL, F., and DICKINSON, G. L., *Goethe and Faust* (London, 1928).

STEPHEN, BARBARA, *Emily Davies and Girton College* (London, 1927).

STEWART, EDITH (Marchioness of Londonderry), *Henry Chaplin: A Memoir* (London, 1926).

STRACHEY, PHILIPPA, *Memorandum on the Position of English Women in Relation to that of English Men* (London, 1935).

STRACHEY, RAY (Rachel), *The Cause* (London, 1928).

—— *Careers and Openings for Women* (London, 1935).

SWANWICK, H. M., *I Have Been Young* (London, 1935).

THACKERAY, WILLIAM MAKEPEACE, *The History of Pendennis* (2 vols.; London, 1849).

*The Ministry of Women: Report of the Archbishops' Commission* (London, 1935).

THOMSON, SIR J. J., *Recollections and Reflections* (London, 1936).

THORP, MARGARET F., *Charles Kingsley* (Princeton, 1937).

TODD, MARGARET, *The Life of Sophia Jex-Blake* (London, 1918).

TOMLINSON, MARY, *The Life of Charles Tomlinson* (London, 1900).

VACHELL, H. A., *Distant Fields: A Writer's Autobiography* (London, 1937).

WELLS, H. G. *Experiment in Autobiography* (London, 1934).

WHITAKER, J. (ed.), *An Almanack for the Year 1937* (London, 1937).

WRIGHT, ELIZABETH M., *The Life of Joseph Wright* (2 vols.; London, 1932).
YEATS, WILLIAM BUTLER, *Dramatis Personae* (London, 1936).

# EXPLANATORY NOTES TO
## *THREE GUINEAS*

155 *Arthur's Education Fund*: Thackeray, *Pendennis*, i. 174.

*the Pastons*: A Norfolk land-owning family, the subject of an essay by Woolf, 'The Pastons and Chaucer', *Collected Essays* (4 vols.; London, 1967), iii.

158 *until the year 1919*: in *The Cause*, Ray Strachey writes: 'Until 1919, when the Sex Disqualification Removal Act was passed, some of the regular professional openings were entirely closed to women' (p. 44).

161 *the Scarborough Conference of educated men, the Bournemouth conference of working men*: the Conservative Party Conference was held in Scarborough, 7–8 October 1937; the Labour Party Conference was held in Bournemouth, 4–5 October 1937.

164 *they are photographs of dead bodies for the most part*: the photographs show casualties in the Spanish Civil War. The Spanish Civil War (1936–9) was the result of a revolt by sections of the Spanish Army, aided by Italy and Germany, against the elected Republican Government. It became the focus of international resistance to Fascism. VW wrote to Julian Bell on 14 November 1936: 'This morning I got a packet of photographs from Spain, all of dead children, killed by bombs.' Julian Bell was himself killed in Spain, driving an ambulance for the Republican forces, in 1937.

166 *as before in France*: VW is referring to the First World War.

169 *Duchess of Devonshire ... Lady Ashburton*: Duchess of Devonshire: Lady Georgiana Spencer (1757–1806), Whig hostess, friend of Fox and Sheridan, writer; Lady Palmerston (1787–1869), political hostess; Lady Melbourne: Elizabeth Lamb (d. 1818), Whig hostess and improving land-owner; Madame de Lieven: Dorothea Lieven (b. 1783), wife of the Russian Ambassador in London; Lady Holland: Elizabeth

[ 427 ]

Fox (1771–1845), Whig hostess; Lady Ashburton: Lady Harriet Baring (1827–1903), political hostess.

169 *Pitt . . . Gladstone*: William Pitt (1759–1806), Tory politician; Charles James Fox (1749–1806), Whig politician; Richard Brinsley Sheridan (1751–1816), dramatist and Whig politician; Robert Peel (1788–1850), Tory politician; Henry John Temple Palmerston (1784–1865), Prime Minister 1855–65; Benjamin Disraeli (1805–81), Tory politician; William Gladstone (1809–98), politician.

*Macaulay*: Thomas Babington Macaulay (1800–1859), historian, poet, and cultural critic.

*Carlyle*: Thomas Carlyle (1795–1881), writer, historian, and social critic.

176 *the veil that St Paul still lays upon our eyes*: St Paul insisted that women should be veiled when praying: (1 Cor. 11: 4–15).

181 *we can refuse all such distinctions*: VW herself turned down the offer of honorary university degrees, and declined to be made a Companion of Honour (*Diary*, 25 March 1933, 19 May 1936, 3 March 1939).

182 *asking for money with which to rebuild a women's college*: VW received a letter from J. P. Strachey in 1936, asking her to join the committee of patrons of Newnham College, Cambridge, which was launching an appeal to fund new buildings.

184 *Although I enter not . . . Angels within it*: Thackeray, 'The Church Porch', in *Pendennis*, i. 315.

187 *Bishop Burnet*: Gilbert Burnet (1643–1715), Bishop of Salisbury.

188 *the oracle is not dumb*: the phrase 'the oracles are dumb', is from Milton's 'On the morning of Christ's Nativity', l. 173.

*at Oxford and at Cambridge*: Girton, Newnham, Lady Margaret Hall, and Somerville were all founded between 1869 and 1879.

189 *without a garden in the middle of a noisy street*: this

[ 428 ]

—

information comes from B. A. Clough, 'The Starting of Newnham College', in *A Memoir of Anne Jemima Clough*.

190 *Gray's Ode*: Thomas Gray, 'Ode to Music'.

191 *she gave £1,000*: the donor of £1,000 to Newnham College was a Miss Ewart.

204 *tripos*: the final examinations at Cambridge University.

210 *a society to help the daughters of educated men to obtain employment in the professions*: the London and National Society for Women's Service, described by Vera Brittain as 'a lively body of young professional women' (*Nation*, 31 Jan. 1931).

213 *WSPU*: Women's Social and Political Union, the militant wing of the Suffrage Movement.

215 *the income of the WSPU . . . was £42,000*: VW is inaccurate here. The income of £42,000, according to Swanwick, was that of the National Union of Women's Suffrage Societies, the non-militant wing of the Movement.

217 *Cleopatra's Needle*: an obelisk, brought from Alexandria in 1877, and now in London.

*Whitaker's Almanack*: J. Whitaker (ed.), *An Almanack for the Year 1937*.

225 *a board is not made literally of oak, nor a division of iron*: a board is a civil service committee; a division is a grade within the civil service.

227 *neither marrying nor giving in marriage*: the phrase 'marrying and giving in marriage' is from Matt. 24: 38.

229 *her husband, her children and her home*: extract from a speech by Adolf Hitler, *Sunday Times*, 13 Sept. 1936, p. 23.

*curled up like a caterpillar on a leaf*: cf. 'The caterpillar on the leaf | Repeats to thee thy mother's grief' (William Blake, *Auguries of Innocence*).

238 *oh, of whom? as the poet says*: Malcolm's response to the information that his father has been murdered is 'O!, by whom?' (*Macbeth*, Act II, sc. iii).

238 *the mulberry tree*: 'here we go round the mulberry bush' is the refrain of a children's singing-game.

239 *the Pensions Bill*: there was a campaign against the introduction of differential income limits for men and women in the government's new Pensions Bill. Philippa Strachey was very active in this campaign, and in the London and National Society for Women's Service, and could thus be seen as the implied addressee of this second letter.

240 *Hansard*: printed official report of proceedings in the Houses of Parliament.

242 *the lion and the unicorn*: the Royal Arms.

245 *Whitehall*: the administrative centre of government.

*Harley Street*: a street in London which houses many leading medical specialists.

*the Royal Academy*: founded 1768, for the purpose of improving the arts of painting, sculpture, and architecture.

246 *Doctors' Commons*: an association for practitioners of canon and civil law.

250 *Pierpont Morgan*: John Pierpont Morgan (1867–1943), Chairman of Morgan, Grenfell, and Co.

251 *Rockefeller*: John Davison Rockefeller (1839–1937), millionaire philanthropist.

*the truck system*: system of paying wages other than in money.

256 *Dean Alington or Dean Inge*: Very Revd Cyril Argentine Alington (1872–1955), Dean of Durham; Very Revd William Ralph Inge (1860–1954), Dean of St Paul's.

264 *Contagious Diseases Act*: an act which forced prostitutes to submit to medical examination for venereal disease.

265 *Bourget's The Disciple*: Paul Bourget, *Le Disciple* (1889), a melodramatic narrative exploring the limits of atheistic materialism.

268 *Florence Nightingale*: (1820–1910), nurse and health

reformer. She wrote of her life and education in 'Cassandra', in Ray Strachey, *The Cause*.

272 *The* Antigone *of Sophocles*: in this tragedy, Creon, King of Thebes, refuses to allow Antigone to bury her dead brother Polyneices. She disobeys him, invoking a divine law whose dictates have greater authority than the laws of any particular state.

279 *to protect culture and intellectual liberty*: VW did sign the manifesto of the International Peace Campaign in 1936, which included the statement that 'Modern war and preparations for war are hostile to the arts, and most of all to writing.'

281 *Seule la culture désintéressée peut garder le monde de sa ruine*: 'Only a disinterested culture can save the world from ruin.' VW saw this headline in a French newspaper, and kept the cutting in one of her Notebooks.

284 *Grub Street*: a street in London inhabited by popular writers.

297 *the criticism that Ben Jonson gave Shakespeare at the Mermaid*: the popular belief that Jonson and Shakespeare met frequently at the Mermaid tavern to discuss literature finds its first expressioin in Thomas Fuller's *Worthies* (1662).

302 *turtles*: VW may be referring to the turtle soup which is traditionally served at civic banquets.

312 *Air Raid Precaution*: the government had established an Air Raid Precautions Department, which tended to increase perceptions of the inevitability of war.

329 *those also serve who remain outside*: VW echoes the final line of Milton's sonnet 'On his Blindness': 'They also serve who only stand and wait.'

334 *Lydia and Chloe, Euodia and Syntyche, Tryphoena and Tryphosa and Persis*: Lydia is the first known convert in Europe (Acts 16: 14); Chloe, the mistress of a Christian household at Corinth (1 Cor. i: 11); Euodia and Syntyche, Tryphoena, Tryphosa, and Persis were all women who engaged in evangelical work (Phil. 14: 2, 3 and Rom. 16: 12).

344 *whose dog Rover has died*: Crosby is a character in Woolf's *The Years*. She is a servant who has been with the Pargiter family for years, but is forced to retire and to leave the Pargiters' house in Abercorn Terrace, in 1913. She has a dog called Rover, who dies shortly after Crosby's retirement, leaving her alone.

345 *Ismene*: Antigone's sister, who claims a share in her guilt and punishment.

351 *Queen's College, Harley Street*: established in 1848 to educate women to be governesses, using lecturers from King's College, London.

357 *tears—angry tears*: the anger modifies the original phrase, 'Tears, idle tears', from Tennyson's *The Princess*, IV, Second Song.

   *Josephine Butler's label*: Josephine Butler (1828–1906), writer and political campaigner.

363 *Holloway*: many Suffrage campaigners were held in Holloway Prison.

369 *a well-known passage*: the Preface to *Pendennis*.

370 *Lysistrata*: in Aristophanes' play, Lysistrata argues that women should take control of state affairs and bring an end to war. Her weapon is the refusal of sexual relations.

375 *a private bequest*: J. M. Keynes, 'Review' of M. D. Forbes (ed.), *Clare College*; Vera Brittain, 'A Woman's Notebook'; both in *Nation and Athenaeum*, 17 Jan. 1931.

381 *Gibb's Buildings*: part of King's College, Cambridge.

392 *Est-il cependant . . . On ne saurait l'affirmer*: 'Is it absolutely impossible, however, that Saint Paul had contracted a more intimate relation with this sister? One cannot be sure.'

413 *Trouver une forme . . . libre qu'auparavant*: J.-J. Rousseau, *The Social Contract*, Bk. I, chap. 6.

   *a quotation from Walt Whitman*: from 'Thought', *Complete Poetry and Prose* (2 vols; 1928), i. 260.

414 *Toutes les existences . . . devient de l'histoire*: 'All human lives are interdependent on one another, and any human

being who presents his existence in isolation, without attaching it to his fellow-creatures, offers only an enigma to be resolved ... This individuality has neither meaning nor importance in itself. It assumes some sort of meaning only in becoming part of life in general, in blending with the individualities of all my fellow creatures, and it is by this means that it enters into history.'

*The Oxford World's Classics Website*

**www.worldsclassics.co.uk**

- Information about new titles
- Explore the full range of Oxford World's Classics
- Links to other literary sites and the main OUP webpage
- Imaginative competitions, with bookish prizes
- Peruse the Oxford World's Classics Magazine
- Articles by editors
- Extracts from Introductions
- A forum for discussion and feedback on the series
- Special information for teachers and lecturers

**www.worldsclassics.co.uk**

**American Literature**

**British and Irish Literature**

**Children's Literature**

**Classics and Ancient Literature**

**Colonial Literature**

**Eastern Literature**

**European Literature**

**History**

**Medieval Literature**

**Oxford English Drama**

**Poetry**

**Philosophy**

**Politics**

**Religion**

**The Oxford Shakespeare**

A complete list of Oxford Paperbacks, including Oxford World's Classics, Oxford Shakespeare, Oxford Drama, and Oxford Paperback Reference, is available in the UK from the Academic Division Publicity Department, Oxford University Press, Great Clarendon Street, Oxford OX2 6DP.

In the USA, complete lists are available from the Paperbacks Marketing Manager, Oxford University Press, 198 Madison Avenue, New York, NY 10016.

Oxford Paperbacks are available from all good bookshops. In case of difficulty, customers in the UK can order direct from Oxford University Press Bookshop, Freepost, 116 High Street, Oxford OX1 4BR, enclosing full payment. Please add 10 per cent of published price for postage and packing.